Skylark

Ruthie Morgan

Lucky Arbuckle Publishing

Copyright © Ruthie Morgan 2014

All rights reserved.

The moral right of the author has been asserted.

No part of this publication may be reproduced, stored in a retrieval system, or transmitted, in any form or by any means, without the prior permission in writing of both the copyright owner and the publisher of this book.

All characters in this publication are fictitious and any resemblance to real persons living or dead is purely coincidental.

First published in 2014 by Lucky Arbuckle Publishing.

ISBN 10 0473289180

ISBN 13 9780473289188

Cover Illustration by Kate Louise Powell

Ebook formatting by www.ebooklaunch.com

For Richard –
Who always told me to write

"The song of the Skylark is fast, variable and sustained, delivered as it hangs suspended from considerable height. At the close of song it soars steeply, head to wind before its dramatic drop earthward."
Falla, Gibson & Turbot: A Field Guide to Birds of NZ & Outlying Islands, 1966

Prologue

The keyboard gleams as she poises herself on the edge of the seat, hands hovering, ready to transcribe the key paragraph she knows must come soon. Sucking in her breath, she leans back on her chair, pressing damp palms against tired eyes. She wills the words to come.

Late summer nights are the hardest to bear with the heat of day settled in the dimly-lit room with its cane sofas, brightly patterned cushions, and the woman in the corner at the desk. Windows and doors are open to the still, heavy night that lies wearily over the hot haze of day. A ceiling fan turns listlessly, cutting the fragrant air heavy with blossoms and earthy dampness, but no breeze comes. The humidity of day seems to rest here in this room; a thick blanket of darkness and insect sounds.

11:59 p.m.: The computer screen's bright glare announces one last precious minute of the day to make a difference, to do one last thing that might somehow make her more. She jerks from her thoughtful repose, fingers on the keyboard in one fluid movement. She taps urgently, as if slowing down may let whatever thought has arrived slip away again. The tap-tap sounds a beat with the chorus of tree frogs and the drone of mosquitoes, and there is life here in the little room in the heat and darkness.

12:12 a.m.: Another noise joins the chorus, jostling for its place in line, but its entry to the symphony signifies an end, and she instinctively jumps in her seat. A wearied look of frustration superseded by concern passes over her face. Removing her glasses, she flicks off the desk light and pads across the bare wooden floor to the urgent cry of a baby awake.

* * *

Chapter One

Billie
St. Cloud 2006

"My name is Billie May Skylark, and I'd like to send my manuscript in for consideration… it's a fictional work, yes… no, not as yet. Sorry, can you hold for just one second?"

I take a breath and cover the mouthpiece with my hand, turning to one of my eighteen-month-old twins who is attempting to climb inside the dishwasher. "Sunny! Get out of there now, that is not a toy! Mommy is on the telephone."

Grabbing the wriggling terror, I placate him with a cracker as I return to my phone call. "Sorry about that… no, that's correct. I haven't yet published a novel… no, I have had a few poems published, and I currently write a column… oh, ok… no, that's quite alright; I understand. Thanks for your time." I stick my tongue out at the receiver as I place it back into its cradle, wondering how it might be possible for a writer to ever get published when no one will look at your novel unless, duh, you've already published a novel.

"I give up!" I announce to the dishwasher; although I know that, really, I won't.

The truth is that I may never get my book published, but I know, deep down, that even if I remain the frustrated, undiscovered writer forever, the simple act of writing has saved me. Amidst nappies, pureed foods, and tantrums, I manage to hold on to a hidden identity which allows me to believe I'm somehow more than the groundhog day pattern my life since babies has become. I tell myself, sometimes out loud whilst cleaning the highchair, soaking the laundry, or playing peek-a-boo for the zillionth time, I am also a writer, I am also a writer, I am also a writer.

"Sunny, sweetie, where's Evie?" one of the twins is no longer in my peripheral vision, and this is always a bad sign. "Honey, where's Evie?" Sunny gives me his dimply double-toothed smile and waddles away, wearing only a nappy and singlet. "Evie... Evie, where are you?"

As usual, I begin the triage search, starting with the places I know most likely to be the site of some awful accident. I race around the house calling her name, trying not to sound like a frantic freak of a mother. Did I close the door to the laundry? Are the baby gates on? Did I leave the garden gate open? Meanwhile, Sunny toddles around after me, giggling as though we are now in a big game of hide and seek.

Reaching the twins' bedroom, I find the lower drawers of the tallboy open and every item of clothing and bedding on the floor. *She's been here, but she's not here now.* In the bathroom, rolls of toilet paper are unraveled, covering every surface. No baby, but I'm on the right track. Laundry door definitely closed. I exhale a breath of minor relief. Out into the front garden, still no sign, but the dog food dish has been emptied into the plant pots. Down the side lane to the backyard, I'm calling her name loudly now. "Evie, Evie, where are you?" Long grass itches bare legs as I run through the overgrown yard we never seem to find the time to care for.

Panic takes hold, changing in an instant what was irritation and mild concern to the icy chill of raw fear. If Evie has gotten this far down the yard, then she might reach the dilapidated fence... which leads directly through the bush to the cliff.

The yard is half a kilometer long, most of it thick with overgrown grass, the rest beyond the fence is dense bush. I had never thought it possible that an eighteen-month-old could make it this far down the yard, but kids surprise you every day. Shit, why was the baby gate to the garden unlocked?

This and a zillion other panicked, terror-stricken and self-flagellating thoughts bounce around my head as I tear through the last few meters to the fence. "Evie!" I scream this time, the pitch in my voice stifled by the heavy bush which waits beyond the fence. There is no sign of a baby; no sign at all.

"Billie! Hey Billie, over here." I turn to the sound of the voice my chest heaving, overwhelmed by panic and the sprint through the long grass. Searching for the source, I shield my eyes from the glare of the midday sun.

"Jack, I've lost her, Evie's gone." His silhouette appears at the crest of the hill leading down to the fence, he is carrying something and I sink to my knees in relief.

"Here's Mommy. Now, what do you guys think she's doing down here?" Jack walks calmly toward me, and I open my shaking arms out to the giggling bundle of mischief he brandishes. I hold her wriggly body to mine as tightly as possible, relief sparking tears as I scold her lightly.

"Where have you been monkey? Mommy's been looking everywhere for you." She smiles and puts her thumb in her mouth, nuzzling into my breast as though it should still hold some sustenance. "Thank you Jack; where was she?"

He smiles down at us; Sunny is on his shoulders, tickling his ears. "I think maybe the dogs have burrowed a hole under the fence. She was in my garden pulling up the flowers."

"Oh, I'm so sorry, I was on the phone for a few minutes, and then she was gone. I thought for a second…" I stall gesturing toward the fence behind me. "I'm a disaster. Women like me should be given compulsory birth control. I don't know how to do this."

"Yes, you do." He puts a work-scarred hand under my elbow and guides me to my feet, Evie almost asleep in my arms, exhausted from her escapee adventure. "You just need a break."

I take a breath and wipe my damp brow with the back of my hand, hair sticking to my forehead. "Thank you Jack, for everything."

He smiles and we make our way back up through the long grass to my open French doors. All is as it was. I carry Evie to her cot where I pull up the rail, should she wake from slumber and decide on another expedition. Jack takes Sunny and lays his compliant little body down on the adjacent cot. We tiptoe from the room and I flop on to the sofa, wondering when life became so very tiring.

Jack returns with a glass of ice water, places it on the table, and tells me to have a rest. "I can see your halo glowing from here, Mr Kelly" I sigh. "My very own guardian angel right next door."

He smiles, making for the door. "Have a nap; I'll get that hole in the fence sorted this afternoon." He leaves with our dog, Toby, trotting along at his heels, and I watch him go; a strong, solid, reliable frame. He stops, bends down to pat Toby's head, then rubs his belly, turns briefly back toward my house and then is gone.

Jack Kelly is my neighbour here in St. Cloud, the South Pacific Island furthest from just about anything and anyone I have known before, a small dot on the map that is now our home.

To find St. Cloud, you might take a plane to Costa Rica then head south, down just past the equator line. Or you might head to Peru and travel north; St. Cloud lies somewhere in the expanse of blue ocean that lies between. We moved here shortly before the birth of our twins, and without Jack, the change might have been too much for me. Jack is a rock, always around with a calm word and a smile. He's like the pied piper for animals and kids. Wherever he is, there's bound to be a dog or two in tow, and whenever he's here, the twins are laughing. Jack is low on the drama factor, and as I'm married to a guy like Evan, any relationship that doesn't involve drama is welcome.

Being a single male in St. Cloud is a precarious position as there are, it seems, more women than available men. Jack keeps a low profile. He's been burned before. I tell him it's only a matter of time till one of those single ladies on the island manages to reel him in, but he isn't interested. After meeting his ex-wife Claudia, I knew the reason why. I think after a few years with her, any good man would need at least a decade of celibacy. She's a piranha with highlights and long legs, and on the few occasions I've seen her, I surmised that she's the sort of woman who doesn't like women.

They divorced two years ago, although Claudia seems to think it was more like two weeks ago. She tries to keep her talons in Jack's life any way she can. The story goes (and here in St. Cloud, you quickly become privy to most stories) she trapped Jack into marrying her by pretending to be pregnant. Jack's a good guy, old fashioned in a way and would have insisted on doing the right thing. Of course three months after the wedding, he discovered there was no baby but there you go. Jack's a "believe the best in everybody" kind of a guy and made a go of things. They say he wanted a family and she didn't, and well, the rest is history. It was a simple divorce; Jack gave her everything, and she now lives in a beach villa overlooking La Misere, St. Cloud's most beautiful beach.

Jack built a house here on Frontiere Point on the opposite side of the island. His house is next door to us, although I'd say "house" is a stretch of the term. His "break-up build" is more of an open-plan man cave atop a large work shed; basic but functional.

Claudia's penchant for expensive, soft furnishings and designer wallpaper ensured Jack will have a lifelong aversion to anything but the basic comforts. He maintains he doesn't need much, and his studio room above the work shed reflects this housing: only a woodstove, bookshelf, radio, and sofa bed. Jack's passion is boats, and he works day and night drawing, building, and restoring them in his work shed below his man shed, along with his two dogs, Louie and Bets, for company.

* * *

Closing my eyes, I let the heat sink into my bones. I stop fighting and let it soothe me into the hazy place between wakefulness and slumber. I can hear the sound of the ocean beyond the end of our yard and the constant buzz of insects. St. Cloud is always sleepy in the heat, but an undercurrent of activity thrives below the surface of its overheated community; it is a hive of people and life. A community in a bell jar.

Sleep comes quickly and I am soon lost in a dream. I am making a speech, thanking people, shaking hands and signing books, but it's raining, and I realize someone forgot to put up a canopy. Words on pages run till everything is blank. I look down at myself and my literary demeanor has changed to mother coffee group attire; braless and in sweats with baby vomit down my front. Jack is in the crowd stifling a laugh and Evan stands, arms folded, embarrassed and disappointed.

Evan.

The telephone rings and rings, and the dream dissolves with the downpour. With half of me still at my dream book signing, I scramble for the handset only to hear the sound of two hungry cries from the bedroom. "Hello?" I sound pissed off because of course I am, the phone has pulled me from my so needed nana nap and woken the twins simultaneously. I clear my throat and answer again. "Hello?" More warmth in my tone.

"Hey baby, where were you? I was about to hang up."

"Evan." It's always good to hear his voice. "I fell asleep with the twins, we've had a busy morning. How's work?"

"Oh, you know; it's good, but I'd rather be there sleeping with you."

I hear the smile in his voice and return it with one of my own. Evan was born with the gift of the gab and as he speaks, his soft persuasive tone slowly pulls me from my sleepy funk. Since I have known him, he has always been able to sweet talk anyone, get himself or others out of a fix with words and charm, and somehow always win me over no matter how mad I might be. Evan is Irish with all the accompanying cheeky humor and charm you might expect. He is my weakness; dark haired, green-eyed, tall and lean, he was and is my first love. We are here, with our babies in St. Cloud because of him. I have followed Evan since we met: a journey equally satisfying and terrifying, depending on which day you ask me.

"When are you coming home?" The sound of the twins yelling for me gets louder every second I ignore them.

"I'm not sure sweetheart, I have some plans to finish before I cut out."

I'm used to this. Evan's job in Becketsvale (St. Cloud's only city) means he leaves before the sun rises and generally returns home after the sun sets, usually smelling of a few local after work cocktails. He is happy in this new job, so I don't make a fuss, even though the days are long without him. His happiness feeds mine.

"Do you think Evie can climb out of her cot yet?"

"How would I know?" He sounds vacant. "It wouldn't surprise me."

I hear a thump in the bedroom and a bang at the closed door. "I can't believe it; she's out! I gotta run Evan. Oh, and you have to do something about that old fence at the end of the yard. I thought Evie had gone off the cliff earlier."

"You'll turn yourself grey with all that fretting. It's practically a kilometer's hike. There's no way they could get down there".

"How do you know that? Evie is practically catching buses on her own!"

Evan laughs. "Go have beer baby; the twins are fine. I'll see you later."

I hang up, rolling my eyes. A beer is Evan's answer to everything; a beer, for crying out loud!

I walk toward the source of the commotion and find Evie has climbed up and into Sunny's cot; she has a crayon and is trying to draw on his dimpled cheeks. I shake my head and stifle a laugh. "What am I going to do with you two? You, my girl, are your Daddy's daughter." I lift curly-haired little Evie into the air as she giggles and charms me with her beaming smile. She is light and wiry, where Sunny is dimpled and chubby; he is fair while she is dark, and seeing them together, it is almost impossible to believe they can be related, never mind twins.

Baby gates secure and double-checked, we three head to the living room floor where I lie on my tummy with the twins and their toys, watching them play and intervening when one looks set to clobber the other with a building block. I love this, watching them together and seeing them explore and learn. I love their need for cuddles and reassurance and love that I am the one who can always give them that. I love all of this yet the voice that nags, "It isn't enough" won't leave me alone.

If my physical body were to reflect my lack of balance since the twin's arrival, it would look like this: swollen feet, skinny legs, oversized milky boobs, and a head that is shrunk from lack of stimulation. A brain once of good size and function reduced to the size of a walnut. Maybe I should do a quick mirror check just to be sure this hasn't actually happened yet ; the head shrinking bit that is. The boobs, the feet; that's all a given.

The air has changed, and a rare wave of cool rolls over the heat haze. My skin prickles with the unfamiliar sensation. In no time at all, a thunderclap sounds, and we gather at the windows to watch the show; St. Cloud hosts the most dramatic thunderstorms this time of year. The twins watch in awe as the dark sky is sliced with lightening, and for a split second, their wide eyes are bathed in white light. We count the seconds till the thunder rolls and they squeal in delight, burying their little heads in my lap as the booming noise shakes the sky.

Storms have always smelled like change to me; something coming, a warning to be ready, a signal to assume the position. It was a night not too dissimilar to this when my life course last jumped tracks, but I wasn't ready. If it hadn't been for that storm, I'm not sure how life might have worked out. But the thunder and lightning that night in London, the smell of change, and warning to be ready were for me, I just didn't know it then. At the end of that stormy night was Evan, and I would wait for him in the rain then follow him to shelter.

* * *

Evan
St. Cloud 2006

He's always liked the rain. It falls heavy in St. Cloud, downpours washing the heat from the day, cleaning and smoothing as they go. The sound overpowers the fusion of music, laugher and talk in the small beach bar, and as the storm heightens, the battering rain on the tin roof becomes deafening; a high-frequency drumbeat that crowds out competing sound until the rain is all there is.

Evan leans back on his chair, one arm lazily slung around the empty seat beside him, the other reaching for the half-empty bottle on the table. There's nothing to be done but wait out the storm, and for now, there's nowhere else he'd rather be. Here, no one needs anything, and he doesn't have to be anyone but the guy who wants to wind down after a long day. It's a guilty pleasure; he should really head home, but for the first time all day, he feels relaxed, the beer working its way through the tension and stress.

Scanning the small bar, he watches the faces; his artist's eye taking in detail carefully, storing away features, expressions, profiles, and angles: the stooped posture of the drunk, the raised face and flushed cheeks of eager new love. Hands gesticulating, fingers pointing, palms raised to the sky in surprise. People all around, yet he's happy to sit alone for now. He'll let the first few drinks work their magic then he might be social.

It should be hard to feel lonely in a place like St. Cloud. Its tight-knit community is a comforting blanket of new best friends and family. But Evan's default position is lonely; it's always been this way. Despite friends and a growing family, there's a space inside him that's always alone. The feeling is almost comfortable; its familiarity welcome in a head whose thoughts and moods swoop and dive like birds riding pockets of thermal air in summer skies.

"You want another beer Evan?" The barman smiles in Evan's direction, gesturing to the now-empty bottle in his hand. "It's a real good St. Cloud storm out there. You'd be wise to hang here till it passes. You don't want to be driving these roads in that." As if on cue, a loud clap of thunder sounds, followed closely by a bright flash of white as lightning splits the charcoal sky. Evan nods in agreement, attention quickly shifting from the familiar faces in the bar to the light show over the ocean. The cold beer arrives, and he traces a finger carefully down the dewy glass before raising the bottle to his lips; eyes still fixed on the drama unfolding in the St. Cloud skies.

This is his sort of weather; big, loud, unafraid and dramatic. Storms here are unrelenting, but short-lived, wild and unrepentant, yet apologetic in departure, a perfect sound bite of nature's great contrasts. The fiery fury is short-lived and the watery sunlight that follows fills the island with a beauty that always feels like the first day of spring.

By nine, he knows he should go home. Billie will be waiting. He drinks the last sip of beer from the bottle then lifts his phone, fingers working quickly on the illuminated screen.

"Hey baby, on my way now. Love you. Ex."

The rain has eased a little; the storm passing, and he knows that if he stays for another, he won't be safe on the road. Heading out of the bar into the moisture-heavy night, he jogs to reach his truck, jacket over his head and keys in hand. The fall of rain is still heavy, although the intensity of before has faded. The red Ford starts first turn. Evan flicks on the lights and reverses carefully from the parking lot before hitting the stereo and turning up the volume.

Falling rain on the roof, the low beat from the speakers and scraping metronome of windscreen wipers form a chaotic symphony in the confines of the truck as it winds its way around the dark roads. Evan drives steadily, carefully, his eyes focused despite the low buzz of beer in his bloodstream. The truck descends down into the darkest part of the road; the base of a gentle dip in the land before the gradual climb skyward. Bright headlight beams carve a narrow path through the darkness, and dense bush rises on either side of hot tarmac. Here the sky is barely visible as overhanging ferns and palms create a dark canopy.

The route turns inland and begins to climb gradually out of the dense valley, winding slowly up around the hairpin bends toward the island's highest point. The truck climbs and slowly gains speed as the road stretches out to traverse the island. Here the rain seems harder, a pocket of the storm lingering, reluctant to leave. Sheets of rain and gusts of warm tropical winds buffet the truck around, and Evan struggles to see the road ahead. There is no other traffic; no other lights to break the darkness.

Taking a hand from the wheel, he distractedly pushes back the damp hair that sticks to his face as rain streams in the half open window; the stormy drive suddenly seems less like a good idea.

He glances down at his cell phone thrown carelessly on the passenger seat. He'd left the bar feeling invincible, and a drive through the storm hadn't seemed like a big deal. The weather is worse than he'd realized and he knows she'll worry. He'd call her to explain, but there's no reception here. He should pull over and wait it out. The truck is buffeted again, and the tires slip and skid on the dark, slick road.

"Fuck." The cuss is barely audible amidst the rain on the roof; he bangs the steering wheel with the heel of his hand and flicks the headlights to bright.

Eyes straining ahead on the dark road for a safe place to stop, he doesn't see it, and blinded by the sudden glare of headlights in the dark, it doesn't see him.

One image flashes bright before impact: a crystal-clear frame of color, mid-flight and a flash of dark eyes in the moment life meets death. Color and feathers clearly defined, wings outspread, the angle of the head and sheen of the beak. A Scarlet Macaw. He knows every bird on the island and even in the moment of frozen panic, he recognizes the form. Evan hits the brakes and the truck screams to a halt, skidding and turning on the slick road.

The sound of breathing is louder than the rain, louder than the screech of tires and louder than the sound of his voice and the words that will come too late. He fumbles with the door, hands shaking uncontrollably and runs through the heavy rain to the spot where the bird lies—a muddied pile of wings and once bright primary colors that seem to leech and dilute on the rain-soaked road.

"Oh Jesus, I'm sorry. I'm so sorry." The words drip and pool on the tarmac. He knows it's too late; the damage done. The bird lies awkwardly, crushed and broken, and Evan sinks to his knees by its side. Headlights from the truck shine over the scene: the rain beating on his back as he bends over the Scarlet Macaw, palm outstretched to lay a hand on its heart.

Life flickers, the spark of spirit trying one last time to restart the broken body. The bird's dark eyes are fixed on Evan; no trace of fear or pain as the last essence of life flickers and dies. The bird stiffens imperceptibly under his open palm; and he feels it, the very moment the heart stops and life leaves. Rain falls relentlessly, and he sits there at the side of the road with one hand on the heart of the bird that grows colder with every passing second.

An hour, a minute, or only a moment passes, and he sits, unable to move, unwilling to go back to the truck and drive away. Where did the life go; that force that propelled the bird forward in the rain to meet its end so meaninglessly? Where did it go, and what was the point? All that beauty, a life, nurtured, grown and lived moment by moment… where was it now, and why was it him that took it away?

He picks up the broken bird and holds it to his damp shirt, walking slowly back to the truck. The noise of the rain is an angry drumbeat on the roof as he sits in the driver's seat, shocked and shivering, with the Macaw's colored feathers drooping dully on his knees. Fate, chance, or circumstance, he took away life and felt it leave. Mud-spattered hands rise to his face, and he weeps, not knowing if the sadness is real or imagined.

That life can be so fragile, so easily given and taken away, that one action, one decision can be a catalyst for catastrophe. That life is a spider web of consequence, and we are all at the mercy of one another. The spill of tears triggers grief unexpressed in a lifetime of occasional sorrow. He cries, and the relief of tears leaves him calm and washed out—how much later he doesn't know.

When he opens his eyes again, the storm has passed, the rain a mere drizzle, the wind all but gone. "Billie." He needs to get home to her, feel her next to him, and let her remind him there's meaning in the chaos. Before Billie, it was always this; life as a series of chaotic events with no reason or meaning. She'll smile and make him laugh, and somehow within the madness of just being alive, it'll all be okay.

It's how she's always been, it's who she is for Evan; a brighter, happier half that finds something good in everything, even him. She'll make it right, just like she's always done from the very beginning. He needs to get home to her and that single thought lays the lifeless bird by the side of the road and turns the key in the ignition to make the careful drive home.

Maybe it's the rain and overwhelming emotion, the feeling of being out of control and the storm, but the drive home sees Evan follow a series of memories: a stormy night not so long ago, rain in summer, birds in flight, and Billie.

Chapter Two

Billie & Evan
Five Years Earlier (London 2001)

"Pens down and wait at your desks, please. You may not talk or leave the room until instructed to do so." The exam invigilator must love this phrase. He can stop pacing the rows, looking over our shoulders, and sit with a good British cup of tea before the next wave of terrified students arrive to seal their future in the last exam of finals.

I place my pen down and exhale slowly, desperate to be outside in the fresh air of freedom. My head throbs from three hours of frenzied essay writing; my fingers ache, and I would like more than anything to lie on the grass and look at the sky. Witness the world outside academia. A door is finally beginning to close as a new one opens; goodbye undergraduate life, here I come into the world of adults. An educated, university-qualified adult, no less. I'm on the threshold of a new beginning, and despite my heavy head, I feel a buzz of new life, of new direction fire up inside. I glance around at the sea of faces; some crumpled, some elated. Whichever way this may have gone for each of us, one thing is certain; we are done.

Cheers and car horns sound as we emerge from the great hall of pain. The last exam of our undergraduate study finally complete, the final paper in the four year degree we all so desperately wanted. Now that it's over, what will we do?

"Over here, Billie!" My vision is still a little hazy from long hours of concentration and little sleep as I turn to find my best friend Iris wearing a smile that speaks on its own.

"We did it! We did it, holy crap, can you believe it's all over? We're done!" She throws her arms around me as we are engulfed by a wave of similarly elated students; everyone is cheering, and as if from nowhere, beer flows. Warm beer in plastic pints is handed out and we drink deeply, barely stopping for breath; the haze in our heads replaced quickly by the warm buzz of booze.

"Jesus H Billie, this is the best day of my life," Iris announces, lying on the grass a few hours later wearing a toga and still drinking beer. "What'll you do?" She props herself on one elbow to face me. Her tone might be asking what I'm having for dinner not what I'm doing with the rest of my life.

"I'm not sure I know where to start." I exhale a long, slow breath. "I'm thinking maybe I'll write the next great novel of our time." I examine my open palm as though looking for a life line to confirm my prophecy. "I'll aim for the Booker Prize next year, and soon after, a whole section in the library under 'W'. Billie May Worthington a writer for our times!" I flop back on to the grass eyes closed smiling wistfully.

"Well, that sounds easy enough, send me a copy of your first best seller." Iris is smiling, her eyes focused on her own projected future. "Yep, good luck with that Billie, but I'm getting myself a job pronto. There's no time to fanny around! I'm heading straight to make some big bucks. Jesus, I've student loans coming out my arse." Iris is also Irish and has a way of expressing herself that can equally horrify and reduce me to howls of laughter.

"Iris, what the hell kind of a job do you think you're going to get with a degree in literature? I doubt the stock market will take you." I laugh.

"Ah, just you watch Billie girl, the world's my lobster, it's up, up, and away from here," she announces, all excited smiles.

"I think you'll find its oyster," I correct, shielding my eyes from the sun.

"Oyster? Who said anything about oysters, for God's sake? A bag of crisps would do nicely." Iris flops back on to the grass, moaning. "I'm peaking too early, it's not even five. Okay, no more beer for an hour and forget the crisps. I need a sausage roll."

8:00 p.m.: Hot shower, sausage roll on board, and a pint of water for Iris, and we are ready for the night of partying we so deserve. In the halls of residence bar we drink cheap cocktails, debrief the year, and swap tales of woe on our performances in today's exam.

Just after nine, our artist-in-residence friend, Derek, or Dez as he prefers to be called, swans into the bar. "Ladies and not so attractive men, you are all looking fabulous tonight!" he announces, red curly hair bouncing as he waves his arms at us. "Accompany me, your cultural guide, into the depths of the city's art scene this fine evening. Our taxi awaits."

We raise our eyebrows, someone throws a crumpled crisp packet at him, and we carry on our conversations.

"Oh, come on you lot." He looks deflated, alter-ego diminished for the moment. "I booked the cab. It's outside. Who's coming to the opening with me? I promise you'll love it, pizza's my shout on the way home!" He awaits the rush to the doors, but gets no response; everyone is quite comfortable, ensconced with their best friends, drinks, and a DJ in the corner.

"Oh, poor Dez. Come on Iris, let's go with him." I nudge her in the ribs, gesturing toward Dez, who pouts by the door. "The poor guy's going to shed a tear if he has to go by himself." Dez has a crush on one of the artists who happens to be part of an opening in a swanky art gallery in town; we had promised him we'd keep him company on his love mission.

"Oh okay, as long as there's free bubbles," says Iris, only half-reluctantly. "I can do art." She applies more lip gloss to her already glossed pout.

"Yes!" Dez punches the air as though Arsenal has just won the league. "Let's go babes." He motions to us, and then pauses, looking carefully at me with the critical eye of a fashion consultant. "Don't you want to change Billie?"

Hands on hips, I turn to face his frizzy hair and nose ring. "Why, is there a problem, ginger nuts?" It's hard having flaming red curly hair. Dez has many nicknames, and not surprisingly, "Ginger nuts" is one of his least favorites.

He raises both palms to face me and stutters, "No ma'am…" He looks at the others, who are stifling smiles and raises an eyebrow. "I'll just go saddle up your horse." Everyone is laughing now, including me; my unchanging dress sense is often the butt of many jokes.

It wouldn't be so funny if I weren't called Billie May. It opens me up to a whole realm of country and western gags. You see I'm rarely seen out of leather cowboy boots and some well-worn Levis, and as I am originally from Kansas, the name slots me right into that Midwestern country girl stereotype. The cowgirl gags are something I'm quite used to.

My Dad is a Londoner, and my mom is from Kansas. They divorced when I was barely a year old; country life was not quite what my Dad had envisaged. Mom died of cancer when I was fourteen, so I came over here to live with Dad. These days, I'm as much Londoner as Kansas gal; a strange blend I guess. So my jeans and boots are all Kansas, and my shirt is usually an expensive designer something-or-other, a bid by my stepmother to glamorize me. I like to think my feet are still in Kansas with my mom, and the rest of me is pretty much Anglicized. The prairie girl twang of twelve-year-old me now replaced by a strange blend of Dorothy from the Wizard of Oz and Anne of Green Gables.

"Leave her alone Dez, and get your fecking beret on," says Iris. "Let's be off to critique some art."

"More like get Dez laid!" hollers a voice from behind as we head for the door.

We step out into the still-humid night air, unseasonably warm. These balmy days that stretch into evening are usually reserved for August and early September; summer's last dash before autumn. But here in June, the warmth feels aged. The air smells thick, but not fragrant. These are hot city smells—individually indistinguishable, of the color grey. Iris and Dez are arm-in-arm up the steps and along the sidewalk to the waiting cab with its shiny black exterior and yellow light atop. I dawdle behind, needing a second to take in the evening, relishing the smells and sights. This could be the last evening like this; here with these friends. I'm ready for change, but nostalgic as always and resolve to hold as much as I can of this last evening to memory. I will write about it later, as I do with mostly everything; journals with descriptions, short poems, sketches, the odd photograph, concert tickets; collages of place and time in images and words.

"Get a move on Daisy Duke; the meter's ticking!" cries Dez from within the taxi, a shiny black beetle, wings open and ready for flight. I hop inside, and the driver pulls away from the curb with the confident air of a true London taxi driver. He drives with the conviction that he is invincible and the road his own. We three must seem an odd bunch huddled in a row; Dez in his second-hand suit and Doc Martens, Iris in a seventies dress and platform wedges, and me, straight-Sally with jeans and ponytail.

The city flashes by; the light waning and the traffic thickening. Stop-start, stop-start, car horns and sirens, roundabouts and underground signs, everywhere there are people.

Dez peers through the glass divide that protects the driver from us, his custom. Checking the neon numbers on the meter, he says. "All right, mate, pull over here if you will."

The driver clicks his tongue and, with a slight shake of his head, pulls in to the curb. Cars behind honk their annoyance.

"But we're not here yet Dez." I'm confused.

He leans in conspiratorially. "Sorry, gals, I've run out money. This is as far as we go." He grins, and we roll our eyes, protesting, as we emerge from the shiny beetle, and Dez parts with a rolled up ten pound note.

Iris whacks him on the arm. "What about the pizza on the way home, you tight cockney?"

He laughs and does a little skip.

"You might not see me on the way home ladies; I'm wearing my lucky undies!"

My turn to punch him on the arm. "How far to walk, then Romeo?"

"Just a few blocks this way." He links arms with us, and we trek through the city to find the much anticipated gallery opening.

"Now just so you two don't look as entirely clueless about the art scene as you so obviously are, let me fill you in… " Dez nudges me. I am lost in one of my favorite hobbies: people watching. "The location is totally amazing," he enthuses. "It's worth a visit just to check out the building. It's the old synagogue near Baker Street, fabulous architecture. They've converted it into three floors, plus there's a loft space and a basement, so there are five exhibits."

Iris is searching in her bag for gum, and I'm still busy watching the scene around me, the people, the bustle, and the feel of night in the city, wondering where each person is going and what their story might be.

Dez doesn't notice our distraction and carries on enthusiastically. "Now, I think there's a mix of painting, sculpture, and architecture;

22 | *Skylark*

models and stuff. Anna is a sculptor. She's amazingly hot, and wait till you see what she can do with her hands." He's breathy in anticipation.

"Christ, I didn't think it was that kind of show," says Iris.

"Her sculpture, you daft cow," says Dez. "Although I think there are a few penises there."

"She sculpts penises?" I ask, trying not to sound too straight.

"Oh yes, in fact, she held interviews to find the right male models for her work."

"She was paying young blokes to show her their willies?" says Iris, aghast. "Can't you get arrested for that?"

Dez ignores her. "I was going to go along myself, but then I worried I might get stage fright and not be able to get it up on command; then she'd never go out with me."

We all laugh. "Does she only want to sculpt stiff willies, then?"

Dez doesn't register my tone. "You know Billie, that's a good question; I can't say I'm sure. Let's go take a look."

We are still two blocks away from Baker Street, Dez having hugely underestimated the distance, and Iris's platform wedges proving to be a hindrance to our pace.

"For fuck's sake Iris, did you have to wear those God-awful shoes? It'll be midnight before we're there."

"I'll kick your arse with one of these here shoes if you're not careful 'Mister I'll get us a cab and pay for the pizzas on the way home!'"

I zone out of their squabble as a cold prickle of temperature change laces my skin with goose bumps. "You guys, I think it's going to rain. We should hurry"

They don't hear, so caught up in a dialogue over the role of platform wedges in the fashion revolution. A sudden flash of lightening stops us all in our tracks; in one blink, the city is all white reflected light and we are monochrome shadows of ourselves. Thunder follows closely, and heavy rain that washes the heat from the day.

"Run!" yells Dez, his voice high-pitched amidst the deep growl of thunder.

We run as commanded, convulsing with laughter, sinking into the hysteria that so often accompanies a storm. Iris pulls off her platforms, and we dash through the rain, squealing like three preschoolers until drenched and breathless; we arrive at the gallery, dripping wet and bedraggled into the foyer.

Iris has barely stopped to look around before she bellows out to anyone who might listen, "Fucking hell, its bloody wild out there! Anyone got a towel?" For a second, all is deathly quiet, glass clinking and hobnobbing stops. All eyes turn in our direction. The art crowd, momentarily ruffled quickly recover their composure at the uncouth disturbance and progress to ignoring us.

Dez is mortified and guides Iris and me to the ladies' room while he scoots off to hang up his sodden second-hand coat (which incidentally smells really bad now) and find us some champagne.

We smooth our hair and take turns standing under the hand dryer. "Okay, that should do Iris, let's find the bubbles." I pull her toward the bathroom door, but she insists on applying some red lippy to both of our pouts.

"It's much more alternative than pastel shades darling. We'll fit right in." We emerge only slightly less bedraggled than we entered to find Dez with his red hair all a frizz deep in conversation with an attractive brunette. He is holding three bubbling pink glasses whilst sipping clumsily from another.

"Ladies, come meet my dear friend Anna. She's the sculptress I've been telling you about." The brunette turns to us and says hello with what appears to be more of a shoo-fly hand action.

"Dear friend my arse," whispers Iris. We take our drinks and politely tell Anna the sculptress we are off to look at her willies. She doesn't flinch.

Dez is quite right; the old synagogue is breathtaking despite the modern renovations to convert it to a gallery. We walk around, enjoying the sheer spectacle that is the world of art; one I would so like to understand but remain on the fringes of. I know what I like and equally know what I don't, but don't ask me to discuss relevance, theory, or influences behind a body of work. I'd consider the question carefully then tell you I like the color.

Despite our lack of education regarding the nuances of each exhibit, Iris and I take our time enjoying the glorious pull of passion in creativity. Well, I do. Iris is fiddling with her mobile phone, and then suddenly turns to me, agitated and a little apologetic. "I've just had a text from Marcus, he wants me to meet him at ten." Her cheeks flush. Marcus is her latest love interest, and she's trying to look unflustered.

"You're leaving me?" I ask, knowing the answer.

"Ah, you'll be alright, you can talk to anyone, and I've seen quite a few of those art ponce types giving you the eye, all rosy cheeks and blond hair. Now, you have a grand night. Say cheerio to Dez for me, and I'll see you back at the ranch… maybe," she finishes with a smile. "Oh, don't look so forlorn, get yourself another glass of free bubbles and mingle. I know you secretly love this stuff." She pecks me on both cheeks and makes a dash for it before I can answer. I'm not that fazed; this situation is more than a little familiar to me. Iris has no loyalty to friends whatsoever when it comes to men. She will dump her girlfriends at the drop of a hat if the chance of a quickie with a new flame arises.

"Be seeing you then," I say mostly to myself and head for the waitress with the tray of filled glasses. I take my time knowing I have nowhere to be and am now effectively here on my own, sad git that I am.

Art ponce guys checking me out, as if! Iris has a clever way of always making it seem like she's trying to do me some kind of a favor when she's off on a love mission. Of course! What was I thinking? She just wanted to free me up for the man of my dreams who must be floating around all these alternative artsy types just waiting for the chance to sweep me off my feet. I laugh out loud, the bubbles going to my head. Oh well, this is good; it's something different, and I don't have to make small talk with anyone. I can't help but keep a tiny eye out for any surprisingly handsome art types who I might want to make some of that small talk with, but it's only the highly unattractive ones who seem to be here tonight.

I have been on a man famine. In fact, I don't want to think about how long it's been since well, you know. I've been a little caught up in studies; this is what I tell myself when the truth is I have no interest in any of the types of men that seem to be interested in me. Of late, it has been beef head rugby blokes or the nerdy anorak types straight from "University Challenge," and presently, I am not desperate enough for sex to go down those roads.

"Single it is!" I toast myself; I am one strong woman. I don't need a man to make me feel good about myself. In fact, I just finished my degree today, and I rock. Oprah would be standing in applause. This is a "you go, girl" moment. "Wooo!" I whoop, giving my thigh a good cowgirl-style slap and am instantly mortified, realizing I may have had more bubbles than I care to admit. I catch a few glances and examine my thigh like I was swatting a bug.

"You must like this one a lot," says a deep, heavily-accented voice behind me, there is humor in the tone and I jump, ready to defend my feelings for the exhibit I am whooping amongst. "Sorry, didn't mean to make you jumpy and all, it's nice to see someone appreciating the work."

I turn to face the voice and find myself close, too close to his face. He is smiling and about to laugh, you see in all my self-reflection, I hadn't realized I was whooping in the room of sculpted willies. I slap my hand over my mouth, afraid I might laugh out loud or have my jaw drop and my tongue loll.

He is beautiful.

"My name's Evan." He holds out a hand; his fingers are long and slender, and I stare at them for far longer than is polite before reaching my own hand out to clasp his.

"Billie May." I feel color rise to my cheeks. My gaze has now traveled from his fingers up to his face and all the small talk I should be making has left the building. I'm writing a soliloquy in my head to the beauty of this man, all dark, wavy hair flopping over one eye, strong jaw, and clear green eyes. I have been holding his handshake for too long, and now I'm not sure just how long the staring thing has been going on. Crap. I say a silent prayer for serenity, plus some irresistibleness, if it's not too much to ask.

"Are you an artist Billie May?" he asks.

"No, and you can just call me Billie." I smile and flatten my hair, not sure whether to run or stay. "I'm just here with a friend." He stares, still smiling that lop-sided grin and I'm afraid if he doesn't stop I may do something worse than the whoopee thigh slap.

"Do you really like the penises?" he asks, and I quail. He just said penis to me, and now I can't stop thinking about his. Internal face slap moment. *Billie May, you are twenty-two years old, and you can do this.* I channel my grandma and look up to answer the penis question without a glimmer of fantasy.

"Not really, I just…" Oh crap, will he think I don't like penises at all now? "Well, not these penises, I mean… oh fuck, can we talk about something else?" I'm a disaster; he will run for the hills wondering who let the mentally-challenged hillbilly in.

"Did you just say fuck?" he asks only loud enough for me to hear, and in his perfect pronunciation of the word 'fuck,' I realize that accent is of course Irish. He is laughing at me, and I can't help but laugh too. He leans in. "It's a little stiff in here, if you'll excuse the comparison, but they don't like bad language. You'd better come with me." He takes me by the hand and leads me out of the room of sculptures and guides me through the crowd. People recognize him and say hello as we pass. He nods and replies, remembering everyone's name, and I am reeling—following him, holding his hand, and wondering who the hell he is.

This moment bears testimony to the sheer pull of physical chemistry.

I know nothing of this man I met moments ago, but I do know that from the instant I saw him, heard him, and touched his hand something changed. Not a small sort of a change like a weather front or a mood flip and not a mild attraction, but something large, something strong and dizzyingly powerful. I've never taken drugs, rarely been really drunk, but I can only imagine this feeling; this sudden high and overwhelming need must be similar to that of an illicit high. Suddenly and unexpectedly plugged into a power source I didn't know existed; a thrilling new sense perception never expected to be in the realm of possibilities.

From zero to one hundred in a few short breaths, my heart rate and blood pressure are operating at warp-speed, and I try to breathe calmly and convey none of this mad mixture of feelings threatening to overwhelm me. Regardless of the fear that I have suddenly lost control of something vital, I have no choice but to continue. I walk with him, holding his hand; this intoxicating stranger who appeared from nowhere. The feeling is so heady I pray he won't let go, and as we walk through the crowded room, my crazed imagination projects wildly forward to a future scenario involving him and a few small dark-haired, green-eyed babies! Oh my God, what am I doing? This sort of thing does not happen to me. I should shake off the weirdly possessive hold he has taken of my hand and gather myself. But of course, I don't. It's the absolute last thing I want to do.

We pass the bar, where he grabs us two glasses then takes me to the lift where we ride to the loft; the only exhibit I haven't seen yet. I stand in the lift, back to the wall, and he mirrors my pose, standing opposite, looking intently at me. He doesn't say a word and neither do I, but I return his stare and relish every second of it.

The doors open with a loud "ding" announcing our arrival to the art lovers in the attic. In an instant, I shift from infatuated to awe-struck as I exit the lift into what feels like another world. This room is full of light, light from all angles giving the impression of daylight. No, something brighter, almost cleaner than daylight. A light unfiltered by pollution and smog, something clean and pure reflecting and bouncing off every surface. The ceiling is arched and high above our heads, and models hang everywhere; large and small, paper thin, and proportionally perfect. All machines of flight, old--fashioned, and in differing shapes and sizes, all neutral and as bright as the light, so we had to stand still to see each one properly, as the slightest movement sent prisms of light to blur the edges of each perfectly-formed aircraft.

The room is crowded, but the light makes it feel less so, people are quiet, respectful; walking, then stopping to stare, walking some more, and then sitting for a time on one of the folding chairs assembled at various perfect vantage points.

I turn to look at Evan to thank him for bringing me here to see this, but he has slipped away, and for a moment, I'm crushed. A hushed voice speaks; a recording that's the voiceover for this work, a description of what it means and the influences of the artist. Closing my eyes for some relief from the overwhelming sensory assault of light, I hear the words more clearly, the same sentence repeating as though part of the work itself.

"I am fascinated by flight, the notion of escape, freedom in wings," the sentence repeats. I open my eyes in recognition, and he is there in front me, the half-smile, the voice, his voice. "I am fascinated by flight, the notion of escape, freedom in wings."

I can't explain exactly why at this moment I am afraid, but fear rolls over me like a breaking wave, crushing and cold. Something strong and powerful urges me to leave, to run, and not to look back, but it makes no sense, and riveted to the spot, staring at all this beauty, I stay. The feeling passes so quickly I wonder later if I imagined it; the adrenaline and anticipation of the moment confusing my overwhelmed senses.

I reach out a hand to him. "Evan the artist, freedom in wings." He looks embarrassed, then quickly recovers. "You're not going to swear, are you?" he asks, smiling.

"I love it," is all I can say, and we walk then together through his pride and joy; him describing each model and what it means to the whole work, me mesmerized.

If there was ever a question about this man I met barely an hour before, it was gone; the strange and confusing fear gone, too, replaced now by longing. I follow him, and I wait for him, and we leave for his apartment. I wave goodbye to Dez, his arm now around Anna; he winks and points to his lucky undies, and I leave without question.

I hardly know him, and it doesn't matter.

Arriving at his studio apartment, amidst the debris of models that didn't make the show, he tips my chin and kisses me hard on the mouth. "I can't explain," he says, and I believe him because neither can I.

Pushing me against the wall, he pins my arms above my head, kissing me with rough urgency. I respond with the same, surprised by own fearlessness. *What am I doing, what am I doing, what am I doing?* The question bounces around my usually sensible head, but I don't care to answer. In fact I know exactly what I'm doing, and God, it feels great. There is heady pleasure in surprising my measured mind with its set responses and careful understanding of the world. For a moment there are two voices, and the new Billie is loudest; she's carefree and confident, whilst the Billie I'm used to stands open-mouthed and horrified at the unfolding scene.

He removes my still-damp clothes with expert dexterity, then when I'm breathless, wearing only bra and knickers, he smiles and slips my leather boots back on. Hair falling around my shoulders, cheeks flushed with lust, I embrace my inner cowgirl and let him kiss me all over until I can't take it anymore.

Overcome by him and so aroused I might explode, I remove his jeans as slowly as I dare. He is before me, hair tousled, green eyes sparkling with something deeper than humor now. For a moment, I remember how the evening started, the discussion of an erect penis, and here I am... .

He is on me, unfastening my bra and tossing it behind his head, moving to my breasts hungrily. There are no thoughts now aside from this moment, and I am lost in the sheer pleasure of being touched by him.

Eyes closed, Evan's hands move over me as though committing form to memory. His mouth, soft and soothing, covers the trail of his hands. Fingers stroke a subliminal message, and I am molded, shaped and reformed under his fingertips and mouth to his version of perfection. He speaks quietly, whispering; his accent thicker than I can understand as he slides his hand between my legs, and I cry out, unable to hold back.

But he shakes his head, kissing me again, the kiss harder now; his teeth biting down on my lower lip as his hand and fingers find their target. In moments, I feel desperate and wild, unable to wait.

He steadies me, bringing both hands to my shoulders and pushing me back on the bed. There is a pause in the onslaught, and as I lie back, breathing heavily, I hear him fumble; a packet rips, and somewhere in my lust ridden daze I register relief and fleeting disbelief that I forgot to insist on protection.

I reach out and hold firmly to the sinewy forearms supporting his naked body above. Eyes locked on mine, he eases himself inside me, and I cry out again as he throws back his head, hovering on the edge of control. "Jesus Christ, Billie… " His eyes are dark and hair damp as he takes a long, slow breath before sinking down toward me again, face inches from mine, hands pushing against the bare concrete wall the bed lies against. He thrusts hard, again and again, and with each movement, I slowly unravel, forgetting everything and knowing this could be all there was and it would be enough.

Reaching hands into his hair, I breathe his name, back arching as I come closer second by second to climax. Slipping into his rhythm, I follow thrust for thrust, breath for breath, till finally we come together and collapse, tangled and undone, to sleep till morning. This was the changing storm and turning point, an end and a beginning, a love story and a tragedy, birth and death all starting out that night amongst the broken models and beer bottles.

I wake early as sharp fingers of sunlight pierce the shadows in the room. Windows without curtains leave us exposed and naked above the city, and the distant sounds of London waking up rise and filter through sunlight and sleep. Evan lies still on my chest; his breath even, one hand in my hair the other wrapped around the small of my back. Pinned to the bed, the evening flooding back, I stare at the top of his head in wonder that this is not in fact a dream. Cramp in my lower legs soon takes hold, and reluctant as I am to spoil the scene, I move myself gently from underneath him. His eyes flash open, and he grabs my shoulders, all traces of sleep gone. "No you don't," he whispers, and the rest of morning went something like that.

"Love is the opposite of wisdom." I should know who said that, being a Literature graduate; someone who no doubt loved someone like Evan. I was, from that morning, no, probably from the night before, from the very first conversation in the room of penises, in love.

I had feared that it would wane, like most things that start so dramatically and without warning, but it didn't. I wanted to be with him every minute, and as of course that was impossible, I thought about him all the time. If I wasn't with him I was thinking about him and just thought of him was like a shot of something illicit. I could raise my heart rate simply imagining his face.

All of this haste and mad passion were so unlike me, my friends worried briefly for my sanity, then quickly got sick of me mooning around and accepted that aliens had taken over the body of straight arrow Billie. Every part of me knew all of this was unwise, but I didn't care; Evan was everything I wanted, and the best part of it was he wanted me too, as badly as greedily, and as urgently as I did.

Social experiences at university seem to operate on a slightly different time spectrum to those in the outside world. Friends made over a few intense terms can feel closer than those childhood friendships nurtured for years. Maybe it's the pace and promise of life on the threshold of opportunity; stresses, studies, first loves, and heartbreak, all while trying desperately to climb the ladder to the adult life you want. My short relationship with Evan soon felt mature; the intensity of a few short weeks akin to a year on the outside.

I had climbed the study ladder, hit every rung to reach the graduate spot, and now I seemed to have grabbed on to a wild stray rope, tying it deftly to mine, soon believing it had always been there. Had I hopped onto Evan's path or him to mine? It didn't matter. In no time, it was a given that we were a couple. I had, without fully understanding, relinquished my single self and become part of something beautiful but complex; something that would bring me to my knees, but give me more than I dreamt possible.

* * *

Chapter Three

London
August 2001

Grey light from the small dimpled glass window bathes the bathroom in monochrome. Everything is concrete or steel, no soft edges or fluffy towels, and I'm thankful that it's summer because Evan's apartment has no signs of heat. I wonder how in the world he made it through the winter.

A cast-iron tub stands on four claw feet against the bare concrete wall, the white interior chipped and cracked, and a trail of wet footprints on concrete lead to where I stand, examining my reflection. The sink and toilet are stainless steel and I can't help feeling like an extra in *Prisoner Cell Block H*. Evan's warehouse attic apartment is basic, and the rent cheap. I'm not entirely sure it's supposed to be residential, more like a studio space Evan sleeps in post-creative bursts.

I rub more steam from the mirror and critically assess my flushed face, which, of course, critiques me right back. At least he has hot running water! I towel off and decide this Billie is quite preferable to the Billie pre-Evan. The bubble of hazy lust, although I'd optimistically call it love, has not burst, and flush-faced seems to be my new look. I go about my day with the self-confident air of one recently shagged by the most gorgeous man on the planet, and that's usually because I just have or am about to be. I somehow entirely skipped the 'playing hard-to-get' bit with Evan, and thankfully, he skipped the "aloof-playing-it-cool bit," and we haven't spent much time apart since the night at the gallery.

I lean forward to scrutinize my reflection, still waiting for the moment where the alarm goes off, and I wake up with braces on my teeth and no boyfriend. I pinch myself hourly, and so far I'm still in this reality; so far, I have only woken up with him beside me and so I walk each step on happy feet. If I had the voice for it, I'd sing, but honestly, I don't think that would do my love life any favors, so I hum softly as I finish examining my flushed reflection in the steamy mirror. With a cheeky wink to self, I thank my lucky stars once again for art galleries and sculpted willies and Irish men and general good fortune.

Fully dry, I grab some sweats hanging on the back of the bathroom door and wrap a towel around myself "à la movie star" style before heading through to get changed. Evan's back is to me at the concrete bench against the window. His kitchen is compactly comprised of a bench, a plug-in two ring electric burner, a small fridge advertising "Bud Light" (no doubt acquired from a bar), two small saucepans, and a wooden chopping board. The smell of coffee wafts through the studio, and the espresso pot bubbles excitedly on the burner.

"Do you think there's any water left in Greater London?" asks Evan without turning around. I ignore him, slipping into my clothes and heading to the enticing coffee smell. Two small red cups sit on the bench, and Evan pours out equal measures of dark creamy espresso and a heaped teaspoon of sugar into mine.

He stirs steadily. "Do you take an hour-long bath every day?" His eyes sparkle as he hands me the sweet-smelling red cup.

I shrug. "I like water."

He nods, watching me as he raises the cup to his lips and sips slowly. "What else don't I know about you?"

"Heaps," I answer, smiling brightly. "In fact, I'm incredibly deep.

You may need to spend quite some time trying to unravel my psyche... you know, figure me out."

He is still nodding, going along with my humor; a small smile plays on his lips. Carefully, he puts the coffee cup down and laces his fingers together, bringing index fingers to his lips as though in great contemplation. "I see, it could take some time then."

"For sure." I nod. "You might need to focus on me full-time for a while just to get a real handle on things. In fact, you might want to make me your muse." My expression has no flicker of a smile, and for a second, I panic and wonder if he thinks I'm serious and he's hooked up with a narcissistic crazy girl, but I catch his eyes twinkle.

"My muse?"

"Uh-huh, do you have a vacancy? I could lounge around half-naked, eat grapes, and recite my poetry for you; that sort of thing." He is silent, watching me, and I'm waiting for him to laugh. "I'd do that for you... just to be helpful..."

"I don't know if it'd be helpful at all." His mouth smiles, but his eyes are all serious. I know that look.

"Okay, I'll forget the grapes."

He takes the coffee cup and places it on the concrete counter, then grabs my waist, and throws me over his shoulder in one mad move. I scream while he laughs, slapping my bum, heading purposefully toward the bed, which is only really a few strides from the kitchen.

"Okay, okay, I get it. You don't need a muse." He slaps my bum again, and I yelp, "Ouch! I would so not even be your muse if you asked me! That hurt." He throws me back on to the mattress, and I raise my hands, warding him off, while he grabs my wrists and pins them to either side of my head.

"Don't worry, I'll kiss it better." I laugh at the cheesiness of his reply, but my trousers are already off, he's as good as his word.

36 | *Skylark*

"Evan, I just…"

He stops. "You just what?"

"I just had a bath." I pretend to push him away, but of course I'm not really serious.

"I know, you smell great."

"And, we have stuff to do… "

He pulls the tattered Lonsdale hoodie I found in his bathroom over my head, and my words are muffled in the heavy fabric of the oversized sweater.

"What did you say you wanted me to do?" he asks when my head finally emerges, face flushed, hair everywhere. The smart comeback I'm about to say is lost as he carries on doing what I hoped he'd do all along.

Much later, no further forward with our day, I jump from a doze that may have lasted a week, entirely naked and disorientated. Evan is no longer beside me, but on the other side of the studio, sketching and making notes. I pull the hoodie on and pad over to where he sits, wearing only his jockeys, hands black with charcoal.

"Hey."

"Hey." He smiles up as though he'd forgotten I'm here. "Turns out you might be my muse after all."

Moving closer, I lay a hand on his shoulder and look down at the sketch. He continues in some sort of hurry to get the image that has appeared in his head onto paper. It's a figure, arms outstretched, face undefined. The charcoal edges are smudged, giving an impression of movement, perhaps flight. It hangs suspended, and as I watch him work, the elegant arms blur into wings.

"She's beautiful."

He carries on without looking up, seemingly oblivious to my hand on his shoulder. The wings become more obvious, less human, more bird, feathered perhaps, and stunningly beautiful. I don't want to break the spell that has him drawing as though in a trance until unceremoniously a telephone rings, making me jump, and I remember I have a life outside of this blissful bubble. My mobile lies on the bench ringing loudly and I panic wondering what time it is realizing I really do have 'stuff to do' today.

"Hello?"

"Billie, what time are we supposed to be there? The bloody tube has broken down, and I have to walk to the next station."

"What time is it now?" I'm trying not to sound entirely disoriented.

"It's twelve, for God's sake; tell me you've picked our robes up?" My eyes widen in horror that I could be so incredibly dizzy and lose track of myself this way. Our graduation ceremony is at 3:00 p.m. "Don't panic, I'm on it. I'll meet you at my room at one-thirty."

"Okay." Iris sounds marginally relieved. "What a palaver, honestly. Mam and Dad will be gutted if I don't have the robe and funny hat; they've probably been parked on the front row seats for hours."

I hear a car horn beep in the background, some muffled swearing, and then Iris is back. "Better run, I've a taxi driver with road rage after me. See you soon." She hangs up abruptly.

"Shit." I lay a shaky hand on my forehead.

"What's wrong?" Evan has snapped out of his mad sketching frenzy and looks up with concern.

"'I can't believe I almost forgot!" I dash around, scooping up abandoned clothes, trying not to panic.

"What?"

"It's graduation ceremony today! At three!"

"It's not even one; you're not late," Evan answers, looking confused at the flap I'm in.

"I know, but look at me. I still have to pick up the robes and… never mind, I've got to run."

"Okay, will I see you later?"

I pause only because I'm not sure what has been organized for the night. There was talk of some post ceremony drinks and nibbles for friends and families, but I hadn't taken much notice as I hadn't invited any family to come along. To be honest, it hadn't felt like a big deal, and I wasn't too wound up about the whole thing. That said, half of Iris's family had planned a summer holiday around the event and would be there to see her take the stage and become a graduate.

"I'll call you."

"Can I come?"

I stop rushing around for a second and look at him. "I didn't think you'd want to."

"Why wouldn't I?"

"Well, it'll be boring as hell, and you'd have to sit on an uncomfortable seat for three hours watching hordes of people you don't know get a little certificate to tell them they can go make their way in the world."

"You're right, boring as hell." He watches me as I scurry around trying to locate a missing boot while tying my hair up in a ponytail. "Billie, I've had this great idea."

"Uh-huh." I am only half-listening, suddenly struck by the thought that the robe shop on campus may close at lunchtime.

"Move in with me." I stop midflight and turn to him. He shrugs, and I let my breath escape slowly, trying not to look fazed. He waits, watching, but I'm overwhelmed and it shows. I have of course been entertaining the fantasy, but in those love-struck daydreams, that bit happens later. I'm late and panicked and so rather than say the immediate "yes" that feels inevitable, I suck in my breath, close my eyes, and press my hands together, trying to gather my thoughts.

"What's wrong?"

"Nothing, I just need to go right now."

"Is that a no then?" His expression is unreadable and his usual humor has left the building.

"No… I mean yes." Now I'm all flustered and suddenly feel unsure of everything, not how I feel about him, but the pace that all this is progressing. It's not the way I do things. Momentarily confused, I shake my head and scoop up my bag. "Today, I'm going to graduate, and then I can think about tomorrow."

He watches me, unblinking.

"It's not a no, Evan, I'm just a little freaked out." He still doesn't answer, and the moment is so unexpectedly tense I feel claustrophobic and need to leave. I grab my bag and head to the door, turning briefly to him. He looks out the window, back to me, arms folded.

"Bye." My voice is small and apologetic, and as the door closes, I feel the hot prickle of tears and hurry to the elevator, afraid I might give myself away. As my proximity to him lessens, the physical hold he has over me lets go its grip a little, and my confusion turns to anger. I replay the short scene that unexpectedly turned the mood on its head. I can't believe he's angry I didn't immediately say yes, jump into his arms, and tell him he is the man of my dreams. Despite feeling he really might be that guy, his cold response to my confusion has thrown me, and I'd like to yell at him for making me feel shitty for wanting to take a little time over a fairly big decision. At the same time, here I am tearful and afraid that somehow I may have ruined things and punctured the perfect bubble I have naively been living in for the past three weeks.

* * *

The auditorium is packed with family members and loved ones, bottoms in Sunday best squashed on to row upon row of folding chairs and I wish just for a moment I had someone here, too. A proud face in the crowd to nod and think, "That's my girl. Didn't she do well?" It's my own fault, of course. I didn't bother telling anyone about the ceremony, didn't feel like the fuss or tension between Dad and Step Dad; an extra reminder that Mom, always the peacemaker, isn't here. So, here I sit in a row of similarly dark-robed friends with funny chalkboard hats listening to the university Vice Chancellor's speech about education and future potential and promising careers.

Slowly, slowly, row by row, we take the stage and walk left to right as our name is called to be congratulated and presented with a rolled certificate. It's all a little tedious, and I can't believe anyone in the room, aside from the proudest of parents, is having a good time. Iris's family (as expected), sit near the front, turning regularly to catch sight of her and give a wink or a wave. The audience have been asked to keep their applause till the end of each class division to prevent the event running on till midnight, but when Iris takes the stage, there's an outburst of wild cheering as Mum, Dad, brother Gav, and Aunty Agnes stand for a full ovation. Iris gives a dramatic curtsey to the Vice Chancellor, a thumbs-up to her proud family, and skips off the stage, clutching the roll of paper she hopes will make her fortune.

Suddenly, my cheeks are red, and my eyes threaten to spill over as waves of emotion take me by surprise; a family of sad and happy thoughts and memories buzz around my dramatic head, and as my name is called, I'm dabbing at my face with the edge of my graduation robe. Dez nudges me from behind, and I rise, taking a deep breath, and head down, praying I don't embarrass myself with a quivering chin as I do the steady walk from left to right. Conscious of the heat and heavy, expectant silence, I let one foot lead the other, step by step toward the Chancellor, and smile in what I hope appears a gracious manner and take my ribbon rolled certificate.

"Congratulations Billie May, and best of luck for the future."

The words almost set me off again, but I focus on his polka-dot tie and manage to keep the waterworks at bay. We shake formally; he has cool hands and a kind smile, and I smile back, surprising myself with how important the moment feels. It's my final step in academia and first step into the real world; a rite of passage and a new beginning.

Still smiling, I exit left when there's an obnoxiously loud wolf whistle from the back of the hall. Heads crane around in the direction of the noise, and there is much "tut-tutting" as people rubberneck to see where the disturbance has come from. The whistle sounds again, this time followed by a very loud, well-oiled Irish voice.

"Billie May… I love you… did you hear that? I love you…" The next drunken word is intercepted by campus security, and there's some commotion and swearing as Evan objects to being ejected. I'm frozen on the stage, unsteady legs only just keeping me upright as I conduct an internal debate from eyes and ears to brain. What I can see and hear cannot be happening; Evan wouldn't behave this way, wouldn't make a fool of himself like this, wouldn't sabotage my ceremony. Eyes wide, hand covering my mouth, I watch in horror, unsure whether to laugh or cry. All around the audience swivel heads from me to the figure at the back of the hall still slurring words of love as he is forcibly removed by two swarthy security guards.

I walk steadily to my seat, my cheeks burning. Iris and Dez are in hysterics. The Vice Chancellor taps the microphone and professionally settles the auditorium before continuing on with the next long list of names, praying, no doubt, that there are no more drunken delays to keep him from the free champers outside.

"Oh my God, Billie, that was pure class!!" Iris hisses in my ear. "He is one crazy fucker!" She can barely contain her giggles.

Dez leans in, mimicking, "Billie May, I love you, too… " I jab an elbow back in his direction, but he carries on regardless. "Bloody hell,

I need some of what he's had. There'll be no action in the sack tonight, girl, that boy'll have to go sleep that one off!"

I shush them both, gesturing at the stage while the rest of the ceremony carries on uneventfully. I want to laugh about it too, like them, make light of the whole thing, but I can't. I sit preoccupied, furious with him, then worried about him, and then frustratingly a tiny bit flattered that he made such an ass of himself for me.

I try not to lose sight of the nostalgic feelings I was enjoying only a short while ago and hone in on the last few robed handshakes and speeches from academics, all the while hoping he is asleep at home working up the hangover he will no doubt be nursing by midnight.

* * *

The crowd has been ushered from the stuffy auditorium to a huge canvas tent set up on the cricket pitch where family members hug flushed new graduates and drink bubbles in plastic flute glasses. Iris is giggly and a little drunk already; her Mum and Dad bustling around looking proud, and Gav chats with Dez, eyes scanning the marquee at the mass of gorgeous girl graduates ready to party.

"I can't believe Evan did that Billie. That guy's crazy?" Iris's eyes are wide as she relives the scene in the auditorium. She claps her hands together in glee, loving that Evan appears to be crazier than her.

I shake my head in disbelief; I still can't decide whether I find the incident appalling or quite funny. "He is." I don't know what else to say; he is, as Iris says, entirely mad.

"Pure class, escorted out of graduation by security. I love it!"

"What will they do to him?"

Iris slaps my arm like I've just made a hilarious joke. "Well, he's not off to Barlinnie, if that's what you mean! Don't worry, Billie;

they're not about to arrest him for getting pissed and telling his girlfriend he loves her at graduation. He'll be down the pub by now waiting for you."

"You think?" I frown, still part worried, part mad, but heading toward 'part drunk,' and really just desperately want to see him.

"What's up with you? You're acting weirder than usual."

I take a large glug of my fake champers and screw up my lips. "Yuck."

"Here, have another; that'll help." Iris pushes another plastic glass into my hand before I have time to object. "Spit it out then, what's up?"

"I don't know, I've never met anyone like him before…" Iris rolls her eyes and then makes a gagging face. I nudge her in the ribs and continue. "He wants me to move in with him, but it all feels so fast."

"And the problem is?" Iris looks at me like I'm the mad one now.

"Well… I really like him."

"And?" She looks at me in disbelief.

"And…"

Iris raises a hand and interrupts me. "And, nothing! Will you get over yourself Billie, and quit thinking everything through? Make a few rash decisions. So what? You really like him!" She raises her voice. "Why the hell shouldn't you? He's gorgeous, and he's Irish; what's not to like? Go have fun, for Christ's sake, you bloody well deserve some!"

She stops for breath and turns around as though expecting some applause for her motivational soliloquy. Jim, Iris's Dad, stands beside us, nodding and looking interested. He's traded the bubbles for a pint of something frothy and dark brown and raises the glass to me.

"Aye, cheers to that, so you do Billie! Away and tell that boy how you feel!"

He nods sagely and slurps a great mouthful of frothy beer, then tries to disguise a gassy belch. I suddenly see the funny side of everything. Maybe it's the company, the bubbles, or just the moment but soon we are all laughing and my worries leave with the first of the robed graduates heading for the pub.

* * *

By twelve-thirty, we have lost the cloaks and the hats, have drunk more than we should, and are ready to go dancing. We file into our usual haunt, 'Crystals', a sticky-floored student nightclub where the music is great and the drinks cheap. I keep expecting to find him waiting somewhere for me, ready to laugh off the wolf whistling scene, and whisk me away to his apartment where we'd forget all the tension from before, and I'd "get over myself," as Iris so nicely put it and maybe make a few rash decisions. That could have been my hesitation with the move-in thing. It feels that the only decisions I've made since laying eyes on him have been rash ones and I freaked out. Just asking for time to think it through shouldn't have been such a big deal, right?

He's not here, the nightclub is packed, and there are sweaty bodies everywhere. That feeling of claustrophobia is all over me again, and I suddenly need to leave. I don't worry about goodbyes, no one cares much at this stage of the night, and most are too sozzled to notice. I slip out of the exit into the cool night air and decide that if he's not coming to me, I'll just have to go to him.

The confidence and bravado I felt in town is long gone by the time I reach the door to his apartment. I am now substantially soberer than before; a combination of the cool night air and the brisk walk. Suddenly unsure if I'm doing the right thing, it takes a long minute of almost pressing the buzzer before I finally do. The tinny sound rings loudly on the quiet street, and I imagine the shrill noise upstairs that might wake him; it is 1:30 a.m.

The automated latch opens as someone inside the apartment block (Evan, I hope) lets me in. The thought of the dark elevator creeps me out, so I take the long stair climb, also creepy but at least dimly lit. By the eighth floor my legs are shaking, and I'm breathing so heavily I'm sure I might wake someone. There is a light on in Evan's apartment; it shines through the high glass panel above the front door, and I take this to be a good sign. Knocking tentatively, I wait, still gasping for air. Nothing. I knock again, louder this time, and as the door clicks open, I jump.

"Come in," says the retreating back. Not the, "Hello, hey baby," "So glad you came over," sort of a welcome I'd been hoping for. He disappears around the corner, and I follow, waiting nervously at the edge of the studio while he stands, still facing away from me, stirring something in a cup on the counter. All this way in the night to see him, and I'm lost for words, wondering why I came and wishing he'd just turn around.

"I was waiting for you in town," I say hesitantly to his back. An old white shirt hangs loosely over jeans, and his feet are bare.

"Why?"

"I thought you'd come out and meet us after…" I have a sudden flashback to the wolf whistling and calling. Evan at the back of the auditorium, hands in the air, making a scene. He has obviously sobered up but I don't see signs of the hangover he deserves.

"I was busy." He still hasn't turned around, and I'm beginning to feel freaked out.

"You were busy?" His flippant reply irks me. "So after making me feel like a total ass in front of the entire university, you decided you'd go find something better to do?" I can feel myself bristling and just want him to turn around!

"Look." He pauses, seeming to gather himself before carrying on. "I'm sorry, that was stupid. I didn't plan it. I came down to see you, I wanted to watch… I'd had a few drinks and well… story of my fucking life."

Is this supposed to be my explanation? "Will you shut up and turn around?" His shoulders sink a little, but he does and I hear myself do the dramatic girly gasp as his face catches the light; one eye is swollen shut, his upper lip is gashed, and cheek grazed. Frozen to the spot an awkward distance away, I reach out an arm, the other hand covering my mouth still wide in shock. Although only a second has passed, it feels like an hour before I find my voice.

"What happened?"

"It was my fault." He looks away ashamed. Finding the use of my legs, I move to him, grabbing his hand, which I now see is dressed and bandaged.

"You were in a fight."

He looks at me with the one eye he can actually open. "Billie, I'm bad news; you should go."

I shake my head, grasping on to his good hand as he tries to move away. "Have you been to hospital?"

He lifts the bandaged hand. "Twelve stitches, then an escort to the cop station".

"Shit Evan, what did you do?" I shiver involuntarily, and he walks to the bed and grabs a blanket, throwing it round my shoulders, then passes me the well-stirred hot tea he'd been hovering over. I sink into his one armchair as he sits on the bed, his head hanging like a sorry dog.

"I can hardly remember. I'm a fucking idiot." He brings his hands to his face, and then winces, everything too sore to touch. "After you left this morning, I painted and drank too much, and then it seemed like a good idea to come along and tell you all the reasons why you should move in with me. As you can see, I made a total arse of myself and managed to show you instead a whole lot of fucking reasons you should steer clear."

He attempts a small smile, but his swollen lip isn't playing. "Those security fuckers decided to kick me out, and I got myself all fired up, knowing I'd managed to screw things up again. So I went and got myself in a good fight… and here we are."

"Here we are." I pull the blanket around me and wonder, not for the first time, where the other Billie has gone and if she's ever coming back. My head is jumbled, tangled thoughts and conflicting feelings battle for a place in line. All noise and chaos, but over everything, the loudest and most insistent of shouts is the one that says, "Listen… stop and listen. His words are true. He loves you."

Another long moment as we both stare at the cool concrete floor and the world slows down and stills. "What you said, before you got kicked out and got yourself beaten to a pulp… the bit you shouted after the whistle." My cheeks flush again, despite the chill. "Did you mean it?"

I'm wondering if I should re-word my question to, "Do you remember what you said?" Then follow it with: "Is the insane behavior and mad drinking a regular thing and were you serious when you said I should run for it?"

I don't say any of those things because my heart is heavy looking at him sitting on the edge of the bed, all broken and bruised, as though he won the lotto and lost the ticket. I want to fix him and make it better, and in that second of quiet contemplation, I make a decision on a deeper level that will shape my future.

The question has thrown him, and he looks up with his one good eye fixed on me. "I did."

I feel the confusion and fear sort of slipping away in the darkness, leaving me strangely calm and full of hope, despite the scene. Despite the drunken, mad behavior and the bruised face, despite the intensity and the anger and his total unpredictability thus far, his passion and honesty are real. That he loved me enough to shout it in front of

500 strangers today fills me with joy rather than horror, and in that moment, all the flashing strobe warning lights dim to candle flickers.

I decide to let myself love him back.

"Will you say it again…?" There's a flicker of hope in his face as he watches me carefully, then says it quietly this time, for an audience of one; not for attention or to make a scene, but because he means it and I need to hear it.

"I love you."

I close my eyes. The words fill me up, but I'm afraid to trust myself.

"How can you be sure?"

Evan rests his palms on top of his head, still staring at the floor, unable to look at me.

"I can't explain. I told you before; I just know, and it's making me crazy. I don't know what to do with it, and I'm afraid of fucking up."

Pulling the woolen blanket with me, I sit on the floor by his feet, and he strokes my hair with his good hand, movement careful and unsure.

"I love you, too."

I sit beside him on the bed and hold shaky hands on either side of his bloodied face. His hands cover mine, and for a time, we sit together, letting the moment rest before moving slowly back to lie on the bed, face to face, chest to chest, too sore and bone-tired to do anything but touch. We talk quietly till the sun comes up and then fall asleep entwined; his head on my chest, my limbs wrapping him in a promise that tomorrow will be better.

* * *

I wake before Evan and lie still, gazing around the studio as the light changes and brightens on every surface. In the dim haze of last night, I noticed only Evan and the bruised, bloody face he tried to hide. Now I see the walls covered in a breathtaking collection of charcoal drawings. Huge sheets of torn paper, the winged woman of before in varying poses, her posture elegant, then suggestive, graceful then ugly; her features emotive, eyes large and expressive. And no matter how many times I rub the sleep from my eyes or tilt my head to view her from a different angle, from every place in the studio it is my face that stares back.

* * *

Chapter Four

London
January 2002

"Let's do it Billie; screw what anyone says. I sure as hell don't give a fuck!" He takes a deep breath before continuing, reigning in the anger which is beginning to surface. "Come with me, you won't be sorry. We'll make it work. Say you will."

I wait in silence for the break in Evan's persuasive speech; he finally runs out of steam, stopping for breath and placing a hand on his forehead before sighing, eyes raised to the heavens. "Do you always have to be so fucking pragmatic?"

I take a moment to enjoy the power. He is waiting for me to call the shots, and although I know my answer, I drag the moment out just a bit longer. We stand in the middle of Evan's studio, and I can see his breath; icy white puffs of frustration as he waits for the answer which will determine our future.

"I will."

"You will?"

"I will."

"You'll come?"

"That's what I said. I'll come."

I can't help but smile at the incredulous look on Evan's face. Did he really think I'd let him go? His furrowed brow is gone, and he has the look of a little boy just given a lifetime supply of ice cream. "You can't change your mind; you've said it now." He folds his arms across his chest, warily smiling, but still unsure.

"I know." I fold my arms across my chest, mirroring his 'don't mess with me' pose and try to convey a certainty I don't feel.

Evan has been offered a job in Paris; not just any job, but a great job. A dream job. One that is tempting enough to lure him from this drafty loft space studio to a downtown Parisian apartment and nine to five hours in a suit. I can't imagine the transformation or how it will fit Evan, the complete non-conformist, but this is the chance he has been waiting for, and he wants me to pack up and move with him.

We have known each other six months, and I have no doubts that Evan was sent to this planet for me. Life before him has faded into some non-descript haze of blahness, and an imagined future without him is not an option. But I find myself thrown by the news that things must change. I'm reluctant to give up our idyllic existence here where I write by day and waitress by night, where Evan makes art, and together, we somehow scrape together enough money to pay rent and buy bread, wine, and coffee: the essentials.

We have been living together in a perfect bubble of each other and dreams for our separate, creative future ambitions, unhindered by any real responsibility, fuelled by an imagined future. It's a bubble where anything feels possible and all of life is presented as an opportunity. With Evan, I believe I can do anything; I will become published, and in my love-struck haze, I write with new passion. I am wordsmith and nothing escapes an evaluation in long verbose descriptions in my head. Thankfully, by the time my words reach paper, they have been reduced to something more concise and, I hope, less sappy.

Every day I wake up surprised to find myself here beside Evan and constructs from his flying world. We are happy together, and since graduation, which already seems like an eternity ago, there has been little to wobble the pedestal I place Evan on. That I could be this fortunate takes my breath away. And so I begin each day with a long, deep breath, some good sex, and a big hallelujah to whoever is up there looking after me. Being a strong believer in karma, I figure I must have done some pretty selfless things in a life before this one, and I'm hoping all this selfish pleasure isn't screwing me over in the next life.

Evan rugby tackles me before I can change my mind, and I fall backward onto the tatty sofa, yelling in protest but actually not trying terribly hard to fend him off. A coffee cup smashes to the floor, a flailing limb toppling its contents over a newspaper opened to the careers section. There is a thud on the stairs, followed by several more, and a loud bang on the door.

"Ignore it," growls Evan in my ear, and I do until the banging persists and Iris's voice is heard in perfect foghorn pitch.

"Quit shagging you two, and let us in!"

Evan flops on top of me, sighing in resignation, while Iris continues her barrage from the stairwell; she is not a force to be messed with. "Are you coming to the pub or not? Me and Dez here are just about dead walking up those bloody stairs! When are you getting a real flat Evan? C'mon, let us in. We're taking you two for a pint!"

I push Evan off, laughing and rearrange my clothes.

Iris and I link arms as we make our way to the local pub; 'The Barley Mow'. The night is cold and damp, and we huddle together talking conspiratorially. "Hope you haven't made a decision yet," Iris says, the boys trailing behind, out of earshot, talking music.

"Well…" My hesitation speaks for me.

"Oh, c'mon, Billie, I thought you were going to give it some time, a few weeks at least! What about your internship? I thought you had that all planned out." She lectures out of concern, and her worry merely mirrors my own, but I've made my decision. "I know, and I've thought it all through. It's the right thing."

Iris throws me a questioning look. "I swear to God, Billie May Worthington," she uses my full country and western style name for effect, "I'd believe the body snatchers had taken you in the night and replaced you with Barbie!"

I tug my arm from hers, laughing, and give her a friendly punch to the arm.

"What happened to 'Billie May… make some rash decisions for once?'" I impersonate her in my best (really quite bad) Irish accent. She frowns momentarily then a light goes on as she remembers. "Oh, that? That was just the champers talking; you didn't think I meant it, did you?"

I laugh, and we carry on, walking down the dark, cold streets, past terraced houses and corner shops.

"Anyway, you really can't talk, can you, 'Mrs 'never made a rash decision in love before'!'"

"Me?"

"Yes, you, Iris O'Neill! You are one fat hypocrite. You have thrown deadlines, plans, and friends out of the window more times than I can remember the minute your latest love interest gives you the thumbs up."

"Watch it cowgirl. I'll have you know I've a romantic heart is all, and by the way, I resent the fat bit. I may be a hypocrite, but this arse can still squeeze into size ten jeans from Topshop!"

"You've got to be kidding me!" I squeal. "Is that with or without high control support pants?"

Iris screams with laughter and punches me back, her Beyoncé--size bottom always a topic for teasing. At all the hilarity, Dez and Evan descend, keen to share the joke. Evan slides between me and Iris, throwing his arms around both of us. "Break it up ladies." He is all smiles; the victory from my earlier decision fresh on his face.

"Feck it, here's Ken!" says Iris, frowning up at him. Evan looks bewildered as I laugh and Dez strides ahead to open the door to the pub.

Inside, the sights and sounds are familiar and comforting. Lots of university friends crowded into corners, around tables topped with pint glasses and empty packets of potato chips, laughter and music.

"I'll sort the bevies out," says Dez, as he weaves his way through the crowded bar. Iris heads for what looks like the last free table. The pub is full of people from university who, a little like us, haven't quite moved on to the next phase. In between graduation and new careers, they stay here and string out the university experience just a little longer, ignoring the responsible world till start dates demand they consider mortgages and pinstriped suits.

The night is one of laughter and memories of good things from our times here at this point in our lives. Strange that within a year mostly everyone will move on to somewhere else, to a different phase of their lives where student days will seem distant and strangely carefree, despite the pressures of study and exams and a future reliant upon good grades and job applications. We all fit; this cross-section of life, all with hopes and dreams, all on the brink of the adventure that 'grown up' life holds. We are a bustling, drunken collective of tomorrow's potential lawyers, doctors, artists, writers, teachers, accountants, dreamers, and drunks. Anything is possible, and with that thought in mind, we are excitable and overconfident; tomorrow we could do anything, but tonight we enjoy this moment when possibilities bubble in the froth of our beer.

* * *

Any indecision on my part soon fades as the momentum of our move to Paris gains speed. There are so many loose ends to tie up when leaving one life to begin another. My internship at Baker & Marlow publishing house was to begin in six months within the editorial department. Giving up this opportunity is huge for me, but I know opportunities will be waiting elsewhere. My path with Evan will take me there, and so I decide that in Paris, I'll learn French and focus on my writing. I conclude that the time will give me the chance to see if I can write a novel worth publishing.

Evan's company, Sans Limites, is an international pioneer in ethical architecture based in the heart of Paris, and already, an apartment in the city waits. I move through the process of packing and goodbyes with a strange mixture of excitement and anxiety. All around, the old life is changing, everyone preparing for new challenges, careers, and locations; it's time for me, too, and wherever Evan went, I would inevitably follow; this much I knew.

Evan's art is sold, packed, or discarded to be ceremoniously burned, and with the money he makes, we are to set ourselves up in Paris before the first paycheck arrives. The models of flight from the exhibition on the night we met are packed; some boxed whole, the others carefully disassembled and laid piece by piece in layers of cotton.

On our last night, Evan makes a bonfire in the shared grass patch mistitled "garden," overgrown and untended by the busy commuters and students who live on the block. We gather with Iris, Dez, and the usual crowd to pay tribute to the great Gods of fortune who are to send us on our way into the world. The January night is cold but dry, and the sky glitters bright, a touch of frost in the air. Evan stands before us, glass in one hand, matches in the other, behind him is the tall pile of paper sketches, old canvases and wooden structures (some half completed), and others that seemed to me to be perfect and unworthy of the funeral pyre. Anything considered in any way imperfect by Evan was to be sacrificed to the fire. Friends had asked him to let them keep the odd model or sculpture lying nervously awaiting the flames, but Evan had refused; only perfection got to stay and be admired, the rest would go.

"… And so my friends… thank you for coming here on this fine London evening to celebrate this offering to the great God of art, good fortune, and good times. Before I light this fucker and warm us all up, I'd like to say thanks to you all for your friendship, and good luck for whatever comes next."

"Get on with it you Irish twat!" shouts Dez from the wings. Evan laughs, undeterred, bowing in recognition. "That I am… and so in good Irish tradition, I'd like you to raise your glasses." Evan is loving the stage and ceremony. We lift glasses and bottles to the darkening heavens.

"Happy trails!" shouts Evan and throws the lit match into the waiting pyre. It responds with a flash of brilliant light, a crackle and hiss as paper, canvas, then wood ignite; one following the other to a great crescendo of orange and red light. We cheer, and Evan takes a bow as the melancholic sounds of Jeff Buckley singing "Hallelujah" float around the scene, speakers propping open Evan's studio window high above.

Much later, lying on the grass with Evan, I wonder hazily about that fire—the way the flame traveled as though it had always known where to go, what to do, and who to follow. Waiting to be ignited, and then becoming for a time all there was, consuming in mesmerizing brightness and beauty all it touched, only to be extinguished into ash and smoke then nothing at all.

Evan strokes my bare arm as we lay side by side, with the fire out, the air is cold. Smoke blends with the smell of charred wood and grass sticking to my clothes and hair; the smell of childhood camping. Propping himself on one arm to face me, Evan touches my cheek.

"You know I wouldn't have gone without you."

I open my eyes and reach over to hold his hand, stained with ash from the fire. "Really…?" I reply, smiling in the dark. "Not even for an apartment in Paris, dream job, fat salary, and Parisian girls? Not to mention the great croissants."

He strokes his chin and turns his head thoughtfully to the side. "Well, I hadn't thought of it that way… now that you put it like that…"

I throw a handful of leaves at his playful expression, and he grabs me at the waist, straddling my horizontal frame, pinning me beneath him, then folds his arms and looks down at me menacingly. I return the stare, trying to look unfazed by the heat I feel move through me as his weight pins my hips down. He falls forward, hands on my shoulders, face above mine but not close enough to touch. I have gone from sleepy to adrenaline-fuelled in seconds. I think momentarily about who might still be around, but the quiet assures me that all have left or are drunkenly asleep.

There's a danger in Evan that is intoxicating and a need in him that passes to me. I close my eyes, leaving the Billie that I am accustomed to behind, sipping her tea, wearing her cardie. The Billie who inhabits me in these moments with Evan is awesomely unfamiliar. She is my 'Go Girl', daring and wild, knowing just what to do when cardie-wearing Billie would be cringing in disbelief.

"Fuck the croissants." He says, unwrapping the blanket around my shoulders, pulling one strap of my singlet down slowly, carefully, touching my breast then moving to the other strap. With both breasts free, he stops and watches me half-naked in the small, smoky backyard, covered in grass and ash. Our breath trails white in the creeping frost, but for now the cold is forgotten. I wait, the dark night heavy with smoke and anticipation; I watch him and wait. He looks up at the half moon, a cloud obscuring the silver light, breathing in deeply, he runs both hands through his dark hair then moves to me. My cares of where we are and who might be watching are hiding in the hedge, embarrassed. Billie the Goddess is in the house, and as Evan unbuttons my jeans and moves his hand inside, I am captured by the power of physical chemistry and the pull of sex. He closes his eyes and a low sound escapes from somewhere near the back of his throat; it's a cross between growl and a moan, the simple sound of a hot-blooded man about to get his rocks on. Unintentional and animalistic, a basic sound of anticipation and pleasure; the rumble before the eruption.

It never ceases to amaze me the time it takes some men to go from foreplay to "here I am in your pants; let's get it on!" How is it possible in the throes of passion to maneuver a belt, jockeys, and a penis so deftly then negotiate the quagmire of a woman's usually tight clothing and underwear? A thought crosses my mind that Evan must have had much practice at this skill, his timing to take off stunningly fast, but sassy Billie pushes the thought aside carelessly and enjoys the ride. This sex was an unspoken promise, a plan for our future, a new beginning, and a pledge to ride together wherever our "next" took us.

* * *

Chapter Five

Paris

It is dusk when he leaves the building, light slowly draining from the day, followed closely by flickering streetlight; the glow illuminates his path. The dull yellow light gives a jaundiced tone to the area, and Evan pulls the collar of his jacket higher, hands sinking deeply into pockets as he makes his way home.

Early autumn in Paris is crisp and smells of the city settle with the earthier fragrance of tree-lined streets and leaves on the ground. Deep in thought, he walks toward their small apartment—an easy fifteen minutes by foot. Startled by a siren, he stops, looking up for the first time as a police car races past, its flashing light breaking his train of concentration. The scene suddenly folds around him, thought moving quickly now from the architectural puzzle that consumes him to the present moment.

The street, the smell of the air, the car, bright and intrusive, and a single fluttering object that catches his eye as he stands rooted to the edge of the leaf littered street. It turns and soars downward, rotating in perfect arcs of motion, flight-guided, the landing softened by its delicately woven wings. It stops gently by his feet, the gradual, fluttering descent protecting the precious seed from damage; nature at its most practical and beautiful. Evan stoops to pick up the helicopter seed, marveling at nature's feat of great engineering. The seed lies flat in his palm, and the soft glow of the yellow street light seems suddenly brighter as an internal light bulb of understanding flickers and illuminates his crowded head.

The answer is simple and it lies here in his hand; freedom in wings.

Evan sits heavily on a wooden bench by the side of the road and pulls a notepad and biro from his pocket. He scribbles and sketches, then folds the seed, whose wings have inspired his solution into the notebook. He shakes his head, knowing he has found the last design solution in the architectural puzzle he has been stewing over for weeks. He stands, puts the notepad and pen back in his inside pocket and follows the tree-lined street to the intersection where the city's bars and cafes begin their treasure trail to the heart of Parisian nightlife.

There is a moment's hesitation as a shift takes place on a deeper level; a decision made before the question has consciously arisen. Just a quick drink on the way home to wind down, quiet his busy head, help make the transition from uptight, anxious Evan to the more relaxed, less absorbed Evan Billie needs him to be. A beer or two should do it. After all, he's just figured out the final link that will bring the project he's working on together. He deserves it.

The change in direction is subtle but definite. Evan walks purposefully into the small, crowded bar on the street corner, tables lining the pavement outside, people spilling onto the street from the smoky interior. Just one and he'll head home.

* * *

"Hallo pet, or am I supposed to say 'bonjour?'" Cameron's comforting voice is akin to a hug via telephone.

"Cam! It's great to hear from you. I was just thinking I should call and check in."

"No bother love, just thought I'd ring for a wee chat. The weather's terrible over here, how's it in Paris?"

"It's beautiful, Cam, colors are changing, and it's starting to get cold. Does it snow in Paris in winter?"

"Aye, I'm sure it does, but not as much as here in Arrasaigh, and if you can manage a winter here, Paris will be easy. But tell me, Billie, how are you getting on?" Just picturing Cam in the farmhouse, with a fire on and his dog Samson no doubt curled up at his feet, makes me happy.

"Everything's great. Evan's still busy at the new company, and I'm, well, I'm still enjoying Paris. There's still so much to see. Honestly, I can't believe I get to live here; I have to pinch myself some days. I don't know how I got so lucky Cam. I just love it." I carry on excitedly, throwing my arms in the air as I explain despite the fact he can't see me. "I'm still struggling a little with the language, though, and I know I must sound like such an uncultured prat with my terrible French and weird accent. I guess that will just take a while. I'm still writing, and my book is going pretty well… I think; not that I've let anyone read anything so far." I'm so happy speaking to Cam I prattle on, barely stopping for breath.

"You sound happy Billie; that's just great."

He's right. I am.

Cameron was my mother's partner for most of my life until her death when I was fourteen. I grew up knowing that soft, gentle voice and faithful man as my father until the world turned upside down with Mom's cancer and her sudden death. None of us could have prepared for the shock and grief that shook our world during that time. Her death tore our world in two; not only did I lose my mother, but also Cam. He was the only father I had known. My real father (and

I use the term "real" although it doesn't seem quite right to me that he should be deserving of such a description when he only provided the gene pool) left Mom in Kansas shortly after I was born, and then brought me back to London when she died. Cam was left alone and grieving, having lost both Mom and me within one terrible month.

Cam moved back to his native home, a small Scottish island he'd left as a young man to find a world outside the farming and fishing community he had grown up in. He'd traveled the world, working in farming or fishing along the way. He would often joke about the fact he ended up in Kansas; of all the exotic places he had traveled, between Scotland and America, that he should end up living in a place like Kansas was a standing joke. "That's the pull of true love," he'd tell me.

One of Mom's jobs was writing feature stories for the local newspaper. She had an idea to write a book on "the people that farmed our lands." She had a romantic vision of pulling together a book of stories, personal tales of each man and woman who found their way to our area in Kansas and lived their own lives on the land. She would recount their joys and tragedies, births and deaths, hardships and bounties, all accompanied by black and white photographs and historical detail for each family and place. Of course, in the research phase, she met Cameron, a thirty-something handsome Scotsman who had been working on a neighboring cattle farm for a few months.

The rest, as Cam tells it, was very simple; he swept Mom off of her feet and moved into our small house, where we somehow made our version of a happy family. Where he worked and paid our bills, where Mom wrote and worked on that book, and where I grew up to be a good-hearted, small town girl.

That was the warm, fuzzy part. The part where Mom gets sick and they find out too late what's wrong I won't elaborate on. The part where we watch her fade away and our hearts are good and broken, then there's the part where Cam and my "real" father scrap to see who gets to keep me. In the end, I had to come to London, and Cam, who had no real reason to stay in small town Kansas, took his broken heart and went back to Scotland, where he bought a small holding on the little island where he grew up. He lives there alone now, farming as he always has done, still there for me whenever I need him.

My gene pool father, "Graham," isn't coming out of the telling too well. It's not that he's a bad guy; in fact, I love him too; he's just different. He never quite grew into the "being a father" role, and although he does his best and I know he loves me, I often think he's far happier in his city apartment with his own life; his new wife Melanie, his wine collection, and restaurant outings. He's there for me in a "let me write you a check, Billie" sort of a way, but he's not the "let's talk" type, and I'd never dream of telling him how I feel, let alone cry on his shoulder. Like I said, I love him, but I am very aware of his limitations.

"So, is the apartment warm enough?" Cam asks.

"It's perfect. I wish you could see it. It's so old-fashioned, you know, high ceilings, big, old sash windows and those really old radiators that creak when the heat comes on… and did I tell you we even have a housekeeper? Can you believe that?"

Cam laughs. "Well, if I remember your ability to keep your room clean, I'd say that's not entirely a bad thing."

"I was never that awful, was I? Well, honestly you should meet our housekeeper. She is straight from… what was that awful mock French show 'Allo Allo?'" I don't wait for an answer but barrel on. "She's just like Rene's mother, all French widow in black with a feather duster and a frown. She calls me Madame and tut-tuts as she dusts around my stuff. I told Evan we don't need her, but he tells me to enjoy the luxury before Sans Limites find out he's a fraud and fire him. Of course, he's joking. He seems to be doing a great job and just loving it. I wish his hours weren't quite so long… Cam? Are you still there?"

"I am, I'm just enjoying listening to you. I'm wondering if you've spoken to anyone in English today." he teases with a laugh.

"Oh, sorry, I am struggling a little with not speaking much French, and you know how I love to chat. I can't get much further than, 'Comment ca va?'"

"You'll get there, just keep up the writing and be sure you call me whenever you need." His words are comforting as always; the gruff Scots accent failing to hide the softness in that big heart.

I sit a while on the window seat after hanging up the phone, staring out at the city's twinkling lights. The glass is cool to the touch, and I press my cheek against it, closing my eyes, waiting, waiting for Evan to come home.

It's ten-thirty when I hear his key in the lock. I'm on my laptop, struggling through chapter four, but finding it difficult to concentrate, fluctuating as I have been for the past two hours between frustration that Evan isn't home yet and worry that something has happened to him. This is a pattern my life with Evan will follow, but thankfully, I have no knowledge of the evening as a beginning.

I steel myself not to turn to him with an accusatory stare; I don't want to be the demanding girlfriend. I keep my eyes focused on the words on the screen. Evan kisses the back of my neck and swivels my chair to face him.

"Before you ask where I've been, I need to tell you that I think I've just completed my first major project, and it's ready to submit to the board. I know they'll think I'm some kind of new upstart, but I know it's perfect…" He holds both of my hands and talks with such passion, my frustration leaves via the fire exit, and I listen happily to his animated news. "I know it sounds mad Billie, but the truth is until now, I wasn't even sure that I was good enough for this job. I mean, I was never sure that I'd fit into the world of suits and offices and board meetings, so I said to myself that I'd give it six months and wait for the magic and if it didn't come, I'd quit."

"The magic," I repeat after him, wondering if it's the whisky on his breath talking, but he doesn't seem drunk, just joyful.

"Yes, the magic; you must get that Billie, you know? The force that comes from a place you don't understand? When you know the answer or have the solution and it all fits and you don't know where it came from. It's like when I'm building a model or doing a painting, I start with something, a seed of something, and I don't know what it will grow into and I just turn up. I make sure I'm there letting the magic work somehow through these dumb ass Irish hands." His eyes fill as he goes on, letting my hands go to examine his own as though for the first time. "With art, it doesn't matter to mostly anyone apart from me and the odd rich bastard who might buy it. It doesn't change anyone's life, not really; it's just eye candy. With this stuff now, I see how ideas can make a difference, can change lives when they become something real, something available to anyone, regardless of their wealth. Tonight, I realized that same magic was working here in my job, and I could do it and do it well. Jesus, I'm ranting like a madman, but I feel like finally I can do something positive, pull my own head out of my arse and use what I have to do something good for a change."

He stands now, pacing back and forward, emphasizing each point with his hands. I have never seen him this way and never for a second would have believed he had held his own gifts in such low regard.

"Evan, everything you do makes a difference; nothing is wasted. You couldn't have been here, doing this until now, and your art? Your art does change lives, maybe not in the same dramatic way that this work does, but in a subtle, beautiful way. Art touches people, it inspires them; it makes them appreciate beauty, and not just beauty that's conventional and measurable, but beauty that's raw and gritty;

beauty that challenges the way we think." I stop, finding Evan no longer pacing, but staring intently at me, arms folded across his chest. I blush at his close scrutiny "… and I don't think your head has ever been up your arse… I would have noticed." We both laugh now, the seriousness of the conversation dissolving as Evan pulls me from my chair to hold me, burying his face in my hair.

"Don't ever leave me," he whispers just loud enough for me to hear. I take his hand and hold it to my cheek, shaking my head.

"Never."

* * *

"Nous avons… vouz avez…" The voice in my headphones is sending me to sleep, and I sit upright, pinching myself, hoping I actually haven't dozed at the reading desk.

Evan's company, Sans Limites, found us the apartment in St. Germaine des Pres. It's a perfect location on the left bank of the Seine at the northern end of the sixth arrondissement. The area is beautiful, classically French and vibrant; known historically as a meeting place for bohemian artists and intellectuals. I love to walk the streets and soak up the atmosphere. From here, I walk or sometimes catch the metro to the library in La Sorbonne, home to Paris's oldest university. Trying to encourage my inner writer and squeeze my more intellectual self to the fore, I do my best to channel Jean Paul Sartre and Simone de Beauvoir, who walked these streets before me.

The library has become my place of study; I come here once a day as a break from writing and put on some oversized earphones, to listen to some guy with a bad accent teach me French.

I drum fingers on the hard wood table, mind drifting off as I gaze at my surroundings. All these books and all that mental energy;

everyone here is studying or reading, noses stuck in texts, scribbling notes, rubbing chins thoughtfully or massaging temples. Libraries are possibly my most favorite buildings in the world. It doesn't matter whether they are the old historic kind: high ceilinged, dark wood, musty-smelling with green leather chairs or the light, airy modern type, all glass and light; an equal mix of books and computer screens. All these words and pages, stories and facts in one sacred place… all the words are overwhelming; each book the product of someone's dream, creative vision, passion, and hard graft. I hope that by sitting in libraries long enough, I will somehow absorb just enough creative juju to make my own writing worthy of a place in a library one day.

I pull off the headphones, winding the wire around the headset, and hang them back on the hook. My French is moving along fairly slowly; my flair for languages somehow not concurrent with my general love of words. Exiting the revolving doors on to a bustling street, I head for my favorite café. Café au lait and warm pastry will be the fuel to assist me in this afternoon's writing quest.

"Bonjour Madame." I am greeted by François, who smiles warmly as he works behind the counter. Café Florian is always busy, and he never seems stressed or unhappy to be constantly serving others; people like me with the luxury of spare time enough to stop for coffee made by someone else.

"Bonjour François! Comme ca va?" I ask confidently.

"Bien merci, et tu?" he replies with raised eyebrows.

"Bien, tres bien." I know François will expect no more in the way of conversation; just greeting and ordering are about all I can manage without self-conscious checking of my French dictionary. He spares me the pain.

"Pain au chocolat avec le café Madame?" Feeling quite French for a moment, I beam at him, taking off my heavy coat.

"Mais oui, François, s'il te plait."

I sit down and enjoy the bustle. The cafe is small and intimate with as many seats on the sidewalk as inside. The weather is getting cold now; it's late September, and the sky is grey and heavy. All café action is indoors.

I watch François at the espresso machine; this is a sight to behold. The machine is unlike any I have seen before. Golden and shiny, it rises to a peak above head height, and perched on top is what looks like an eagle. Lower down are the many spouts where creamy espresso flows into numerous white cups. Milk frothers extend alongside gleaming and ready-to-puff jugs of flat, unsuspecting milk into creamy clouds of foamy white. Francois works the machine like an experienced engineer and pats her lovingly: his prime racehorse.

Taking out my notebook. I scribble down ideas, words, anything I want to remember; phrases that spring to mind, descriptions, characters I see in passing imagining their story. I record details of my life and others greedily, storing them up, knowing that if needed, they will emerge into my narrative at the perfect time. This is Evan's magic, and this is the way I know it works for me. When I write, so many times the words come unbidden, the plan forgotten, the magic taking the story where it needs to go.

François sets my coffee and pastry beside me on the small round table, placing a hand on my shoulder.

"Voilà Madame."

"Merci, merci," I reply as the sweet smell of buttery pasty wafts upward, and my tummy rumbles accordingly. Taking the delicate silver spoon, I swirl the contents of the cup, watching dark mix with light. Some things cannot be rushed.

I count my blessings. For now, I am a lady of leisure; I drink coffee in cafes, walk the streets of Paris, write and live in an apartment with my gorgeous boyfriend. How did I get to be this lucky? I linger for maybe an hour then bid François goodbye, packing my notebook and French text back into my oversized backpack. Pulling on my winter jacket and woolen hat, I am not the picture of French elegance, but that's okay. Feeling full of hope and happiness for my life and future, I begin the short walk back to our apartment.

All around are Parisians and tourists alike, some meandering but most walking briskly, purposefully; the weather too cold to linger. Just ahead of me is a group of four or five well-dressed men and a woman walking in the same direction, talking intently. There are many hand gestures and voices raised then lowered, a passionate discussion of some kind. They stop outside a bar and continue their talk. I love to watch body language and try to read situations, creating the story. With a jolt, I recognize a familiar stance; head down in thought, hands deep in pockets, a mess of dark hair. Evan.

I'm about to shout his name and run toward him when the woman in the group reaches out a hand to him. With a gentle, deliberate touch she strokes his back twice, then touching his arm, kisses him on the cheek.

I stop in my tracks, sure that what I have just witnessed must not be what it seems.

The street is crowded and my abrupt stop causes a gentleman with a briefcase to collide with my backside. He stumbles and drops the briefcase and I topple over, landing in a crumpled heap on the cold sidewalk. The small commotion causes the group ahead to turn around and there I am, ashen-faced, woolly hat askew, on the ground.

"Billie?" shouts Evan, jogging toward me while his colleagues look on, bemused. "Are you okay?" He looks like he might laugh, but the expression on my face stops him in his tracks. "What are doing here, and how did you get down there?" He doesn't have the look of one having committed some act of adultery and I quickly pull myself together, letting him help me to my feet

"I was on my way back from the library, I just stumbled… I…" I feel a perplexing mix of anger and embarrassment as I scold myself for imagining what looked like an intimate exchange, and try to dust off the leaves stuck to my clothes. I have as yet never met Evan's colleagues, and this was not the introduction I had hoped for. Evan hugs me to him, kissing my cheek.

"Come and meet a few people. We were just going in for an after work drink." He doesn't look to be hiding anything, and I squeeze his hand, wondering what in the world could have made me distrust him even for a second. Then I see her, and I know.

"Meet Guillermo, Pierre, David, and Stephan." He makes the introductions, and I smile, shaking hands with the friendly faces, all concerned for my well-being after the unglamorous tumble. "… and this is Juliana" Evan finishes as I turn to meet her… the woman of back-stroking, cheek-kissing fame.

"Bonjour Billie, so lovely to finally meet you." She is devastatingly gorgeous; blond hair settling around her shoulders, red lips, and small tortoiseshell glasses. She is one of those women that make the rest of us descendants of Eve feel somehow inadequately masculine. Everything about her is small and beautiful, clever and exquisitely feminine.

"Hi," is all I can manage, not even a "bonjour," just a "Hi." When I take the hand she has reached out to me, I imagine myself as cavewoman taking the delicate porcelain hand of Betty Boop. Everyone makes small talk for a minute while I smile politely and try to swallow my unexplained aversion to the divine Juliana.

Evan speaks in French, and I am quite taken with how amazing he looks and sounds; professional Evan with his suit and French tongue. I gather he's telling them he will walk home with me rather than go for drinks. Juliana responds with a quip in French that of course I don't understand, but I'm sure it goes along the lines of, "Yes, you'd better take care of that clumsy oaf of a girlfriend." I bite my bottom lip in annoyance and vow to double my French lessons at the library!

They shake hands again, and although I know the French are supposed to be amorous and physical, there is something in the way she looks at Evan. And then, as an afterthought cloaked in sincerity, smiles at me. She kisses Evan on both cheeks goodbye and does more of the cheek brush on both sides with me. I find myself smiling goodbye with a grin that doesn't reach my eyes. I don't like her and hate myself for feeling this way. Was I always this possessive? I wonder.

Evan laughs and waves goodbye.

"What did she say?" I ask, trying to keep the accusatory tone from my voice.

"She said, young love is a beautiful thing."

"Yuck. How patronizing," I murmur, gripping his hand as we head home.

"Well, actually, she asked how you managed to score a hottie like me," Evan says, not missing a beat. I punch him playfully, the last of the winter sun fading in the sky, golden streetlight flickering on as we pass.

* * *

(Three weeks later)

The banner behind the small podium reads "Architecture Sans Limites."

The room is brightly lit, and the well-dressed crowd sits respectfully at white damask-covered tables, champagne glasses to the ready; some expressions expectant and others bored. People watching at its best. Suits and cocktail dresses trained in the art of polite small talk clap in the right places and air kiss the right people.

Sensing Evan's gaze, I turn to meet his eye, and he winks while managing to look absorbed in the animated conversation of a sparkly older woman. I sip champagne and smile, feigning interest in the gentleman beside me who's been chatting about the relevance of architecture in the third world since we sat down. He was quite interesting for the first thirty minutes, but now, my mind is wandering.

Applause fills the crowded room as a tall, lean man with greying hair and pale eyes taps the microphone and introduces himself. His manner is engaging and friendly, and he speaks passionately in heavily-accented English about Sans Limites and their mission.

"… architecture that is relevant to those who are marginalized or living in poverty… architecture that embraces social and environmental agendas… " He leans heavily on the chest-high wooden lectern, oozing commitment to the cause. I imagine a great weight balancing on those well-dressed shoulders. He speaks sincerely and with an intensity that leaves us wondering why we'd never realized before how architecture can change lives. So absorbed in his passionate speech am I, imagining myself in third world countries doing my humanitarian best, I jump when people clap, and the general tone shifts from admiration to expectation.

Awards time; more clapping, glass clinking, and presentations in various categories. Mock surprise and genuine astonishment as the company's most talented, most dedicated, and specifically skilled in differing areas are praised and acknowledged by all. I clap and raise my champagne glass several times, feeling ever-so-proud of Evan for being part of this very grown-up world where people work hard and seem to really care about making a difference. Another hush as the room awaits the recipient of the next prestigious prize. I smile at Evan, who is distractedly fiddling with his cuff links; black tie is not his ideal attire.

"… and this year's award for 'Sans Limites' newest and brightest talent goes to Evan Skylark! Come on up here Evan… This young man has demonstrated the kind of passion we are all about, and that passion combined with great talent has made him our young architect of the year. Congratulations, Evan!"

Mr Passionate CEO points across the room to our table, and we all turn to look at Evan, who for a second looks like he might run for the nearest fire exit. Stunned and flush-faced, he makes his way through the room to shake the hand of Gerard Fournier, the company's French CEO. He receives many pats on the back and words of congratulations as he weaves through the obstacle course of fellow architects and their partners. He nods shyly at the audience and accepts his award. Wide-eyed and incredulous, I beam at him as he returns to the table clutching a glass plaque and an envelope. He smiles sheepishly and shrugs his shoulders.

Evan's star is rising.

* * *

In this new world of pressured careers and ambition, sleep is becoming a distant friend. I think of her fondly and miss her restful, easy presence, but she just doesn't come by like she used to.

We have made the transition from 'student, tatty couched, low--level responsibility life' to 'long hours, high expectations, and career ladders to climb life'. Well, I guess it would be more accurate to say that Evan has; I'm sort of riding on his coattails for now, writing determinedly by day, hoping that the universe will comply with that wonderful law whereby energy out equals energy in. I write and write, read, study French, and write some more in the hope that my writing will become the career path I will follow, and the ladder I might climb to keep up with Evan on his vertical shimmy upward from obscurity to architectural greatness.

And although my tiredness is no comparison to that of the sleep-deprived mother; for me, the girl who loves to sleep, this current lack thereof is playing havoc with my drive for greatness.

A manila envelope thuds on to the doormat, sending small puffs of dusty objection into the air. "Don't get up," I plead with Evan, pulling halfheartedly on his arm as he rises from bed to check the mail. Gone are the days when we would linger till mid-afternoon in bed. Evan is obsessive about work and finds it difficult to wind down on our precious weekends.

He returns with the mail, dropping the newspaper on the floor and climbing back in beside me, clutching an envelope addressed to me.

"Mailman's here baby," he whispers in my ear, spooning my frame and placing the envelope under my curled arm.

"I don't need the mail," I complain. "Let me sleep."

"Are you sure sleep's what you need?' he asks, running a finger along my leg.

"Evan, is there ever a moment when you don't feel like sex?" I ask, voice laced with sleep.

"Is that a trick question?" he replies, hand moving to target.

"Please, I am so honestly asleep. In fact, this must be a dream, and you must be Brad Pitt." I pull the pillow over my head, and he laughs unwilling to let me drift back.

"I'll be whoever you need, and I do think about sex a lot of the time, but only when I'm with you… oh… and only with you… I promise," he protests as I swat him with the pillow.

"Well, I'm awake now Brad; show me what you got!" The manila envelope is forgotten as Evan needing no encouragement pulls me up and on top of him.

Later in my "afterglow," I see the envelope lying partially covered by my underwear. Reaching over to grab it I settle on my stomach and rip it open. Pulling two thick sheets of paper from the envelope, I read carefully before shrieking with delight. I read then reread the letter, jumping up and bouncing on the bed, yelling for Evan.

"Holy Christ, what is it?" he cries, entering the bedroom from the bathroom to find me hopping on the mattress, starkers with the letter in my hand. I stop bouncing only for long enough to get the words out.

"I'm published."

"What?"

"I said I'm published!" My words gush desperate for delivery. "The poems I submitted… it's a book, a poetry anthology, Harper Collins… they want to pay me for four poems to be printed in the book!" I wave the letter at Evan, who stares at me. "I mean it's only a few poems but still; I'm published and they'll pay us!" I continue.

"You're amazing," he says, smiling, and I know he's proud. This is what I have wanted more than anything, some kind of acknowledgment, however small, that my words are good ones. Evan beams at me, and I reflect the smile right back until I remember I'm butt naked, standing on the bed with the curtains wide open. I suck in my breath, diving for a sheet and Evan laughs striding the length of the room… similarly naked, passing the windows proudly, sporting an impressive woody.

"Evan!" I squeal, part mortified, part turned on, pointing to the window. He ignores the plea. "You'll have to help me out here," he says huskily, "all that bed bouncing with your tits out and being published and all, I've no choice but to fuck you."

I slap my hand to my mouth in horror "Watch your mouth! I'm a literary lady now."

Evan raises an eyebrow as he continues to advance, smiling his half smile, "Will that be okay with you?"

I throw my letter at him; he catches it, tosses it behind him and keeps walking. Laughing, I raise my hands and sigh.

"If you must. Is it because I'm published? I feel a poem coming on."

He grabs my outstretched arms and slaps my naked bum. I yelp and give in quite willingly, his Irish accent thickening as he whispers in my ear. "Recite it to me Billie, let me hear the words."

"Tell me you love me."

He does, over and over, and I recite the words amidst orgasmic breathy interludes.

And after the madness, after the sex and the words and joy in the smallest achievement, Evan says, "Marry me Billie."

And I say yes.

*　*　*

Chapter Six

A Wedding

"You have got to be fecking kidding me!" Silence. "You're not kidding. Christ, married? Billie, are you sure? I mean, this is Evan. What's gotten into the pair of you? Are you up the duff?" Iris's shock manifests in incessant fast-paced talk, and I can't get a word in to even begin answering her barrage of questions. "I just can't believe it. I mean, it's not like I'm all against the marriage thing necessarily, it's just I never thought you, or Evan, I mean I just never thought you'd both…Christ, you're too alternative for that nonsense, are you not?" She's still talking, and I hold the receiver at arm's length for a moment to give my poor ear a rest. Evan smirks from across the room, thoroughly enjoying the shock our engagement has brought our close set of friends. I take a deep breath and bring the receiver back to my ear. "Billie? Are you still there? Billie?"

"Yes, I'm here," I answer with resignation, anticipating the lecture I'm about to get.

"So… before you say any more I just need to ask you a few questions," Iris continues.

"Um, okay."

Iris is at home in Belfast, and I'm calling her from Paris. Prone as ever to drama, I had anticipated Iris's overreaction to our news. "By the way, one answer will suffice. There are no bonus questions, and you can't call a friend." She is all serious. "Number one: is your name Billie May Worthington or am I speaking to an imposter?"

"This is Billie May Worthington." I stifle a giggle.

"Number two: are you up the duff?"

"Definitely not."

"Number three: have you recently found the Lord and become a Christian?"

"Negative."

"Has Evan?"

"Negative, was that number four?"

"Yes and don't interrupt… Number five: any history in the family of early senile dementia?"

"Not so far. Are we done?"

"Last one… is there a party and will there be a free bar?"

Evan rolls his eyes as I laugh with Iris, who, after the initial shock is planning us a party. I am trying to explain it won't be necessary, but she is so funny and I miss her. So, I enjoy her hysterical chatter and let her ramble on.

"Iris, it's not such a big deal. In fact, we had planned to do something real simple maybe next week."

"Are you kidding me? Next week? How am I supposed to get a hat in time?"

"I know it sounds a bit mad, but Evan has booked us some flights and we'll be in Belfast next Friday so I can meet his Mom. His cousin's a priest, so he's going to marry us on the weekend. Real simple, a few family members, a few drinks in the local, and back for work on Monday. Will you and Dez be able to get there?"

"Is that a trick question? With bloody well bells on! Now that I'm over the shock I'll get on the blower and get Dez organized. I'll book him on Aer Lingus, and he can sleep in my brother's room, and oh, I'd better get off to the shops and find a frock. I'm all of a fluster now Billie." After much excitement and laughter, I hang up and flop back on to the sofa, feeling a little steam-rolled.

Evan's spontaneous proposal was only last weekend and here we are planning a wedding next week. In usual all-or-nothing fashion, Evan wanted to go ahead and get married the next day, find a registry office, and be Mr and Mrs Skylark immediately. Although I wasn't keen on a big affair either, the suddenness of all this was a little too much for me, and I persuaded him that marrying the next day might seem a tad impetuous. I managed to negotiate a two week delay from proposal to ceremony, and even this short delay felt like a small victory. When Evan sets his mind on something, he's hard to sway. I wonder on some deeper, less secure level if maybe he's afraid he'd chicken out and change his mind if we waited.

But we aren't waiting, we're racing ahead as usual, flights are booked and we are to run off to Ireland to get hitched. I'll meet Evan's Mammy (as he calls her), Cam will fly over, a few of Evan's brothers will come along, and now Iris and Dez.

It would be perfect. Evan's family had seemed entirely unfazed by the whole affair and his Mammy "Mary" had reacted as though he'd told her he'd be home at five for tea. His cousin, Liam (the catholic priest), would do the honors in the local church then we'd all head to the pub. It is all entirely mad and of course entirely perfect, so I run along with the idea of being Mrs Skylark like I'd known my whole life I would be. This new road on my life course feels perfectly natural, and I trust this intuition to be a guide. Although marriage might be a little spontaneous, my love for Evan is the opposite. It feels old and enduring, like I've known him forever and understand him as I understand myself. With this as my anchor, I sail happily toward my imminent wedding day and a new life thereafter.

* * *

Belfast 2002

It's the middle of October, the beginning of winter; a season that seems to sit so comfortably here in Belfast. Sunnier warmer days seem like weather that happens somewhere else, on the continent, in movies, but not here in Belfast where the grey of winter seems timeless. There is a cold dampness to the air that clings and a lack of color that tries to press down my elevated spirits unsuccessfully; today is my wedding day.

Waking up in Evan's sister Sinead's old bedroom, I lie still in the narrow single bed for a time, listening to the little house wake up. Muffled voices through the walls and groaning pipes of the old hot water cylinder in the bathroom next door. I hear a familiar voice cuss loudly; the hot water has run out again. I picture a sopping Evan standing in the little bathtub reaching for a pink frilly towel.

Posters of teen bands still cover the walls of Sinead's room. The duvet cover is emblazoned with the teenage faces of Take That. I feel old. The air in the room is stale and smells of moth balls and lip gloss. Evan's mother lives alone now in the terraced council house, but the rooms her children used to share stay as they were. Small museums to the family life that once was.

Her husband Frank has been dead for eight years, and Sinead left home five years ago. Mary's house is neat as a pin. Downstairs, I hear the radio blaring and a kettle whistling. Kneeling on the bed, I rub the condensation-covered window to clear a small screen of vision. The street outside is quiet; a paperboy throwing newspapers into gardens, a couple of barking dogs, and two scallywag kids kicking a ball against a fence.

I wonder that it's possible for a scene to be so colorless. Everywhere is grey, from the sky, to the road, the houses, and the concrete gardens. All the bright hues and shades sucked out by what? Unemployment? Depression? Poverty? Violence? So many dark shades, yet something bright and vibrant oozes from every scene I see here in Belfast. I rise and slip on some clothes, and as I brush my hair in the mirror, I hear Mary bellow up the stairs.

"Evan? Are you awake, son? There's some sausages in the pan, and I'm just popping round to Betty's. I've ran out of milk." I hear the door slam and catch sight of Mary walking down the path in her dressing gown, her hair in rollers, slippers on her feet. It is the people I conclude, smiling to myself. It's the people here that bring the color and somehow make everything brighter; the scenes are monochrome, but the people beautifully bright.

Sitting round the Formica kitchen table, Evan shovels sausages down like he's never eaten before. I watch, amazed, hands wrapped around my tea mug which boasts a picture of the Queen Mother.

"Any last minute jitters?" Evan asks mid-mouthful. I'm about to answer when Mary comes bustling through the door with a glass bottle of milk, its shiny foil top reflecting light on her chin.

"There yez are." She smiles. "Have you made me a cuppa Evan? I'm gaspin'." She plops herself down on a chair and looks carefully at me. "Billie, now have you had a sausage? Evan, did you not leave the girl any sausages? For Christ sake, it's her wedding day; she needs her strength."

Evan looks up guiltily. "She didn't want one Mam; she's fine. Did you want one?" he asks as an aside. I shake my head.

"I'm fine Mrs Skylark; I'll just have—"

"Away, you're not fine at all; you look like a sausage would do you the world of good." She's up at the frying pan, and I really don't want a sausage.

82 | *Skylark*

"Honestly, Mrs Skylark, I really am fine. I'll just have a bit of toast if that's okay."

"Fine? Look at you, you're marrying this eedgit," she gestures her head affectionately toward Evan, "you're not fine at all, get a sausage into you."

"Mam, she's fine. You're fine, aren't you?" says Evan, looking perplexed. I want to laugh, but I nod and shrug at Mary's bustling behind; she is tying a floral apron around her waist and frying sausages for Ireland. Evan shakes his head and kicks me under the table.

Mary Skylark rules the roost and for a few years now, has had no roost as such to rule. With all five sons and one daughter flown from the nest and no husband anymore, she relishes the opportunity to cook and fuss over us. She chats over the hiss and crackle of the fry pan, updating Evan on the local news and family gossip: what the neighbors are up to, who's pregnant or in jail, and which brother is doing what and where.

News of Evan's brothers is told on a most favorite to least favorite son basis, I can tell. Evan's oldest brother, Frank, is an accountant living in Dublin, he's sober, has a "nice" wife and two kids.

The next brother is Owen, a traveling freelance photographer currently working in Spain (although according to Evan, Owen is the family's second drunk. His father was number one). Owen is on the eternal holiday in Ibiza and hasn't taken a photograph in years; thankfully, Mary seems not to have heard this version of events and so boasts on about Owen for a time before continuing on to Michael.

Michael is the family's almost priest; he entered the seminary at nineteen, then changed his mind right before he was due to take the Catholic brothers' vows. He's now a window cleaner in Killarney with a great fondness for Guinness with a whisky chaser.

Finn lives here in Belfast, started a degree in philosophy, dropped

Ruthie Morgan | 83

out after a year, and is now unemployed, claiming on the benefit and taking prescribed methadone to wean him off 'un' prescribed heroin.

Evan is the youngest boy, followed by miracle of miracles, the family's wee surprise Sinead, who now has a wee surprise of her own; a fourteen-month-old baby girl called Clodagh whose father is apparently serving time for GBH.

No one talks about Evan's Dad Frank. He was, according to Evan, "a fucking drunk"; never one to mince descriptive. I don't know too much more about Frank senior. Evan did tell me that Frank left Mary four times, returning between sojourns to impregnate her before taking off again. He finally left for good after Sinead was born, and Mary raised the children alone. It seems amazing to me that a woman of such obvious resilience and strength could be weak enough to allow a philandering, drunk husband back in to her life time and time again, knowing that the odds were history would repeat itself.

Raising six children alone on a meager income in a small home would be the end of most women, yet Mary Skylark managed and stands here in her floral pinny smiling and frying sausages like she's the luckiest woman in the world. No one mentions Frank senior, and there's no evidence of him anywhere in the house; no photographs that include his face, nothing to suggest he was ever a presence aside from two large, rusty bird coups in the backyard. Frank kept canaries, and from what I can gather, he loved those little birds almost as much as the booze. Evan once told me his father was obsessed with birds; he knew every species that landed in their garden and loved to sit in a deckchair smoking and watching. He'd study them, those flying free and alighting on the garden fence and his own in their cages, talking to them in a way I'm sure he never spoke to his children.

Apparently when Evan was born, shortly before Frank's third departure, he changed the family name by Deed poll to "Skylark," his favorite bird in the summer skies. Appalled, Mary had refused to use the name, but the community who loved the carefree drunk thought the whole thing a fabulous joke and the name stuck. Soon Mary was Mary Skylark and the children Skylarks too.

The name changed, but the problems remained. Frank Skylark flew away sometime after, and the silence around his name is louder than the radio which always plays in the little kitchen in Belfast. And I can't help but wonder what he might have looked like and if his face is mirrored to Mary every time she looks at Evan.

"Aye, and so Finn and Michael will be at the church and will come over for a pint afterwards, Sinead and Clodagh will be along, so will auntie Sal and your cousins, Bill and Brigid. What's wrong with yer face; are you not happy they're coming?" Mary holds a greasy spatula in front of him as though ready to strike.

"I'm happy Mammy, how could I not be?" Evan stands and gives his Mom a bear hug, which takes her by surprise; she swats him with the spatula. "What's gotten into you?" She's smiling happily. One of her boys is back.

"Now, Billie, is there anything you need doing before this afternoon? Shall I iron something for you? What about yer hair? Yer nails? Sinead's awful good with the hair straighteners. Shall I call her to come early?" Having seen many framed photos of the glamorous Sinead, I quail in horror at the thought of her and the hair straighteners.

"No, no, that'll be fine, Mrs Skylark; I'm keeping it pretty simple."

"Simple?" She looks disdainful. "You are wearing a dress, aren't you?"

"Yes, I'm…" Evan returns to the kitchen with a newspaper in his hand saving me from further future mother-in-law interrogation.

"Right Ma, am I washing these dishes for you or not?" Mary looks as though Evan has just spoken a foreign language; obviously the offer of help in the kitchen is an unusual phenomenon in the Skylark household. "Don't sit there with yer mouth hanging open,

Ruthie Morgan

pass me yer plate now." Mary chuckles and obliges while Evan waves me off. "Go on and have a rest before the mad crew arrives." He winks, and I thank Mary for breakfast, escaping upstairs.

Propped up on a pillow on Sinead's bed, I take out a pen and my trusty journal and begin to write; there is so much inside me that needs to find words. Here I am about to be married to a mad Irishman I met barely a year ago, I live in Paris, I am finally published, and I'm madly in love. Life is racing. I want to slow it down and take stock. I scribble away until the excited haze in my head becomes a little less cloudy.

Amidst all the happy feelings of great fortune and love and the future and possibilities, a thin tendril of grief wraps itself around my happiest thought and grows. Joy and grief side by side, the feeling is familiar; sad yet strangely comforting. Reminded once again that in my moments of greatest happiness there will always be a shadow of loss, a reminder that the person I want most to share the happiness, the one that brought me here into the world, can't be here now.

Thoughts of Mom in times of joy are always with me, and I know I will learn to welcome her memory, but for now, the hole where she was still swallows me for a time. There's a quiet knock at the door, and Evan pokes his head around its frame.

"Can I come in?" His expression is soft and I smile at his sheepish face.

"Since when did you ever ask?" He smiles his lop-sided grin and slips in, clicking the door closed behind him.

"Room for another?" He slides on to the bed beside me and nuzzles his head on my stomach.

"Always."

"What are you doing?"

"Writing."

86 | *Skylark*

"Another poem about me?" he teases.

"It wasn't directly about you!" I say, swatting him.

"Really?" He sits bolt upright. "Then who the hell else was all that about?" Several of my published poems had focused on love and loss and passions of the physical; of course, Evan now believes they are all inspired by him.

"They are about love, the concept of love and... "

"And sex."

"And sex." I laugh.

"Sex with me." It's a statement rather than a question.

"Well, sort of, but..."

"Sex with me, I knew it... all this time, you thought you were my muse, but actually, it's the other way around; admit it!" He pushes my journal and pen to the floor.

"They're much more subtle than that..."I try to explain, but he's not listening. He kisses my neck, and I carry on determined that he should understand. "They're about the force of love and..." He moves to the top of my collarbone, his right hand stroking my thigh.

"Uh-huh?"

"... and what it does to us, to everything..."

"Carry on." Evan's fingers pull gently on the waistband of my trousers.

"What we do for love, what we do to keep it... what we do without it, once it's lost." My breath comes quickly, struggling to focus on my poetic integrity as Evan moves his hand inside my underwear.

"We'd do anything to keep it," he whispers.

"Evan, your Mom is downstairs."

He is undeterred. "The radio's on, I'll be quiet."

"Evan."

"I love you Billie." He peels my underwear down just enough to slide inside and moves slowly, carefully, hands covering my mouth,

Ruthie Morgan | 87

eyes locked on mine. Outside kids swear and kick a ball, downstairs Mary vacuums enthusiastically, and here in the small bedroom, we make love and that bright, vibrant light is everywhere and the glare is too much. I press my eyes tightly closed, knowing that in a handful of lifetimes there are few moments as perfect as this.

* * *

St. Joseph's Catholic Church has seen better days. It is cold and draughty, and the yellow and blue paint peels like old skin from the stone walls. The worn wooden pews are bare of cushions, but today, several bottoms clad in Sunday best grace the seats. It seems bizarre to me that not only am I about to be married, but I'm to be married in a church.

My family has never had any religious tendencies. Mom was spiritual certainly, but prayed more to Mother Nature and the stars, being a hippie girl. Cam's just philosophical, and "gene pool" Dad, Graham, is pure atheist so the "family religion" thing is really quite foreign to me. Aside from the deep intuition that all of our lives mean something, I have little leaning to any religion or deity and this immersion into Irish Catholicism is interesting to me on so many levels. I enter the small church parlor with Cam and feel sure someone will ask me for ID, expose me as a catholic impersonator, and tell me I'm not permitted entry. I haven't said any Hail Mary's today.

Cam's arm is steady, despite his reservations about my impending marriage. Impending as in "about to take place in about three minutes!"

"Are you all right love?" he asks, giving me a quick sideways glance.

I look up to meet his sparkling brown eyes, concerned and full of love. "I'm fine." I squeeze his arm. He's wearing his best suit, and I realize this may be one of the few times I have seen him clean-shaven.

The church smells of old things, old air, old wood, old bibles and benches, and probably mostly old people, all tinged with a hint of incense. Cam rolls his eyes and smiles. "Your Mum would be laughing at you here getting married in a church!"

"She would, wouldn't she?" We both smile at the memory and together, without a word, take a step into the small church where we're greeted by a handful of flushed faces, best hats, and the clumsy notes from Evan's little cousin Sheila's recorder. The flush in their faces spreads to mine, and I am suddenly self-conscious, aware I am definitely not the traditional bride. I wear a sleeveless sundress, despite the season, pale green with small pink flowers. I have let my hair out, and it falls down my back; my only makeup some pale pink lipstick. I refused Sinead's offer of her best stilettos and chose to wear converse and my own small extravagance: one fresh flower in my hair.

I feel all those critical female eyes bearing down on me. Cam squeezes my arm, and I channel my confident, brave mother, take a deep breath and smile, then make my way to Evan—who just this once waits for me.

Sheila's recorder toots out the last few notes of "Amazing Grace" tunelessly as I reach Evan, all slicked and suited, clean-shaven, and smiling. All Irish confidence, not a stitch of visible nerves or uncertainty, he looks me up and down and grabs my hand, pulling me away from Cam before sweeping me into a movie star, back-arching kiss. Everyone cheers, and the recorder stops mid-note.

"Hey. Hey! Wait a minute, that bit comes later!" exclaims Niall (another of Evan's cousins who has actually taken his vows). Evan releases me and, squeezing my hand, repeats the words of the Niall the priest, as do I, until we are officially allowed to do the kissing bit again. Everyone claps, the aunties in hats dab their eyes with embroidered hankies, and the uncles make a path for the pub. There is much congratulating, cheek kissing, and back-clapping as we walk back up the aisle together, emerging onto the stone steps to be greeted by the blare of an electric guitar. Frankie, one of Evan's friends who aspires to make it like the guy from The Frames, serenades us down the steps to a loud rock song he composed hoping to enter the next "Ireland's got Talent." Everyone is laughing and shouting, and poor Frankie gets a few missiles aimed in his direction as we all walk arm-in-arm for the pub around the corner.

Much later, the hats have come off, the sandwiches are finished, salt and vinegar crisps are crushed under the heels of dancing aunties as the juke box blares, and the whisky flows. Dez seems to be in some drinking competition with a few men at the bar, and Iris is dirty dancing with Evan's brother, Michael. "Any excuse for a party, eh?" Evan slings his arm over my shoulders and looks around at the heaving pub scene of mad relatives and friends dancing, drinking or in deep conversation.

"Is that why you asked me to marry you then; for the party?" I run my hand through his dark hair, which has lost the slicked back look of before, and he pulls me backward through the crowd to dance. Soon we are lost in the mayhem; the sounds of rock music and laughter spilling over into the grey streets; the cold Irish night and warm Irish people celebrating life and love. A voice echoes over a loudspeaker amidst the music and madness. "Raise your glasses to Mr and Mrs Skylark!"

We do, then we kiss and everyone cheers as Mr and Mrs Skylark take the floor.

* * *

Chapter Seven

A Turning Tide
Paris, 2002

"Do you have to go?" I ask, trying not to sound too pathetic and forlorn. It's early November, winter in Paris, and our apartment is comfortable and warm. The old radiators are fired up from a central boiler downstairs, and I am ensconced on the old leather sofa, immersed in a novel.

"I have to." Evan grins down at me, fiddling with his tie. "I promised; the tables are all booked and paid for."

I pull another Kleenex from the box and blow my stuffy nose unglamorously. "Okay, I'm sorry to let you down, but I'd be terrible company tonight." I have the flu and am clad in flannel pajamas, my hair hangs limply around my face, and my nose is a shade of red more commonly associated with a ripe tomato. "Come here and let me fix that." I gesture to Evan, and he squats down beside me in his tux. I straighten his tie and push back his hair. He leans in, smelling of cologne and toothpaste. "Don't kiss me, I'm too sick."

He laughs, planting his lips on my hot forehead then straightens up and checks the clock. "All right, Cinderella, I'm off to the ball."

I sneeze in reply.

"Have fun then hurry home to me," I croak. The door clicks closed, and I settle back into my book and cup of chamomile tea.

Evan is on a high; work with Sans Limites has gone from strength to strength. He loves his job and colleagues, his French is perfect, and the projects he works on are inspiring and fulfilling. I keep waiting for the "but," for the "the only thing is." This is my modus operandus ever since Mom got sick so suddenly. I can never quite rely on happiness or good fortune lasting. In fact, I'd say that happiness, although quite wonderful, scares me senseless. I am terrified to get used to situations, circumstances or people that bring joy in fear they may be taken from me.

My counselor (paid for by Graham so he wouldn't have to talk to me about it) said this was trauma; a natural reaction to unexpected loss and grief. So I recognize that my feelings are irrational and try not to act on them, and instead do my minute-by-minute mantra. I must only cope with one minute at a time, ever. Such a simple truth, but somehow so difficult to get your head around when a busy brain worries about every possible eventuality and potential loss all the time.

I think about Mom every day. And although I know that by now I should be better at dealing with the knowledge she's gone there are days when her loss feels fresh and keen all over again. Like the shock of her untimely death somehow stunted my mourning and here I am stuck with feelings maybe I should have processed in my early teens. Even now, nine years after her death, grief comes to find me when I am least prepared. It never gets any easier; the feeling never any less intense or physically crippling, but the difference is now that I know it passes. I must just see one minute through to the next, and eventually the feeling will move on, and I will remember that there is hope and love and light in the world, and that sadness and death touch us all.

Evan knows my story and does his best to understand. I try not to lay my grief on him or make him the focus of my fear of abandonment, but I struggle. This is the fear that for me goes hand-in-hand with love. So, as Evan heads off to another of work's fancy dinners, I swallow my fear, try to enjoy the solitude of the evening's quiet then decide to cheer myself up by calling Cam.

The phone rings for a time before his familiar voice answers, a slow and deliberate greeting, always the same. "Cameron McMahon speaking."

"Hey, that took a while. Where were you?"

"Hullo sweetheart, I was just coming in from the paddock. The weather's terrible here, just wanted to check the gates were properly locked. The wind's howling." Closing my eyes, I imagine the farm on the hill surrounded by majestic Scottish mountains and bordered by wild, grey ocean.

"Isn't it lonely, Cam?" There is a moment's silence, and I realize the question has brought back an entire lifetime we rarely talk about.

"Sometimes pet. I keep busy." He waits a moment, then asks, "How are you? You sound all stuffed up."

I pull the cotton quilt around myself. "I'm fine, just a cold." I follow this with a well-timed sneeze.

"Where's Evan?" Cam asks in an accusatory tone.

"He's at another company dinner. He had to go, a fancy black tie affair."

"Weren't you both just at a fancy awards dinner? Aye, I'm sure you just told me about one where young Evan got some award. My, your life in Paris is a bit more glam than mine over here," he says, laughing. "The closest I get to a night out is an invitation to Mary Black's house for a cuppa, and to be honest, that makes me a bit nervous. I think she's looking for a new husband." He chortles again.

"Doesn't Mary Black already have a husband?"

"Aye, but she's checking out her options for the new model before the old one pops his clogs!" We both laugh, the island is full of characters, and the small population means everyone knows everyone else's business. "Anyway, you didn't fancy the night out tonight, eh?

Thought you'd catch up on the local gossip with me instead? I could tell you about the specials down at Crusty's Bakers. Oh, and Maureen Kirk's daughter just had twins."

"Okay, Cam, that'll do. I'll let you go, and I'll get back to lying on the sofa. I think I'm actually too snotty and miserable to deal with the island gossip." I moan.

"Well, you must be sick then! Shouldn't Evan be home with you? You shouldn't be alone when you're not well," says Cam, protective as always; unfortunately this means he is always ready to criticize Evan. It's not that he doesn't like him, but he's hard on him, never quite believing that he does enough or is good enough for me. He tells me that's what Dad's are for, and I think it strange that my real Dad is so very indifferent to Evan. I often feel he is just relieved I've found someone so he can breathe a sigh of relief that I am no longer his sole responsibility.

"It's just a cold, Cam; I'm not dying." I catch myself on the last word.

"I know, love, just be sure you're eating properly, eh? When will you manage a wee trip over to see me?" he asks. It has been too long since my last visit, and I hang up later promising to organize a trip the next time Evan can get some holidays.

Evan is working on a team project with some fellow architects in the firm. It's on a hospital in India. The funding is coming from a charitable trust, and the design and construction has to be efficient and economic. It is to operate in a poverty-stricken area and will potentially change the lives of the surrounding community. Evan has been working with his group tirelessly, driven to see the project complete, and, more importantly, to create a structure that is viable in such a community. Evan's work with energy utilization has been instrumental in the entire design and structure of the building; it must run from as much solar energy as possible, and its shape, contours, positioning and so forth are all crucial in its energy footprint. The evening's dinner is a farewell to a respected firm member, and Evan will enjoy relaxing a little with his colleagues. They have been working so hard, and the break tonight is well-deserved.

I've met his team on several occasions, the first unfortunate encounter being the face plant outside the cafe. Meetings since have been much more civilized, and I have grown to like his colleagues and their partners very much. Unfortunately, I still have some weird female issues with Juliana of petite French gorgeousness, but I realize this is probably my own insecurity speaking.

It doesn't take long before I fall asleep on the sofa, book in hand, and as I doze, I imagine myself at the ball; Cinderella without the ball dress. Juliana is center stage pirouetting like a tiny porcelain princess. I feel shaky and uncertain and look for Evan who is holding my hand, smiling adoringly at me. Exhaling my relief, I reach up to stroke his back tenderly but catch my reflection in the crystal champagne glass he raises to his lips and see Juliana stare back at me. I am Juliana, and Evan bends to kiss me.

I wake up with a fever, disoriented, but grateful for the reality surrounding me. 10:30 p.m. I pop a Panadol, and as I take myself and my flannel pajamas to bed, I say a silent prayer for peaceful slumber and leave the light on for Evan.

* * *

"… Love is not love which alters when it alteration finds, or bends with the remover to remove. Oh no! It is an ever-fixed mark that looks on tempests and is never shaken."

Shakespeare; Sonnet 116

Temptation lives within us all; it takes many different forms, its disguises are endless. Temptation is cunning, without conscience or empathy as it asks us to risk everything for the tiniest taste of something. The pull of temptation is the first step into the padded room of betrayal. Once within those walls, no amount of guilt will remove the taste. It remains on the lips long after the thrill is gone. It follows like a shadow and taints every taste thereafter. And here, the ever-fixed mark of love stains like a tattoo; it remains despite the tempest, it remains quite contrary to the laws of sensibility. Like a quiet curse, love becomes painful and jagged; its edges smoothed only with the passage of time and the steady belief in love itself.

* * *

The buzz of a city at night has always felt intoxicating to Evan; the bustle and lights amidst darkness and anonymity, anticipation of a good time, and of possibilities beyond the confines of a nine to five day. There is a relaxed feel amongst the crowd; they have left the stresses of the workday behind. The talk, the banter, the music, the feel of the alcohol creeping through his veins… it has always been the same for Evan. The memory is still sharp from a first stolen taste of his father's whisky; the first sip such a jolt to his young senses, invincibility that followed the high, the feeling that he could do anything, and that the world suddenly made sense.

Evan knows he has always danced on the edge of addiction, but so far, he's managed to balance on the right side. The side where people tell you what a fun drunk you are, what a great guy to have at the party, what a hoot. The socially acceptable side where drinking is encouraged, that's what we do, we deserve it, and there's no need to explain. He'll stay on the right side; there's too much to love about life to fuck it all up over the booze like his father and his brothers already have. He'll stay on the right side, but it's a fine and dangerous line.

The trouble is maintaining the high. How do you keep on feeling the glorious sensation that comes from the first drink? The beautiful stillness that trickles over the body and mind as the first few sips hit the bloodstream and the alcohol takes hold. It's impossible and trying to achieve that feeling is why we all get drunk and keep on drinking, only realizing it's all too much when it's too late.

Evan's tie is loosened, and his shirt sleeves rolled up. He sits on a bar stool, Whisky Sour in his hand, face relaxed, posture at ease. "Ok, mon frère, it is my round non?" Guillermo claps a hand on Evan's shoulder and signals for the bartender.

"Sure, another one should wrap the night up nicely," Evan replies. They laugh; this has been Evan's response to the past few rounds of drinks, and as yet, no one is making any moves to go home. The four men have been working hard and feel they deserve a night out. Things are going well, their project is running to timeline, and there's much to be happy about.

In the bar scene, Evan is the light around which the moths flutter. It's always been this way. He's charismatic, people like to be in his circle, and he is gracious and funny; he entertains and includes, he is a good listener. He is on form tonight and guiltily enjoys being out alone without Billie. He loves her, but when she is with him, she becomes his focus, and he loses sight of this side of himself; party boy, carefree Irishman, no pressures or commitments just for a short while.

Juliana enters the bar with another crowd of colleagues from Sans Limites. She is breathtaking in her black backless dress, hair tied up, classically beautiful. Her eyes scan the crowd, looking for him, and he can't help but return her stare. She is very attractive, and he is male; she has made a career of flirting with him since he began at the firm. He has of no intentions of following anything through, but enjoys the attention, and tonight, under the influence of a few too many whiskies, he flirts right back. Green light on, Juliana decides what the evening's outcome will be, and she is a woman quite used to getting what she wants.

At midnight, the crowd leaves the smoky bar and heads further into town; some deciding to call it a night and others determined to find a nightclub. Guillermo leads the way. "Vien ici, come on! We may be getting older, but the night is young, my friends!"

Evan laughs. Guillermo is in his late fifties, balding and plumper than average, and he is determined to go dancing.

"I'm done lads." Evan salutes the crowd, wobbling a little as he points in the general direction of his apartment. "I'll be seeing you all in the morning." The crowd urges him to carry on, but Evan feels good. He is happily drunk and proud to be on the right side of the line he so carefully marks for himself.

Jacket draped over one shoulder, he takes his turn and begins the slow, measured walk of the happy drunk heading home.

"Evan, wait, I'm going this way too." Juliana runs to catch up and threads her small, delicate arm through his.

"Oh… right." He takes a breath, feeling an uncomfortable shift of direction in the evening's course. They walk in weighty silence until he feels Juliana's grip on his arm tighten and pull. Sensing danger, Evan stops. His head is spinning, he knows his weaknesses. "Do you live up this way Juliana?"

"No, but you do," she murmurs without looking up. He should not be alone with her when he's this drunk. The pull of temptation is strong and he doesn't trust his control. "Juliana, I've got to get back to Billie. She's not well."

"Why are you here then?"

"What do you mean?"

"I mean, why are you here with me, making it perfectly obvious to all that you want to sleep with me."

"Holy fuck, Juliana, it's not like that! Christ, I didn't mean to give you the wrong idea. I'm sorry, that's not it at all. I mean… you're beautiful, but I… I'm sorry. I'm drunk, and I need to get home."

Evan runs his hands through his hair, trying to center himself. She is so delicate, yet everything about her manner suggests the opposite; her direct come on is an uncomfortable turn on.

"You could come home with me," she says, facing him as he backs up against the wall.

"No." He throws the word out then takes a deep breath before continuing "… No… it wouldn't be right. I've got to go." Evan's tone shows an internal battle is underway; Juliana sees momentary weakness and goes in for the kill. Pushing Evan roughly into a darkened doorway, she is on him, pressing her mouth against his and pushing her small, determined body into him before his rational head has time to object.

Evan's total loss of control is complete, and for a few moments he forgets himself, forgets Billie, and forgets his career. No thoughts to cloud the first few moments of deceit. He responds quickly to her body, an instinctual need that overwhelms his senses. Drunken haze mists the experience in a dream-like quality, giving permission to action through the misty consciousness of the dreamer. Juliana wastes no time reaching for his belt, her intentions clear. In an action that suggests anger rising over passion, Evan pulls back her hair and kisses her small mouth, grazing her lips with his teeth. It's Juliana against the wall now, and in the quiet, dimly-lit street, Evan is stepping solidly over the forbidden line so carefully drawn on the Parisian sidewalk.

"I want you to fuck me," she whispers, still in control. She pulls herself higher on to Evan, drawing her dress up and twisting her legs around him. She's naked from the waist down, and Evan is lost. There

Ruthie Morgan

is nothing but sensation and need; alcohol convincing him he has no choice. It paints reality red, and all he can see is her. He acts without thought, conscience, or fear of repercussion, responding instinctively to temptation; the barrier of self-control maintained in sobriety gone. Hands on her bare thighs, he pulls her in as she deftly releases his belt and trousers, never taking her mouth from his.

A sudden flash of red and blue illuminates the alleyway, bathing the seedy scene in bright light. Evan freezes, a chill of reality washing over his drunken senses. The siren blares and the police car speeds past, unaware of the act it has only just interrupted. As the light grows dim around them once again, Evan releases his hold, pulling abruptly away from her.

"Jesus Christ, I'm sorry." His head is in his hands and she remains motionless against the wall. "I shouldn't have… oh fuck… this was wrong… I'm sorry."

Juliana pulls her dress back into place and flattens her hair, steely gaze never leaving his. "You will finish this." The words are icy-cold, controlled, and clear, laden with contempt. Her voice cuts through his confusion, and any hopes that this is a dream are gone. Evan recoils, suddenly aware of the unraveling; he has crossed the line, and the thread that held him upright frays. A slow but steady undoing of everything set in motion by this drunken moment of indiscretion.

"I made a mistake; you need to go now. I'll take you to a cab. I'm sorry, I just… I fucked up; this is wrong." Evan's face is fallen. His composure crumpled, and all glimpses of the charismatic man of moments before are gone.

"I don't need a fucking cab, you Irish bastard." Juliana pulls her jacket over her shoulders and strides away from him. "This was a mistake." She practically spits the words. "Your mistake, Evan." She walks away, heels resounding, and he knows she's right.

Suddenly sober and filled with self-loathing, Evan throws his jacket to the ground and starts to run. He doesn't know where he is running to, and it doesn't matter. He runs and he runs, the physical punishment only the beginning. He runs through the city along the pathways beside the Seine, out past the suburbs, stopping only when the light lifts and the first rays of morning sun break through a clouded sky.

* * *

Chapter Eight

Betrayed

Night time pulls our demons from the darkest places. Impossible fears, rational in daylight, creep insidiously into the realms of real and possible in the dark corners of night time imaginings.

At 4:00 a.m., I know he is not coming home; by six, I'm convinced he is either dead or has run away forever. He is gone, and we are done, and in the night's deep darkness, I know this to be the truth; my worst fears taunting me with every tick of the mantle clock. *He is not coming back, and you are alone; you did this, you've done it before, and you are alone again.*

No one wills the people they love away, but as a teenager, I believed somehow I had contributed to my mother's death. In my childish understanding of the life, I believed the world and those in it revolved around me. This being the case, it made sense it must somehow be my fault that my mother had suffered the way she did and had been forced to leave life before she was ready. This was the feeling that sat heavily on my young shoulders rather than a statement in my head. I never said the words "it is my fault," but the feeling that I played a part in her suffering was with me always.

Now as the dawn approaches, the irrational and overwhelming feeling that I have driven Evan away pokes and prods me into daylight. When finally a watery grey light filters through the tall windows, a sense of reality creeps into my altered night time state, and although the fear does not leave entirely, it creeps behind a curtain of worry that something terrible has happened. Something terrible must have happened to keep Evan out all night without a call to let me know he is okay.

I hadn't closed the curtains last night, enjoying watching the sight of the street and views of the city from the window. A vicarious night out from the comfort of my sofa, wrapped in my duvet, sneezing into a cotton hankie. I should have gone. I should have made the effort to go with Evan. He wanted me to, and instead, he went alone and now he's not home. I move wearily to the small kitchen and put the stovetop espresso pot on to brew. I slept very little, waking intermittently to check if Evan was home, then struggling to fall back to sleep after 2:30 a.m., that bad feeling settling like a mist around me.

The city is waking in the near distance, and outside in the street, windows spring to light one by one as Parisians move into their day. A solitary man braves the wind, and semi-dark, wrapped tightly in a wool coat, leashed dog by his side—a little furry form skipping its joy to the cold morning. He walks briskly, dog at his heels, his face down and hiding from the wind… the little dog looking up, the cold wind delicious to its eager face.

The coffee pot begins its slow boil, bubbling thick dark espresso into the silver pot on the little gas stove, and I listen to the comforting sound and watch the window. The man, the dog, the leaves, the lights. Looking for Evan.

I check my phone again. No messages, no text, no missed calls. Rubbing my eyes, I head for the bathroom where harsh light reflects my pale image. Bedraggled hair falls in my face, and grey shadows line my eyes. After splashing tired eyes with cool water, I pat my face dry with a towel and re-examine the worried image staring back questioningly at me.

Hearing a key in the lock my heart jumps wildly. I round the bathroom door and am down the hallway in three long, perplexed strides. Evan has his back to me, his feet are bare and blistered, his shoes in his hands. He drops them roughly to the floor and before I can say a word he growls.

"I don't want to see you Billie."

"What are you talking about? Are you alright?" My fear turned to anger has turned back to fear. "Where have you been? What happened?"

"I said I don't want to see you. I can't talk to you right now." His voice is strangled and I don't know whether he is about to yell or cry. "Evan, I…" I move toward him.

"Get the fuck away from me Billie, can't you fucking hear? I said leave me alone."

Stunned and confused, I step backward, leaving one hand reaching out to his back. Head down, he turns and pushes past me to our bedroom and slams the door. Feeling as though I am in some weird dream, I place both hands on top of my head and breathe out slowly, and although my guts say *give him time, he will come to you*, I can't listen. I follow him.

"Evan, what the hell is going on?" Nothing. "I've been up half the night worried something had happened to you. Talk to me." Nothing. "Evan, please…" Still nothing, the closed door stares impassively at my anxious form. I push it open and find him sitting on the edge of the bed, head in his hands.

"Don't you ever fucking listen?" His tone is no longer angry; it's deflated like something vital has been sucked right out. He looks smaller, almost fragile. "I'm bad news. You should run, you should pack a bag and leave me."

The dramatic line is stingingly familiar. "What are you talking about? I'm not going anywhere. What happened? God, look at the state of your feet!" They are blistered and bloody, red with cold. "Where have you been?" I sink down on my knees in front of him but he can't look at me. "Talk to me, Evan."

"I don't know what to tell you."

"The truth."

"I can't."

It's at that moment I know for sure, I know and the sudden understanding is like a blow to the chest. I know, and it is all I can do not to break, not to stop breathing right there on my knees on the hard wooden floor. The words he will tell me will be more than I can manage, but I need to hear them.

"Tell me." My voice is steely now, a strong shiny front to the weakness that lies underneath.

"Billie, I…" The words are a plea, and I shake them away. He reaches a hand out, and I shrug it off, and he raises his eyes for the first time; sparkling green replaced by broken fragments of guilt and despair.

"Tell me."

"You'll leave me, you should leave me, oh fuck." His hands are on his face again. "I made a mistake."

I'm staring at his blistered feet, red with cold, and my mind is racing in circles of what ifs and what nows. I can't lose him, but will I be able to forgive him? Pride and anger, love and betrayal, once the words are spoken, he can't take them back, and I won't be able to pretend I haven't heard them. Once said, it all changes. But already, in this moment, things have irrevocably changed. Something fragile shattered; the illusion in the perfection of love and its tenacity.

Stale alcohol and cigarette smoke seep from his pores, the pieces of the puzzle fall into place one by one, forming a picture I don't want to see. Why should it be such a shock to me? I know his weaknesses better than he does; I know because I see them every time he is with me, in me, and it's a vulnerability that frightens him. The losing control is the thing he fears most. I know what has happened before he has to tell me, but I want to see him suffer. I want him to break a little more.

"Man up Evan, tell me, or should I tell you?" Anger fuelled by pride washes over self-pity, and I'm fiery and ready to fight.

Evan takes a breath and looks at me. "It was Juliana."

And although I should have expected this, should have known, trusted my intuition, the confession hits me like a punch. I'm frozen, staring at his face, mute with shock—then suddenly wild with red rage, ugly and unfamiliar. I swing for him, and he raises his face, ready to absorb my feeble slap. I swing again and again, he takes the blows; the fourth time he catches my wrist and holds it.

"Stop now Billie. I deserve it, but stop and listen to me." He doesn't let go, I struggle for a moment, then relax into his hold, sobbing pathetically.

"She doesn't mean anything, nothing, you must know that."

"Do you hear yourself? You are a fucking cliché Evan."

"I was drunk, I didn't mean for it to happen. I'm a stupid fucking drunk."

"You are a stupid fucking drunk. That is not news! You are now an unfaithful fucking drunk!"

"It was barely a kiss and would you believe that she seduced me?" That he thinks I might find any of this mildly amusing enrages me all over again, and I try for another slap. He grabs my wrist tightly now. "I swear to you, I didn't mean for any of it. She came on to me and..."

"And you think that's an excuse? She came on to you? I don't give a crap, you came on right back. That's why you stayed out all night, and that's why you came home here this morning with your tail between your legs." I have lost all control, and my words tumble over each other in my craving to hurt him. "You could have said no, you could have pushed her away; you could have stopped for a moment in your drunken lust to remember me, your fucking wife, waiting for you here at home. I'm always fucking waiting for you, Evan!"

"I wasn't with her all night. It was one stupid kiss, and I ran. Billie, I couldn't come home because I couldn't face you."

"You should have kept on running. Get out."

My voice is strong, but my resolution weak. I know I'm about to crumble, and I need to be away from him. He doesn't move but stares at me, willing to take whatever punishment I will give him.

"Get out, Evan."

My shoulders sink, and I feel the shudder of my heart's last beat before it breaks in a million pieces etched with his treacherous name. He rises slowly to his feet and leaves, bare feet and all. He walks out the door, not stopping for a coat or shoes, no car keys, wallet or backward glance.

Evan leaves.

The clock on the mantle ticks on, oblivious to the weightier seconds it has witnessed; each moment passing just as before, despite the upturn of my world. I curl in a sobbing ball on the floor in the same spot I had only moments ago embraced my full angry female tiger and hit Evan three times in his sorry broken face. I cry for all of it, for the love lost, for the treachery, the deception. I cry out of self-pity, frustration, and plain sadness at the breaking of something once so beautiful.

It could have been days, hours, or merely minutes later that I pull myself up, cold and aching, from the floor, unsure where to put myself or what to do. The light has changed and the grey day is slightly brighter, the light stronger and more resilient. Such a contrast to my shaky self. Have I slept? I'm not sure but feel disoriented and dreamlike as I push myself on to the sofa and pull on a soft blanket.

Despite my flushed cheeks and hot forehead, I am cold and miserable. Grief does not numb my cold toes; they are numb already, amidst the night and mornings drama I neglected to click on the thermostat firing the old radiators that hang on the walls. Without their reliable heat, the high-ceilinged apartment is cold in winter. I want nothing more than to stay under my blanket, but acknowledge that heartbreak doesn't prevent chilblains so drag my blanket-wrapped self up and toward the hallway to click on the thermostat.

Passing the window, I stop in disbelief. Evan sits down on the street, across the road on a garden wall directly opposite our window. Elbows on his knees, palms pressed together he rests his chin on his index fingers, swinging his legs like an impatient schoolboy. He is jacketless and his feet are still bare, and he sits with the inevitable expression of one waiting for a late running bus; unhappy certainly but sure the bus will come. An old lady passes and looks quizzically at him. He smiles and salutes her. She responds in French. He smiles again then returns his gaze to this side of the road.

Sighing, I bring a hand to my face as another fat tear gives me away. The movement in the window attracts his attention, and he starts, looking up directly at me. I return his stare for as long as I can then step backward out of sight before I become weak. I know Evan, and he will stay there now until I go for him. "He can stay!" I announce loudly, my voice sounding braver than I feel.

* * *

6:00 p.m. Evan is still on the wall, and I can't bear it; there's a cold wind, and he is half-dressed. Torn between anger and despair, I debate what to do. To let him back in says "I forgive you," and I'm not ready to do that, though I can't help but feel he is my responsibility. If I leave him out there, he will contract pneumonia and die anyway, then the whole forgiveness thing will be somewhat of a moot point.

"Oh, fuck it!" I scramble around until I find a marker and some paper. In bold print, I write "GO AWAY EVAN." Stomping to the window, I press the paper up against the glass. I hear him a moment later yelling and I can't make out the words. I open the window a crack, hoping he can't see me.

"Billie, it's upside-down!"

I put a hand over my eyes and moan under my breath. Is just a shred of dignity too much to ask for? Scowling, I turn the paper right-side up, underline my message and push it against the window then sink to the floor. This must all be a bad dream, and in a minute, the alarm will go off and Evan will swear, throw the clock somewhere then nuzzle into me and ask me to help him wake up. A loud, pathetic "thank goodness no one can hear me" sob escapes my lips, accompanied by much sniveling and nose blowing. Moving to my happy place, the soft, warm sofa and the plaid blanket, I curl up and fall instantly asleep; a black sleep of total escape from reality.

* * *

Outside, Evan sighs, claps his freezing cold hands together and takes a last long look at the upstairs bay window where her scribbled poster remains. His feet are beyond cold, and after a night of no sleep and 30ks of barefoot running around the city, followed by a few smacks to the head and a cold, miserable day on a garden wall, he feels desperate enough to curl up on the cold sidewalk under the shelter of the oak tree. Instead, he takes the smarter option and walks the few kilometers to Guillermo's house where he requests a "no questions asked" bed for the night. Guillermo, confused but learned in all matters of domestic disputes (he has three ex-wives), kindly obliges.

* * *

Bathed in moonlight, I run barefoot through the streets. There's a feeling I have to get away, I must get away. I must run and run, and an icy fear creeps up from the chill in my bare feet to my throat where it sticks as I try to yell out. Turning, I see another smaller running figure in the shadows, and I know I need to run faster, be smarter, and get out of sight. Pain rockets through my aching legs, and I look down to see my feet bloodied and dripping. I am so cold, and my pace slows like a toy action figure running out of batteries. My movements stutter to a stop, and I am stuck frozen as the figure approaches. "Parlez-vous français?" she whispers delightedly in my ear as her small, nimble figure passes me and sprints on ahead closer and closer… to what? I can only watch as she reaches a taller shadow, and they embrace in the dark. He says in a stage whisper, "Seduce me." She giggles and falls into his arms as he looks up at me, his face thrown momentarily into light. "No! Evan, seduce me! Me! Over here!" I yell, stuck to the spot, but of course, Evan has now turned into Mr Whippy with lips, and he's singing like Elvis. "Please release me; let me go."

I awake with a jolt, sweaty and disoriented, gradually steadying my breathing I try to relax, relieved not to be a battery-operated action figure stuck in a park with Evan posing as Mr Whippy.

My tummy growls, in the day's despair I forgot to eat, and now, all I can think about is a tub of Häagen Dazs in the freezer; comfort eating at its best. I wrap my blanket around me like a toga and head for the kitchen, flicking off the radio which I had accidentally left on. It's the night time golden oldies show, of course Elvis is singing and still wants releasing. The clock above the oven says 2 a.m., and with a flash of inconvenient memory, I am overwhelmed by all the reasons I'm alone at 2 a.m. about to eat a pint of ice cream listening to Elvis Presley.

At this time 24 hours ago, Evan would be cheating on me with her. I want to scratch her mascaraed eyes out and then steal her designer clothes, not that they'd fit me. Bitch. I want to slap Evan a few more times then probably kiss him where I hurt him right after.

I hate and love him in the same breath. I know he would never have meant for this, I know he loves me, I know he hates himself right now, and I know ultimately, he would not have initiated the act. However, I can't push away the thought of them in my mind. Of them kissing… the intimacy shared in a kiss, that he shared that with her and no doubt wanted more. That the kiss was one initiated through shared desire, and that desire was not for me.

How long will I punish him? I don't know. Can I forgive him? I think I will in time, but I know I won't be able to forget or erase the image of them together.

Are love and lust so separate? Should I view his indiscretion as something unrelated to me in that it bears no reflection on his feelings for me; a stupid decision made in lust with the impeded judgment of the drunk? Do men view these things in entirely different ways than women, or am I making excuses for him? Shouldn't love create a boundary that lust for another, no matter how strong, cannot pass over? What about our marriage vows? Were they taken so lightly? I work my way through the crowded mess in my brain while spooning chocolate Häagen Dazs into my mouth; not the best snack on a belly that hasn't eaten in 24 hours, but hell, it hits the spot. Comfort eating comes close to sex on the pleasure stakes when done rarely and the food chosen wisely.

Inevitably, I reach the bottom of the tub too quickly and am left feeling nauseous with the same sad thoughts as before the ice cream experience, although the anticipation of ice cream made my situation somewhat more bearable. I blow a long breath out and head to bed rather than the sofa, but change my mind and return to the reliable sofa when I realize the bed still smells of him.

It's early when I wake the next morning, and as I pull open the curtains to greet another grey day, Evan is already perched on the wall. He smiles up at me and waves, and I shake my head in disbelief. At least he has found himself a sweater and some shoes.

I make coffee and pull a chair up to the kitchen table where I take out my laptop. Every now and then, I glance sideways; from here I can see him, but he can't see me. He is still there, looking up from time to time, reading a newspaper, writing or sketching in a journal. I feel like a spy. After a few attempts at writing, I log on to my e-mail. My thousand words for the morning may be a struggle today. I have so little focus.

Inbox: Billie Skylark

11:30 p.m. FAO Mrs Skylark from philanderer husband: Billie, you're killing me. Please forgive me, I hate myself, please let me come home. I've frozen my bollocks off on that wall today, and I'm afraid another day of the same treatment might jeopardize our chances for Skylark babies. I love you. Please forgive me. EX

1:03 a.m. FAO Mrs Skylark from miserable husband: Billie, I just dreamt you ran away with a big bloke with a hairy back. Don't do anything rash. I'm an asshole, but you're the best thing that ever happened to me, and I haven't the words left to tell you how sorry I am for hurting you. I'm on Guillermo's lumpy couch, and it smells bad and he snores. Rescue me. P.S. Men with hairy backs are terrible in bed… I heard that somewhere. Please let me come home to you. EX

2:37 a.m. FAO Mrs Skylark from lonely husband: Billie, the truth is I could never love anyone like I love you. And the other truth is I did fancy Juliana. Of course I did; all the men in the office like to look. We think with our dicks unfortunately, but I promise you I had no intention of ever cheating on you. I drank too much and made a stupid arse choice but stopped in time. It was no more than a kiss and a grope. I'm so sorry. That's the truth and there's no more to tell. You deserve the truth, and if you want me to leave the company, I'll do it. We can leave Paris and start again; just say the word. I'm so tired I could cry for ma Mammy, but who'd listen? Don't forget I love you. Please forgive me in the morning. EX

4:50 a.m. FAO Mrs Skylark from sorry husband: Billie, I've slept for two hours, and I've blisters for Africa and a crick in my neck from this fucking sofa, but it all feels about right, like I deserve it. I keep thinking about your face after you slapped me; all wild and crazy, crying and yelling and fighting and you know, although I hate myself, I'm proud you're so strong. I don't deserve you and I don't deserve to be forgiven (that was a bit of negative psychology at work… is it working?) I'm like a dog without a bone. Tell me to come home. I love you. P.S. The mad slapping thing was a bit of a turn on. EX

6:03 a.m. from my blackberry: FAO Mrs Skylark from husband bearing coffee and pastries: Billie, when you get this, your coffee's at the door, and I got you one of those chocolate twisty things with the crumbly pastry. P.S. I'm on the wall when you're overcome with forgiveness. EX

My heart's heavy, and I'm not sure whether to laugh or cry, staring at the illuminated screen of the laptop. I smile through the hurt and know that somehow we'll make it.

I wait another hour to be sure I'm ready, and then head to the window to watch him. He is chatting to the man with the happy dog from yesterday. Evan nods and gesticulates with his hands and smiles in response to the man, bending down to ruffle the dog's fur. He seems to sense my stare and looks suddenly up at the bay window where I have taken down my "GO AWAY EVAN" poster and replaced it with one that says "Come Home" in smaller, less angry lettering. Evan jumps to his feet, clapping the man on the shoulder happily, he beams a thousand-watt straight-toothed smile at me and limps across the road.

There is a knock at the apartment door a moment later and I stand awkwardly on the other side. "Evan, I'm not ready to forgive you, but I want you to come home."

"That's good enough for now."

"I'm opening the door."

"I can see that." I hear the smile in his voice.

"Don't come in yet. I need to say a few things first."

"Right." I open the door. Evan tries to look seriously at me but he is so happy. He knows he has won. "Go ahead, Billie; I'm ready." He is part-teasing and part-nervous at what I'm about to say.

"Don't think about touching me and don't think we're back to the way it was, because we're not and we won't be… ever. I'll do my best, but I can't make myself forget, and I don't know how I can trust you again."

"Okay." He looks steadily at me and I feel myself weaken.

"And… you'll have to sleep on the sofa till I say."

"Till you say what?"

"Till I say you can sleep with me."

"Right."

"When does the touching start again?" He is definitely teasing me now, but I stay firm.

"When I say."

"Will you keep me posted?" he asks. "I mean on how I'm doing, and when I can touch you… it's going to be hard for me." He's trying not to smile, pointing to my breasts, a finger briefly making contact with my nipple. I am, to my shame, still in flannel pajamas and a singlet; braless, I have left myself open to his teasing. Stepping backward, I close the door on him.

The voice from the corridor: "Sorry, Billie, I promise to be good. Please let me in."

I open the door reluctantly, frowning at him, wanting to be mad but feeling the anger slip away by the second, replaced by my need for him. Evan steps inside, lets out a long slow breath, closes his eyes and says, "I love you."

"I know, go shower. You smell."

He does as he is told, and I throw some clothes on and make him some coffee. By the time he emerges fresh-shaven and clean, I am back on my laptop feeling good again. I know that today my thousand words and possibly more will flow freely after all. I can't change what has happened, but I have to believe in love and second chances and forgiveness and forevers, so I smile as he settles on the sofa drinking his coffee and watching me from a distance. I'll nurse my wounded heart till it mends and be stronger in the end.

* * *

Much later, after a day of small distances and careful words, we sit together on the sofa, some cheesy sitcom breaking our silence. I am carefully ensconced at one side, and Evan at the other; there is still no touching.

"Billie?"

"Uh-huh?"

"How am I doing?"

"What do you mean?"

"I mean, do I get to hold your hand maybe?"

I pause for effect. "Maybe."

Evan looks down at his hands and smiles; he edges over on the sofa, his leg just touching mine, and takes my hand in his. I hold my breath feeling the onset of tears and close my eyes. "Is that okay?" he asks tenderly, all traces of humor gone. I nod, and we sit there like that for a short time. "Billie, I…"

I silence him with my hand, pushing a finger against his lips. He bites down softly on my fingertip and closes his eyes. His free hand feels for my hair and lets it loose, and I let him kiss me and kiss me until I forget that once, just once, he kissed her.

Evan undresses me carefully, like a doll he might break, and tenderly touches every part of me like he might never see me again. Our love making is gentle and slow, hushed and tender, and we come together, collapsing afterward into deep and dreamless sleep.

* * *

Chapter Nine

Fallout

From under the duvet, I hear the telephone and wonder who in the hell is calling at 5:45 a.m. I push my head under the feather pillow and will sleep to return as the answer phone in the living room records a message I can't understand, all in French. Some wrong number, no doubt. I close my eyes and try to bring back the dream I was enjoying, featuring me accepting the Booker Prize for my latest work of fiction.

Reaching to Evan's side of the bed, I find it cool and empty. He's on a fitness and health regime, and is out for an early morning run. Since throwing him out after the Juliana incident, Evan is sworn off alcohol and has morphed into "respect your body" yoga guy. He has run every morning and, in the evening, insists I join him in his yoga routine. I objected at first. I'm too restless to sit still and meditate. But I gave it a go and quickly found a mere half an hour of being alone with his own thoughts made Evan horny. The sex that followed was quite spectacular, so I'm pushing through my yoga phobic phase for now.

At 6:30 a.m., I get up anyway and head to the shower, emerging towel-clad as Evan arrives back from running. He's sweaty and full of the joys of life. He comes up behind me and kisses the back of my neck. "Argh, get off! You're all sweaty!" I swat him away with my hairbrush then begin to get brush out the tangles.

Evan sits back on the bed watching me. He looks like a geek. Some people go running with their newest gear, all matching Nikes and fancy runners. Evan is sporting a faded grey t-shirt that celebrates a U2 tour in Belfast about a zillion years ago and a pair of baggy shorts, ankle socks, and Adidas trainers that might have been cool back in the seventies. "Someone called there's a message on the answer phone." I continue brushing my hair.

"Uh-huh." He sits back, arms behind him, sweaty hair falling over one eye, sinewy thighs and… ankle socks!

"Evan, did anyone laugh when you were jogging this morning?" I ask.

"Why would they laugh?" He frowns, pretending not to get my joke. "Besides, I wasn't jogging, that's what you do. I was running. There's an important difference. I was too quick for them to notice my stylish seventies attire."

I throw the hair brush.

"I do not jog; I run too, you know. In fact, I bet I'd kick your ass any day!" I'm truly outraged. I have, over years of jogging, honed my skills and nowadays consider myself a runner rather than a jogger.

"Really? Kick my ass? Come over here and say that." He looks menacingly at me, and I stare him down, towel clad, skin pink from the hot shower.

"I don't want to kick your ass right now. I'm clean, and you're all sweaty." He fakes a wounded look and edges toward me. "God, I need my ass kicked," he murmurs with a smile, pulling me to him and dropping my towel to the floor.

"Evan, you've got work… and I…"

"You've what?" he asks, moving lower, his head easing between my thighs before I can object further. I suck in my breath, his mouth and tongue cold against me. He moans, sucking the warmth from me. Pulling me down on to the bed he works his magic, eager to please, every action a tiny step away from the guilt of betrayal. I lie back and let him, let him make it up to me the best way he knows, for now this is enough. In the heat of heady pleasure, all is forgotten, and I let him bring me closer and closer to exquisite release. I marvel momentarily at the many pleasurable functions of the tongue, but return swiftly to my body, where tension builds and I shudder and buck, coming close to climax.

Evan stops suddenly, pulling himself up, eyes on mine, baggy shorts somehow lost. "Evan," I exhale his name as his hand continues to stroke and prime.

"I know, baby, come for me."

"I can't, it's…" I am breathless and close to desperate. "It's the ankle socks…" His lips are on me, but I feel the smile. Ankle socks gone, he moves into me, hard and fast, and I am ready. I cry out a moment later, and he carries on, his new identity as endurance athlete taking over. He moves rhythmically, heading toward his own release until he cries my name and collapses, our sweat combining, ankles socks forgotten on the floor.

Evan leaves a little late for work but with a smile on his face. It's only days since the world turned upside-down, and I had contemplated life without him. Now in the face of love, mistakes and second chances, we move on, trying to put it behind us. Me, keeping as busy as possible, and Evan trying to have as much sex, with me, as possible. The ways we cope with life's traumas, so different, yet essentially with the same goal in mind: distraction.

I move on with my day, and Evan his; this is his first day in the office since the "Juliana night," and although he looks nonchalant, I know he feels anxious as to what might follow. After that evening, he had taken a few days holiday, his first real days off since beginning with the firm. He had simply e-mailed the office informing them he'd use up some accumulating holiday, personal matters to attend to, etc.

Human resources had given the okay, so we'd spent the time together, hoping to cement over whatever damage had been done. And although I know the reality is that we have a ways to go, I also know we will make it with time.

Today at work, Evan will see her, and the thought makes my insides clench with an emotion I can't quite label. I think a blend of fear, anger and jealousy just about covers it. I hate thinking of her working with him; all of it makes me nauseous. But as Evan reminds me, he is close to completion of his current project, and Juliana will no longer be in his immediate team. This gives me only minor comfort.

I kiss him goodbye, knowing that we have borne the worst; we will never be in that situation again.

After showering for the second time, I sit at my laptop, coffee in hand, and thank my lucky stars for life's ups, downs, and heartbreaks. Its richness flows into my writing, and today, my characters come to life beautifully, leading me through the story rather than the other way around. Today, I will somehow channel all this emotion into words on the page. I plan to write all day, my perfect day really. My first novel is coming along nicely. I'm eight chapters in, and when it all flows like this, I get to feeling entirely irresponsible for what comes out, like being possessed; I write the words, but the story tells itself.

9:10 a.m.: Feeling like I lost and gained my entire world in a weekend, I need to talk to Cam. I pick up the phone. The red light flashes; message waiting, and I remember the early morning call I chose to ignore. I press play, and the sound of a male voice speaking in French moves through the room. His tone is serious, and I am unnerved despite not understanding exactly what is being said. I hear Evan's name, much more serious French, and then a severe sounding click as the speaker hangs up on the other line. I'm shaken, although I have no reason to be. Standing with my back against the refrigerator door, I close my eyes and try to decipher the French I am struggling to learn. I listen again but still make little sense of it and decide I must be overreacting to most things right now as a result of my traumatic few days. I dial Cam's number, knowing his steady voice will bring me back to calm.

* * *

Paris is cold in winter, and an icy wind cuts through the commuters as they walk briskly, heads down against the elements. Evan decides not to take the Metro today, despite the cold. He'll walk; the air feels good and he feels good. These mad few days have been a turnaround. There will be no more drinking. Billie deserves better, and he owes it to her and to himself.

It's time to clean his act up. He's never been able to drink like other people do. He's always known, and his love affair with booze is the reason he's never tried the hard stuff. It's tough enough to stay on this side of the line with booze, but on drugs, he knows his story would be very different. There'd be no happy endings and the thought shakes him from the nagging fantasy that clouds his vision: how would it feel to be that high?

The sheer escape provided by a narcotic is a fantasy he tries not to entertain, but it's there nonetheless. Is he really so different from anyone else? To seek escape from the pressure of expectation and desire is understood. We each do our best with what we have and pray it's enough. He's far from perfect but he's doing his best and the thought carries him forward toward the office and another day. Today, he decides, he is good enough. He walks briskly along the tree-lined street, knowing that today will be a new start. Turning the corner on to Avenue Marceu, the impressive frontage of Sans Limites looms before him, its height casting a shadow on to the street, blocking the early morning sun. Despite a small knot of anxiety in his belly, he's sure things will be fine. Juliana will probably be feeling like him: embarrassed and guilty. She will want to pretend it never happened, and they will ignore each other for a while and then move on.

The revolving doors transport him from the frosty street into the warm lobby of Sans Limites. The gleam of white and steel is bright, and Evan blinks, adjusting his eyes to the glare, and his body to the heat. Relaxing, he unbuttons his coat and greets the receptionist with a smile. A glass elevator takes him to the sixth floor where his office waits, and his day will begin.

The elevator doors open and chime for the sixth floor. Evan strides out into the reception area where Matilde, the secretary who works for his team, is busy behind her desk. "Bonjour Matilde." Evan smiles warmly as he exits the elevator and strides past her desk.

"Bonjour, Monsieur Skylark." She stands quickly, trying to catch his attention, but he's already down the corridor on the way to his office. "Monsieur Skylark!" she calls again as he reaches the glass frontage looking in to his office space. Sitting at his desk is an unfamiliar face, a man he has never seen before. The shelves are bare, apart from a few framed photographs of unfamiliar smiling children. Confused and disoriented, Evan stops, looking left and right. Has he come to the wrong floor? Has he walked past his own office?

The name on the door has a temporary sign. *Pierre Devereaux*. Evan shakes his head, bewildered, and pushes the temporary sign on the door to the side. Underneath, it says *Evan Skylark*.

"What the hell's this?" By now, Matilde has caught up with him, her cheeks red and her expression flustered.

"Monsieur Skylark, I tried to tell you. There has been a change. I was told to ask you to wait in reception when you arrive; Monsieur Bertrand wants to speak with you."

"What's all this about? And who the hell's this guy?" he asks, pointing to Pierre Devereaux, who is trying to look terribly busy and ignore the commotion outside the glass wall.

"Monsieur Bertrand will meet with you I am sure and discuss everything," says Matilde, perplexed.

"This is crazy," he answers, running a troubled hand through his hair. He follows Matilde back to the reception area where he sinks on to a soft seat. Matilde anxiously bustles around, brings Evan some coffee and resumes her typing behind the safety of her desk.

Time passes slowly as Evan waits, confused and frustrated, jacket still on and briefcase on his lap. His colleagues come and go, greeting him awkwardly as they pass, heading to their own offices with their own names on the doors and their own framed photographs on the shelves.

Finally, Guillermo arrives, having been at a meeting on the tenth floor. Seeing Evan, he blanches and looks as though he might run in the opposite direction. "Guillermo! Do you know what the hell is going on?" Guillermo looks embarrassed, then apologetic.

"I'm sorry, I don't know." He comes closer to block Matilde's view of their conversation. "It's not looking good for you, my friend."

"I don't get it."

"Well, let's say Juliana is a powerful woman."

"Fuck."

"Yes, 'Fuck' would be the right word. Good luck, my friend." Guillermo pats him on the shoulder as the intercom buzzes, and Matilde motions for Evan. "Monsieur Bertrand would like to see you in his office."

"Right." Taking a breath he heads for the elevator, once again experiencing that dream-like sensation that none of this can possibly be happening. He presses the button for the 12th floor, and a French female voice tells him they are going up. His head throbs, and his heart is heavy.

The 12th floor houses the four main executives who control and run Sans Limites. This floor is different from the rest of the building. Instead of bright white, large windows, and chrome, the lobby is darker, thickly carpeted, and the door's heavy mahogany. Another receptionist, this one old enough to be his Granny, greets him with a prim smile and asks him to sit down. "Why the fuck is everyone looking like they know something I don't?" he thinks. Evan chooses not to sit, but instead paces back and forth, a trace of his nervous footsteps left in the pile of the thick carpet.

"Monsieur Skylark, would you care to come in?" Jacques Bertrand stands in the doorway and beckons him inside. Nodding, Evan walks into the large office, more heavy carpet and dark wood. "Can I get you a drink, Monsieur Skylark?"

"No, thanks, and Evan will do fine. I just want to know what all this is about so I can get back to work. I've a lot to do, and there's some guy in my office! What's going on?"

Jacques Bertrand takes his time and walks round to sit behind his oversized desk. Evan feels he's back at school in the headmaster's office for smoking behind the bike sheds.

"Evan." Bertrand says his name slowly then pauses, obviously getting a kick out of the drama and his power over Evan. He strings it out just a little further. "Evan, we tried to spare you the embarrassment this morning and called you at home to tell you not to come in today."

"Not come in? Why would I do that? I've a deadline I'm working on with the others."

"Don't worry about that for now Evan; we have Pierre Devereaux up to speed on the project. He will take your place."

"Take my place? What the hell is going on? I'm leading the fucking project!" Evan tries to gather himself. "Sorry, but it's my project. We're not far from completion, and you can't have someone else take over."

"Actually, we can… and we have." Bertrand sits back in his chair, hands laced together, index fingers pressed against his lips. "There have been some serious allegations against your conduct, and we do not like bad publicity."

"What allegations? What's this about? I'm a great architect; I work my ass off. What the hell is going on?"

"There has been an allegation of sexual harassment, and here at Sans Limites, we take these things very seriously."

Evan's eyes are wild, and he breathes a long, controlled breath, trying not to reach over the desk and punch Bertrand's smug face. "It's not true Jacques, I can tell you now. Whatever you've heard, it's not true."

"Is it true that last Friday evening you left a bar with Juliana Dupont?"

"Yes, but I…"

"Is it true you tried to have sex with her, and when she refused, you struck her?"

Evan pales, blood draining from his face. "No, that's not true! Absolutely no fucking way; none of that happened! Is that what she said?" Something heavy sinks inside his chest, a physical pain accompanying the knowledge that his fate is sealed.

"Juliana has written a statement of exactly what happened and has requested you be released from the company; on this condition, she will not press charges."

Evan jumps to his feet, his briefcase falling to the floor. "This is fucking madness. Honestly, I swear to you; nothing like that happened. She's lying, she's the one that came on to me, and now she's pissed off because I turned her down."

"Listen to yourself Evan," answers Jacques. "Put down your ego.

Juliana is a beautiful and powerful woman in this company. Did you even know her husband is on the board?"

"I didn't know she had a husband."

"Of course you didn't."

"Jacques, I swear to you; it's not what happened. I did not come on to her, and I would never, ever hit a woman"

"Have you seen her since last Friday?"

"No, you know I wasn't in last week, and you've had me waiting in fucking reception all day."

"She had a black eye; she claims you gave her it. Her husband wants you charged, but you are lucky she does not want the police involved. She just wants you out."

"I don't believe this is happening. Can't you see through this? There's no proof! She couldn't fucking involve the police anyway. I'd like to see her try. There's not a shred of proof."

"You did leave the bar with her, and according to your colleagues, you looked to have designs on her all night. I'm sure on closer examination they'd find your prints all over her clothing. Do you really want to go through that?"

Evan sinks back in his chair, his head in his hands. "This can't be happening."

"It's already happened. Your things are boxed and waiting in the lobby, and you will receive your contract termination in the post. This meeting is over."

A red haze settles over him as he leaves the office and makes his way to the revolving doors in the main lobby for the last time. He wants to see her, look her in the eye and see if she's happy now, see if this is what she wanted, but he doesn't trust himself. His anger is all there is. Every step is controlled and measured as he tries to rein himself in; God help her if he sees her now.

Guillermo is in the lobby talking with a client, and he stands when he sees Evan, but stiffens, noting the expression on his face. "Evan, where are you going?"

Evan doesn't answer but pushes past him, needing to be outside so he can breathe again.

"Monsieur Skylark, there is a box here for you!" calls the petite receptionist behind the main desk as Evan strides past.

"Keep the fucking thing," he mutters and exits on to the cold Parisian street. He walks and walks, feet still blistered from the weekend's barefoot run. He keeps walking till he can't take any more. A neon Cafe/Bar sign flashes respite from a side street and without thinking, he enters, sits at the bar and orders a double.

"I fucking deserve this." He shakes his head, overcome by the chaos he knows he's created. "I fucking deserve this." The bartender stands before him, brandishing a shot glass apprehensively; Evan takes the glass without looking up, knocks it back and orders another.

* * *

It has been one of those days where everything goes beautifully: from this morning with Evan, to my completion of chapter eight, to the weather. The air is cold and brisk, but the sun came out around 11 a.m. and the sky is clear and blue. All this and I'm even having a great hair day! I spot my reflection in a shop window and admire my bouncing long locks, not frizzy or wayward, but shiny and sleek. The ashy tones of my blond hair always made me feel washed out, but today in Paris I feel stylish and sexy. There is a skip in my stride as I make my way along Rue St. Benoit. The world is good and full of potential.

Headed for Marche Maubert, our local street market, I take in the sights around me for a moment, appreciating where we live and what I have. I must not take any of this for granted. Color and fragrance greet me as I reach the busy market and meander from stall to stall. Vendors sell hot crepes lathered in sugar and lemon. The smell is intoxicating. Other stalls boast fresh pastries, colorful fruit, and dried meats, cured and hanging from strings on stall roofs. Vegetables burst from wooden barrels; oranges, tomatoes, courgettes, red onions, and pumpkins too big to carry. There is a crowd around the fish stall; people queuing for fresh scallops and langoustine. One busy stall devoted entirely to olive oil stands like a glass monument—bottle after bottle of varying shades of pale green oil.

The vendor gestures to me. "Madame! Vien ici.'" He beckons me over to sample his wares, he has me figured as a tourist no doubt "Try some Madame, please, I insist."

Always a sucker for good manners and free samples, I smile broadly and step forward, taking a lump of ciabatta bread and dipping it into the earthenware bowl of oil. The taste is divine, rich but clean, and I imagine the farm where the olives grew. I close my eyes savoring the flavor and can picture the wandering vines and the dark red soil. "Magnifique!" I pronounce to his joy, and I clap my hands together to emphasize my point, leaving with a bottle wrapped in a brown paper bag.

I'll spoil Evan tonight. I will cook something fabulous, light some candles, put on a dress and surprise him. Happy with my little plan, I go from stall to stall, selecting my produce carefully. I'll make scallops in garlic and white wine with spagettini, we'll eat fresh tomatoes, basil, and buffalo mozzarella drizzled with my olive oil, and mop up the juices with some fresh ciabatta.

Loaded with my wares, I walk through the crowded market toward home and notice for the first time a small shop on edge of the square. Its sign swings in the breeze and is written in English rather than French. 'Blackbird.' The image below is of a small bird singing on a perch in a gilded cage. Intrigued, I stroll to the window. The sign is so beautiful I want to see what they are selling. With the sun no longer casting a bright glare on the shop window, I see the vintage display of dresses, bags, shoes and gloves; divine cuts and fabrics from an era past.

Fashion has never given me the buzz it does for some women. I like to look good, but I tend to stick to what I know. The dresses that hang in this window are more than just fashion; they are stunning works of art, and each carries a story of the women who wore them before. I imagine parties in the twenties in Paris; cloth caps, long gloves, and raucous jazz, cigarettes in long black holders, and women with red lips and martini glasses. Intoxicated, I step inside, and a bell signals to the owner. She emerges, tacking pins in her mouth and needle in hand. "Bonjour Madame."

I smile, gesturing to the gorgeous little shop. "I love your store."

She places the pins on the counter and smiles broadly at me. Her hair is dark red and pinned in tight curls on one side.

"Please, look around," she says in heavily-accented English, and so I do.

Half an hour later, I emerge with another bag. This one contains a vintage dress in colors of antique cream and burned orange. After trying it on, I had no choice but to buy it. It's possibly the most beautiful garment I have ever worn. The fabric heavy silk, pinched under the bust in an empire line, falling to the knee, the skirt cut on the bias. The back is low, a scoop revealing more than I'm sure was prudent in those days, but I love it and for the sheer hell of it, I bought it. I'll wear it tonight just because I can. Just because life is good, and every girl deserves a perfect dress.

The light grows tired and low in the sky as I head to the apartment; still smiling, my mood unsquashable. Evan won't be home for a while, so I unpack my wares and put the dress on a hanger, hooking it on to the curtain rail where I can admire it until I wear it.

There's time to write for another hour, and I flick on the lamps and settle down at my laptop. Time races away as it sometimes will when you find yourself completely absorbed. When I next look up, it is almost seven-thirty. Glued to the screen, typing ferociously, I have lost track of time; I must fix my surprise dinner before Evan gets home. In fact, he should be back already. Good thing he is running late.

I busy myself in the kitchen, chopping and frying, stirring and slicing, until the smells that fill the apartment cause my tummy to protest at the meager lunch I had hours ago. "Good to go," I announce, grabbing a hunk of bread and taking my gorgeous dress to the bedroom. Slipping it on, I feel like a million dollars. I sweep my hair up with a few bobby pins and apply a little lipstick and mascara. Skipping barefoot into the kitchen, I lay the table, light a few candles and find some old Edith Piaf to fit the mood. Now, I'm ready. Where is he?

9 p.m. and still no sign of Evan, a thread of worry knots my brow. He will be here soon. I hate waiting though. I know this about myself, and perhaps that's why I'm almost always late. Waiting seems like such a precious waste of time. I'd rather fill my moments completely, but then find that the things I can fit into a narrow window of time take longer than I had anticipated. I am terribly reliable, but usually ten minutes late.

"Humph." At this rate, the candles will be all burned out. Oh well, I think, it's good to be forced to feel what other people must feel every time I keep them waiting.

Wine, that's what I need. The light from the fridge shines on my silk dress and despite my rumbling tummy and my mild frustration at being kept waiting, I still feel divine. A bottle of dry Sauvignon Blanc from New Zealand was my choice for the evening; I know Evan has sworn against the evils of alcohol, but I figure he'll probably want to share a glass, just a glass over dinner. I meant to buy local wine, but the Sauvignon Blanc from New Zealand's South Island is my current weakness, and I shamefully chose it over a local Chardonnay.

Feeling the happy buzz of wine race through me, I twirl over to the stereo and change the music to Ryan Adams (you can't take the country out of the girl) and dance around like a giddy teenager. I clap my hands and whoop, knowing no one can see me and feeling the joy that floods you when music touches something deep inside that nothing else gets near.

Lost in my disco moves and musings, I don't hear the doorbell the first time. When it rings insistently three times in a row I stop dead and punch the off button on the stereo, feeling disconcerted and anxious. Evan wouldn't ring the bell, and why isn't he home yet?

As I head to the door, the hallway clock ticks 9:45 p.m.

"Guillermo," I say, surprised.

He stands sheepishly in the doorway, hands in overcoat pockets, shiny head gleaming under the pale corridor overhead light. "Billie, I am sorry to disturb you at this hour, but I wanted to speak with Evan, please." His English is perfect, if a little formal.

"I'm sorry, but he's not home yet." I'm worried now. "I was waiting for him." I'm suddenly self-conscious in my vintage silk dress, all made up and alone.

"He has not come home?" says Guillermo.

"No, I assumed you were all working late."

Guillermo pales realizing he will not be able to leave now without explaining. He brings a hand to his chin and rubs it thoughtfully.

"Were you not all working late then?" I ask, feeling stupid.

"No, Billie. Can I come in?" He sounds apologetic and his tone scares me.

"Yes, of course, I'm sorry. Come in." I usher him into the corridor, closing the door behind him. Something's not right, and I feel the air being sucked from the balloon that has held me high today.

I follow Guillermo into the apartment and watch him look around at the candles and the covered food, his cheeks flush, and he hangs his head imperceptibly but I see it.

"Sit down, please." I motion him to the sofa and he does as bid, his overcoat making him look larger than life; a small, shiny anxious head on a body that takes up the two-seater. "Where is he?" I should take his jacket and offer him a drink, but I know this is not a social call.

"I had hoped he would be here with you."

I breathe out and sink into the chair opposite his bulky form. "Did something happen? I know about Juliana, Guillermo."

"Yes, I know. He spent the night on my sofa on Friday." He gives me a half-smile and turns his palms up. "I knew you would want me to let him in, even though I agree he behaved like an imbecile." There are some words rarely used in English, but that said with a French tongue work perfectly.

"Yes, he did, and thank you, Guillermo, for taking him in. I was too angry to think straight."

"Rightly so, Billie. I understand, but you should know that he was not entirely to blame. Her name may sting, but Juliana is bad news. This is not the first time she has behaved this way, I'm afraid, and I wish I had warned Evan before this happened."

"What do you mean?"

"She has done this before, and the young man in question left the company too. When your jealous husband is on the board of directors these indiscretions are taken care of, let's say."

"What do you mean, left the company too? Guillermo, what happened to Evan today? Where is he?" My heart races as Guillermo relays the news he has only just heard via office gossip. Evan was released rather than face charges of harassment and assault. I breathe into my hands covering my mouth; red lipstick traces on fingertips. Words stick in my throat, and an array of emotions vie for their place at the front of the line. Outrage wins.

"How dare she? Evan told me what happened. What is she trying to do?"

"Save face," answers Guillermo. "Like I say, she has done this before. I wouldn't be surprised if her husband gave her the black eye, that has happened before also."

"Oh my God, they fired him?"

"Well, they gave him no choice; either he chose to leave or they threatened to press charges. I'm so sorry to have to tell you all of this. I should have warned Evan about her."

"Evan shouldn't have needed warning." I am momentarily confused by anger then pity; Evan has really fucked up this time. I want to kill Juliana, but first I need to find Evan. A sudden jolt of anxious energy gets me to my feet, and Guillermo jumps too.

"Where are you going?"

"To find Evan." I grab a coat and my boots and pull them on roughly, with Guillermo at my heels.

"I'll come too Billie, maybe I can help."

I don't answer and out on the street, run toward Sans Limites; my anger at Juliana fuels my speed. I try to think like Evan and know that a bar will be the most likely place he will hide, afraid to face me with this new development in the big Evan fuck up.

I go from bar to bar, not caring what I look like, vintage dress and cowboy boots, wild-eyed and worried. Guillermo couldn't keep up, and I don't know where he is anymore. What ifs barge around in my head like angry flies. Evan has such a dark side, such a tendency toward drama and depression. What if? My mind flashes forward, despite my efforts to keep it present, and I see a falling body, arms out, falling willingly into the fast-flowing Seine. Giving myself an internal bitch slap, I shake my head at my own dramatic imaginings. I will try one more bar and then go home and wait.

The flashing neon sign looks seedy, and I almost change my mind, but intuition tells me to go ahead and make this the last bar. I walk the cobbled alleyway, my boots echoing. Inside, the bar is crowded and warm, loud music blares from a corner, and the air is thick with smoke. My eyes take a moment to adjust to the dim light, and I weave my way through the crowd to the bar. I see him in the corner, slumped and alone.

My heart nosedives, although I know it should soar having found him alive and well, if drunk; but the picture of despair he forms is such a contrast to the buoyant, confident man who left our apartment only this morning. It's a heartbreaking scene, and despair washes over everything in the moment of recognition.

A body jostles behind me, and I move through the crowd around the bar to him. Someone wolf whistles, and I remember my overdressed attire.

Evan raises his head momentarily, and I catch his eye. The barman leans over and says something to Evan in French. His gaze clears for a moment, and he recognizes me. In that instant, all of it washes over his face; a brief view into the complexity behind his eyes. Disappointment, failure, grief, and self-loathing; all of it. But the eyes are those of a little boy confused and afraid, unsure of how he got himself in this fix and unsure how to get out.

"Billie, I'm so sorry," is all he can say before he passes out. A few hefty men carry him to a cab for me and I take him home, cradling his drunken head in my lap, crying a few bitter tears along the short ride home. I tip the cab driver, who helps me drag him upstairs to the dimly-lit apartment, the candles long since burned out. I undress him and manage somehow to drag him onto the bed. I see life flash ahead of us, this scene many times over, but dismiss the thought as angry and unfair. He murmurs in his sleep, and I lie with him, curled behind his drunken, sleeping form wondering what next.

* * *

Chapter Ten

Escape
Scotland, 2003

Mom always used to say that change was healthy, and everything that happened to each of us was working just as it was supposed to; every life, every action and decision was a part of our own little road to somewhere. I try to hold on to that when the burdens of life's decisions and unexpected changes become too heavy. Looking back, I wonder if her words were merely to help guide me through the rigors of childhood, because these days there's no joy in thinking I can't change anything in my path. That it might all be pre-determined is not a comforting thought. I want to be able to steer us to stability and happiness, and I can't handle the thought that it might all have been decided for me.

The cold rail is strangely comforting, its icy grip reminding me all of this is real. I hold tight, the wind whipping my hair around my face, shaky legs wobbling as the boat plows forward on course for the Isle of Arrasaigh.

Paris is behind us, and we are beginning a new adventure; we will start again, and we don't know where yet, but for now, we'll spend a few months on the farm with Cam. We need a clean break from the stresses of the city, and Evan needs a total change in order to regroup and move on.

Our last few months in Paris were unhappy. Evan tried to pull himself out of the dark hole he fell into after the accusations and termination of his contract at Sans Limites, but without another job and no means to pay our rent, our options were limited. Evan tried for several other positions, but word of the minor scandal had spread through the network, and despite his resume and credentials, he couldn't get an interview. Paris became a reminder of everything he'd done wrong, and his depression grew darker the longer we stayed.

It seems crazy to me how life can turn on a dime; one incident, one bad choice and everything changes, but here we are. The thing with Juliana seems so insignificant now compared to the repercussions following in its wake. Evan's drinking binges, a near breakdown, and his professional reputation in tatters.

We could have waited it out. I tried for a time to persuade Evan that maybe I should get fulltime work, he could make a studio in the apartment, sell his art; people would forget, another small scandal would become the focus, and Evan could start again. But pride is stubborn, and Evan wanted to work in his field, where he was beginning to make his mark. He wanted to draw buildings, plan structures, help engineer designs that people would use, and I realized he would step no further forward with this until we left Paris behind.

We told no one what had happened, not that they wouldn't on some level have understood, but more that in sharing the story and explaining the move over and over again, the process of moving on became more drawn out. We packed our belongings and put them in storage, taking only what we needed in two suitcases, and told Cam we had to have a holiday. I hate to lie, so I told him a variation on the truth; Evan no longer saw eye to eye with the company and had decided to move on. We were in between jobs and could we come and stay for a while?

Cam was delighted, although I'm sure a little concerned; the

Ruthie Morgan | 137

old-fashioned attitude that a husband should always have a job to support the wife and so on. We would both help out on the farm, and this would give us a chance to figure out what came next.

"Aren't you cold?" Evan's arms circle around me from behind, his head resting on my shoulder.

"It feels good." I look out at the mist and soaring seagulls swooping and squawking as they follow our trail. The air is damp and smells of seaweed and engine oil, the boat is quiet, and most passengers are inside in the cafe or bar. Evan lowers his head, burrowing into my neck, kissing me gently.

"Are you okay?" he whispers, needing reassurance.

I turn to him and place my palm against his cold cheek, his strong jaw line disguised under a layer of stubble. "I'm fine." A thin veil of rain settles over the boat, and we head inside, hand-in-hand, to watch from the round port hole windows as the coastline slowly fades and we head into open sea.

Arrasaigh is only a two-hour ferry ride from the mainland, but once there, it's easy to believe you've stepped back to the fifties. Time seems to have stopped somewhere around that era, but it adds to the little island's charm. It's not a tourist destination; the climate is cool and usually damp. Its hills and valleys are breathtakingly beautiful, and it's greener than anywhere I have ever been.

My last visit to Arrasaigh was too long ago, two years at least. During my student years, visits were less frequent than Cam would have liked. High school and university saw my life become crowded with study and social events. Time to make the long trip north was neglected. Cam, never complaining, came to visit me regularly, but coming back now makes me realize how much I've missed him and how good time here would have been for me then.

Mom didn't want to move to Arrasaigh with Cam. She blamed the climate, saying she could never live in a place where it rained 300 days of the year. Cam had to agree, and they were happy together in Kansas where it rained hardly ever. Mom wrote, and Cam farmed. I realize now that Kansas was never home to Cam; Mom was home to Cam. With her gone the only thing to do was to come back to Arrasaigh where he grew up.

Soon, the windows of the boat are so smattered with rain we can't see whether the island is approaching or not. I curl into the crook of Evan's arm as we sit in a booth looking at the view we can't see, polystyrene cups of watery tea on the table in front of us.

"We're doing the right thing," says Evan, and although he tries to make it sound like a statement, I know it's actually a question.

"We're doing the right thing Evan."

"I wish it were different, I wish I could…"

"Stop! This is the last time we will have this conversation! The pity party is over!" I sit up and face him. "We are moving on; this is a new adventure for us. Who knows what things might open up for us now? Life is full of possibilities!"

"Okay, I get it." Evan rolls his eyes. "And no more self-help books for you; you're beginning to sound like Steven Covey."

"That's more like it. I mean it. Can we move on now? We won't ever if you keep beating yourself over the head with the guilty stick. This is our new start, and I don't want you spoiling it by making me think of the evil witch again."

"Right," says Evan. "No more evil witch…" He laughs into my hair as I snuggle back up to him.

"What?"

"Sorry, I'm just reliving the slapping scene."

I blush. "Stop it, I'm not proud of that."

"Oh, but what I'd have done to have seen it."

"It was over pretty quickly."

"And the evil witch didn't try and claw your eyes out?"

"No, she didn't have time to; I sort of slapped and legged it."

"Billie, you're a legend."

"You shouldn't be so proud! As your devoted wife, I had no choice but to defend your honor, and now she's probably trying to figure out a way to press charges against me!"

Evan's smile is incredulous and, although he was flabbergasted when I told him I'd given Juliana a good slap on the chops, he was more proud than shocked. Now it sends him into convulsive laughter every time he thinks of it.

I have to say it was the last thing on my mind as I left that morning. I had planned a nice de-stressing run before another day at home with a sorry-for-himself Evan. As I plodded along in my own happy world, I actually bumped into her. I was jogging, I mean running (because that's what I do) in Bois de Vincennes, my most favorite park, iPod on, feeling feisty, listening to Joy Division (the particular track, if I remember was 'Love Will Tear Us Apart'). She sat on a bench looking perfectly gorgeous, takeaway coffee in hand and chatting intimately with a man in a suit.

When I realized it was her, I felt sure she was put there at that moment just for me; a tiny bit of heavenly closure. I ran right up to her, all breathless and sweaty, the lyrics of Joy Division reverberating in my head. "Juliana," was all I could say.

She stood up with a smug smile, ready no doubt to say something smart and leave me feeling like a cumbersome sweaty she-man. Before she had time to utter a word, I took the coffee cup from her hand and gave it to the man sitting bemused on the park bench. "Hold this will you mate?"

She stood, open-mouthed, and before I even knew I was going to, I deliver a classic bitch-slap to her rosy little cheek. Then I gave her a thumbs up and sprinted off before crumpling into a bush out of sight experiencing heart palpitations at my sheer madness.

The story has become Evan's favorite of all time, but in the retelling, we have to mention her name, and as of today, she is a no-talk zone. I have officially put the tiny bitch to rest. The stupid husband has suffered enough, and it's time to get over it.

A huge horn blast sounds that the ferry is coming into dock, and we jump to our feet to look out of the blurry window. Gathering our things, we head upstairs with the other passengers to await docking and our first few steps on Arrasaigh. Evan looks nervous, and I squeeze his hand. "It's going to be great." Standing on my tiptoes, I kiss his cheek, and he smiles that gorgeous lop-sided, hair-flopping-over-one-eye smile. For the first time in a while, I feel like the luckiest woman alive.

* * *

The sun sets as we head down the gangplank with the other passengers. Most heads are down, sheltering from the cold wind and drizzle. I look up for Cam as the soft rain coats us like a damp blanket, sealing in the island's spell and pushing out all that came before.

I don't care that it's wet and windy or that it's too dark to see the coastline and the way the mountain towers over the bay. I see Cam at the end of the gangplank, watching us disembark, shoulders back, head held high as always.

"Cam!" I throw my arms around him, smothering his welcoming words in a hug. He detaches himself, smiling a moment later, never comfortable with too much open affection.

He beams at me. "Welcome darlin', yer home for now." He shakes Evan's hand, clapping him on the back like an old friend. "Come on you two. Let's get you inside; the weathers bloody awful."

We bundle into Cam's truck, cases tucked under a tarp in the back where Cam's faithful Border Collie, Samson, sits guard. I slide into the back, and Evan sits up front beside Cam.

"Aye, it's good to see the pair of you." He starts the engine and begins the short drive up the hill to the old farm house where Nell, his housekeeper, waits; a warm fire burning in the kitchen grate, and the table set for tea.

Nell has worked for Cam on the farm since he returned, and I wonder what he would do if she left. I don't think he knows how to do much in the kitchen aside from making porridge.

We hang our wet coats in the hallway and kick off our shoes by the mucky farm boots sitting under the coat rack. "Come in, come in," says Cam, trying his best to be a good host, but I know he has little experience of this. He hardly knows Evan, and all of this will feel strange for him, too.

Nell sees me and rushes forward, sweeping me into a hug, and after pressing me into her warm bosom, she holds me at arm's length.

"Oh, Billie May, look at you, all grown up. And married!" She drops her grip and moves to Evan. "And you must be Evan, oh my, I can see what our Billie sees in you; what a handsome chap!" I blush.

Evan smiles broadly, turning on the Irish charm, which I haven't seen in a while. "Something smells wonderful, Mrs Mills."

"Aye, well, you'll all eat once you're settled in, let me show you to your room."

For an awful second, I imagine that Nell will show us to two adjoining single rooms, being that the last time she saw me was a few years ago and I was unmarried. We follow her down the dark corridor, where framed pictures of family and landscape decorate the walls. She turns at the end, heading up a narrow staircase which curves and stops at a small landing before continuing up to a second floor. "Gosh Nell, I can't remember the house ever being quite as big."

"Aye, it's too big for one man. I keep telling him he needs to find himself a lady friend, but oh no, he's fine on his own." Nell shakes her head. "Never mind, here we are." We're at the end of the upstairs corridor, and Nell opens a heavy wooden door to a large bedroom; its walls are thick stone and a fire is burning in the hearth. A large double bed with a patchwork quilt is against the far wall.

"Oh Nell, it's beautiful."

Nell smiles, looking bashful. "Well, I wanted you to feel special. It's been such a long time Billie. Come here. Let me give you another cuddle." She embraces me again, and I wrap my arms around her warm, soft body. She smells of scones and lentil soup.

Nell leaves us with a wink. "Get yourselves unpacked now; there's plenty room in the wardrobe, and I've clean towels in the bathroom next door. Cam's gone out to finish milking, and dinner will be in an hour." She nods and smiles, the door clicking behind her.

There is no place like home, no place like home, no place like home; I am Dorothy from the *Wizard of Oz*. I drop my case and flop backward on to the bed, eyes closed, filled with dizzying happiness at being here. Here, where love is unconditional, where there are no monsters in the cupboards or witches in the boardroom, where the bed has clean sheets, there's a hot bath waiting, and lentil soup for tea. I could cry with joy but instead hug myself then spread my body out like a star on the large patchwork quilt.

Later at dinner with Nell home at her cottage just around the corner, we sit, all three of us, at the old farm table with the fire roaring behind us and the rain battering the windows. Cam's hair is wild, and he wears an old knitted jumper, jeans, and pair of woolen socks with a hole in the toe. "So Evan, you know anything about farming?"

Evan looks up from his bowl somewhat sheepishly, a hunk of bread soaked in soup halfway to his mouth. "Uh, no sir, I don't, but I'm good at taking orders… I mean, I'm married to Billie after all." They chuckle together, agree that Evan won't call Cam "sir" anymore, and settle into a discussion about farming. Then weather. Then religion and politics. Cam stands and pours them both a whisky, and I can't help feel a little tension around my temples as the amber fluid flows into the crystal glasses. Evan hasn't drunk for a while. The alcohol had seemed to make his depression worse, but I know he won't say no, not wanting to seem less of a man, and it's not my job to refuse for him.

I'm too happy to let the worry sit with me for long and have soon joined them. We sip a Glenmorangie and chat, laugh, debate, and share news. I feel like the world is just as it should be, and maybe it's Mom's presence; maybe she's beside Cam now saying, "I told you so Billie, it's all meant to work out, just hang in there." The two men I love most in the world are talking like old friends, and something in me that's been tied in a knot for months is slowly unraveling.

Rosy-cheeked and blissfully happy, I say my goodnights at eleven and go up to our room, where the fire still glows in the hearth and the big bed waits for me.

I light a candle and slide into the cool covers, knowing for now all is well. In the dim light, I look around as shadows from the fire and candle play on the old stone walls. I'm not sleepy, just deliciously happy; I wait for Evan.

Half an hour later, the door clicks open then closes, and I see his shadow move quietly, undressing, trying not to wake me. He undoes his belt, letting his trousers slide to the floor. He turns and smiles, feeling my stare. "Mrs Skylark, I thought you'd be asleep."

"Are you disappointed?"

"Should I be?" He walks to the bed, eyes on mine.

I shake my head, mouth suddenly dry. Am I just goddamned lucky that I can still feel this way about him? That I can make him look at me with those eyes, and I know what he's thinking? I lie on my side, eyes still on his approaching form, his hair falling that way it does, the dimple on the right side that always makes his smile look devilish. He pulls the covers back, about to slide in beside me. "You're naked." He holds the covers back to look at me, and I lie still, unflinching under his gaze. Stepping out of his jockeys, he stands before me, eyes dark and body ready.

We have not had sex in weeks, our heads in different places, too angry, frustrated, or guilty to touch one another. I reach for him, arms outstretched, fingers clenching, beckoning. He moves toward me, touching my face tenderly, and then moving gradually downward; carefully, urgently, then desperately. Unable to wait for him, I guide him inside me. His eyes are closed, and his expression unreadable. In one hard, desperate motion, he thrusts deeply, hands pushing mine further back, mouth on me lest I cry out. We move together, and there is no anger, no frustration, no sadness; only joy and something else; hope for a new start.

He whispers in my ear, hand on my mouth, "Let's make a baby, Billie."

I moan and come as he says the words, not realizing that he really means it and there are no condom packets on the floor to be scooped up in the morning. That as he says the words, those little Irish sperms are racing their way toward my hysterical egg, who is running for cover, screaming, "Not now… are you kidding me? I'm not ready!"

* * *

I wake early as the soft grey light filters around the corner of the heavy drapes. Evan is wrapped around me like bony blanket. I'm warm but stiff, and wriggle out from underneath him.

"Where are you going?" he mumbles sleepily. I ignore the question, propping myself on one elbow, staring at his sleepy form.

"Evan, what you said last night."

"Uh-huh?" His eyes are closed but there's a smile forming around the edges of his lips.

"You weren't serious, were you?" I try to make this question sound like a statement because I'm sure there's no way he could possibly have been serious.

"I was." He opens one eye and reaches an arm to pull me into him, but I resist.

"Evan! There's no way we're ready; we're miles from being ready." I'm insistent. "Honestly, can you imagine us with a kid right now?"

Evan, fully awake, props himself on his elbow facing me directly. "Yes, I can, and that's why I think we should. Why wait, Billie? There's never a right time."

"You're mad! It's the home cooking and island air. It's made you mad for your own barefoot pregnant wife and troop of little farmers." I get up from the bed, knowing Evan will have changed his mind on the topic by tomorrow. I get dressed, wanting to help Cam with the morning chores; I can hear him outside and already smell coffee downstairs. "Oh, I'm so glad we're here!" I exclaim, rushing over to kiss my broody husband on the head before running downstairs to see Cam.

* * *

Our days pass in a happy haze of physical work and fresh air. There is much to do on the farm, and now that we are both here mucking in, I'm in awe that Cam manages this alone. He tells us that when things are busy, he gets a few lads from the village to help, but still it seems likes so much for one man. What strikes me is how quiet the life is, how in contrast to the city life we came from. The only stresses are the weather and the odd gate left open or an occasional sick sheep. The island's community are mostly farmers and, the vet lives close by in the village so Cam's flock is well taken care of.

We fall into a pattern of eating and working together, and when we can, Evan and I walk into the hills exploring the island's rugged beauty and magnificent trails. Every morning after milking and breakfast, Evan sits on his laptop, always frustrated with the slow internet connection, and searches for jobs in his field. He has a headhunter based in London who seems confident she will find Evan a new and exciting post. Again, the issue with references and employment history are a worry, but Guillermo has promised to be his referee. He's been promoted in Sans Limites, and his credentials should be enough.

Every morning while Evan searches for our next chapter, hunched over his laptop at the old kitchen table, I put on my trainers and go out to run in the cool, clean air. It's easy here to run a different trail every day with access to forest paths and woodlands right on the doorstep.

Today, I decide on the beach. The wind is sharp and the sky threatens more rain, so I bundle up and leave the farmhouse clad like an Antarctic explorer: bobble hat, gloves, rain parka, and tights. Running down the gravel driveway, an uninterrupted view of the bay opens, wide and welcoming; a sweeping semicircle of ocean and pebble bay. The tree line frames the land's edge, sloping gently upward to the foot of Ben Druach, the island's tallest mountain which towers over everything. Its imposing form is thick with lush green pine for the first third of its climb to the sky, then as the tree line breaks, barren heather, moss, and bracken cover the remainder of its path to the summit.

Reaching the foot of the drive whose battered sign points the way back to Cam's farm, I turn left and begin my jog through the quiet village streets. It's late winter; spring comes just a little later here than on the mainland, so the trees are bare and there are no buds or blossoms in the flowerbeds outside the cottages. The winter light doesn't change much from morning to late afternoon, and although it's 11 a.m., most household lights are on, and the village seems fairytale like as I run past each glowing window my breath white in the frosty air. There is a sudden yap at my heels, and I jump, lost in my own imaginings. Samson has decided to follow me. He falls into step, and we run together. I am happy for the company, and he's thrilled for the extra walk.

The main street houses a pub, a post office, a baker, and a butcher. These establishments are the social gathering spots for the small community. At any one of these places, you're sure to bump into more than a few familiar faces and have a chance to find out any island news you might have missed. By the pier where the ferry comes in, there is a small supermarket where you're guaranteed to find one variety of mostly anything you might need, all at three times the price you'd expect to pay on the mainland.

Samson and I make our way past the baker's, the smell of warm, fresh bread intoxicating. I nod, greeting the few locals who pass carrying baskets filled with produce, sausages, lamb chops, and brown paper parcels to post. It's like a time warp, and I'm sure that on returning in a year, two years, even five, the scene would be the same.

We cross the road to the grassy verge that leads to the pebble beach and head down to the water's edge, where we follow the curve of the beach around the bay toward to foot of Ben Druach. Here, the air is distinct, having lost the smells of the village. Baking bread is replaced by damp woodland and seaweed scents. I breathe deeply, the action double purposed: to stop my lungs from exploding from exertion and to hold the air longer in my body. It feels that every breath in helps push out something less pure, something stressed and anxious in my exhale.

Feet crunching on the pebbles and washed-up broken shells, I try and keep rhythm but Samson, thrilled by the unexpected opportunity to chase skimming stones in to the ocean, runs circles around my feet, getting in the way, urging me to stop and play.

"I give up!" I laugh, happy for the excuse to stop and catch my breath. I pick up the roundest stone with the flattest side and do my best to skim it out to sea. Samson barks ferociously, racing ahead, jumping over the first breaking wave, and then stopping, turning back to me as the stone sinks unimpressively after two bounces. His head tips to one side, and if he could talk, he'd definitely say, "Was that it?" Laughing, I try again, this time marginally more successful. Samson decides that my lame throws are not worth swimming for after all and trots back to shore, dropping belly-down on the sand to chew a piece of drift wood. The ocean is the color of cold steel reflected from the grey sky, which goes on forever from where I stand. From here the line separating the sky from the sea is barely visible, and it's only when I see the silhouette of the ferry heading toward us that the sea becomes distinct from the sky.

The coming and going of the ferry twice a day is crucial to most things in Arrasiagh. Islanders await newspapers, post, people, produce, and pretty much everything that cannot be grown or bred. The island relies on the smooth operation of the ferry; in wintertime, people can be stuck for days or even weeks till the wind or rough seas calm enough to allow the ferry to run. Cam has missed many pre-arranged trips to see me due to the ferry being unable to sail. Worse is being stuck on the mainland, unable to get home to your farm. This explains why islanders tend to isolate themselves, and the smallest stories become big news.

Word that Evan and I had come to live with Cam spread around the village in quite a hurry, and already in our first week, we'd had many visitors, well-wishers, and good old nosy neighbors wanting to meet us, wondering why we were here. Already I felt like I'd met, drank tea with, and eaten the home baking of most women in the village. Lovely as that was, my morning runs were becoming necessary; there are only so many scones one can eat without traveling up a jean size.

That said, the physical farm work has been comparable to a hard daily session in the gym. The first few days made my body ache like I'd run consecutive marathons, but now the strict prescription of fresh air, mental rest, and home cooking leave me feeling healthy and glowing.

We run away from the sea, heading for the tree line, and take the first trail that leads up through the forestry track on to the foot of Ben Druach. My thighs burn as we ascend, but Samson looks like he could run this pace for three days. The air in the forest is damp and heavy, the smells intensified by the low-hanging branches and thick ferns. The light filters green around me, and if it weren't for the very real ache in my muscles and burn in my lungs, I'd be sure I was lost in a dream world.

My goal is to get to the edge of the tree line where the forest ends and the barren mountain path begins. It's a struggle, but thankfully my mental stubbornness often makes up for my physical limitations. I slow my pace and feel Samson have a doggy eye-rolling moment. The trail becomes steeper and more undulating, and I know I will have to slow to a jog if I'm to make it to the edge of the forest.

Soon, my legs are screaming for mercy, and Samson has run off ahead as I stagger uphill, still determined to make it to the tree break. It can't be far because the light begins to brighten, losing its dense, green, dream-like quality. The air becomes lighter, thinner and less damp; the trees become sparse, and the path drier underfoot. In less than a minute I can see the clear pathway ahead, a sudden absence of trees and the beginnings of brown bracken and gorse. I am going to make it. I've been keeping my head down until now, focusing on my footsteps, not wanting to look up and see how far I might have to go, but now with the clearing within reach, I look up feeling a surge of pride that I will make it.

A movement startles me out of my sweaty haze, and I stop dead in my tracks, trying to control my breathing, slow my racing heart and not draw attention to my presence. Standing maybe ten feet away from me, blocking the track, is a stag; a fully-grown male, liquid eyes so dark and wide they seem out of proportion with his handsome face, which is angled toward me. Antlers fully grown, grand and imposing, rise from his statue-still head; his body frozen, assessing danger as we stare each other down.

For a short time, nothing moves and all is still. There isn't a breath of wind or single sound within the tiny bubble of awareness circling our two unsure bodies. Me—half-awestruck, half-terrified, the stag giving nothing away, staring with those eyes that might be a thousand years old. It could have been an hour, a minute, or just a few short seconds as I looked into the knowing face of the stag, his eyes sharing the history of the hill, his land, his honor, and his fear in that instant that I might be a threat.

A loud bark sounds to my left, deep in the undergrowth as Samson crashes toward me, a dead rabbit hanging limply from his mouth. His expression is deliriously happy. The stag is gone by the time I turn back from Samson's approach to the spot he had stood seconds before. I bend down to stroke Samson's head, my heart beating wildly in my chest, the whole incident becoming more surreal with each passing moment. Walking to the spot where he stood, there's no trace of his presence or his timeless wild stare. He is gone.

Filled with indescribable joy, I turn and jog back down the trail, the descent fast and exhilarating compared to the exquisite agony of the climb. With a pounding heart, an overjoyed mind, and a soul that weeps at nature's great bountiful beauty, I am a wild woman. A female version of Richard Attenborough crossed with Eckhart Tolle, experiencing a moment of Bear Grylls-style ecstasy in nature and adventure.

*　*　*

"And so when I got to the top, you know, the clearing, well he was there, sort of waiting for me."

"Waiting for you?" Evan smiles but doesn't look up from the computer screen. He has brought the laptop up to our bedroom and sits at an old wooden table by the window.

"Yes, exactly, that's what it felt like, sort of the presence of the mountain letting me know he was watching or something. It was beautiful." Still red-faced, cheeks chilled from the cold, I pad over behind his hunched form and wrap my arms around his shoulders. I sink my nose into his hair and breathe in a smell that is uniquely Evan.

"You're freezing!" He covers my hands with one of his.

"How's the search?" Looking at the computer screen over his shoulder like this, I can see what seems like another job description. "S'okay," he answers, a little sourly.

It's been three weeks now, and so far, Evan has applied for three posts, two in England, one in Switzerland. No interviews so far. It seems strange, given Evan's success when applying for a job the first time around. He had three interviews immediately, and three jobs to choose from in the end. It's the big elephant in the room, and both of us hover around the topic, not sure whether we should discuss the fact that Evan appears to have been blacklisted within the European architectural circuit.

Do we discuss the elephant or tread carefully round it for now, hoping it will move on soon? Sensing Evan's annoyance at my question regarding his luck today, I ignore the elephant once again and use distraction as my best weapon against his imminent slide into despair.

"Have you eaten?" I ask innocently; food always such a great distraction, and Nell's home cooking is truly something to brighten the day. Here there are no rushed breakfasts or snack lunches, there's no running out of the door with a travel mug realizing you forgot to have breakfast, and there is no such thing as a takeaway. We sit down every mealtime with Cam and sink into easy conversation, enjoying some wholesome fabulous dish that Nell has conjured up with basic larder ingredients and a whole lot of fresh produce. There's no pecorino cheese here or pine nuts, no sun-dried tomatoes or polenta; just good, old traditional home cooking, usually made slowly and lovingly in a crock-pot on the range stove. Nell bakes bread every day, and with homemade butter and jam for spread, I haven't even missed my daily chocolate fix!

This in itself is a minor miracle; my affection for chocolate coming a close third behind my addiction to good coffee in the morning and a nice glass of wine in the evening. My usual routine sees few days pass when I don't feed my need for a little chocolate, usually mid-morning in between breakfast and lunch, or naughtily late at night when those fat calories make a sprint for my hips and bed down while I head to sleep.

Nell slow-roasts lamb and beef, she serves whole chickens stuffed with sage and onion, mashed potatoes and turnips lathered with rich gravy, and steamed puddings with golden syrup or jam roly poly covered in creamy custard. Evan and I are spoiled entirely by her food, and it's easy to distract him now. One gesture toward the kitchen, and he's off the chair, sniffing the air like a hungry dog.

"Jesus, that smells good." The tense furrow on his forehead is gone, and he rubs his hands together like an excited little boy. Overcome with joy at the culinary pleasures to follow, Evan scoops me up, holding me like a small child. My legs wrap around his waist and feet cross behind his back. "I think something's about to happen!" he says with a smile.

"What's that supposed to mean?" I laugh, lacing my fingers behind his neck, looking directly into his eyes. He has the distinct expression of one hatching a plan.

"It means that something's shifting. I dunno, I can't explain. I just have that feeling." He pauses. My face is close to his and I resist the urge to make fun of him, he looks so sincere. "It's like I can feel that something good's happening, that this is where we should be right now, you know? Like it's part of the plan. Something good is around the corner for us."

There are days when I wonder if Evan's guilt and sense of responsibility for the way things turned out in Paris will ever go away. Although we have agreed the chapter is over and we'll move on, it hangs over him like a rain cloud. There are moments when the sun beams through, but even so, every good feeling is still tempered by a "but if." I can practically see the subtitles behind his green eyes. "If only I… things could have been… what would have happened if I hadn't… will I ever… what if?" and so on. He's doing his best to convince me, and by doing so, convince himself that we are on some cool karmic path, that all is as it should be, that this is a stepping stone to something else, something better that wouldn't have been possible if we hadn't had to leave Paris.

Here's the thing: I already believe it; he doesn't have to convince me. I have never been happier. Although I would erase the Juliana incident tomorrow if I could, I can't. It's a fact, and Evan has paid his dues and, come to think of it, so have I.

Part of me lately wants to thank the vindictive little cow. If she hadn't seen to it that Evan was fired and his reputation tarnished, then we wouldn't be here, enjoying this little idyllic chapter in our mad life.

Like a dream within a dream, I like this part a lot, the part in Paris at the end—the bad dream part? I didn't like that at all, and so I've tried my best to move on.

Here in this little slice of paradise with family that love me and nothing but nature, fresh air, and good food around, it's hard to feel any of this isn't a good result. I hate that Evan endures the weight of guilt, but I can't take it away from him no matter how many times I tell him how happy I am. By acknowledging his guilt and barely disguised attempts at convincing me it's all working out to the big master plan, I'll be acknowledging that I see through it. I see through the front and know he still carries it. We have talked over it so many times; I am done with the topic. I am done with the rehashing and the bitterness. I take no convincing about our new path and direction because truly, right now, I believe I've never been happier. I think this really is where we're supposed to be and for now, that's all I need to know.

"I think what's round the corner might be bacon and egg pie and jam tarts!" I kiss his forehead. "Let's go, you know how quickly Cam eats. We don't want to miss out."

All thoughts of guilt, fate, and possible lack of job opportunities are momentarily gone, replaced by the concerned look of one with a rumbling belly. "You're right, although I'll bet Nell has already served me a slice." Evan nudges me as we head downstairs toward the kitchen. "Watch out, Mrs Skylark, old Nell has a soft spot for me."

"Shh." I poke him in the ribs. "Don't call her old! Anyway, I'll bet you a $100 she serves Cam before you."

"You're on!" He pats my behind and whispers, "I'll raise you… you owe me a blowjob if my pie is waiting on the table."

I feign horror at his suggestion, then wink. "You're on."

Arriving at the table, I flush red. At Evan's place is a plate with a large slice of warm pie and mug of cold beer.

"There you are, Evan love, I know you've had a hard morning. Tuck in," Nell calls over as she fusses by the stove. Cam and I lock eyes in mild amusement as we sit down to serve ourselves from the large, perfect pie in the center of the table. The first slice, lovingly cut, is already on its way to Evan's mouth.

"Oh thanks, Nell, you're an angel." Evan says affectionately, and then winks at me as he bites down.

Cam shakes his head, smiling, and pulls his chair in, thankfully none the wiser to the bet I have just lost. "What happened to the days where I was the man of the house Nell?" he asks, mock-disappointment in his weathered features.

"Oh for goodness sake, you two aren't guests, you serve yourselves," Nell tut-tuts, pulling the jam tarts from the oven.

I shake my head. Evan's magic working beautifully as usual on the ladies.

* * *

My leading man, my main character, is not behaving himself. I sit back on my chair and take my glasses off, rubbing my tired eyes, hoping that when I open them he will do what he's supposed to. I have a plan that I have painstakingly worked through, drawn out, created timelines around, bullet-pointed, and then carefully drawn up, chapter by chapter on note cards. With all this in mind… why, oh why is he not doing what I want him to?

As my book progresses, my storyline has more or less followed the careful path I have set out. Inevitably, it may stray off course, but usually because it's found a slightly different angle from which to be told, a better angle than I could have planned. So, it sways a little and eventually settles back roughly onto the course I had hoped it would.

My present problem is that my main man, Connor Sinclair, seems to have developed a will of his own. This wouldn't be a problem if I liked where that self-will of his appeared to be leading, but the direction he's taking me is not at all what I had planned, and I'm not sure I like it. I'm not sure how to weave this new direction in with the plan or with the relationships I have so carefully been constructing with my other characters. In fact, the truth is I'm not sure what to do at all. Should I press on with my plan and ignore this new development, pull him into line and make him follow me, the writer? His creator! Or do I follow his lead? Is this the essence of creativity; that often the plan has to be thrown by the wayside to accommodate a story which begins to tell itself?

I have been staring at the screen for twenty minutes and am no further forward. It's not unusual for me to develop an affection for the characters I write about; to think of them as real people I know, friends I might have. I talk to them, sometimes dream about them, but never has one actually disappointed me. What to do?

Okay, this is a moment for tea and a late night snack. When in doubt, eat something; not a philosophy I am entirely proud of, but it really tends to work quite well for me. I save the little writing I have achieved tonight and leave the study to head along the quiet hallway to the kitchen.

A grandfather clock ticks my passage down the long corridor, its loud relaying of time the only noise I hear. My woolen socks are soundless on the worn, dark red carpet runner that travels the length of the hallway's thick wooden floor; the dark green walls are dimly lit. On a side table, a small tiffany lamp casts its glow on the framed photos hanging above.

I stop here, as I almost always do when no one else is around, to look at the photograph hanging in a central position, framed carefully in heavy, gilded, plated gold. Cam and Mom stand on our porch in

Kansas. Cam looks directly at the camera, smiling broadly, towering over Mom, his arm around her shoulders. He has the look of an old-fashioned military gentleman, unused to having photos taken, best smile on, shoulders back, showing off his prize possession. Mom's posture is much more relaxed, her face in profile as she smiles up at him. The look is one of knowing; the look you give the person in this world you know best, you love best, you understand and adore. She looks up at him, smiling; the sparkle in her eyes suggesting she's about to laugh. One hand is on his tummy, the other wrapped around his back.

I remember taking that photo, and everyone being impressed that it had turned out so well. It was almost a year before Mom got ill, and we were all happy. Not necessarily happier than most, or worry free. It wasn't the Walton's. We had our fair share of minor family dramas and money troubles, all the usual stuff as far as I can remember, but essentially we were happy. Life was good, and then one day, so very suddenly, it wasn't.

I wonder if I look like her, if I look at Evan the way she is looking at Cam, and I wonder if together Evan and I can hope to be as good parents together as they were for me. Lost in my own reflections, I jump when I hear voices in the kitchen.

Who could be here? Cam is out at the pub with a few fellow farmers, and Nell has gone home for the night. Walking toward the heavy oak door, I hear the conversation more clearly.

"We are hoping to hire in six weeks' time and will need to know within the next two weeks if you are interested," the heavily-accented voice continues. "We have a very reliable team here and rarely hire outside, but we feel it might be time for some new blood, some new ideas."

Who is in there? I wait, eavesdropping, unsure of whose conversation I might be interrupting should I continue. Evan's voice now clear and professional, his tone formal and polite, says, "Well, I appreciate your consideration, but I will need some time to think it all through."

More words from the other speaker, harder to understand now, and I realize Evan must be on Skype, the reception suddenly poor. Evan again: "Yes, thank you, I appreciate the extra time to consider the post." The other voice speaks again, continuing on for a minute or so, and I feel a little guilty listening. I should quietly pad away but am intrigued and too nosy to leave now.

"Okay, Mr Evander, it's been great speaking with you and thanks again." Pause. "Yes, I'll be in touch within the week." Evan's chair scrapes on the stone floor as he gets to his feet. Torn with the dilemma of barging in and asking him what all that was about and revealing myself as a sneaky eavesdropper, or slipping back to the study and feigning innocence, I hop from foot to foot in indecision until the door opens and Evan stands looking at me in surprise. "What are you doing out here?"

"Ahem, I was just on my way in… for tea; yes, some tea. I was coming through to make tea. Would you like some?" I ask, eyes wide, feeling silly.

"Okay," says Evan slowly, eyeing me suspiciously. I slip around him into the kitchen where I busy myself filling the kettle and setting it onto the stove. I feel the need to whistle, but this might be taking the "I'm all innocent" thing too far. I glance up briefly between putting tea bags in mugs and getting the milk from a jug in the fridge.

Evan watches me, arms folded, legs planted shoulder-width apart, his eyes slightly narrowed. "Okay Billie, how much did you hear?"

"Hear about what?" I ask. "Don't tell me you've been having it on with Nell on the sly after all! I swear, I didn't hear a thing. It's just that, well, those big pie slices and extra pudding every day… it was a bit of a giveaway."

"Billie, have you been listening outside the door?" Evan's arms are still folded, his head tilted to the side. I can practically hear his brain cogs whirring around, figuring out if this might be a problem.

"Well…" I take a long breath in, my brain, like his, weighing up if this is an issue. "I was coming in for the…"

"Tea," Evan interjects.

"Yes, the tea." I point to the two cups and the box of tea bags in front of me to corroborate my story. "And I heard voices, and I didn't want to interrupt, so I waited outside and then, well, then there wasn't a good moment to come in and…" I trail off. "Yes, I was listening."

Evan smiles at me and shakes his head. "Why didn't you just come in and say hello?"

"It sounded important. Was it? Have you just gotten a job I should know about?" I'm not sure why, but my tone is hesitant when I know it should sound excited. It's not that the thought of a new opportunity for Evan isn't wonderful, but I selfishly have been enjoying this interim and I don't want it to end quite yet.

"No, but I think there might be a good one waiting if I want it."

"Wow. That's great news Evan!" I give myself a quick internal slap so as not to jeopardize any excitement Evan may be feeling. I'm wondering if he was trying to surprise me and that's why he was Skyping in secret.

"Well, there's a lot to think about, so I'm going to sit on it for a bit, do some more research before we decide."

"Is it a good company?"

"Uh-huh"

"Is it an exciting position? Not council offices or shopping malls?"

"No, it's a great position. It's really great."

"So what's to decide?"

Evan looks unsure; he unfolds his arms and sits down again at the kitchen table as I hover, tea kettle in hand, wondering why I have a weirdly ominous feeling in my guts. He's studying his hands, playing with a fingernail, nodding his head in silence, obviously privy to some internal discussion I can't hear.

"How do you feel about the South Pacific?" His tone gives nothing away despite his left field question, but my tummy takes a strange lurch, and I'm no longer listening. Closing my eyes, I will my sloshing insides to calm down. Did I eat something?

Evan is still talking, oblivious to my sudden internal rumblings "... I know it's a great company and don't ask me why they'd have their only office in the Southern Hemisphere there, of all places. Lots of potential for structural development, I suppose... Billie?"

I clutch my mouth, my face clammy and pale. Evan stands, a look of concern on his face as he moves toward me, but I'm too quick. I sprint for the bathroom knowing Nell's clean floors are within an inch of disaster. I practically push Evan out of my way, reaching the bathroom in record time, and heave dinner and anything left from before into the white ceramic toilet bowl.

"Christ Billie, are you okay?"

I groan, feeling very not okay, waving him away with my hand. "I'm fine, must have eaten something. Go." I shoo him out. There are few things as undignified as vomiting.

When its feels like there can't possibly be anything left to throw up, I slide down the tiled wall and sit on the floor, a cold flannel against my mouth. What was that?

Evan is at the door. "Billie, are you okay? Was it the South Pacific thing? Listen, it's just an idea. I knew you'd hate it. We don't have to move anywhere you don't want to."

South Pacific? I can barely remember the conversation now. I crawl to the door and let him in. "No, it wasn't the South Pacific. I must have eaten something weird. I feel okay now. Maybe I've picked up some bug. Anyway, why are you talking about the South Pacific?"

Evan gets on his knees on the bathroom floor beside me. "Oh, forget it for now. Here, let's get you to bed." He scoops me up and carries me along the corridor past the happy gilt-framed faces and up the steep stairs to our bedroom. "Come on, you just need some rest. Maybe you're too fragile for farm life." He peels my clothes off and tucks me under the cool sheets. "Or maybe Nell's trying to poison you so she can keep me for herself." He laughs and kisses my forehead, and I smile and swat him weakly with a free hand.

"Goodnight Evan."

"Goodnight Billie."

"Thanks for taking care of me."

"That's my job."

"I love you."

"Me too."

* * *

Chapter Eleven

Revelation

The town hall has been transformed, tables are candlelit and covered with thick cloth and pastel-colored rose petals. Balloons hang in bunches like oversized floral arrangements and colored bunting is strung from the ceiling beams. A banner reads "Congratulations Stuart and Siobhan" and glasses clink to signal quiet for another speech.

We have been invited to Nell's grandson's wedding, and the church hall has been lovingly revamped by friends and family to become the reception venue. The best man stands to make his speech, a tall, sandy-haired man in a kilt. We all listen, waiting to laugh appropriately at the inevitable jokes at the expense of the groom. I take a deep breath, hoping the speeches don't last too long. The rich dinner hasn't settled well, and I conduct an internal assessment of my exit path to the bathroom. Maybe I have developed an allergy to something I've been eating here on Arrasaigh; for a few weeks now, I have been plagued by unpredictable and overwhelming nausea. When I feel the signs, I need to be in sprint range from a bathroom.

Evan chortles and claps with the crowd as the best man tells another story about the groom, who now has a red face to match his red hair. Each story so far has revolved around the groom's inability to hold his alcohol. Poor man, I can relate. Just the thought of the glass of bubbles in front of me sends my tummy into spasms. Everyone raises their glasses to toast the bride and groom, and I join in, letting the champagne touch my lips, but even the smell is too much. I do a quick situation evaluation. Do I draw attention to myself by running out of the room amidst the speeches or cause a real scene by spewing on the table? Easy decision! Bile rises in the back of my throat, and I panic, standing too quickly. My chair falls backward, knocking on the hardwood floor, and the other guests turn, eyebrows raised, expressions disdaining.

Slapping my hand to my mouth, I spin on my heel and try to run to the loos, a movement comedic to watch, being that I'm wearing a long dress too tight to stride out in. I stumble, grabbing the shoulder of a kilt-wearing gentleman at the table beside who is wide-eyed but smiling, thinking no doubt I have drunk too much whisky.

The best man stops in the middle of the long (really quite boring) joke he is telling and all eyes are on the stumbling, apparently legless guest making the undignified exit. My stomach lurches, and the muscles begin to contract involuntarily, and it's like the slow-motion beach scene in *Chariots of Fire*. Me striding desperately for the finish line (which happens to be the exit door to the loos), and there the similarity ends. There's comedy rather than beauty in this scene, and Eric Liddell ran for the greatness and glory of God. Here I am in an equally desperate race, but only for the privacy of a toilet.

Having lost all dignity by now, I really don't care about the best man, or the bride and groom for that matter. I lunge into the toilet, and the wedding feast sees the light of day again before plunging into the toilet bowl. Crostini with blue cheese and caramelized onion, stuffed pheasant, and Cranachan lost; its exit an undignified contrast to its earlier presentation on white china.

Doubled over, hands holding my hair out of the firing line, I vomit again and again until, heaving for breath, I sink to my knees on the tiled floor of the church hall toilet.

Taking a moment to gather myself I lean heavily against the cubicle wall, wiping my mouth and pressing a cold hand against my clammy forehead. It must be dairy; that's it! The blue cheese must have done it. I'm on a farm, my system isn't used to all the milk and cheese and lactose-heavy stuff. It must be the lactose.

"Um, Billie? Are you in there pet? Is everything okay?"

The voice is Mrs Monroe's, the owner of the local post office. She is a kindly widow in her sixties who lives on the main street in a small cottage behind the post office. The post office is a bit of a social hub here on Arrasaigh, a small but busy shop which doubles as a stationer, book shop, and has a handy sideline in hardware. Mrs Monroe has been running the post office for thirty years, she lost her dear husband to cancer six years ago and still refers to him as though he's around. Funny how, in a short time here, you quickly get to know the summary background of most people on the island.

"I'm fine." I smooth my hair and check my front for vomit splashes before opening the door. "I'm not sure what happened. I think it was the cheese. It didn't agree with me."

Mrs Monroe has a concerned look on her rosy-cheeked face. "Did you drink a wee bit too much champagne, love? I tell you, the same thing happened to me once; I'm not used to the bubbles, better off sticking to a wee sweetheart stout. Did you know it's full of iron? They gave me a half pint every day in hospital after I gave birth to our Ian. Aye, they said it was good for recovery. Can you imagine all those poor, tired women having just had babies, tipsy in the wards on doctor's orders? Aye, how things change. Anyway, love, your Evan's outside the door. He asked me to come and check on you. You made a bit of a scene dashing out like that. The poor best man lost his thread a wee bit, couldn't remember the punch line of his best joke. Now they're all booing at him out there, poor lad."

I'm glad Mrs Monroe is fond of talking; she hasn't noticed I'm chalk-white and still struggling to compose myself. Turning the taps on, I run my wrists under the cold faucet, and then splash my face. "Thanks for checking Mrs Monroe. I'm fine now. You're probably right, too much champagne."

She smiles knowingly and pats me on the arm. "Right then, I'll be getting back in there and see how the speeches are faring. I'll tell your Evan you'll be out in a minute. Lovely boy so he is, lovely boy." She bustles from the bathroom, the smell of lavender and laundry powder wafting around behind her. Gripping the sink, I take a quick look at my reflection. My eyes are glassy and lips pale.

"Hey Billie? I'm coming in. Ladies be warned, man in the vicinity." Evan rounds the corner of the partition between the door and the sinks. "Are you alright?" His expression changes from amused to worried when he sees me gripping the edges of sink, pale and bedraggled. "What happened?"

"I'm okay." I hold a hand up, warding him away, sure I smell of sick. "I must have eaten something; I think it was the blue cheese."

"The blue cheese?" Evan wrinkles his forehead. "You love blue cheese. I've seen you eat a block in one sitting. How much did you drink?"

"God, will people stop asking me that? I am not drunk!" I glare at him. "I've barely touched a drink tonight. I'm not well. I'm going home."

"But the party's just starting!" Evan's worried look has changed to disappointment and it makes me cross.

"You stay then! I need to go and lie down. I don't feel good."

He moves toward me and pulls me in, stroking my hair and back. "Tell you what, how about we go back in for half an hour, and if you don't feel better, I'll carry you home myself."

I look up at his twinkling eyes, feeling the nausea fade. I sigh "Half an hour?"

"Half an hour." He leans in to kiss me.

"Get off!" I push him away. "I need a toothbrush and my lipstick."

Moments later, he is back with my handbag and an after dinner mint. I fish around for my lipstick and apply a coat of pale pink sheen, which instantly lifts my sickly pallor. Popping the mint in and bouffing my hair a little, I follow him back to the hall where the lights have dimmed and the band has started up.

"There she is!" The voice is Cam's, nicely relaxed with a few whiskies on board. "Belle of the ball. Are you all right, pet?" Cam wears a kilt, knee-high woolen socks, traditional black crisscross laced shoes—the look complete with a small dagger just visible down the side of his sock.

"Fine thanks." I change the subject, sitting down beside him and his best friend, Archie, asking about the rest of the speeches and hoping to divert attention from my embarrassing exit. Luckily, people are too busy having fun to care, and as the band kicks off another tune, the dance floor fills and there is plenty of action to distract us all.

"Christ, would you look at that?" says Archie over the bagpipes and electric guitars. He gestures to a few local ladies on the dance floor, short skirts and low-cut tops, bouncing around, handbags in the middle, amped and ready for a good night. "That's Eileen McManus, she works at the dairy. Bloody hell, who'd have believed she had a pair of…"

"Aye, nice girl. Another drink, Archie?" Cam nudges him in the ribs as he stands, nodding toward the bar.

Archie having momentarily forgotten that I'm part of the conversation jumps, flushes red, removing his gaze from the large-breasted dancing girl to his almost empty pint. "Aye, that would be grand, Cam. I'll have another."

Smiling, I ask Archie about his family, and we launch into a comfortable chat about his children on the mainland and his farm up the hill. I lean in close to hear as the band turns up the volume and the newly married couple take the floor. We all stop to clap and cheer, wolf whistles fill the air, and the groom bows, looking dapper in his kilted ensemble.

The lead singer, also wearing a kilt, accompanied by a leather jacket and Dr Marten boots, steps up to the mic, congratulates the couple, and launches the band into a Big Country cover.

Like I say, Arrasaigh is a major step back in time.

The groom rocks out as his bride looks on happily, not quite sure how to dance in her long, tight wedding dress. Before long, the floor is filled, and the bride has thrown her headdress up in the air, pulled her dress up to her knees and is dancing madly with the rest.

The happiness is contagious and as my nausea fades, I find a second wind of energy and drag old Archie up to dance with me. Evan watches, smiling from the table, a line of drinks before him, happy as a clam. I dance with Cam, with Nell, even with Mrs Monroe, and then finally with Evan. Having reached the level of drunkenness necessary to get him up on the dance floor, he jumps around with me in his usual "so geeky it's sort of cool" dance style.

At eleven, the band takes a break, and the four-tiered wedding cake is rolled out on a hostess trolley to the middle of the dance floor. The guests make a circle around the towering cake, a miniature bride and groom delicately sculpted from icing standing atop the fourth tier, all smiles.

By now, the life-sized bride and groom are good and sozzled. We clap and cheer as they lean forward together, holding the knife, ready to cut the first slice. As the knife touches the white royal icing of the bottom layer, the trolley lurches forward. Someone forgot to put the brakes on and it shoots toward us, the bride and groom following in an unfortunate belly-flop. Together they land face-down on the dance floor, and the cake trolley with the knife safely embedded in the bottom layer hurtles across to the waiting crowd. Reaction times are a little delayed; too much has been drunk by all and the cake trolley plows straight into Mrs Monroe.

The direct hit sends all four tiers tumbling to the ground. Guests lunge forward, attempting to catch what they can before it hits the floor; some successful, some not.

The aftermath is an icing-covered, sponge-filled, marzipan-coated horror show. Best dresses and kilts are covered in cake, blobs of sponge and sugar frosting reside in hairdos. The bride gains her footing and for a moment sways between laughter and hysterical tears. Thankfully, after the initial horrified silence there's a hoot of laughter, and soon everyone is in hysterics. The band starts up again, and people dance, eat, and wear cake. What a night.

It's two-thirty when we stagger home; I carry my shoes, feet aching from dancing. Evan is drunk and happy. "So much for half an hour." I giggle, stepping carefully along the pebble beach leading up to the gravel road to Cam's. Evan slings an arm around my shoulder, more to steady himself than as a mark of affection.

"Billie Skylark." He leans into my ear and slurs a little. "Take me to bed." He tries to twirl me around Frank Sinatra-style but his legs aren't paying attention. "That was a good night, we should get married again just for the party. What do you say? Marry me again, Billie."

"Which is it? Take you to bed or marry you? Come on, we won't be home till morning if you don't hurry." I pull him along, and he objects, stopping, eyes raised to the heavens.

"My God Billie, do you see that? Look at those fucking stars. Just look! "Evan stands, feet planted firmly, shoulder width apart, his head's tilted back, eyes wide. "That's God's work you know. Look at it, real fucking beauty, untouched, right there. You know, tomorrow

I'm going to paint. My head's been in my arse for too long. Tomorrow I'm going to paint the stars."

He reaches his hands to the heavens, divinely inspired, drunkenly impeded. I watch as he gazes upward, pontificating at the heavens' great beauty. Slowly at first, so I might be imagining, he tilts backward ever so slightly, then suddenly drops like a sack of spuds on to the pebbles, hands still raised to the skies.

"Evan! Are you okay?" I race over, and he looks up brightly at my concerned face, before I can say another word, he laughs like he might never stop. I sink onto my bottom beside his convulsing body, sigh heavily and roll my eyes. "How am I to get you home?"

"Leave me here, Billie! I'm grand. Come get me in the morning."

"Oh, for God's sake." I slap my hands on my thighs, stand up and attempt to pull him to a sitting position. Stronger than he ought to be while this drunk, he lets me grab him around the wrists, but when I bend to heave him up, he tugs sharply on my arms, and I fall on top of him. Thankfully, we are the only mad pair on the beach at this hour; Evan, back on the pebbles, laughing up at me… now on top of him, chest to chest. I squirm to get off but he holds me firm, suddenly in control of his body. "Evan, get off! Come on, this is crazy. Let me take you to bed," I plead, but he holds me fast. He grins cheekily and his eyes glint. Incredible, the sobering effect of a possible shag. "You're too drunk."

"Everything's working baby."

"Not here, anyone might see."

"I don't care, let's give them a show."

"Evan…" He cuts me off mid-protest, kissing me hard tasting of whisky and cigarette smoke. Pulling free, I half-heartedly object again, but my body seems to be doing one thing and mind another.

His hands are underneath my dress, and I move to meet him. Predictably, he is ready to rock; trousers already undone, he guides

Skylark

himself inside me, and I suck in my breath; the sensation always a thrill.

It's easy, this part; no words, no thoughts necessary, and for a short time, the total loss of control and self-conscious thought. We could be anywhere, and anyone could be a watching, but as the pull of sex lures me in, I forget it all and let his body tell me what to do. A force beyond thought, I move to him, and he moves to me, deeper, slower, with the intimate knowledge of lovers' whose bodies and responses are familiar. Here, on the pebble beach in the darkest part of night we make love, and when it's over, and Evan shudders and pulls me to him, we fall asleep for a time, right there on the pebbles, the waves a few short meters away.

I wake later to the feel of moist air and wet clothes. The clear night sky has clouded over and a soft, fine rain falls as the light turns from black to grey. We walk back up the hill hand-in-hand to Cam's farmhouse where everything is still and asleep; the fire dead in the grate, and the lights all out. We creep to bed, sandy and bruised, and I'm overcome with bone-aching exhaustion. As I fall asleep, I hear the morning chorus begin. I sleep as the world wakes.

* * *

A small child calls my name, the sound insistent and irritating. Initial joy at the sound of the child has been replaced by annoyance as the voice goes on and on saying the same thing again and again. I don't want to answer, but know the voice will keep calling my name until I respond; the trouble is I don't know what to say. I don't know what the voice wants, but it keeps calling in that demanding tone suggesting I must have the answers, but I'm withholding, purposely not paying attention. I've had it and decide to tell that kid so, but I can't see him. He must be here somewhere. His voice is so close and insistent. "Will you shut up?" I shout, knowing it's wrong to yell at a kid, but man, he's got me all wound up. "Yeah, you, shut up already, I've had enough of your whiny voice. Give it a rest and leave me alone!" His voice has changed and he's pulling at my shoulder. I shrug the hand off but he won't let go. The voice is now deeper and somehow familiar.

"Billie... Billie, you'd best wake up. It's after lunchtime. Come on baby, wake up."

Billie is asleep; she'd best wake up, and I'd best tell her. Wake up, Billie. Hang on... A thread of reality weaves its way into my heavy dream; I swat it away, preferring to stay curled in a ball under the feather duvet. Why is that so familiar? Billie...

I slowly become aware of light, fingers of brightness edging under my eyelids. I am Billie, and I must wake up.

"Billie, come on now; its three in the afternoon. Nell's getting worried."

Evan. My eyes spring open, and the sudden shock of light and reality take my breath away. I try to sit up too quickly and, having been curled in a ball for many hours, my limbs are on strike. Opening my mouth, I find my voice has been transformed into a chain--smoking version of Bette Midler. I close my mouth and let my head flop back onto the pillow, shielding my shocked eyes from the light streaming in the half-opened curtains.

"How're you feeling?" Evan's hand is on my cheek, and I'm about to answer that I feel okay, considering I slept half the night on a pebble beach in the rain and have sand in my crotch, but the words stall on their way from brain to mouth as I feel another unwelcome rush of bile. Scrambling on to unsteady feet, I run to the bathroom and again only just make it through the bathroom door before vomiting violently into the toilet bowl. What the hell is happening to me?

Slowly and carefully, treading with the wary steps of a visitor unsure of his welcome, truth arrives plain and clear, shaking his head apologetically. Stunned at the obvious explanation I have managed to avoid until now, I cover my open mouth, sitting down on the toilet seat before my shaking legs give way. Of course, how could I not have realized? All the pieces fall into place, and the jigsaw puzzle picture of a cherubic baby grins toothlessly up at me.

For a moment, I can't breathe, and every ounce of adrenaline in my body is released into an overwhelmed blood stream. I cannot steady my shaking hands nor can I get up from the toilet seat. Could I be wrong? The rational side of my brain says not to panic, to get a test before I get all crazy lady, but every other part of my severely freaking out body screams, "That's it! Of course! You're pregnant, you idiot! You're pregnant! You're pregnant!"

"Billie?" *Evan at the door; shit, what do I do? What do you mean what do you do, you tell him! But what if he freaks out?* A mad internal debate rages. No matter what Evan might have said before, this is such bad timing. We aren't, might never in fact, be ready. This was not in the plan for now. Shit. What do I say?

"Are you okay?" Poor Evan, it seems he has been standing outside of bathroom doors waiting for a word of reassurance from me for weeks now. The latch is unlocked. Bolting myself in was the last thing on my mind as I raced for the loo, and he pokes his head around the door. "What's up?"

I raise my eyes to meet his; concern meets panic and right then in that single exchange, the answer passes without need of words. His eyes widen, and the sounds his lips are trying to make are lost. A hand moves involuntarily to his mouth, and we stare at each other for a moment before I let out a small sob.

"You're pregnant." The words lack intonation or expression; a statement of fact, nothing to betray how he feels about this shock revelation.

"I think so." I blink and wait, blink and wait, wondering if at any moment I might wake and find this is just a continuation of my dream. He closes the bathroom door and leans against it, lacing hands together and pressing palms on top of his head. Seconds pass like minutes as we each absorb the life-changing exchange that has just passed between us.

Shock passing through and settling followed closely by assessment of the other and how they might be feeling; this dance around each other's reactions and emotions adding another layer to the complexity of the new dynamic. After the time of quiet shock and many deep breaths, Evan blows a long exhale and comes toward me. I still cannot move from my seat on the loo. He kneels down, taking my face in his hands.

"It's okay baby." He whispers the words and I nod, keeping my eyes focused on his, praying that those words will seep into me and assure my terrified self that it will in fact be okay. "It's okay." He repeats the words again and again, pulling me to him, pressing my head to his chest. "It's okay."

We stay on the tiled floor for a long time; Evan pushed up against the wall, me on his lap, and we don't talk about it anymore. We stay there, each alone in our thoughts on what to do and how we will manage, but together in the knowledge that somehow we will.

* * *

At the pharmacy there are at least seven different varieties of pregnancy testing kits, and I try to choose one without looking like I'm choosing one. How to discreetly pay for something like a pregnancy testing kit in a small local pharmacy where the lady behind the counter is Nell's sister-in-law? Confidentiality up the spout! I know as

I discreetly check the options, that if I am to buy one, Cam will know in approximately three hours.

At this stage, having not had any official positive test done to confirm my theory, I'm trying not to think about the "what ifs." What will we do? Where will we go? Can Evan get a new job? How the hell can I be a mother, and how the hell can Evan be a father? What do I tell Cam? Do I even tell Cam right now? What about my book, my career? How the hell do you change a nappy and how good are the labor drugs?

Yes, I am trying not to go down the overwhelming road my terrified head is already halfway down. First things first: how do I buy the kit without the entire village knowing?

"Can I help you love?" Till lady has noticed me hovering, and I try to direct my gaze to the stand of hair accessories as I smile and tell her I'm just browsing, thank you. Who browses in a pharmacy for heaven's sake? Feeling ridiculous, I head home five minutes later, having purchased only a hairbrush.

"You have to get it for me!" I plead as Evan looks confused and turns distractedly away from the laptop screen.

"Why?"

"I just told you why!" I answer. "I don't want the village to know I might be up the duff."

"Well, if you're up the duff, they're going to know soon enough anyway," he answers with a half-smile.

"Evan, will you do it for me please? I'm going to have to psyche myself up to tell Cam if I am, and I don't want the old gossipy girls getting stories back to him before I have a chance to think it all through."

"What's to think through? If you are, then you are. We'd have done it sooner or later, right?" He pulls me on his lap, and I glance at the screen. Looks like he's answering e-mails.

"I know, I know, and you're right, it's just, well… if I am, I want to tell Cam on my own, in my own time."

"Okay, I get it."

"I just can't believe you're being so calm about all this."

He smiles a smile that doesn't quite reach his eyes. "Someone's got to."

Evan arrives home with the pregnancy testing kit half an hour later. In my desperation to pee on the stick and confirm one way or the other if I am actually, in fact, pregnant, I hadn't thought through how he would get away with purchasing the aforementioned kit. I mean, as I said before, everyone here knows everyone.

I swat the thought away like an annoying fly, hands on the kit, heading to the loo with the determined stride of one who needs to know her destiny. Evan follows me and let me say, there are few things as undignified as peeing while trying to hold steady a floppy piece of cardboard under your urine flow for ten seconds (in front of your loved one!). I pee, Evan watches. I pass him the white cardboard stick and turn to the wall. I can't bear to watch it develop those telltale lines in one window or two.

How many women have done this before me? How many have sat on cold toilet seats awaiting the declaration of their future, a future that might have been decided through one mad unprotected shag; two lines or one, two lines or one? I breathe out through my mouth, focusing on the shiny white tiles; the instructions say leave for exactly one minute before assessing the results. I breathe like one enduring a long downward dog yoga pose; in through the nose and out through the mouth. Focus on one line, focus on one line, I repeat silently, hoping I might will the result in my favor.

Evan stands behind me, arms folded, staring at the stick intently, waiting and watching the two windows. His serious expression gives nothing away. "Did you say it takes a minute?"

"Yes, we shouldn't see anything for a minute. No, hang on… actually there should be a line in one window to show its working and then we have to wait a minute to see if another line appears. Yep, that's right; I'm sure it said that in one minute another line will appear in the second window if I'm pregnant."

"So am I looking for one line or two?"

"You are looking for one Evan! Only one, just one little line in the first window. Close your eyes and think one line."

"Billie?"

"Uh-huh?" My eyes are closed, visualizing the one line in the one window that will say "sooo not pregnant… oh my gosh, you are so not pregnant. You are barely even fertile… better luck next time" and so on.

"There are two lines."

My inner monologue stops abruptly. "Evan, it's been twenty seconds… there can't be."

"There are two lines."

"What?" I turn around; my outrage over being duped by the instructions momentarily overwhelming my terror at the very positive result I should have had another forty seconds to prepare for. "But it said a minute…" My voice trails off, as I realize that minutes, seconds, a week, whatever, it really doesn't matter. I appear to be very pregnant.

* * *

There is much thoughtful silence in the farmhouse over the next few days. I wander, unable to focus on any one task, lost in future projection. Evan is suddenly busy. He's either out doing extra hard graft on the farm for Cam or on the computer busy researching or searching, his manner focused and intense. Cam seems oblivious to our altered state and carries on reliably, usually catching up with us only at meal times. Nell hovers around me with the watchful gaze of one in the know.

Since confirmation that I'm really and truly impregnated, with child, up the duff… and so on, my body seems to have charged ahead with its newly confirmed pregnant persona. I can feel myself expanding, my boobs have doubled in size, and it's becoming increasingly difficult to explain my nausea.

There are so many questions over our future and so many things to consider that I haven't allowed myself to think about what is happening inside me. That as every second passes, another miracle happens in my burgeoning belly. Cells divide, fuelled by a magic we may never understand, and a little life blossoms within, growing and changing moment by moment, knowing exactly what must be done. In nine months, we will have a baby. I should feel joy, but I'm unprepared and unsure. I'm barely twenty-three.

Evan is stewing. The signs are there: distraction, distance, intensity. I am too absorbed in developing my own coping strategy for now to manage his. We will come back together soon enough, and together, we'll figure out what comes next.

For now, we move though the days separately, coming together at night to physically share what is impossible in words.

* * *

Chapter Twelve

Decisions

"March roars in like a lion and out like a lamb."

Cam is the king of proverbs, clichés, and words of wisdom deemed from old Scottish wives' tales. March does roar in with wild weather and events for me that are wilder. That I am seven weeks (or thereabouts) pregnant is wild, and the gale force winds that leave the island's population stranded and farm animals distressed seem in keeping with my head space. This March, the lion forgot to leave, and Cam is concerned when his ewes show signs of lambing in the bad weather.

It's just after 7 p.m. when Cam comes in from milking, hat dripping with icy rain. I sit at the kitchen table, all woolly socks and cable knit sweater, scribbling senselessly in a journal. No thoughts worthy of contributing to my book of late, I make do with journaling, the act of writing a small relief. Nell fusses around at the stove, preparing the last touches to the evening meal.

"Evan, I'm going to need your help, son. A few sheep wandered up to the gully, and there's a chance they'll labor tonight. I need to get to them. Lambs will die overnight in this weather."

Evan looks up from the computer screen, glasses gleaming. "Sure, are you going now?"

"Aye, best get up there before it's too late."

"I'll come. I can help," I say with more enthusiasm than I feel. Evan shoots me a look, but before he has a chance to speak, Cam answers.

"No, it'll not take all three of us. You stay here and give Nell a hand. You're looking pale, lass." Evan heads for the hallway to don a heavy wax jacket and boots. They are off out into the night before I can say much more.

Nell glances my way, and then stirs her casserole. "Are you feeling all right, love? Cam's right, you are awful pale, and I can't help but notice you've gone off your food."

"I'm okay, thanks." I'm a terrible liar. At this moment, I would love to confide in someone, share the load, talk to a woman and get some advice.

Nell appears to hear the debate in my head as she stops what she is doing, wipes her hands on her apron and looks at me. "Well, it's one of two things, love. With the look on your face this past while, I'd guess at heartbreak or pregnancy."

I drop my pen and stare up at her knowing face.

"Now, I don't want to stick my nose in where it's not wanted, but God knows I've seen it all before. You're looking at Evan with those big doleful eyes, you're moping around like a lost soul, sleeping more than a newborn, and the sight of food sends you racing for the loo. Tell me pet, how far gone are you?"

I press fingertips to my lips and close my eyes, feeling the hot rush of tears. "Maybe seven weeks." Nell's arms are around me, and I sob into her apron front. She strokes my hair and after all the crying is done, I feel better.

* * *

The mountains are shadows looming black and ominous over the damp valley, contours of land only just visible in the dark night. The two men walk steadily in silence, heads down to the wind and rain. Evan enjoys these times with Cam. Nothing too much is expected of him. Cam tells him what to do, and he does it; milking, feeding, driving the tractor, all uncomplicated and achievable.

He likes Cam but often feels that Cam isn't sure about him, but then no one would be good enough for Billie in Cam's eyes. The quiet time spent together in physical labor, tending the farm and the animals will help Cam see that Evan is good and responsible. He likes Cam's sincerity, lack of bullshit, and the simple life he leads here on Arrasaigh has been quietly captivating. The real world is beckoning, though. He must find a good position. They need security, especially now.

He was serious about babies and wanting them with Billie sooner rather than later, but the sooner has happened sooner than he anticipated. His own fault, he wasn't careful, and he didn't tell Billie he didn't use a condom. That's a trouble with booze—dumb decisions. A few too many whiskies and it seemed like a good idea to let nature take its course. Billie wasn't ready, and he gave her no options.

He needs to make it all work.

"She won't be far from here," Cam says, pointing to the close ridge, visible amidst the low clouds and heavy darkness which have settled over the valley. "If she wandered, she won't have gone beyond the ridge. They never do." On route, they have already found two wandering ewes and shepherded them back toward the farm, but one heavily pregnant ewe is still missing, and they must find her before the rain turns to snow.

Heads down to the rain and cold, they search on, knowing the pregnant sheep cannot have ventured far, not when so close to delivery. The wind picks up, and Cam motions for Evan to follow behind, leading the way over the top of the ridge where shelter can be found as the sweep of land forms a natural barrier to the northerly gusts. Catching their breath, they lean against the rock face, the sound of the storm muffled behind the wall of stone and moss, the quiet louder than the wind before.

A small pasture stretches beyond the sheltered spot where they stand and in the corner, the huddled form of a ewe alone and distressed is clear; a white contrast to the bleak surroundings.

"There she is." Cam breathes a sigh of relief, and they move to the ewe who, despite her distress, acknowledges their presence. Large pain-filled eyes rise to meet them as she labors to rid herself of the weight she's carried for days. Together they crouch beside her, and she doesn't try to move, channeling her last ounces of strength into the delivery of the baby lamb, which struggles to enter the cold, wet night.

Evan watches Cam with total admiration as he helps pull the slippery baby into the world, a tiny creature that knows immediately what to do, moving to its exhausted mother for comfort and sustenance. As the lamb is licked and fed by the ewe, the men watch in silence, each alone with his own thoughts.

"We'll have to carry them back," Cam says, eyes on the mother and baby. "Let her rest awhile, the wee one won't make a night out here in the cold and without her mother, she won't thrive."

Cam runs the back of his hand over his brow, shaking his head. "Why they wander so far when they know their time is close, I'll never understand. There's always one or two, every season." He sighs and they sit, backs to the stone ridge, sheltering as best they can from the wind and rain. They watch the mother and baby.

"It must be a female thing, can't settle till she's found the perfect mossy bank to have her babies on." Evan realizes the irony of his comment only after the words have been spoken.

"Aye, that'll be right, females are funny like that." Cam says, shaking his head again, eyes still on the ewe and lamb. "What are you going to do, son?" The question shakes Evan and he stalls, wondering what exactly Cam is referring to. Which sheep he will carry down the hill? Which job he might apply for next? Which direction his life path is headed, and how the hell he will support his beloved Billie? Cam turns to Evan and pats him on the arm as though to somehow reassure. "… about the baby. What are you going to do?"

A long silence fills the space between the words, interrupted only by intermittent bleats from the baby lamb. "How long have you known?" Evan talks to his feet, head down, elbows on bent knees. He doesn't want to turn to Cam, unsure of what he might see in his eyes. Anger, blame, worry?

"Not long. I knew something was wrong. She's barely spoken to me this past week. She used to do it when she was a wee girl, hiding a secret; she wouldn't look at me because she knew I'd figure it out."

"Did she tell you?"

"No, I guessed, but she doesn't know I know."

"We'll be fine, Cam. I have a job in the pipeline, a good one; we'll get on our feet, and I'll take care of her."

"She's far too bloody young, barely left her teens. Do you have any idea what this means for her? For you?"

Evan winces at Cam's words because they're the thoughts he's been nursing since the day they found out.

"We'll be fine Cam. I love her; I promise you that. I love her, and we're married. We're not teenagers; we've got a future planned. I'd do anything for her."

"I know son, I don't want to lecture you."

"I understand how you must feel, but I promise you I'll take care of her."

Cam shakes his head, lost in thought. "Her mother was the same age when she had Billie and it wasn't easy. She never finished her studies, never really had the chance to do much for herself. Once a baby comes along, she'll forget the hopes she'd had for her future, and the baby will be all there is. I don't mean that it's wrong." He rubs a work-scarred hand over his tired face. "It just seems like you pair had a lot of living to do yet."

"And that's about to stop?" Evan bristles, hating to be judged, hating to feel he is being blamed for somehow compromising Billie's life and future. "It's a baby, not a terminal illness."

Both men fall silent; Evan composing himself, and Cam struggling to keep the grief from his face, 'terminal illness' the analogy is not a good one.

Evan cradles the bleating lamb in his arms; its new skin still warm and wet, so small and vulnerable. Cam hoists the ewe over his shoulders. Exhausted and compliant, she doesn't struggle.

The wind has calmed since their ascent, but a steady rain falls as they trudge down the steep path and through the valley. A mutual understanding settles between the men, and there is no need for further talk. Cam has said his piece and Evan understands what is expected of him. He won't tell Billie of their discussion. It would only make accepting the situation harder, and she is having trouble enough.

Light from the small farmhouse windows guides them through the rain, and soon mother and baby are comfortable and dry. They leave the two together—baby suckling, mother barely awake. At the front door under the shelter of the overhanging porch, Cam takes off his hat, raising his eyes to Evan. "Take care of her son." Not a request but a command, five simple words. Evan wears them, meeting Cam's eyes, nodding. He will.

* * *

Well-thumbed copies of Women's Weekly lie scattered on the table, forming an island in the middle of a rectangle of plastic chairs in the waiting room. I read the notice board for the fourth time. "Dog walker available, weekends and evenings. Reasonable rates. Phone Kenny on 373693." "For sale: Ford Fiesta, good condition, one lady owner, low mileage. Call Esther on 372846." "Tarot reader available for in-home reading and parties." The list goes on. Do people have tarot reading parties then? The things you learn in the doctor's waiting room.

I stare down at my hands, twirling my wedding band round and round, a nervous habit I seem to have developed. Evan is beside me, looking like an ashen-face possum, grey in pallor but wide-eyed. His palms rest on his thighs, and his right foot taps on the carpet; a nervous habit he seems to have acquired.

"Mrs Skylark?" A tall, grey-haired man in his sixties pops his head around the corner and I give a small wave. "Come on through." I stand, feeling a brief rush of nausea, take a breath and follow him, Evan in tow.

We walk down the dark wood-paneled corridor, heels echoing on floors, till we reach a room which looks like it might have once been a master bedroom. The doctor's surgery on Arrasaigh is housed in a two-story granite stately building which must have been home to a wealthy family once upon a time.

"So, what can I do for you?" The doctor looks at me with kind eyes, waiting for me to tell him what he has already guessed. There's a brief silence while I rattle through a few one-liners that might have been appropriate in an alternate universe; "I'd like a sex change, and this will be my same sex partner… I think I have syphilis, and this is the guy that gave it to me… I'd like his nose… do you have qualified plastic surgeons on the island?"

Instead, with no grace or ceremony, I blurt out, "I'm pregnant."

The doctor continues smiling and nodding, makes some notes on paper, then looks at me, and then at Evan "… And this is?"

"Sorry, I'm Evan… the husband." This sounds so sitcom funny I giggle, and the doctor turns his attention to me again, probably wondering if I'm much younger than I look.

"Nice to meet you Evan," says the doctor genially, taking some more notes. "And, have you done a test yet… Billie? Yes, Billie, isn't it?"

"Yes and yes, five actually. I've done five tests, and all have shown up positive."

The doctor smiles again, and by now, I feel marginally annoyed; what's with all the smiling? Give me the low down. What happens now? When does the random vomiting stop and when will I grow out of my skinny jeans? Although to be fair, the pinch at my waistband should be answer enough. I have forced on my favorite skinny jeans every day this week in protest to my expanding waistline. What I mean to prove with this is a little vague, being that my tummy continues to subtly swell and the waistband becomes more and more uncomfortable by the day.

"Okay, well I think five tests are probably conclusive. When was your last period?" Pause. "Do you remember?"

"Yes," I reply as he looks at me, eyebrows raised, pen to the ready. "Actually… no." Now Evan and the doctor both give me the raised eyebrow look, like I should be marking it on the calendar or something, and all this baby business is inevitable if I can't even keep track of my own goddamned period, for heaven's sake! "What?" I say to Evan. "It varies, I've never been terribly regular. I'm not sure… um… maybe… six, eight weeks ago?"

"So you're not sure?" says the doctor, making more notes.

"No."

"Okay, well, I'll have a wee feel about that tummy and check how the uterus feels, then we'll have to book you in for a dating scan on the mainland."

Evan looks like the good doctor has just spoken in Arabic. "A dating scan?" He squeezes my hand as though this might mean something dangerous and painful.

"Yes, if Billie isn't sure when she last menstruated, then we'll have trouble predicting a due date."

Now, Evan looks like the one who might faint at any given moment, just the words "due" and "date" have drained the color from his face. The doctor gestures toward the bed against the back wall, and I approach gingerly. I take in the ornate detail of the plaster ceiling, all flowers and carved leaves around the borders and light fitting, as the doctor pulls my waist band down and feels around my lower tummy with cool, clever fingers.

* * *

Wind whips and pulls at my hair as we walk hand-in-hand back down the main street, armed with a "So You're Having a Baby" mini folder with all manner of information on what not to do for the next forty weeks, and a bottle of multivitamins.

"Well, that's that." Evan squeezes my hand.

"Yep, that's that."

"What now?"

I ask the question as though there should be a perfect solution, another guide book, the next logical step. Evan pulls me toward the ocean side of the street where, despite the low clouds, we can just make out the castle across the bay and a few boats coming in and out with the day's catch. We head toward a lonely wooden bench with a view of the water and pebble beach and sit side by side looking out, awaiting divine inspiration. I lean my head against Evan's shoulder, enjoying the warmth that emanates from his body, despite the chill in the air. He takes a deep breath, looks briefly at my expression then turns back to the ocean one arm around my shoulders and the other resting on my tummy.

"Billie?"

"Uh-huh?"

"I got a job."

* * *

In one month, my entire life has taken a U-turn, and the pace of change leaves me spinning like a pirouetting ballet dancer without the poise or grace; a little clumsier and tummy-heavy, my expression confused rather than focused, unsure of how all of this came about.

From quiet country living—bliss in isolation and simplicity—to stress and impending madness. A young couple on the brink of fabulousness; the fledgling novelist, the wacky artist/architect taking time out from the rat race to choose a new avenue down which they will follow their dreams, to the panic ridden, stereotypical, young couple with a baby on the way.

Of course we're different we say; we were always planning a family, a life together, there's never a perfect time to have babies, etc., etc. Here's the thing. There may not be a perfect time and all of those things may be true, but I can't help feeling derailed by the fact that the time is now. That those babies, the family thing, didn't happen just a little later, a few years from now, when we'd found our feet a little, settled, and decided together that yes we were ready.

I am pregnant; it's a fact, and I say the sentence to myself over and over, trying to make the reality sink in to my still disbelieving head. And now, the new variable, a left hook to follow the right, the shock from both sides that should restore my equilibrium, but instead has sent me into a spin.

Evan has a job in the South Pacific; we leave in a month.

Evan has a job in the South Pacific; we are moving to the other side of the world.

Evan has a job in the South Pacific, and we will have a baby far away from every person we know and love.

Trying not to freak out, trying not to freak out, really trying not to freak out. Soooo freaking out.

I spin around the farmhouse for a day after Evan's bombshell, alternating between hyperventilating *Oh my God, Oh my God* thoughts to moments where in a less emotionally charged space I can stop, catch my breath and remind myself it's a good thing, a positive thing, an exciting opportunity, a new adventure, and so on and so on. Evan seems to have gradually moved on from the shock of impending parenthood to the calm, controlled state of one who is taking care of business. He has found a rescue plan, a great job, a location where we can start again, raise a family; a place to escape to.

Tentatively at first, he told me of the job he had researched and applied for, the island where opportunity was rife, a climate conducive to good living with a great economy. He hadn't been sure about the move until the news that I was pregnant broke the airwaves. "Mr Provider" stormed in after the newsflash and decided this was the way forward, and at that point, I was in no position to argue. I wasn't even sure I wanted to; I wasn't sure how I felt about anything. Overwhelmed, exhausted, and constantly nauseous, I honestly would have agreed to anything.

I have to talk to Cam; but where to begin? "Hey, Cam, do you have minute? Just wanted to let you know I'm up the duff and emigrating." No matter how I rehearse the conversation in my mind, it never comes out right, and I can't shake the feeling that I'm letting him down.

"You need to talk to him, Billie." Evan lies beside me in bed that night. A week has passed since we visited the doctor, and Evan told me about the new job.

"I know." I stare at the ceiling, covers pulled to my waist, hands by my sides resting on the white duvet. "I just wish I knew how to tell him."

"It's simple. Just talk to him. He'll understand. He's always behind you, whatever you do." Evan is on his side, facing me; he strokes hair back from my forehead, smoothing out worry lines as he goes.

"I feel like we're abandoning him."

"We have to leave sometime. You're an adult, for God's sake. We would have moved away for a job sooner or later."

"I know, but it's just so far away, and it's not just that. Think about it. I'm all he has, and I'll be telling him I'm having a baby and I'm off to the other side of the world to have it!"

"And?"

"Evan!" Exasperated, I push his hand away. "If we go, he won't see us or the baby."

Now Evan looks how I feel. "It's not the dark ages. We have planes. He can visit."

I close my eyes, feeling tears approaching. "It's not the same."

"Don't you want to go?" Evan's tone is measured, fearful I'll tell him I can't do it and that he has to come up with another plan, find another job, although nothing in Europe has come through despite his best efforts.

"No." I slap my hand over my eyes. "Yes, I mean… I don't know. I'm just not sure."

"You're not sure." He's still, and his gaze is steady. I realize how afraid he is. He has to make it work; he's afraid and needs my support, just as much as I need his.

I turn to him, reaching to touch his face, stubbly and rough, green eyes troubled. "I'm sorry, I can't lie; it's just such a lot to get my head around. Just give me a little time to feel my way into all of this."

"I know, baby." He leans in to my hand and brings my fingers to his lips. I let him kiss my hand, my wrist, the inside of my arm, working his way to my achy heart and swollen belly.

I let out a slow breath, my skin celebrating the smoothness of his lips and the roughness of his chin. "I'll talk to Cam tomorrow."

"Shhh." A free hand touches my lips to stop the words. He slips a finger into my mouth and I suck, biting down gently as he moves lower. Slowly, slowly, each kiss takes a little of the fear and replaces it with hope, and by the time he reaches the soft space between my legs, I'm practically glowing with positivity for our future and family in the tropics.

* * *

I wake early the next morning, the room still dark, and Evan still sleeping; his long form spans the bed. Moving out from under his arm, careful not to wake him, I tiptoe from the room. Cam will be awake and in the kitchen, lighting the fire and making coffee before milking. I hear him humming as I approach the kitchen door.

"You're awake early, pet; don't you want to sleep a bit longer? It's barely gone five." He's already dressed in dark trousers, a cream cabled sweater, and woolen socks with a hole in the toe.

"No, couldn't sleep." I sit at the kitchen table as he finishes stoking the fire.

He heads to the stove. "Coffee?"

The word plus the smell of the brewing pot combine to produce an instant and overwhelming need to vomit. I raise a hand as if to say,

"Not right now," clasp the other over my mouth and race back out toward the bathroom.

Moments later I'm back, a little red-faced but feeling much better. Cam looks kindly at me. "Maybe a tea instead?"

I nod and sit down once again, this time rehearsing the delivery of the two momentous bits of news I am about to tell him. My words come blundering along—unless controlled by a pen they have limited eloquence.

"I'm pregnant Cam."

I take a deep breath and wait, eyes closed, not entirely sure what I'm waiting for. When he doesn't answer, I open my eyes slowly. He still has his back to me, fixing the tea and coffee, and I wonder for a second if he has heard my thunderbolt.

"I'm pregnant!" I say it again, the lack of reaction strangely worse than the reaction I had imagined.

When he turns around, he's smiling.

"What?" I ask. "Did you hear me?"

"Of course, I'm getting old, but I'm not deaf yet, and I'm not daft either. I've known for a while."

"You have?" I'm shocked and relieved all at once, although the drama queen in me is a teensy bit disappointed her thunder stolen. He nods, sliding a wooden chair out from the table to sit down across from me. "Did Evan tell you?"

He smiles and stirs a teaspoon of sugar into his coffee. "No, I guessed. It wasn't hard."

"Really?" I can't believe my efforts at deception have been so transparent.

"Well, you've spent more time in the bathroom than anywhere else the past few weeks, and you've never been much good at keeping a secret."

I can't help but smile. Smile at how silly I have been to imagine he would be angry, and smile because at this moment I feel such a rush of love for this wonderful man who, like Evan says, is always behind me. "It's a little sooner than we'd planned."

"Well, your mother might have said that about you, too, and look how you turned out." He reaches across the table and squeezes my hand, his work-scarred palms still warm from his mug of coffee. He's doing his best to make me feel better, and I love him for it.

With a heavy heart, I squeeze his hand in return and say, "… and there's something else."

"Well, let's hear it then."

"Evan's got a job."

"Well, that's great news. Why the long face?"

"It's far away."

"Everywhere's far away from Arrasaigh." Cam is still smiling, but his face isn't telling me the whole story. I realize what I am about to tell him is another piece of old news.

"It's in the South Pacific."

I can't look at him, and instead examine the knots of wood in the old farm table, waiting to hear him make a joke about hula skirts and coconuts. When he remains quiet, I chance a quick glance up at his face.

He nods slowly, confirming some internal question I have yet to hear. "Well, is it a good job?" I nod in return. "Is it what you both want?"

"Yes, it'll be a new start; I think it's what we need." My tone suggests I'm still convincing myself.

"Then, it's the right thing to do. Life's short, Billie. Take the opportunity and see how it turns out."

"It's just so far way."

"And that's why you don't want to go?"

"I didn't say I didn't want to go. I… it's just, with a baby coming now, and you here, I'm just…"

"What?"

"I'm afraid."

If I could bottle the love that flows from Cam's eyes as he looks down at my teary and confused face, I'd survive on it for years in his absence. I take a mental Instagram, freezing the moment in time so I could take it out and feel it all over again as the distance between us grows and time ticks on.

He passes me a Kleenex. "What would your Mum say now?"

I take a deep breath, drying my eyes and think a moment, conjuring her face in my head... her smile, the calm sound of her voice. "She'd hold both of my hands like this." I reach across the table grabbing both of Cam's hands holding them firmly. "Then she'd look at me like this." I stare intently into Cam's eyes. "And she'd say, 'Be brave Billie.' She'd pause a moment for effect, then she'd say it again. 'Be brave.'"

"So, what are you going to do?" says Cam, pulling a hand away to wipe his eyes.

"I'm going to be brave."

We smile, then laugh a little at the drama and the tears because that's what Mom would have done. Armed with our senses of humor, we go forth, the little scene around the kitchen table reminding us to laugh at all the things that make us cry and the dramas that accompany just being alive.

*　*　*

The following three weeks pass in a haze of planning, packing, organizing, and visa applications. The new job apparently wouldn't wait; our tickets were booked by Evan's new company, leaving exactly one month to the date Evan agreed to the post. Evan took control while I half-heartedly made arrangements for the packing and shipping of our belongings currently in storage in Paris. The rest of my time was spent surfing the net, alternating Google searches between the two impending life dramas on the horizon—emigration and pregnancy. Life in the South Pacific, what to expect in the first trimester, the island of St. Cloud, the history, the climate, the people, and "how to get through labor." After taking short snack breaks, I'd begin the website trawl all over again, surges of excitement followed closely by waves of anxiety.

I could no longer stomach coffee or tea, and before midday, barely managed to keep the vomiting at bay. The trick seemed to be to graze constantly—saltine crackers became my food of choice. If I wasn't listlessly chewing on a dry morsel, the nausea would begin. It's a terrible affliction, constantly hungry yet constantly sick, and with all the indulgent foods available to the hungry pregnant woman, the only thing I can stomach is saltines. Where's the justice in that? Even the thought of a cream cake makes me dry gag. Where's the glowing part of pregnancy women talk about?

And so, after a leg stretch, another wee, and a few saltines, I would resume my research beginning with: St. Cloud. "Climate and creepy crawlies" followed closely by "track your baby's growth" (a particularly interesting site telling me exactly which part of my unborn baby was sprouting from day to day). The internet makes it terribly easy to overdose on any subject of choice. In a short space of time, I felt I knew more about the small island of St. Cloud than the locals and had simultaneously registered for every pregnancy support website available.

Evan had organized visas, residency applications, accommodation for our first month, boat schedules, airport cabs and car hire; his efficiency was quite remarkable. The fits of darkness and irritability that plagued him for months seemed to lift, and Evan, the positive go-getter, came skipping from the closet full of happy, happy, joy, joy at life and the fortuitous nature of circumstance.

With the sudden change of circumstance, the dating scan to be conducted on the mainland was postponed to be completed in St. Cloud within our first week. Our doctor on Arrasaigh contacted the local hospital on the island and transferred my notes (limited as they must have been; Female, Billie Skylark, twenty-three years of age, pregnant, gestational weeks unknown). Our doctor assured me this would all be fine, the scan would be completed within a few weeks, and as everything appeared to be okay and I was in good health, the scan was only to determine my due date.

All boxes ticked, bags packed, tickets in hand, we were ready to leave, and the prospect of goodbyes fills me with quiet despair.

The morning of departure dawns cold and grey, a damp mist hanging low, blanketing the mountains and sealing in sound. The air is still and heavy with moisture, watery light barely changing as the sun rises higher in the sky. The atmosphere in the cottage is somber. Only Evan bustles around with the excited energy of one embarking upon a new adventure. Cam, Nell, and I amble around the kitchen in silence, knowing we are dragging out a long, painful goodbye, but somehow unable to create distance just yet.

Soon Evan and Cam are carrying cases out to the truck, and I'm hugging Nell, standing on the doorstep of this chapter of my life. She releases me and spins me around, nudging the small of my back toward the waiting truck. The engine hums, exhaust fumes mixing with the grey mist. Samson waits in the back of the truck, nestled between cases and hold-alls. He barks, hurrying me along, and I slide into the backseat, afraid to look around. The truck pulls away from the cottage, Nell, and the happy, safe bubble the farm has become, a short escape from reality, from decisions and responsibilities, from an adult life.

Tires crunch over loose stones on the rough path down the hill to the road, window wipers rhythmically clearing the misty drizzle coating the windscreen, clouding the view ahead. The small lump in my throat is now a large, constricting mass. Silent tears spill over my lashes and down my pale cheeks as the truck drives along the main street. Using my sleeve as a hankie, I push them away, grateful Evan is in the front beside Cam. And it's not that I'm afraid or filled with regret or uncertainty, but simply that I'm aware of the closing of this chapter.

It feels as though this is the real goodbye; a final goodbye to childhood, to teenage dreams, to Cam, to Mom, to Kansas, to Arrasaigh. As though all the sadness of every great goodbye in life this far is condensed into these final moments; leaving on a boat for a faraway island to start a new life and begin a family of my own.

Squeezing swollen eyes closed, I will the tears away, even if for a few moments more. "Be brave Billie, be brave."

The good humor which defends and protects me dissolves under the weight of self-pity, and for now, everything is sad and grey; every word said and hug given is a forever. The boat's foghorn sounds as we approach the ferry terminal, and in moments, we're unloaded and on the gangplank. Evan and Cam do the manly handshake and back pat. Cam mutters some parting fatherly "take care of my girl" sort of line, and Evan nods respectfully before heading on to the boat, giving me a moment's private goodbye.

"I'm always here pet." Cam holds me tightly to him, and then pulls away, looking awkward, still unsuited to emotional displays.

"I know." I keep hold of both of his hands, squeezing tightly and nodding, convincing myself I can turn around and walk calmly up the gangplank onto the boat.

"Call me when you can. Don't worry about the time difference. I'll keep a phone beside the bed."

"And how will you hear it through all that snoring?" I smile half-

-heartedly. Cam's snores have been known to wake the neighbors. My small jibe breaks the tension, and he laughs.

"Watch it you! Now promise me you'll get yourself all checked as soon as you arrive."

"I promise."

"I'll need to know when I'm to be a Granddaddy."

"You will." I throw my arms around him one more time. He smells like home. "I love you Cam." The words come out fuzzy and unclear, my face buried in his thick wool sweater.

"I love you too."

"Thanks for everything."

He shakes his head, unwilling to acknowledge the words that are unnecessary. "There's my lass. Now get off with you before Evan has to go on his own!"

The horn blasts again, and I squeeze his hand once more, then turn and walk up the gangplank one foot in front of the other till I reach the boat and Evan. He waits, hands in his pockets, eyes kind. Together, we move to the rail and stand side by side as the boat pulls away from the dock.

Cam is a solitary windblown figure at the end of the wharf, hands in his pockets watching the boat. He sees us at the rail and raises a hand to wave. I wave back, the gesture a futile attempt to demonstrate a lifetime of feeling in a single motion, a solitary hand moving back and forward in the cold, northerly wind. I stay there in the bleak, early light watching it all shrink away, refusing to go inside until Cam's tiny speck on the horizon disappears and the island is a sleeping giant in the distance.

I follow Evan again. This time further, two journeys on a one--way ticket, destination baby, destination St. Cloud. And although we are floating, buoyant above the weight of water, the sensation of sinking is everywhere. Even though we are starting again, it feels like ending. The beginning of this new adventure feels like escape from an old one. I'm overreacting, no doubt the result of exhaustion and hormones, the need to nest and no nest to flee to. There is nothing to be done but let it all play out as it will. Soon the melancholy will pass to be replaced by some other melodramatic emotion, so for now, I just have to hang on. Hang on and follow Evan.

Arms wrap around me from behind, my eyes fixed on the distant silhouette of Arrasaigh. Evan holds me silently, his gaze fixed intently on a seagull hovering above us, following the ferry's course, soaring up then down, gliding in a perfect display of Mother Nature's infallible engineering. The seagull's black, beady eyes watch us watching him, feathers rippling in the strong wind, course unchanged.

"Can you imagine how that must feel?" Evan's eyes are wistful as he speaks. "Sometimes it seems like everything we do is against the flow, like we're swimming upstream, running into a head wind." He shakes his head, gaze never leaving the flying form before us. "Not him. Look at him, just harnessing what's already there, no struggle, no fighting the flow; he uses it. What I'd give to fly."

I rub a hand along his forearm, leaning my head into his body, firm and steady behind me. "But you'll never know." The wind carries my words away.

"Not this lifetime," he answers. The seagull swoops and squawks, nose diving down to the wake of the boat where the promise of breakfast has drawn him.

We stay there, watching the birds, the sea, and the boat's white frothy trail of goodbyes. Wispy words form on dark clouds of my imagination. "Billie feels trapped, Evan feels free."

Shaking my head to clear the thoughts, I breathe before vomiting violently over the rails.

*　*　*

Chapter Thirteen

Migration: Arrasaigh to St. Cloud
February 2004

"Chicken or beef ma'am?" Startled, I jump in my seat. The question rouses me from another one of my mad dreams. Pregnancy adds another level of bizarre to my already weird and wonderful dream world. In this one, I am swaddling my newborn, cooing and kissing, and just as I raise the baby to my breast, I realize the small bundle wrapped tightly in woolen blankets is actually a baby deer, doe-eyed and still.

"She'll have beef, thanks," Evan answers for me, smiling up at the leggy blond air hostess, who bends over to rustle around in her trolley for a red foil-wrapped tray.

"There we are, beef. And for you sir?"

"Chicken, thank you. Oh, and I'll have another wine when you have a chance." Evan smiles, and the air hostess blushes a little, smiling back, ready to give him whatever he might ask for.

"I'd have liked chicken, you know." I eye his chicken roast, the portion size barely enough to feed a skinny twelve-year-old. "I can speak for myself."

Evan smiles, unwrapping my beefy thing for me. "I know, but you were half asleep, practically drooling on my shoulder, and you need the iron, tubby." He passes me a plastic fork, and I poke him in the ribs.

"It's your fault I'm tubby." I'm accusatory but playful. Although still somewhere in the first trimester, my tummy is protruding quite nicely, competing with the fold-out tray for room between me and the next row.

"I'm sure I remember you having something to do with it, too." Evan replies with a grin.

We are somewhere over Europe, flying Cathay Pacific, destination St. Cloud. Goodness knows when we will actually set foot on St. Cloud, being that the journey there seems not only very long, but complicated. We have several stop-offs and layovers en route and are to finally catch a small domestic flight on to the island from Costa Rica.

The more I hear about St. Cloud, the more I wonder what the hell I have agreed to. I have Robinson Crusoe visions; a lonely lump of ocean-surrounded land and a solo coconut tree. Evan assures me St. Cloud is a busy destination, young population, beautiful varied landscape, thriving business hub, and a healthy tourist industry. Part of the charm appears to be the isolation, slower pace of life, and, of course, the climate. No winter! Well, not in comparison with what we're used to. It's a winter where the temperature barely gets cooler than Arrasaigh summer. So, despite my concerns over a new life in the boonies with no one but Man Friday to chat with, I can't deny I'm a little excited about what lies ahead.

The small plastic trays are cleared away, and the lights dimmed for the night portion of our long flight, but I'm restless and don't feel like sleeping. "So tell me again, when we arrive, what happens from there."

"You are such a control freak. Why don't you relax and let me take care of things?" Evan has taken on sort of a fatherly role of late; the provider/soon-to-be-Dad thing has him talking to me in gentler tones, treating me as though I might break.

Ruthie Morgan | 201

"I am letting you take control. Look at me: barefoot and pregnant, being dragged across the world to an unknown destination and… you just chose my dinner for me!"

"You're not barefoot for a start."

I look down at my feet comfortably sporting the navy blue toweling travel socks the airline provides.

"And, the destination isn't unknown, and you couldn't decide on dinner, anyway. You can never decide on dinner." He pauses, and I smile before his brow creases momentarily. "I'm not really dragging you, am I?" Concern etches across his handsome face, and I feel sorry for my off-hand comments. I know this is a big worry for him. He feels responsible that everything should be perfect, and senses my lack of certainty over the move. I can't pretend I'm one hundred percent sure about anything right now. Life has changed so dramatically in such a hurry.

I smile up at him, giving what I hope to be my most dazzlingly, happy smile, and then kiss him full on the mouth till he pulls away with a glint in his eye. "Easy, Mrs Skylark, don't start something you can't finish."

Laughing, I nudge him in the ribs, and he grabs my hand, guiding it under the tray tables to rest on his crotch. With a half-smile, he raises his eyebrows as he presses my hand down to feel him, hard beneath my fingers. Thankful that we have a spare seat beside us, I press myself closer, relaxing, my hand gently stroking him. Feeling a rush of power, I carefully guide him as close to climax as I dare. Eyes closed, his breathing controlled, I watch him, wondering when this ends. When do we stop needing this from each other, wanting this? Does it stop or change? What will happen when a baby is part of our picture? Always on the edge of a melancholic thought, I wonder if now that I've found Evan, could I ever manage without him? As he comes close to orgasm, I feel an equally electrifying jolt of anxiety rather than pleasure when the answer to my question shudders naked and afraid in front of me: never.

* * *

Long haul flights do terrible things to the brain. I'm sure brain cells are lost during flights through time zones and equator lines. The cocktail of forced air, sleep loss, and daytime-night time confusion leave me woozy and nauseous. But as so many unexpected symptoms accompany pregnancy, I question the authenticity of any feeling or emotion these days; never sure what can be attributed to pregnancy and what's normal. Or just simply the result of change and the general topsy-turvy status of my life right now.

As the small prop plane begins its decent into St. Cloud, my hazy head can't decide whether it's still asleep or not. Am I in some tropical dream akin to the Bounty Bar ad, or am I truly awake and can what I see from the window really be our new home?

Transfixed by the view from the small oval window, I press my face against the glass, the dazzling blue of the ocean and sky broken by lush green ferns and palms rising up from coast lines, valleys, and mountainsides. The clear aerial view of the fast-approaching land explains the island's magic without words. I can feel it from here. There is a quiet peace and celebration of simplicity in the contours of the land and unashamed pride in its beauty.

The pilot announces our imminent arrival, and the seatbelt sign flashes. I lock eyes with Evan and squeeze his hand as the plane heads for the runway. Wheels thud down on hot tarmac, brakes screeching, and engine shuddering as the small plane wheels to the terminal, an unassuming building easily mistaken for another plane hangar. As the heavy door is pushed open and the folding stairwell extended onto the tarmac, we ease ourselves from the sitting position we have assumed for what feels like an eternity. My legs wobble, and Evan steadies me with an arm as we walk down the aisle to disembark.

A wall of heat is our welcome as we pass from the plane onto the top step of the stairs to reach the Promised Land. Moisture heavy, muggy, humid air, such a contrast to the cool, air-conditioned dryness of the little plane. More than the sun and the heat and the color, more than the sounds and the music playing from a tinny speaker somewhere, more than the smiles and welcomes as we hobble our way down the steps and on to the hot ground; it is the smells that surround and overwhelm me. The air is heavy blossom, Bougainvillea and Jacaranda, Musk and Jasmine; it is so fragranced I cough, the perfume settling in my nose and lungs. Floral hues edged with briny salty air, laced with beachy notes of coconut suntan lotion. All this mixed and intensified by the weight of such humid heat. We stand, intoxicated by it all, feet warming on the hot tarmac, hands shielding our eyes from the bright sun, and we follow the small trail of similarly overwhelmed tourists and complacent business men into the terminal to collect our baggage and begin our new life.

Any concerns I may have had over the move evaporate in the heat of those first two weeks in paradise. We get a room with a view of the ocean in a hotel on the beach, our days comprised of sunning, swimming, and sightseeing.

Evan has two days of initiation at the new firm, but they insist we spend the remainder of the week acclimatizing, resting, and finding our way around. We hire a Mini Mok, the island's small, cheap, open-topped version of a Jeep, and we beach-hop around, exploring and discovering the paradise we're lucky enough to find ourselves in.

We are high on our good fortune, new beginnings, and each other. It felt like the honeymoon we never had, and somehow in that long week, whose days stretched forever, I feel happier than I thought possible. Evan is positive and light; every challenge ahead is an opportunity, and the world is our oyster (or lobster in the words of my funny friend Iris).

The baby, whose stage of development is still in question, seems to become a smaller detail than the earth-shattering cataclysmic event pregnancy had seemed just over a month ago. We are madly in love, I'm pregnant; big deal, we will be great parents, and I'll know just what to do… right?

Whether or not I will and whether we are destined to be great parents to the bump of unknown term, I actually have no idea, but in those first happy days, I push all worries aside. In fact, I sit on them, squish them, make them invisible under my gradually expanding bottom (no one tells you your tummy is not the only thing to gain girth). There's no talk of past misdemeanors or dark shadows, drinking, or depression; there's no need. It's as if the time before has faded and we live only in the bright light of now. Shiny and golden, sun-kissed and tropical; as though the physical distance had erased selected memories from who we were before. We start over, a clean slate, a beautiful, flat, charcoal-grey untainted slate on which to draw plans for a new life, a perfect family, a new career, and a perfect relationship. Intoxicated by St. Cloud, and everything she offers, we revel in our first week of dreaming, exploring, and sketching out the new life we are beginning.

* * *

Saturday morning, end of week one. Evan begins work on Monday. Honeymoon week draws to a close. "You know we have two fairly important things to do today." Evan's lips bury into my neck, his body wrapped tightly around mine; spooning, naked, the shuttered windows open, the sounds of the town and beachgoers below still quiet and unhurried.

"It's too hot for important. Can't we just do inconsequential?" I murmur in reply, waking slowly, reluctantly, the light still dim.

Evan's right arm is under my head the left wrapped around me, hand resting on my small, round bump. "Well, depends what you consider inconsequential." He strokes my belly and kisses the back of my neck.

"Let's start with breakfast and work our way up," I reply.

"You're hungry? That's great; normally you're running for the bathroom to hurl around this time of the morning."

"You say the sweetest things."

"I do my best." He flips me over to face him, examining my tummy with renewed interest. "I wonder if this means you're through the first trimester. Don't they say the sickness is worst in the first?"

"What are you suddenly an expert in pregnancy symptoms?"

"Well, I do study you more closely than most, and I'd say you must be past the worst."

"Really?" I answer. "So, the rest will be a bit of a breeze then? I can hardly wait."

He tweaks my nipple. "Uh-huh, I'd say you'll get big and fat now, and these puppies should get up to a D cup." He laughs as I swat him in reply.

"You won't be touching these puppies. They're way too sore."

"Come on, now." He moves closer, fingers tracing the outline of an already swollen breast. "What if I was very gentle?" He circles around then moves lower, taking my nipple into his mouth. I nod, eyes closed, used to this little game.

"Right here?" he asks quietly, and as pleasure overtakes pain, I give up objecting.

I raise my arms above my head and move in closer to him. "… right about there," I answer reluctantly, eyes still closed as he moves from one breast to the other.

"Is it getting any better?"

"Very slowly," I exhale and arch involuntarily.

There's a smile in his voice as he asks, "Is there anywhere else that needs attention?"

I can't help but smile, too, and guide his hand down between my legs. Evan groans, and the day begins as each day has begun and ended so far in St. Cloud, a good start to a new life.

Later after a post coital doze, and the morning's second awakening I realize Evan's right. I am hungry, and the nausea has passed. How far along could I be?

* * *

Hospitals and I don't agree; in fact, that's a mammoth understatement considering the fact that the slightest whiff of hospital disinfectant gives me an instant anxiety attack. Once within the automatic doors of any hospital, a strong feeling of claustrophobia engulfs me, and the need to run away crowds my every thought. I have no doubt this is a result of the traumatic months spent in hospitals with Mom as her condition deteriorated. Hospitals mean only one thing for me, and no matter how much I remind myself of all the people who leave cured, recovered, relieved of pain, fixed, happy, and so on, for me; hospitals are places where people die. And it's rarely a happy, peaceful death; they are there because they have been robbed of life by disease, illness, accidents, and trauma, and there are many, many unhappy endings. For every baby born, there is a life, incomplete, lost.

Smells, colors, and sounds make me flinch; the squeak of a nurse's shoes on linoleum, the roll of trolley wheels, the smell of hospital food, and the uniformity of color and patterned curtains designed to provide a charade of privacy within the open display of human frailty.

It all leaves me searching for emergency exits, needing to flee by the quickest route before my blubbering begins.

In the hospitals where Mom lived her last few months of life, I also lived my last few months of a different life. I watched as she deteriorated and suffered. Cam fell apart, and Mom disappeared into herself, and I could do nothing to change any of it.

I had watched the walls and patterned curtains, pretending to read by Mom's bedside while listening to the noises all around, trying to draw out each second she remained with us, yet guiltily wishing it away. Watching her suffer and knowing she needed to go, dying inside at the despair of our surroundings and the way in which she was forced to spend her last moments, yet wanting to drag it out. Battling emotions and feelings pushed down under the surface of "coping."

Those hospitals weren't awful places. The care wasn't unsatisfactory or the staff unfeeling, none of that, but for a time, I sat at a bedside or walked the corridors, waiting and watching as Mom grew weaker. Few things are more terrible than watching a loved one die. Helpless, I waited, knowing the inevitable was around the corner, but not sure how long the corner might be. Fluctuating from feeling devastated for her—a beautiful life cut short—to self-pitying. How would I manage without her? Guilt that I could do nothing, guilt that I watched, that it wasn't me, and that during all of her suffering, I could feel sorry for myself. Pity for Cam, watching him crumble while trying to stay strong for her and me, all of us pretending that things were okay, that somehow all of this was normal; three devastated people in a hospital day after day watching a life slip away.

We walk hand-in-hand down the corridor toward outpatients and ultrasound, Evan with a skip in his step, me focusing on one foot in front of the other. *Don't freak out, don't freak out, don't freak out.*

Mercy Hospital is modern and, thankfully, air-conditioned. It's the island's main hospital. The other smaller infirmaries feed more serious or urgent patients here. It is our scan appointment, and today we'll find out my due date and possibly even the baby's sex, depending on how far along I am and which way the little peanut is facing.

"You're freaking out."

"I'm not!"

"Your palms are sweaty, and your face is red."

"I'm hot."

"It's practically freezing in here!"

We reach the heavy doors which lead to a waiting room filled with tropical potted plants and a rotund dark-skinned nurse sitting behind a desk. Her smile is wide and welcoming, and it's hard not to lose a layer of anxiety soaking up a little of the warmth she exudes. "Good morning! You must be… let's see." She stops and perches a pair of glasses hanging on a beaded chain around her neck onto the end of her nose, peering at the computer screen. She frowns, clucks to herself then says, "Ah, it's Mrs Skylark?"

"That's us," Evan replies on my behalf. "Mr and Mrs Skylark." He emphasizes the "and" just to be sure she and the rest of the waiting room know we are married.

"Have a seat, Mr and Mrs Skylark," she answers with the hint of a smile, and as Evan turns to find us a few chairs, she winks at me.

Browsing through the collection of outdated copies of *Women's Journal* and *Island Times*, trying to look interested in the random recipes, home baking tips, and articles on the joys of composting, I grow impatient.

"How long do we have to wait?" I let out a sigh, blowing loose stands of hair about my face. Evan has been drumming his fingers on the chair armrest for fifteen minutes, and it's driving me crazy. It seems the week of honeymooning and pushing all baby panic thoughts from our minds is truly over. It seems imperative that I know within the next five minutes that my growing bump is developing as expected. I need some facts, a blurry photograph, or a date to confirm this is definitely happening.

"Can't be long now," Evan answers, his foot tapping in time with his drumming fingers. I'm waiting for a penny whistle and a harmonica to complete the tune to the beat.

"Will you stop that?"

"Stop what?"

"That!" I gesture to his fingers and feet, but he shrugs and continues. I pray for patience.

"Mrs Skylark?" Another nurse's head pops around the corner, her eyes scanning the room of expectant faces.

"That's us!" Evan is up in a shot, striding across the waiting room floor before realizing he's forgotten his pregnant wife. The nurse watches him, arms folded, amused. "Right." He spins around, looking bashful, and comes back to take my hand. I roll my eyes and follow.

"In here dear." The smiling nurse leads us into the dimly-lit room and motions to the bed, an island of white sheets in the sterile space illuminated only by the bleeping many-dialed scanning machines propped against the wall. "Down to your underwear and lie down here. I'll be back in with the technician when you're ready."

"Thank you" I reply. *Breathe, Billie, breathe.*

Evan understands my phobia around hospitals and does his best to be relaxed, but his "relaxed" act today isn't fooling me. He squeezes my hand as the nurse draws the curtain around the bed and leaves us alone. I try to unbutton my blouse, but my hands are shaking so badly I fumble, stop, take a breath and try again. I lock eyes with Evan, and he smiles—not the "I'm trying to make you feel better" sort of a smile or the "you're really funny" sort of a smile—it's the sort of smile that gives hope, lifts spirits, and reminds me that there's one person in the world that gets me, and loves me, and always has my back.

He steps toward me, kisses the top of my head, then unbuttons my blouse and peels off my shorts. I lie back on the cool white sheet, and he grins, then kisses my tummy. "Ready?"

I salute in reply and he heads out to tell the doctor.

Minutes later, the room is bathed in a greenish sort of light and the loud drum of my heart is accompanied in time by various beeping and bleeping machines. Craning my neck to the right, I try to make out the images on the small screen as the technician gently moves the sensor back and forth across my abdomen. His face gives nothing away and the screen looks like a weather forecast for snow. "Hmm." He leans his head closer to the screen and moves the sensor to the side, further down, then over to the other side before squeezing some more pale blue gel on my tummy, and *hmming* some more.

Evan holds my hand, staring intently at the screen looking like he understands the blurry images when I so know he's faking.

"Does everything look okay? I mean, you probably know this is our first scan. We've just moved here and didn't manage to get it done before we left. We sort of think I must be around fourteen weeks, but can't be sure." I'm wittering, and no one seems to be listening. I'd like to give someone a shake, but as I'm lying flat out in my undies covered in slimy blue gel, I try again. "So can you tell how far along I…?"

The technician raises a hand to stop me and takes off his glasses. My heart hits the floor, and in that second I know he's about to tell me something I'm unprepared for.

A frenzy of worst-case-scenarios race around my head as the blood drains from my limbs and creates a pressure pot in my brain. I squeeze my eyes shut and raise my hand to match his, willing him not to tell me there's something wrong. In a heartbeat, the shift is complete; from desperate uncertainty about a baby and its place in our life, I'm suddenly desperate to know that a healthy child is growing inside me. Filled with shame for sending negative energy to my unborn baby, I convince myself in the five seconds of silence that I have somehow been the cause of disaster.

"Mrs Skylark. Are you all right?" The doctor's gentle tone distresses me further. Evan is frozen beside me. "Everything is fine, Mrs Skylark, and your estimations are quite accurate; you are fourteen weeks and four days pregnant."

Covering my face with my hands, a small sob escapes as relief overwhelms me. Gulping air into my desperate lungs, I pull myself from the cliff of despair. "Oh, that's such good news, thank you so much… thank you."

He continues to smile, passing me a box of hankies.

"Your babies will be due around November." He examines my expression, and it takes a moment for his words to get past my relief. I wonder if I misheard him, but Evan's hand holds mine in a vice.

"Did you say 'babies'?" Again, the kind smile and again, the blood drains from my limbs, and my head has that hazy, surreal sensation. Now, rushing in through the flood gates to mix and curdle with all that relief is wave upon wave of shock and a sizeable portion of panic.

"Yes Mrs Skylark, you are having twins." The room is silent again for what feels like a very long time. I cover my mouth with my hands, and Evan sinks into the chair beside the bed. "I take it this is news for you both?" The technician replaces his glasses and resumes the scan as we remain dumbfounded and silent.

"Yes," Evan manages to croak. I can only stare in shock at the screen as I begin to see the quite definite outline of two tiny forms; not one, but two.

* * *

The drive home is quiet, leaving us alone with our own thoughts. Evan's hand is on my leg, the other hand on the steering wheel, as we negotiate downtown traffic and head out over the String Road to the beach, where traffic thins and pace of life slows. There seems no reason to stop; the drive feels good, we can be together without feeling the need to discuss anything as the island flashes by, beach after beach. I look out of the window. Life happening all around and life growing within; two lives—two tiny, vulnerable, dependent lives.

The Mini Mok climbs high, leaving the coastline far below, the air becoming thinner and cooler. We have nowhere to go and nowhere to be today, a day to navigate a new life path. The drive fast-forwards the processing of feelings: shock, anxiety, relief—the myriad of overwhelming responses to the thirty-minute hospital slot.

Eventually, we reach the highest lookout point on the narrow road that climbs St. Anne, the island's highest summit. Evan pulls the car into the gravel parking bay, pulling on the handbrake and turning off the ignition. We sit for a moment longer, both facing straight ahead, lost in the panorama that is the eastern coastline of St. Cloud: shades of dark to light green, textured and abundant foliage meeting sand and ocean. Curving lines where land meets sea changing with tides and time, the effect of sunlight enhancing color, and form leaving sparkling traces from every angle—images etched on my eyelids as I close my eyes, shielding myself against the brightness of life.

Evan releases the steering wheel, eyes still on the ocean, and runs his hands through his hair, nodding almost imperceptibly to himself. "If you were a bird, which one would you be?" he asks, looking ahead, his expression serious.

I bite my lip in thought, eyes creasing a little against the glare of the sun. "That's easy. Definitely a Tui; I'd sing for a living, and all the other birds would love me for my beautiful voice."

He smiles and nods.

"You?" I ask, suspecting his answer.

"A Skylark."

"Of course."

"You know, the flight of the Skylark is probably the most divine thing you'll see in the sky. It's not flamboyant or the most graceful or skillful, but it understands the wind and flow better than any other. It's daring and fearless, and you can tell the Skylark from its flight; it soars and plummets so you think it's about to plunge straight into the ocean, then it about turns, almost cresting the waves, before heading back up for another nosedive."

"I'm sticking with Tui. None of that risky nose diving thanks. I'll sit and preen my feathers in the trees and sing for you."

"And I'll impress you with my stunts."

"Sounds risky. Couldn't you go for Penguin? Then you could keep the eggs warm while I head off gallivanting." The eggs/babies/parenthood link bypasses his wistful expression.

"No point in being a bird if you can't fly Billie."

"Tell that to the Kiwis."

He smiles and faces me. "Do you think I can be a good Dad?" The quick turnaround in topic makes me pause before answering.

"Of course. I know you will be."

"You waited."

"Only because I was thinking about Kiwis." I'm not sure if he's listening.

Shaking his head, he says the word. "Twins." Then repeats it, pronouncing the word slowly and clearly, like it's a different language, something foreign and strange.

"Twins." I echo, trying the word out, my lips hesitating to collaborate with my tongue to make the sound and acknowledge its meaning.

"How do you feel?" he asks, his hand slung around the back of my head rest, leaning in toward me, holding my hand, prizing my tightly clenched fingers out and rubbing my palm.

"Generally speaking, fat and grumpy, but if you mean specifically… I… well, I'm not quite sure. It doesn't seem real. I think maybe I'm in shock."

"Me too, one baby was big news. Two is, well…"

"Double?" I offer.

He gives me the famous half-smile in reply and leans forward to kiss my forehead, pulling me onto his chest. I hold onto him, pressing my face into his t-shirt, inhaling deeply as he strokes my hair and reclines his seat, letting us both lean back, feel the breeze and smell the ocean. Evan watches the sky, profiling each bird that soars overhead, describing in detail what makes each special and I close my eyes and doze, dreaming of birds and flying babies.

* * *

The next few weeks sees our new life start at full speed; as Evan's new job begins, I scour the local real estate market, feeling the need to nest and settle. The new firm and new post mean that Evan spends long days in the offices of Evander Associates, finding his feet, getting up to speed on work projects, and in discussion with the firm's boss as to the upcoming project he is to lead.

The change is such a contrast from our first week in St. Cloud that I'm a little lost at first, missing Evan, feeling suddenly very aware of the huge distance from this new life to the old one. There are no friends to call on or meet with. I have no job to do and so to push the lonely phantoms away, I submerge myself in finding us a home. I write in the mornings and search the real estate market in the afternoons.

Being that having twins is inevitably more complicated than a one-baby pregnancy, I'm forced to address my hospital phobia on a fortnightly basis. Appointments for checkups in the maternity unit are every two weeks, and as time ticks by, week after week I begin to feel more comfortable with pregnancy and the double luck I have growing rapidly inside. Two babies for the price of one; I have no illusions things will be easy, but I'm increasingly overwhelmed by the changes in my body and the sheer miracle that is life blossoming within.

Evan is attentive but absorbed by his new role. The company designs and manages projects throughout the southern hemisphere, and the potential for growth and development in his career is huge. Evander Associates was established in St. Cloud almost one hundred years ago by the great-grandfather of Johan Evander, a migrant to the island from Holland. Initially designing and building only in the then-small main city, Becketsvale, the company grew and diversified over the years to become an international player in architecture, design, and construction. Although the hours are long, Evan is excited to go to work, and there are no traces of lethargy or despair.

In our second month of hotel living, I find us a small cottagey house on the southern side of the island near an array of coastal beaches and bush. The house is basic and small, but has the potential and land we will need to expand in time. We visit the bank, get a mortgage, and buy the little house with its wandering section of land which winds its way to the ocean.

My days are spent sanding, painting, and gardening; the pace of all three activities interspersed with snacking and napping. Evan's days are spent in the office, an office which seems to extend beyond the firm's shiny multi-floored building to the bar across the road. Colleagues regularly debrief their work day over cold beer or cocktails. Evan insists this is part of his bonding process with the new firm and the people he works with, and I'm just happy he's happy.

I've been so tired that most evenings see me asleep on the sofa by nine, or on the luckier occasions when I manage to stay awake, Evan and I spend sunset on the old swing seat suspended from the eaves of the back deck facing our grassy section and small glimpse of ocean. This is the perfect vantage point for sunset and our days form an easy pattern.

* * *

Three weeks after our move into the house on Frontiere Point, I'm in the sprawling garden, which spreads to thick native bush. The sun is bright overhead, and after tackling the weeds for a few hours, I'm hot and perspiring. I wander to the end of the long, sloping lawn, heading for the shade of the bush. There has been so much to do in the jungle of a garden that I haven't yet explored this part of our section, and although I know the ocean is not too far away, I'm not sure if there's a way to get down to the water from our land. Shading my eyes with a hand, I see the traces of a path cut through the dense growth some time ago, the break in trees and vines only barely visible. The cool of the bush is so appealing, and I wander toward the gap with a view to find the route to water. A voice sounds from behind, and I jump, the words a shock within the solitude of my morning.

"You want to be careful down there! The path is pretty rough, and there's a drop right off the end. The fence really needs repairing."

I turn to the source of the voice, its timbre deep and grounded. It's hard to make out a face. My eyes are dazzled by the bright midday sun, but the figure is tall and the voice assured.

"Sorry, I didn't mean to startle you, I was down here doing a bit of work on my side of the fence. I'm Jack."

Jack of swarthy beanstalk proportions steps forward and extends a hand, moving into the shade as he does. I extend a sweaty hand, feeling a little self-conscious; I haven't yet met the neighbor in the house to our left and assumed that he or she would be out at work during the day, like most of the people on the street. I'm wearing denim cut offs, top button gaping open to accommodate my burgeoning belly, and a bikini top. Honestly, the weather has been so hot, and so far in three weeks, I haven't seen a neighbor between the hours of nine and five. Right now, it's all about comfort, and so here I am, sweaty and dirt-encrusted from gardening, wearing a string bikini top and shorts with a bump sticking out beyond my boobs wondering why this might feel a little awkward.

"I'm Billie," I manage, grabbing his calloused hand, which seems to swallow mine as we shake formally. "So, you're next door?" I gesture toward the house that resembles a boat shed.

He nods, his gaze fixed on me, and there's something behind that calm expression I can't quite read. At that moment, two wildly excited dogs race down the grassy slope of his garden toward us, and begin to jump and lick me. "Easy girls, what kind of welcome is that?" says Jack. The dogs quiet to his voice. The black one sits promptly on his feet, and the tan one gives me a cheeky lick on the tummy before sitting to attention. "Sorry about that. They're just excited to see you."

I pat the tan-colored dog on the head. "Well, I don't usually get a belly lick every time someone's happy to see me, but thanks, guys." I bend down, ruffling fur. "… and that's a good thing, of course…" I blush, stumbling over my awkward words.

Jack laughs, and the sound is nice; deep and hearty, genuinely entertained and looking a little confused by me. "How long have you been in St. Cloud?" His gaze is steady.

"Almost two months. Not that long, really. My husband Evan works in the city. We just moved from the UK."

"You don't sound entirely British."

"No, I'm one of those people whose accent can't quite decide what to do. I grew up in the States, then moved to the UK as a teenager, and now I'm married to an Irishman."

"Right." He smiles. "Are you guys settling in well? It must be a big change."

"It's great, thanks, although this heat takes a bit of getting used to." I hope this might explain my attire. "Incubating makes things a little hotter too. I don't know how I'm going to last the summer."

He smiles, gesturing to my exposed belly. "I'm glad you confirmed there's a baby in there. I was afraid to ask in case you're just very fond of the local food," he laughs, and I join in, the awkwardness leaving with the overused "too many pies" joke.

"Actually, there are two babies in there, not just one." His eyes widen, probably wondering what the hell he will have to put up with next door—two screaming mad toddlers.

"Well…" He pauses and scratches the top of the black dog's head. "Should you really be out here in the midday sun pulling weeds and digging?"

"Oh my God, you're worse than Evan. You two should get together and swap notes." I put my hands on my hips, a little insulted. "I'm all good, thank you, and I'm making the most of my mobility before I become beached on the sofa with only ice cream for company!"

He laughs that hearty laugh again, and we fall into the comfortable chat of two people who instantly connect. He seems like a friend from a previous life, a like soul and chatting with Jack makes things feel easier, safer, and somehow the unruly garden and wonky little cottage feel more like home.

Strolling back to the house much later, I feel the happy glow of someone who knows they've found a friend.

That evening, sitting on the deck on the swing seat with Evan, me sipping iced tea, Evan on whisky, I gesture to Jack's house and tell him about the chance meeting.

"He lives on his own there?" Evan's tone is a tad touchy, and I look at him, his brow furrowed and his mouth a little thin as he swirls his glass and looks over at Jack's place.

"He's divorced."

"You two covered a few personal details already?" Evan downs the last of his drink and plants the glass on the table beside the swing.

"What's that supposed to mean?"

"I thought you just met him today."

"I did."

"What else did you talk about?"

"Why are you getting all testy?" I don't like the way the conversation is going.

"Testy? Well shouldn't I be a little concerned that my pregnant wife is at home all day hanging out with the good-looking divorcée next door while I'm out working fifteen-hour days?"

"What the hell? Are you insane? I'm telling you I met our neighbor, we chatted, and he's a nice guy. Not that I want to have his babies, for God's sake! That's what people do; they have conversations. Because he's divorced doesn't have to mean he's some kind of threat to you. Drop the weird machismo thing, will you?"

"Since when did you get so feisty with me, Mrs Skylark?" Evan breaks into a grin which both relieves and frustrates me.

"Since you got me up the duff with two of your offspring!"

Laughing now, he pulls me onto his knees, my legs straddling him, tummy to tummy. "Can I remind you that they're our offspring?" Arms wrapped around my back, he buries his face into my chest, my belly making the maneuver trickier than anticipated.

"And don't give me the having to work fifteen-hour days. No one drags you for cocktails after work."

"But they do. You have no idea what it's like." He kisses the top of each breast.

"Have I ever given you a reason to be jealous?"

He doesn't answer, but plants his whisky-laced mouth on mine and kisses me possessively.

"I hope he's watching," he whispers in my ear, and I push his shoulders away, but he catches me by the wrists and holds me firm.

* * *

Chapter Fourteen

The Arrival

Sex with Evan has always been pretty spectacular. I know how that sounds, but really it has. I'm living proof that damn good sex can still happen with the guy who leaves his dirty laundry in piles at the end of the bed, always forgets to lift the toilet seat, and snores quite regularly. Sex with Evan has been consistently great, which is really quite funny as Evan is inconsistent in so many other ways.

He might drive me crazy from time to time, as any male inevitably would, but the sex has always been good, mostly great. Heavily pregnant sex, however, is not great. Let's just say it's not even good at all. In fact, it's awkward and clumsy, careful, uncomfortable, and entirely unsatisfying.

I am thirty-seven weeks pregnant with a tummy so gigantic I can barely maneuver myself to the loo without accidentally knocking something over, losing my balance or… worse still, not managing to make it to the toilet at all. Late pregnancy is decidedly unglamorous, late pregnancy with twins is a double whammy.

No one believed I would carry the babies this far, and I feel like a science experiment. "Let's see what happens. How far will she go? How big can a little thing like her possibly stretch? When is she going to blow?" Oh, I've blown all right, but not in the expelling-babies--sort-of-way, much to my frustration. I have developed an incredibly short fuse, a nasty temper, and eyes that weep at the mention of anything remotely sad, especially if it concerns small animals or children with big eyes and chubby cheeks.

Beyond uncomfortable, the midwife suggested I try a little natural initiation to get the babies moving, and if all fails she will admit me into hospital for induction at thirty-eight weeks. We could wait, but the babies are a good size, and well, I'm not. The problem here is quite obvious. If another midwife mentions tearing, stitches, and episiotomies one more time, I'll swing for them. I'd rather not give the babies any more time to grow bigger, and from what I can gather from the other Mom's at antenatal class who are only too eager to share their past experiences, being induced is hell. So I'm determined to get things moving along naturally whatever the cost to my dignity.

My midwife's first recommendation was power walking. I tried and lasted all of six and a half minutes before I thought I'd die of heat stroke or collapse from the sheer weight of my enormous tummy. The next idea was to eat lots of fresh pineapple, which I duly did, only to become nauseous and spend much time on the loo.

Her last piece of advice was sex.

Although Evan pretended to be excited by the idea, I knew he was faking. Sex had stopped being much fun ten weeks ago when I had passed the luscious, blossoming phase and moved into the "there's absolutely no comfortable position to do this in" phase. We persevered with good humor, but now had entered the "how is this even possible?" phase. I had stopped knowing where the entrance to my own vagina was six weeks ago.

Nope, in these last few weeks, I have no desire for anything except my babies coming out, in one piece (well two actually), and having my body returned to me. I'm long past being hungry, long past sleeping, moving, all of it; I have become a beached, swollen version of my former self, and all I want is a cool breeze and a strawberry milkshake.

It's 3 p.m. on a hot November afternoon, and I don't know what to do with myself. Everything's uncomfortable and hot, and the pressure on my tummy is so tight I feel the slightest knock might cause a pop of magnificent proportions. Evan is at work, and I'm alone and stranded. I have been warned not to drive, which wasn't necessary as my tummy doesn't actually fit behind the wheel unless the driver's seat is moved back to the furthest position, and then my feet come nowhere near the pedals. I have moments of great humor about the whole thing, but now and again, I'm overwhelmed. I am exhausted and bored of waiting. I've never been good at waiting, and with everything as ready as it can be for the twins' arrival, I'm stuck for things to do.

I should write, but here's the thing: the last ten weeks have seen me incapable of stringing together even a few sentences worth keeping. It's like every ounce of creativity has been used up in the creation of the two babies squished inside me. I'm freaked out, but know it will pass; it's just another of Mother Nature's lessons in preparation for life with babies. There will be no writing for some time once they're born, so she's weaning me off now. It's all very clever, really. Despite being tired and hungry, I can't eat much or sleep. It's another little preparation for what's to come—oodles of sleepless nights and quick snacks between feeds.

I reluctantly joined an antenatal group full of earnest, nice women, all pregnant (strangely) and desperate to talk about it. You see, the thing is that I don't want to talk about it, and I'd rather not think about labor or breast feeding until I have no choice. I'm on the one-day-at-a-time program. I joined the antenatal group mainly because the midwife insisted I do so, and also because despite not wanting to talk about babies and their imminent arrival for hours, I want to do the right thing. I want to be a good mother, and I don't want to mess up. The group has taken it on themselves to call me daily just to check if I've gone in to labor. I'm the first due date to come around; the leader of the pack, so to speak. That and the fact that I'm incubating not one baby but two has made me something of a phenomenon.

The phone rings, and I roll my eyes, expecting to hear Sandie's voice, this week's designated caller, checking I'm not in labor and don't need any cookies delivered. It's not that I don't appreciate the kindness; it's just that I'm not myself. I'm grumpy and quite over being asked how many Braxton Hicks I've had today.

"Hello?"

"Hey, it's me, Jack."

Jack, hurrah! Lovely, funny, hulking, bear man Jack. The closest thing I have to a girlfriend despite him being entirely the wrong sex. Jack is always around, and he's kind and makes me laugh. Just knowing he's always next door is a great comfort to me. I try to "put aside" his handsome features—sort of enjoy them from a distance and accept his friendship as a gift. He's loyal and consistent, predictable and safe. Every girl needs a Jack next door.

"Oh, thank God, Jack. For a minute, I thought you were another pregnant woman checking if I had begun dilating."

"Oh." Pause. "Should I be asking if you're dilating?" Jack sounds confused.

"Oh my gosh, please don't! I've had enough people ask about the status of my vagina lately. Let's talk about something else."

There's another pause, and I a picture Jack's face red and awkward. It's probably not cool to talk about your vagina to the neighbor.

"Sorry, too much information, but just so you know I am not about to push out a baby, much as I wish I were."

"Okay. Well, I was wondering if you needed anything. I know you're stranded in there, and I was heading into town."

"You are?" My tone is wistful and dreamy… ah, town, that place where normal people have lives, do things, shop, drink coffee… another world away from my stuck-on-the-sofa existence.

"Do you want me to pick anything up for you?" I hear Louie and Bets barking in the background.

"Yes! Actually, if you don't mind, I'd like you to pick me up. Can you do that?"

"Literally?"

"Yes."

"That might be a challenge."

"I think you're ready Spartacus. Flex those biceps and come get me. I need to get out of here."

"Should you be going anywhere?"

"If I have to look at these walls for another five minutes, I swear I'm going to have to start knitting baby bonnets, and that would be tragic. Now please, just let me come for the ride. It's so hot, and your car has no roof. It would be heaven." I'm pleading, and it's a shame really. I leave him no choice; everyone feels pity for a large, pregnant lady on a hot summer's afternoon.

"Okay. I'll be over in ten minutes, but just a short drive."

"Yes Dad, just a short drive."

"Ten minutes."

"I'll be the fat one on the sofa. Just come on in with a winch."

"I'll see what I can do."

"You rock, Jack."

The phone clicks as he hangs up, probably regretting calling to ask if I needed anything. I'm sure he wasn't expecting to haul fatty's ass into town in the Jeep. I picture him shaking his head as he climbs the stairs up from his workshop, wondering why he can never say no to me.

I haul myself from the sofa and shuffle to the bedroom where I change from an oversized t-shirt to a cream colored maxi dress, with spaghetti straps and plenty of cool cotton fabric in which to fit my girth. It's the only dress I have which fits, but seeing as I rarely leave the house, my lack of gorgeous attire hasn't been an issue. I brush my hair out and then pin it up into a bun, pushing any flyaway strands behind my ears before splashing on a little fragrance and donning my flip-flops. I hear Jack's Jeep in the driveway and make my way, slowly and steadily, to the front door. By the time I get there, he is waiting outside.

"Ready?"

"Ready," I reply with the determined air of one off on military reconnaissance.

"You look great," says Jack, smiling, eyes fixed on the sundress.

"Thank you." I smile back, feeling a little lighter, which is quite something considering the sheer weight of my belly alone. We walk round the Jeep, and I take a deep breath, wondering how to negotiate the high step up to the passenger's seat. I look at Jack, and he rolls his eyes.

"Don't even think about climbing up there. I'm not ready to deliver any babies today."

"I can manage." Before I have time to continue, he scoops me up, one arm behind the fold of my knees the other under my arms, and places me carefully on the passenger seat which he's already pushed back to its furthest position. Bets licks me on the ear and I laugh. "Thank you." I'm a little embarrassed.

"You're welcome." He hops in to the driver's seat, turns the ignition, and we're off. The breeze in my hair and the cool sensation on my skin is heavenly. Louie and Bets wag their tails happily in the back, and Jack turns on the stereo. The sounds of Ray Lamontagne float beside me, his scratchy voice singing about his "baby" and "coming home." Amidst the lightness in my heart, I feel a flutter of worry about what Evan would say if he could see me. He hasn't taken much time to get to know Jack, and when I mention him, Evan becomes tense and it usually ends in terse words.

My days and much of my evenings are spent without Evan and I would have gone mad if it hadn't been for Jack's company. He's been nothing but a good friend, and although I tell myself I have nothing to feel guilty about, I can't entirely put away the fluttering feeling of guilt that accompanies the happiness I feel around him.

"Where to ma'am?" Jack asks as we cruise along the ocean road, the sun glinting on the waves and alighting on our faces as the Jeep traces the curve of the land before turning inland.

"Wherever you're headed Jeeves."

Jack laughs and drives, and we carry on in comfortable silence, me lost in the scenery, his eyes on the road ahead.

Half an hour later, we pull into Becketsvale: first stop the docks where Jack has to pick up something for the latest boat creation slowly taking shape in his workshop. I stay in the Jeep, leaning back in the seat, sunglasses on, listening to the sounds of the docks. People come and go, boats lap against their moorings, and the water lulls me into a peaceful doze.

I jump, hearing Jack's voice close by, and he hops back into the Jeep, turning the noisy engine on and reversing without a word. Another few errands as I daydream and doze, soaking up the life around me, everything brighter and more interesting after having been cooped up at home for a while. My phone vibrates, and as I pull it from my bag, I see the text from Evan. "Hey baby, how are you? Ex."

I reply as I always do to his regular text checks that I'm fine and that as yet, no action on the baby front. Evan's been nervous about leaving me for the past few weeks, but work has been demanding, and I've assured him nothing is going to happen quickly, and that I'll let him know at the first signs of anything. We play the waiting game, both terrified over what we are waiting for, but what else to do but wait?

An hour later, we pull up outside Beau Jangles café, home to St. Cloud's best coffee and the best place to catch a slice of local life. Jack flicks on the hazard lights as the Jeep stops in the loading zone. "Okay, tubby, are you ready?"

"Ready for what?"

"We're going for coffee."

"Oh God, I can't be seen in public. I'll barely fit through the door!"

Jack takes no notice. He has already hopped out of the driver's side and opens my door. Reaching in to scoop me out, he places me gingerly on the sidewalk. The outside tables are full and the coffee drinkers stop momentarily to stare then carry on with their coffee and conversation. Anything goes around here. Jack finds us a table and makes sure I maneuver my tummy safely to the seat before ordering himself a coffee and me a milkshake. He heads off to park the Jeep.

"Billie, how are you doing? I take it those babies still aren't keen on my coffee." Jed, Beau Jangles' fabulous owner/coffee dude calls over the espresso machine as he whips up our order.

"No, unfortunately, but I'll sure be making up for it once they're on the outside, let me tell you."

"And when can we expect to meet them?" Jed glances overtop of the espresso machine at me and my gargantuan tummy, but is too polite to comment on my size.

"I'm hoping any day now." I say blowing a breath out as my stomach tightens involuntarily. Jack arrives moments later, grabbing our drinks from the counter before sitting opposite me.

"How's the outing going for you?" he asks, stirring his coffee.

"It's very good, thank you. And the milkshake was a good bet. Did I already tell you I can't even drink coffee anymore?"

Ruthie Morgan | 229

"Maybe once a day for the past four months." He sips his own coffee, and I screw my nose up, regarding him jealously. I can't wait to enjoy a good espresso again.

Local faces come and go, and I enjoy the bustle and interaction—and the fact that no one makes a fuss about my tummy. Everyone is busy doing their own thing, having their own break, time out, pick up, wind down. Beau Jangles is a vibrant little hub and a wonderful slice of life. It's St. Cloud in color and smells, music, and energy. I'm happy, and as I pick up my milkshake, bringing the straw to my lips, I feel a surge of good fortune followed closely by a rush of pain. My glass clatters to the table and Jack jumps, frothy droplets of pink milkshake splashing onto the newspaper he's reading.

"What is it?"

"Nothing, sorry. I lost my grip on the glass."

He looks questioningly at me and mops the pink mess up with a paper napkin. I don't want to make a fuss; this is no doubt the practice contractions the antenatal group has warned me about. After a moment of scrutiny, Jack returns his gaze to his newspaper, and I hold the milkshake with two hands, hoping the pain won't return. Suddenly, the labor I have been praying for is a little terrifying, the pain of one minor contraction sending me scurrying up the corridors of imaginary labor wards yelling beseechingly for an epidural.

As Beau Jangles fills with people hungry for lunch and table space becomes limited, Jack suggests we leave. Drinks finished, he stands, giving me his hand to haul me out of the chair. Again, the tightening band of exquisite pain surges through my body, and my legs wobble as I grip his forearm, nails piercing skin.

"Billie?"

I can't answer, eyes closed, willing the pain to recede. I thought I was prepared for this, but now I realize there's no way I could ever have been ready. "Jack, I need to get out of here." I still haven't opened my eyes, and I'm gripping his forearm like it might save me from what is inevitably beginning.

Without another word, Jack grips me under the elbow and guides me, my feet barely touching the ground, through the busy cafe and out onto the street.

"Shit." I hear him cuss, my eyes still closed. "I need to get the car." He sits me down on a bench, calling for Jed. The eyes of the entire café are on my slumped form as I sit holding my tummy.

Jed is soon by my side, arm around my shoulders, and I open my eyes as the pain recedes. "Jack's getting the car. Just hang on. This could be it, girl. Hold tight."

Oh God, now I'm not ready, I'm so not ready. I take it back. I'll live like a beached whale for a few months longer. I'm really not ready.

I squeeze Jed's hands. "I think it's stopped." I'm out of breath. "Maybe it's just a practice run. They say that happens, right?"

"What are you asking me for?" answers Jed, perplexed. "Virginia?" he yells into the café. Most of the customers stare out at the little scene, of course while Jed is out here with me, no coffee is being made.

A tall, slim woman strides from the cafe, all business. "Is she alright, Jed?"

I'm vaguely aware that I've seen this woman before, but have never spoken with her. The accent is English and her manner is earnest and efficient.

"Billie, this is Virginia. She works at the hospital and knows a lot more about this than I do." Jed keeps his arm round me, and as I look up to say hello to Virginia, another wave of pain sweeps over me, and I am rendered mute. Gripping the side of the bench with one hand and Jed's leg with the other, I count the long seconds as my stomach contracts and my back screams in pain.

"How long have the pains been coming?" Virginia crouches in

front of me and takes my hands. There's something reassuring in her presence, and I try to explain that everything began only a short time ago, but the pains are coming quickly. She speaks to me in a knowledgeable, soothing manner as another wave of contractions descend, and everything swirls and dims as I focus on staying upright. "Jed, I think you need to call an ambulance." Virginia is calm and authoritative.

Jed jumps, but at that moment Jack pulls up in the Jeep, its tires skidding to a halt in the loading zone. In a flash he's out of the driver's seat and by my side. "I'll take her to the hospital Virginia. Jed, call Evan and tell him to meet us there."

All around its action stations, and all I can do is press my eyelids shut and steel myself against the waves of excruciating pain that pull me under and seem to be coming closer and closer.

Jack scoops me up and places me in the passenger seat again before setting off at top speed to the hospital, which is only a few kilometers away. Every bump in the road causes me to cry out, and Jack speaks to me in soothing tones, but I don't even know what he's saying. Bets and Louie lie down in the back, quiet and confused at the drama.

In the delivery suite, the midwife strips me down to a hospital gown and examines me. Jack waits outside, pacing like the anxious father-to-be. I try to breathe. That's all I have to do for now—just breathe.

"Okay dear, it looks like you're well on your way, and it's all happening quickly so I need you to breathe steadily and try to rest in between contractions when you can."

Rest? Who is she kidding? "It happened so fast. I thought I'd have a little more warning. I don't even have my hospital bag!" I'm distraught and terrified. Like being on a rollercoaster that's gradually speeding up, heading toward the loop de loop, you're strapped in and there's no way out and you know what's coming but have no choice.

"Don't worry about any of that. Just focus on your babies. They'll be here soon. Sometimes, these things happen quickly. Twins can be unpredictable."

I press my palms into my eyes and cry, hoping Evan will be here soon.

* * *

He runs along the corridor, trying to find the lift to take him to the maternity ward.

What the hell? She sent him a text only a few hours ago and everything was fine. How could it have happened so fast? What the fuck was she doing? Evan's scared, and his worried head goes into overdrive as he finds the lift and punches the button for the fifth floor. The lift stops at each floor to let people come and go, the doors opening and closing over and over as late comers rush to enter. It's torturous, and as the lift moves and stops and moves again, Evan wonders why the hell Jed called him and not Billie and why Jack was the one that drove her here?

Anger is soon crowded out by worry, and as the door opens on to the fifth floor, he pushes his way out and runs to the reception desk where he is pointed in the right direction by a tired nurse.

Jack stands in the corridor, back leaning against the wall, arms folded, head down. He jumps when he sees Evan.

"Where is she?"

Jack points to the door, seeing the fear on Evan's face.

* * *

Evan enters the delivery room like a whirlwind. His eyes are wild and for a moment, despite the pain, I'm scared of the expression on his face. "Jesus Billie, I don't understand. I thought you were okay earlier. What the hell were you doing in town and why the hell is Jack outside?" His words fall out in a torrent of worry and frustration as he crosses the room in two strides.

"I was fine. It all happened so quickly…" I am about to say more, but another wave of pain crashes over me, and I cry out, gripping the sides of the bed, trying to remember to breathe. All the anger is sucked from Evan as he watches, horrified, while I struggle and strain, trying to make it through the contraction.

"Christ almighty, talk to me, baby. Are you alright? What can I do? Tell me what to do?" He holds my shoulders as the pain gradually recedes and I breathe normally again. He pulls my face to his and kisses me gently, realizing he mustn't panic if I am to make it through. "Okay baby, you're doing great. It's going to be okay. I'm here now." He strokes my hair and whispers to me until the midwife returns, bustling into the room wearing a plastic apron.

"Hello, you must be…?"

"Evan, the husband…" he replies, not for the first time.

"Oh, but I thought…" She gestures to the corridor, confused then embarrassed. "Nice to meet you Evan. She's doing well."

A shadow passes over his concerned expression at the confusion over who is my husband, but he recovers quickly, squeezing my hand proudly. "She is. How long does she have to go?" he asks the midwife, and I get my first taste of how things will be for the next twenty-four hours. Everyone will talk about me as though I'm not actually in the room, and although in between contractions when I'm tired but closer to sanity, this bugs me; soon, I won't give a toss. It will fall into the hazy memory of labor and the miraculous, terrifying, excruciating, out-of-control business it really is.

"Well, she's around 8 centimeters dilated, which means she should be ready to push soon."

"Holy shit. I mean, does it normally happen this quickly?" Evan looks at me with concern, but I'm focused.

Another contraction, and I groan and cry out for him, squeezing his hand with all my strength, and then pushing him away when I realize he can't help. No one can.

"It's different for everyone, and twins are never easy." The midwife bustles around, getting things ready like she's setting the table for dinner. Does she realize I'm dying here?

"I need some drugs!" I scream between contractions.

"She needs drugs. Can we get her some drugs?" Evan repeats to the gentle-mannered midwife.

She sits on the bedside and holds my hand and the tenderness sends me into sobs of sorrow realizing what my poor mother went through to have me and remembering her in the warm, caring hand holding mine.

"You're too far along now for an epidural dear," she says, and despite her kindness, I want to jump up and throttle her, all calm thoughts of mothers and compassion gone.

"What do you mean, I'm too far along? I can't do this. You need to help me."

"We will dear. You're doing wonderfully. I've just organized the gas and air for you, and that should help you through these last few big contractions. Won't be long now, and you'll be ready to push."

Ready to push? Who is she kidding? I haven't the strength to see another second of this pain through. I can't do it! How do I tell them all? I can't do it. Can we get someone else to do the pushing bit? I've done my part. I'm all spent.

I cry between contractions and am soon puffing on gas and air, which does nothing but make me feel dizzy and nauseous.

The room is soon busier than before, aside from a moaning and occasionally screaming me. There's pale-faced Evan, the gentle midwife, an obstetrician, and a student doctor. Everyone gathers around my nether regions. Even the handsome young student doctor, but honestly, I don't care. I don't care about anything anymore but stopping the pain, getting my babies out safely and stopping the agony.

"Evan!" I yell, flapping a hand at him like he should know what I need without me having to say it.

"I'm here."

"I'm going to be sick."

"She's going to be sick!"

There he goes again with the repeating thing. The midwife thrusts a cardboard bowl under my mouth, which Evan holds for me with one hand while holding my hair back with the other. I vomit the milkshake, the muesli, the banana and anything else unlucky enough to have been hanging around in my stomach. I puke until there's nothing left, and then collapse into the grips of another intense contraction.

"Okay, that's a good sign. She's in transition."

I am vaguely aware of the positive sounding voices around me as I hold on for dear life, wishing I'd gone to the loo.

"Billie? Okay dear, you're ready to push. I need you to be strong, and with the next contraction, I want you to push down as hard as you can." It's the voice of the obstetrician. He pats my hand and nods to Evan, and I experience terror at the thought of the next contraction, knowing it will be worse than the last.

"That's it baby, you can do this. I'm so proud of you." Evan's hand squeezes mine, and I look into his moist eyes briefly before it hits. I scream and push like my whole body is on fire.

"There's the crown. Almost there Billie. One more push, and you'll see your first baby." The midwife is still so calm.

Terror, joy, and dread crowd around my aching body; I'm almost there, I'll get to see my first baby, one more push but then what? I have to do it all again?

With another wild scream, I push and feel the soft, slippery body of a baby slide its way into life. The relief is instant, and I cry out, exhausted but desperate to see the tiny mite that pushed its way so determinedly into the world.

"It's a boy! It's a wee boy." Tears roll down Evan's cheeks, and he burrows his face to mine as I cry.

The midwife passes the tiny bundle to me, and he lies blinking on my chest. I hold him, sobbing happily until the next wave of contractions begin, and our little boy is taken away as we prepare for the entry of his sibling.

This time the contractions are shorter but more intense. My body knows what to do, and the baby is anxious to be out in the world with its brother. I am exhausted, but the fear has gone. I know I can do it; I must hang on a bit longer. I imagine myself running toward the pain, not fighting it off, but running with it, accepting it as part of the path to my baby.

Ten minutes later with three more strenuous pushes, our little girl arrives bawling into the world. Dark, sticky hair and a tiny elven face, a contrast to the little hairless boy whose tiny face is rounder, his cheeks flecked with the beginnings of dimples.

Our new life as a family begins.

Birth, beginnings, hope, and a future to build together… loss and grief in death filled and smoothed over by the beauty of life in birth. Loved ones mourned and now remembered in part by new life; an expression, the slant of a chin, or a smile. DNA passed from them to us to these tiny babies, their small forms testimony to who came before and the seed of who will follow. Life forever changed, our path irrevocably altered, and our responsibility in this world now weighty and of significance. Tiny lives that rely solely on us and our devotion to them, these two vulnerable, dependent beings whose eyes alight on our faces and feel safe.

* * *

Chapter Fifteen

Change
Eighteen Months Later

The rain subsides, and the sun makes a last-ditch attempt to show its face, reminding us after the day of grey, heavy cloud and storm that it's still there, always there. The attempt is valiant but watery and with no warmth. The air hangs damp and heavy, and I glance outside at the wash line laden with diapers, vowing to get on top of that laundry tomorrow. I cringe inwardly, remembering a life before babies. How different my expectations and awareness of what I might achieve daily, how drastically my plan for the future has changed. Target-setting now for the day might pinnacle on drying the diapers before the next rainstorm. How quickly things change. I laugh to myself, grateful to have the sense to laugh at my own despair.

The wooden floors are warm beneath my feet, and I head for the bathroom, carrying a baby on either hip, singing a little tune that has become my signature "time to get sleepy, kids" song. It never works, of course; where most toddlers might start to wind down come bath time, Evie and Sunny seem to take it as a cue to party. The floor is soon sopping, and there is much gleeful shrieking and throwing of bath toys. I give up on the sleepy song and join in their little water fight.

Sometime later after storytelling and lullabying, the twins are asleep, snuggled safely in their adjacent cots, each with a favorite blankie and soft toy in their painted yellow room. This is the last room at the end of a long corridor from which all rooms in the house leave and to which the open-plan living/kitchen/dining leads.

The house is quirky, its design entirely unintentional; functional, but most definitely not a thing of great beauty. It is a house of the seventies, built originally as someone's holiday home and haphazardly added on to and pieced together to eventually become an oddly-shaped three bedroom cottage sort of house. The twins' room is on a corner and light floods in from windows looking onto thick bush on either side. For now, the pale blue cotton curtains hang limply despite the open windows. Outside the air rests still, recovering from the rigors of the storm.

Green is everywhere here in St. Cloud, and from each window in our house, the creeping bush can be seen; its dense and fragrant growth relentless in its mission to permeate the concrete driveway and brick walls. Agapanthus in purple and white line the roads and driveways. The sea almost always in our sight line is framed by the slope of tea trees and native fern.

I tiptoe along the corridor, knowing that one creaking floorboard could spell the end of my peace. One baby awake usually means two, and the bedtime routine must start again. I know exactly my safe spots to tread as I head into the bathroom, longing for the coldness of water on skin. Half an hour later, still quiet on all fronts, I give myself an inner high five that I have managed this small but quite celebratory goal; twins fed, bathed, and asleep by eight! That and a cool uninterrupted shower are nothing short of a miracle.

Although I know the night will inevitably be interrupted by many bouts of crying and that if I were smart, I would grab an early night and sleep stock, I want to wait for Evan. Turning on the radio nice and low so as not to risk the tranquility, I flick to and from the few local stations available, settling on some local dub reggae band. I like this station; the DJ is actually our family doctor who has now become a dear friend. "Doctor Dan" moonlights a few nights a week on a local music scene and talk show. Dan is jaw-dropping gorgeous. I mean that literally, speaking from experience after an awkward first doctor's appointment with the twins; Dan charming and professional, me ogling at his polished complexion and deep suntan. Very gorgeous and also very gay, to the dismay of the heavily female-laden St. Cloud population. There are many who believe they will be the woman to change all that, but so far he's not interested.

I open a cold bottle of beer which I feel I now justly deserve and sip it, feeling the alcohol spread though my tired body. There is something intoxicatingly forbidden in this small pleasure. That for a time, a bottle of beer can lift me a little higher than my day and help the perspective I so quickly gave away, come creeping back, apologetic and red-faced. Looking out at a burned crimson and ochre sky, I slow down, take a deep breath and thank my lucky stars.

I set the small table for two, light a candle and cover the food waiting for Evan. He should be home soon, and if I am asleep before he gets home, it can feel like days since we've actually spoken. He's busy with his current project, and I'm always tired. He tells me I don't operate on St. Cloud hours, and he'd be right. I don't and neither do the twins.

People do everything later here. They siesta mid-afternoon, a two- to three-hour lull in the heat we have gotten used to. People return home, take a break, go for a swim, surf or maybe just have a nap; it's a nice way to live.

The siesta usually means that people work later, and a workday might finish at seven or eight rather than five or six. People have cocktails then head home for a late evening meal or stay out. St. Cloud is a social place, and there is always somewhere to go have a few drinks and debrief the day with friends.

I know this mostly through Evan because I'm always here with the twins, a fact I am equally happy and frustrated over. I mean, I haven't the energy at present to party or stay out sipping cocktails till late, but I am just a little jealous that this is never an option for me. Having no family here, I am loathe to leave the twins with anyone; a fact that drives Evan crazy.

Evan is of the opinion that I am too soft, having grown up with Mary Skylark and a house full of mad siblings, he's a little more used to this sort of thing. Our different upbringings result in more than a few contrasting opinions on parenting.

Evan is still the party boy. Parenthood has not changed this, and although I hate being without him, I understand he will always need the release of a few drinks and I'd rather he was out with friends than… well, anywhere else. It's not that I don't trust him, I have no concerns over his faithfulness despite our past, but I know he thinks differently following the first beer and can be reckless after a few more.

No one is perfect. My own vices stack up rather nicely these days and so I try my best to understand what Evan needs and support him in the same way he tries to do for me. A few drinks in the bar after work helps him wind down and, I suspect, allow him to be someone else for a while.

Life as a Dad to toddler twins is far removed from the life we had before. It's not something you get used to overnight, and you can't try it for size before you buy it. There's no returning goods with a valid receipt, no changing your mind or deciding that actually, you're not cut out for this sort of thing. That has been a good thing in my case as there have been, and still are, many moments when I might have popped the twins back to the store—receipt or no receipt.

Being a mother is the hardest challenge I have been faced with this far, and there is no practice run. I've lost count of the times I want to run screaming for the hills like a mad woman, yet I am bound to my babies by an invisible thread of love and hope and devotion that remains intact long after the umbilical cord is gone. But as they grow and change and confuse and challenge me, that invisible thread is often colored with guilt, frustration, and self-doubt. Am I doing it right? Am I good enough? How can I be better? This coupled with those awful thoughts of how much easier life was before, remembering that I had a life before, that my days are now just variations on a theme: feed, clean, change, cuddle, pacify, feed, clean, and so on and on.

There are days I think I might not make it till morning tea; those days when I've changed four poopy diapers, cleaned vomit from cot sheets, scrubbed crayon from freshly painted walls, only just prevented two near-death experiences (one twin in a fight with the cat, the other with a raisin stuck in each nostril), flooded the laundry, and burned the toast all before ten.

Where did my other life go, and will it ever return? There are still moments in the night when the sound of a baby crying will send me into a sort of denial. I'll snuggle against Evan, thanking my lucky stars I'm not old enough or responsible enough to have babies of my own, simultaneously hoping that whoever that baby belongs to will make it be quiet. For that brief moment, my dream sucks me back to the old me, and as I am about to slip from half-sleep to someplace deeper, I jerk awake, filled with cold panic that those cries are for me and worse still, that the dream where they cried for someone else brought me quiet joy.

This is life with small children, joy and despair in equal measures and I try to reassure myself and Evan that it's normal and soon it won't be like this and maybe, one day we might even miss it.

"… and so that's it for tonight, island people. The moon waits for no man or lady, so get out there, smell the air, and thank your lucky stars you live in paradise." Dan signs off with a Gregory Isaacs number. My beer has been gone a while and my stomach growls that the romance has left the candlelit table. 9:45 p.m. and still no Evan. I wrestle between relief that he is happy here in St. Cloud, has good friends, doing no more than relaxing after work, and frustration that I'm here on my own again.

Pulling up a cane chair to the hardwood table, I shovel my cold Paella down in approximately 1.35 minutes. I cover Evan's food and wonder whether to succumb to the lure of bed with its cool sheets and a hopeful breeze from the shuttered windows. But then I think of my manuscript waiting patiently on my hard drive, wondering when it might find its conclusion. Its happy ending… or not.

I rub my temples, hoping to massage half an hour of creative juju into my keyboard fingers. Who am I kidding?

I hate that I have become one of those kind of/maybe/wannabe writer people who are eternally "in the middle of a book." Yet here I am living a life where I manage little writing, yet in my head still call myself a writer. I have to you see, otherwise I'd spiral into the pit of full-time mother, coffee group, beige pants, home baking despair that awaits the female post-reproduction.

I am still an "almost writer", because it seems undeserving to take the title without a published book. There is something self-congratulatory in the title "writer." It suggests a known name, available in a bookstore, "googleable," published volumes to list, a small fortune and movie rights negotiations.

I am plainly living in an alternate universe to this clever and wealthy alter-ego and so I keep my writing life private. My writing resume is sparse, and my few published poems and short stories lie dusty in desk drawers. My first book, finished just before we left Paris, sits unread by anyone, a second halfway done. A published novel is the dream that holds me on the runaway train my life has become.

The lure of bed wins once again, and I pad down the hallway to those cool sheets while my horn-rimmed spectacle-wearing, black-coffee-drinking, creative alter-ego frowns her disgust at my retreating behind.

It takes only slightly less time to fall asleep then it did to consume my paella. The sleep is exhausted: black and dreamless, and I barely rouse when Evan slides into bed much later, pores oozing the familiar smell of rum and cigarette smoke. A hand strokes my hair pulling me out of that divine place of deepest black recovery sleep where all is forgotten and everything is silent.

Prising my limbs from the fetal position, I turn to him groggily. "What time is it?"

He answers by locking me in a smoky, boozy kiss, his fingers moving deftly under my t-shirt as I drag myself awake.

"Evan… " I am about to berate him, the nagging wife at home with the kids, dinner cold on the table… *where have you been… didn't you think… it's late… how could you… no sex tonight* and so on. But my body betrays me and responds to his touch, my mind following less urgently, still a little pissed off.

Sometime later with Evan asleep on my chest, I remember that nothing has changed. Evan has always been this way, and it's life that changed around us. He is the way he's always been, and I love him anyway.

I drift off again, feeling safe and happy, wakened momentarily by my writer alter-ego from the room next door who whispers loud enough for me to hear "… and shouldn't he change too? Why is it always you… always you?"

* * *

The night is never long enough, and sleep doesn't hang around; it plays hard to get. I love it passionately, but never know how long it'll stay and when I'll get some more.

The phone rings and rings, and I am wondering why the hell someone won't just answer the damn thing. It feels like hours, and that phone is still ringing, then there's another sound, a baby crying, its volume growing as the cry becomes more frustrated.

I sit bolt upright in bed, sleepy eyes finding focus in the pale morning light. Exhaling slowly, confusion from my dream fades into frustration at the alarm clock, not the telephone which is ringing on Evan's side of the bed.

Reaching over the space where he should be, I slam the stop button and pull myself out of bed, heading to the source of the loud wailing. Pushing open the door to the pale yellow room, I see Sunny standing forlorn, his little fingers gripping the bars of his cot.

"Mommy's here," I murmur. He raises his chubby arms to me, snot running from his nose into his mouth, his cheeks red and blotched. "Come here, sweet pea, what's all this?" I wipe his nose and cuddle him to me. He's warm and clammy. Evie lies curled in the adjacent cot, still asleep despite the mayhem. I head through to the living room, carrying Sunny, nuzzling his warm cheek into my chest.

The oven clocks digital display says 5:35 a.m., and I sigh, patting his little back before pouring some cold water into a sippy cup. "There, there, little man. This will help." Sunny wraps his thick fingers around the handles and drinks. I find some baby Panadol and give him a small dose to bring down the fever. He is teething and has had a temperature on and off for weeks. A note from Evan is on the counter: "Hey, baby, had to get in early. Didn't want to wake you. Call me after your first coffee. Ex."

Evan knows that my words before first coffee are short and delivered with a scowl. I lay Sunny down on the sofa where he drifts back to sleep and return to put my coffee on the little gas stove.

Opening the sliders out to the back deck, I marvel at the gentle break of day. Such a tranquil beginning to what will, no doubt be another twelve hours of heat and blazing sunshine. Last night's storm has left a hazy dew on the surrounding bush, and from here things sparkle and steam as fingers of sunlight warm droplets of moisture on leaf and branch.

From this point I can see the ocean, only just, but it is enough. I love the sea, and each day when I can, I swim just to feel the touch of the cool water, and for a time be pulled by the force of the waves. The ocean feels like escape, an untamable force; joy and fear rolled into each powerful wave as it beats on the shore then pulls back strongly to recoup and return again.

I have a recurring dream, another in my catalogue of dreams to be analyzed one day by some clever psychotherapist who will rubber stamp me as certifiably Doolally. In the dream, I float on my back, head looking at the sky. I can hear the people on the beach, and they are laughing. The water sops now and again over my ears, and I hear something else. A seductive but unfamiliar voice calling not my name, but Evan's, I want to dive down toward the voice, but can only float, looking at the sky. The strange thing about the dream is that although I feel out of control and afraid, the ocean feels like home, and I know I need to stay there… floating, waiting, although I don't know what for.

There is another ring, and this time it's the phone. Phone, phone. Where is the bloody phone? Evie has a habit of hiding anything that looks like it may take my attention; the phone is the biggest culprit. I dash around trying to find the source of the ringing, hoping to get to it before it wakes both Sunny and Evie. I find the offending receiver in the toy box, and grabbing it, I press the connect button, snapping "Yes?"

"Hey, what's wrong? It's me."

"I know it's you. Why are you calling?" I say so bitchily I surprise myself.

"Um… because I wanted to say good morning?"

Evan's explanation sounds like a question. "I'm sorry," is all I can manage. Suddenly I feel tearful and don't want to have to try and explain; 'Hi, yes. It's me, your wife. Sorry I bit your head off, but your alarm woke me and the teething baby at 5:30 a.m., and you're there and not here, and you're always there and not here, and I miss you, and the crying babies are driving me crazy, and I love them because they're our crying babies, but the crying is too much, and I can't take it anymore, and I miss home and… and… and another thing…' and so on. This explanation isn't an option, so I grab a Kleenex, wipe my nose and say, "I lost the phone. Sunny has a fever again. He just went back to sleep."

"Poor little guy. Those teeth are giving him a hard time. Are you sure folks don't let them suck on a whisky-coated pacifier these days?"

"I can't believe Mary really did that."

"God's honest truth. To all six of us. It worked a treat."

"Evan, three of your brothers are alcoholics."

"True, good point. What about a good spoon of honey? Mam used that trick when the whisky ran out."

"He'll have no teeth if we stick to Mary's tricks." We're both laughing.

"Have you had your first coffee?" he asks.

"No, hang on. I'm off to pour it now."

"Good girl, that'll sort you out. Sorry I was so late last night. I got caught up. You know how they do things here."

I pour the smooth black coffee into my favorite cup. "You mean that all deals are finalized at a bar after hours?"

"Well…" He pauses, deciding whether to fib to me or not. "Not all deals… but yes, you're right, quite a few." He's smiling on the other end, knowing I will be softening, first coffee on board and a few sweet words. "I promise I'll be home earlier tonight. I'll cut out before cocktail hour. You've no idea the pressure, Billie. They'll be on at me. 'Evan Skylark, work like a man, get yourself down to this bar and seal the deal,' and I'll be all, 'Sorry, lads, I've a gorgeous wife at home and two babies. I've got to get my arse home'. And they'll say, 'Skylark, you're quite a guy,' and I'll say, 'Boys, I'm just doing my bit—'"

He's teasing me, but it works and I laugh too. "Will you stop already?" I interrupt him. "Listen, promise me you'll fix the fence at the end of the garden on the weekend. I have extra wrinkles this morning after the stress of Evie's escape bid yesterday."

"Relax. I already told you there's no way the twins could get down that far."

"Evan, please, just do it for me then, for the sake of my worry lines."

He sighs before relenting "Okay, okay, I'll get to it on Saturday. It'll be fine. Listen, I'd better go. I'll see you tonight."

I feel like' naggy wife'; tired, edgy, and always grumpy. "Okay, just don't be too late, the kids will be calling Jack next door Dad soon."

This stops Evan in his tracks, and I realize I have touched a nerve without meaning to. "What the fuck does that mean, Billie?"

"It doesn't mean anything." I am floored by his sudden anger. "I just mean they see more of him than you right now."

"Thanks, that makes me feel just great." His tone is flat.

"I'm sorry. I didn't mean it like that. I know you're working hard, I just…" I feel the tears again and know I should hang up before he hears the thickness in my voice. "I just miss you."

"Jesus, I'm sorry too. I don't mean to snap. I'm just tired. Jack's a good guy, and I'm being a wanker. I miss you, too. I'll be home early baby."

"Okay, bye. I love you."

I hang up then have a long girly sob into the tea towel in my hands. Damn these hormones. I sit silently, hugging the tea towel, cradling my coffee cup, watching the last fingers of sun break through to form the day. This will be my only quiet moment, I know this much. As I finish my last sip of coffee I hear Evie yelling from her cot, awake and unnerved that Sunny is not there. At the same moment, Sunny awakens on the sofa, flush-faced and hungry. His cries match Evie's, and I take a deep breath and say a quiet thank you that I had finished my coffee before the madness began.

* * *

9:00 a.m. and the twins are in the sandpit as I hang out another pile of laundry. "Well, would you look at me," I muse aloud, lifting damp diaper after damp diaper on to the heavy wash line, day's goal fulfilled before morning tea despite a rocky start. Twins are happy, no one has cried (well not for long, anyway) since breakfast, I've had an uninterrupted coffee and managed to wash and hang up a load of laundry! Super Mom kiss my ass!

I should know better than to tempt fate this way. No sooner have I stroked my mothering ego, Evie starts to scream as Sunny throws a pile of sand in her eyes.

"Hey mister!" I scoop the momentarily blinded Evie out of the sandpit, reprimanding my tiny thug as I dust the sand off her little head. "That is not okay. We don't throw sand, Sunny."

He looks at me as though I might have said, "Hey Sunny, why don't we throw some sand?!" He picks up a handful and throws it at me with a charming smile on his dimpled face. I'm saved from the ensuing battle by a screech of tires as a red Corvette pulls into

250 | *Skylark*

Jack's driveway. I know I should run for cover, but my life is so dull right now that I crouch down in the sandpit with the twins, unseen from Jack's house while the dreaded Claudia slams her car door and clip-clops up the path in her ridiculously high stilettos. The twins are thrilled I'm getting down and sandy, and all upsets with sister-blinding are forgotten as I feign interest in a plastic dump-truck while training my gossip girl ear on the inevitable commotion next door.

Claudia slaps the door with an open hand, her nails too long to make a fist and knock. "Jack! I know you're in there, Goddammit, open up!"

This is Claudia's welcoming line, and I have grown used to her drama, but it always fills a dull moment, so I eavesdrop.

The door opens. "Hi, Claudia. What could it possibly be today?" Jack's deep voice has the restrained quality of one struggling to contain an angry beast. "Jack, I want to know when the fuck I can expect to hear from your solicitor. You owe me." Her voice is nasal and high-pitched; an overgrown cheerleader on speed.

"I don't owe you anything, and that's why you won't be hearing from my solicitor. Let me tell you again in case you missed it the last twenty times. I don't have a solicitor, and I don't owe you anything, and you won't be getting another bean from me." Jack's voice is weary. It's been two years, and Claudia won't leave him alone. The house and most of Jack's money wasn't enough after their separation. I figure that it's Jack she secretly wants back, but until she figures out how, she'll make a fuss about money.

Claudia changes tack quite suddenly. "Jack, baby, can't we stop fighting? How about I come in, and we have a good talk about how to resolve all this anger?" I think I might vomit and hope Jack isn't about to fall for this.

"No thanks Claudia. I'm busy and so must you be." Jack attempts to close the door, but she sticks a stiletto in the way.

"Now you listen here. I was the best thing that ever happened to your hairy ass. You think about what we had together and tell me truthfully you don't miss me." Her bottom lip sticks out like a sulky teenager and she folds her arms across her chest.

"Truthfully?" says Jack. "Me and my hairy ass are much happier. Hang on, did I put enough emphasis on that last part?" He raises his voice, "*Much* happier on our own, now would you please fuck off?"

I slap my hand to my mouth in shock. I have never heard Jack swear, and for some reason, I blush. I think Claudia might combust. She stomps one foot, turns on her high heel and clip-clops her way to her car. As fate would have it, for sheer comedy value she can't reverse the thing out of the driveway and poor Jack, in his desperation to be rid of her, has to come back out of the house and do it for her.

I am laughing hard and struggle to keep my muffled giggles under wraps. The Corvette whooshes away, and Jack sighs, walking back to his house muttering under his breath. Although quite confident I am concealed behind the Pittosporum bush, Jack's voice rises over the fence.

"Don't think I can't hear you in there Billie May. I'll have you know she was once quite an attractive woman."

I poke my head over the fence, all smiles. "Really? I mean… of course, you two must have been a match made in heaven."

He laughs with me and keeps walking back to his workshop.

"I promise not to tell anyone about your hairy ass!" I yell after him.

He gives me the finger and keeps walking.

Poor Jack, how could such a good guy get so unlucky in love? As I ponder this, I wonder, not for the first time about fate and relationships and how it all works. Are we really destined for one love? One person waiting out there for us, the perfect guy or girl, the perfect love, the perfect relationship, the perfect sex… does it even exist? Can there be one perfect match out there, or are there many, spread liberally all over this world? Perfect loves dotted around our life path. Our final partner simply a result of timing, a love match dependent on where we end up when we're ready? I toy with this idea until I smell something like a dead creature in the sandpit—or a brown offering in a nearby diaper.

Much later that day, waiting for Evan to return from work, I see Jack in his yard throwing the ball for Louie and Bets. Pining for adult conversation, I stroll out to the deck and call his name. On hearing my voice he seems to stiffen involuntarily, but before I can muse on this, he waves, and throws the ball in my direction. I jump, hands above my head, trying, unsuccessfully to catch it. A second later I am bowled over by Louie and Bets who hurdle the hedge in an attempt to beat me to the ball. Jack laughs as I pick myself up scowling at him although I'm not actually mad at all. "You gotta work on that reaction time Billie; I get you every time."

I stick my tongue out then having managed to wrestle the slobbery tennis ball from Louie, throw it back toward him, and he catches it deftly with one hand. "Do you fancy a beer to take your mind off your crazy ex-wife and my mind off my phantom husband?"

He smiles warmly and walks toward the fence. "Phantom?"

"Yep, it's beginning to feel that way. Appears only in the night and disappears before the sun comes up. I'm beginning to wonder if he's a vampire or has developed an aversion to family life."

Jack hops over beside me, and we stroll together to the deck where we sit companionably, legs swinging from the edge, eyes fixed on the glimpse of ocean and late afternoon sun. "It's hard in a new career," he says, "especially in a place like St. Cloud. Everyone knows everyone else's business. It's like an old boys' club. The first few years they'll be milking him dry in case he decides paradise isn't for him."

"Paradise isn't for him? Is there anyone that paradise isn't perfect for?"

"You'd be surprised. There are a lot of people who only last two years in St. Cloud then leave. I guess it's small, maybe too small for some. Things stay the same, even the weather, some people don't like that."

I shake my head, incredulous that someone might want to settle anywhere else after living in St. Cloud. "I do miss the seasons, I suppose, but not enough to stop appreciating the luxury of shorts in December."

"They call them the honeymooners."

"Who?"

"The people who move here for a new life then leave after two years. Like I say, paradise isn't for everyone. The same problems follow you wherever you go." He glances behind us as though expecting to see an unfriendly face.

"I guess. So, you think Evan's company is running him ragged now in case he's a honeymooner and we take off after two years?"

Jack shrugs his shoulders and turns his thoughtful expression back to the sight of ocean at the far end of the garden. "Probably, but it sounds like Evan loves his job, so the hard work won't be a problem."

I follow his gaze to the dancing light on water, reflecting the vibrant blue from above. "If only all that hard work didn't end in another two hours of 'debriefing' at the bar!" I say pursing my lips a little.

Jack laughs. "You got it; this is island living baby, and it's not so bad".

I stick my tongue out and throw him a beer. "Do you have an opener? Mine has gone AWOL like mostly everything else in my house."

Jack grins and uses his teeth.

"That is so bad!" I squeal. "How many frat parties have you been to?"

"We don't do frat parties here," he says, all serious, handing me a bottle. "Where are the twins?" I jump, slipping off my maternal pedestal. Out in the garden drinking beer with the neighbor while the twins could be anywhere!

I catch myself and take a breath. "Oh, they're watching Bob the Builder. Am I a terrible mother?"

He laughs as we look through the sliding doors to two tiny heads, cuddled on the sofa dressed in onesies, mesmerized by a small man with a spanner.

"Shouldn't there be a Bobette?" asks Jack, frowning. "I mean, we don't want them to think that building is just for boys." I can't tell if he's serious or not.

"Oh, don't worry. There's a Wendy, and she builds too."

"Is she Bob's love interest then?" Jack has a sparkle in his eye.

"Possibly, but let's not think about Bob's sex life. Surely he's too busy fixing things to get it on with Wendy."

"Possibly," says Jack.

"Jack, you need a girlfriend!" I say slapping my thigh with conviction.

"No Billie, I definitely do not need a girlfriend," says Jack. "Didn't you see earlier the trouble the last one got me into?"

"True," I reply. "… and I have to say it again… what were you thinking?" I raise my beer to the heavens in horror.

Jack laughs. "There you have it. Like most young men, I was thinking with my nether regions. Had I given the thought time to reach my brain, the story might be different."

"Right. Well, now that you're not so young and tender, maybe the time is right to go find yourself a good woman." I say in an encouraging tone.

"Billie, let me say it again. Until further notice, I am done with relationships."

I can't decide whether or not Jack means this well-rehearsed line. Something in his eyes tells a different story. I take a long swig from my bottle. It just seems like a waste for womankind to not have this guy in the gene pool! It's practically a crime not to spread that seed around! Jack is six-foot-two, all muscly, quarterback, stubbly bear man with a big heart, and a great sense of humor; what's not to be attracted to? I'm staring, and stand up far too quickly, spilling beer down my front.

"Easy girl, you're a cheap date," he teases, standing up and beginning to head back to his garden. "Say hey to Evan for me."

"I will," I call after him a little too cheerily, wondering when Evan will be home.

* * *

Chapter Sixteen

Flight Paths

The sand is cool and clay-like, each step leaving a deep footprint, a trace of our path until the tide comes to wash it away. I walk with Zoe, my closest friend aside from Jack.

I met Zoe a few months after buying the cottage here in Frontiere Point. She is a dynamic, vibrant personality who exudes good energy, and my time with her is both hilarious and exhausting.

"So, how come you got married?" asks Zoe. "You and Evan just don't seem the type. I mean that as a weird kind of a compliment." She pauses, her nose wrinkling in thought. "Just that you sort of seem more like the let's-live-together-and-not-do-the-conventional-thing sort of a couple."

I'm about answer, but Zoe carries on, her train of thought off at 'Zoe pace.' "You know, with Felix and me, it's funny, but the minute I met him I knew we'd get married. He was just the type, you know? That sort of bearish, stable type, does everything by the book."

I look at her, my eyebrows raised slightly.

"Oh." She stops, registering my expression before smiling and reaching for my arm as we walk. "That didn't come out right. I don't mean that Evan isn't the stable type, or that you two aren't perfect." She looks awkward. 'It's just…"

I stop her mid-flow. "You're right. I didn't think we'd be the marrying type either, and truly, I'm not sure why we did. Not that it hasn't been the right thing; more that we'd have been together anyway. You know Evan. Sometimes I wonder if he asked me to marry him because he knew it was the last thing people would have expected of him. He likes to shock."

"You mean he likes to piss people off?"

"No, not necessarily, although to be fair that's sometimes true, but I don't know. I don't think either of us ever thought that marriage was something we should do, then it just was, you know? Kind of a nice reason to have a party and maybe a chance to give a silent finger up to all the folks who never thought we'd last."

"But you did."

"Yep, just like you guys."

"And here we are." Zoe laughs.

"Uh-huh, here we are, living in domestic bliss. Right?" I nudge her, and we laugh, splashing through the tidal beach, each pushing an all-terrain double buggy through the sludgy sand.

Zoe runs, like me (although these days Evan would be accurate calling me a "jogger"). Post-babies, running was slightly less comfortable than it had once been, and although I must resemble a hippo trundling along, I love it and so I run or jog—whichever, because it makes me feel good about myself, the world, and my place in it.

I love the meditative movement, footstep after footstep, the enhanced sound of breath struggling to be controlled, the burn in my lungs, and the ache in my thighs. I love experiencing the environment in a run. It's like concentrated hiking for the restless, those of us who haven't the peace of mind or quiet soul to relish the outdoors in a gentle walk. Everything is enhanced when I move more quickly, the blood pumping through my muscles, my breath forced and regular. Colors are sharper, textures clearer and smells stand out in a way I rarely experience when still. This is terribly "un-zen," but it's the way it's always been for me. I'd like to be the meditation type in the same way I'd like to be green fingered, but it's not happening. So, I figure it's good to know what works for you and what doesn't, and running has saved me many a hysterical bout of hormonal tears or tantrums.

Shortly after moving into the cottage, I would see Zoe early mornings, plodding along the same tracks I chose to walk, too tubby for fast pace as pregnancy advanced. She was usually running in the opposite direction, so we'd nod and say good morning in that gruff way people do when they're not quite awake and not expecting to see another live person. After a while we would stop, have a little stretch and chat, and then carry on separately. Finally one day Zoe turned around, and we joined forces, walking the trail together.

From the start, our companionship has been easy. Honest and easy. Zoe is open and nonjudgmental, she is good and kind and her glass is always half-full. Together we have survived the rigors of being new mothers. Zoe has a one and three-year-old, and I turn to her for advice on all things new and overwhelming in the baby department.

"So, how's work for Evan?" she asks.

"Good, I think, mostly… oh, I don't know. Sometimes he's a little moody, you know? It's like a man period or something!"

Zoe laughs, and I carry on enjoying the chance to vent a little. "He has these moments where he's on top of the world, where I'm the best wife, the twins can do no wrong, and he's the luckiest guy on the planet. He'll have this boundless patience and energy with the twins and be so damn happy about life that I feel like a big, fat downer beside him. Like I'm raining on his bonfire, you know?"

Zoe nods sympathetically.

"Then just when I'm getting used to 'Mr Happy- Go- Lightly,' he nose dives, gets all grouchy and shuts himself away in his workroom building his planes. Oh, I don't know…" I sense I'm over sharing as Zoe's looks concerned and I scold myself for saying too much. "It's no big deal, just work stress and long hours making him moodier than he used to be."

"Than he used to be?"

"Oh yeah, he's always been moody. I mean, when I met him, I sort of thought it was attractive. You know, artistic; dark and brooding."

"And now?"

"It's a pain in the ass!"

We both laugh.

"He's just being a man retreating to his cave; that's what they do," says Zoe knowledgeably, and I want to believe her. "Yup, it's the transition to having little kids, the chaos and noise; Felix goes into hiding with his model trains in the attic. One day I was ready to call search and rescue thinking he must have gone fishing when he was just hiding away in his 'attic man cave.' Trains or planes, whichever, it's the same thing. Escape from the mayhem."

There has been a gradual change in Evan since the arrival of Sunny and Evie. Nothing dramatic, hard to really put a finger on at first until months down the line, I find myself worrying, wondering, "was he always like this?" The dark moods that hovered on the periphery of our happiness have taken a step closer, and I catch myself obsessing, watching, taking mental notes, trying to predict the change and avoid situations which could be potential catalysts to his melancholy. I want to believe Zoe, accept her explanation of men and their behavior in early parenthood. I smile at my friend, the simple action helping convince me that everything will be fine; nothing stays the same, all is normal. Everything changes with babies, of course it does. How could I expect anything to remain as it was? Evan and I are bound to each other. We're doing our best, like every other couple adjusting to the demands of a young family.

Zoe sighs and shields her eyes from the sun, gazing out toward the dock at the far end of the beach. "Yep, don't worry about Evan. Billie, he's a man, he needs a cave. We can't relate, so don't sweat it."

Talking things out, problems large and small, always somehow diffuses them. Worries shared with a friend seem less of a big deal when spoken aloud. My weighty words and anxiety dissipate with the sea breeze, urged along by Zoe's easy presence and ability to make me laugh.

"Man cave, huh? So, that's what it's about. We need woman caves!" I raise a hand and gesture enthusiastically. "We need a place to go, but there isn't one! I can't even take a pee without sitting one of the twins on my lap, then inevitably the other is squawking because they want to sit on my lap too… and I want to scream, 'I'm just trying to take a pee in peace,' but who would listen?"

Zoe laughs, and we carry on with our walk, appreciating the blissful quiet of four sleeping preschoolers.

Further ahead, we see boats pull in and out of the wharf, the last of the day's fisherman bringing in their catch. "Is that Jack?" Zoe points ahead to a figure at the edge of the wharf.

"Mmm, might be, hard to say from here." I shade my eyes against the sun, trying to get a better look. "Man, that Claudia is a piece of work!"

"I know," answers Zoe. "Poor guy. She's a viper."

"And those heels?" My claws are out.

"Not to mention the boob job and the lips!" replies Zoe.

All at once the babies start to rustle. "Dang, that's what we get for gossiping. An end to the peace." I say shaking my head. We jiggle our respective prams, hoping to lull our little passengers back to sleep, but it's no use.

"Oh well, we had a whole half-hour. Who are we to complain?" Zoe sighs as we turn and hurry back the way we came.

We decide to take the kids to the park for a picnic, and I'm determined we should have a good take away coffee to see us through the afternoon. Placating each tiny person with a muesli bar, we head to Beau Jangles hoping to grab the much needed coffee before our park stop.

* * *

"Two cappuccinos and an extra shot skinny latte to go!" Jed practically sings the order as he plants the paper cups one, two, three on the wooden counter. The lineup of thirsty coffee lovers extends out the door of the small café, but he seems oblivious to the pressure. He makes the best coffee in St. Cloud in record time, he doesn't need to feel rushed. He's a master, and people will wait. Bob Marley's voice floats through Beau Jangles, and the familiar reggae beat reverberates up through the floor. Strangely, the little people in our double strollers are quiet, mesmerized by the sights and sounds around them. The air smells of baking pastry and all around is the busy hum of conversation, laughter, debate, and the odd baby crying.

Beau Jangles café is the best coffee shop in St. Cloud, and Jed is the multi-talented "thirty-something" manager, barista, chef, busboy, and baker. I will be forever in his debt; not just because his coffee maintains my sanity, but his calm words held me together in the first few shocking contractions of labor. The poor guy maintains he still has scars on his forearms where my nails pierced his skin as we waited on the bench outside for Jack and his Jeep.

Zoe sits at a table, the two bulky strollers pulled partly underneath whilst we await our takeaway order. I stand by the busy counter watching the spectacle that is Jed in action.

Jed is the energy that locals plug into when they arrive for their morning fix. He knows everyone, the coffee they like, and just enough about their job and personal life to be sensitive and interested without being overbearing. He remembers regulars' orders without them having to ask, gauges the music in tune with his customers' vibe, picks them up or winds them down.

The "to go" order is whipped away by a smiling lady who is quickly replaced by another. I prop myself on a stool by the counter, happily unhurried. Our order could take a while. Zoe is talking on her phone and the little ones are content with their little snack boxes, so I take the opportunity to people watch—still one of my favorite activities.

"Hey, Dan!" I smile and wave at Dr Dan, and he winks and waves back before returning to his newspaper and black coffee. This is a sacred part of his day, the mid-morning coffee break. He'll be hoping he manages at least five minutes of uninterrupted time before a local pulls up a chair and tries for an informal GP session. I've known him to put a small sign on the table which says, "The doctor is on coffee break."

For now, Dan sits alone, sunglasses perched on top of his slicked golden hair. His foot taps to the music as he sifts through the day's news. Stories in St. Cloud aren't too different from day to day.

"Dan, what do you think about this airport business, you think it's a good idea?" asks Jed from behind the hissing espresso machine.

Dan rubs his chin thoughtfully. "I'm just reading about the damn thing here." He gestures toward the newspaper. "I'm not sure; I must admit I can't quite decide which side of the fence I'm on: for or against."

"We know which side of the fence you're on brother, don't worry about that," laughs Jed behind the counter. Dan smirks, takes another long sip of coffee and rolls his eyes at Jed.

Another voice from the opposite side of the café throws an opinion casually into the mix. "Oh, come on you lot; it's a fabulous plan!

Think of the trade it'll bring to the island, the effect on our tourism will be phenomenal." Virginia gestures excitedly toward us, thrilled to have a small audience to hear her position on the much debated topic.

"Virginia, do you have an opinion on everything?" ask Jed. "I already know how you feel; we've all seen the petition." Jed points to a colorful banner-like notice taped to café's front window; 'Say Yes to Progress!'.

"I'm just looking out for the future economy of the island. Someone has to, you all would be happy to carry on here like this forever, living like we're still back in the seventies. Well, not me. I say bring in the tourists, let's shake things up a bit, let's have some market competition. Bring on IKEA!"

"Yeah, and inflated house prices, and McDonalds, and all the bullshit we moved here to avoid," answers Dan, sounding irritated.

"Oh Dan; don't be so negative," counters Virginia. "Honestly, it can only bring progress."

Virginia Gibson: another local I am forever indebted to, another voice of calm during labor and conveniently an expert in all things female down below. Going into labor that day in the cafe just at the exact time Virginia happened to be having a cappuccino was really quite fortuitous. Virginia is a gynecologist working at the island's main hospital.

I eavesdrop on their debate, enjoying the passion locals have for St. Cloud and its future. Virginia, an advocate of all things modern and progressive, has been rallying support for the new international airport since we arrived in St. Cloud. She is an advocate for most good causes and is fond of standing on her soap box and voicing her well--informed opinion. I see Dan trying to unsuccessfully bury himself back into his newspaper.

"I heard through the grapevine that there's a foreign investor keen to push the whole thing through," Virginia adds conspiratorially.

"Oh yeah?" answers Jed, busy with the milk steamer. "Why would they bother?"

Dan glances up again, "Well, there could be a lot in it for a private investor, I mean think about it." He throws a hand in the air. "St. Cloud—the new holiday paradise for the discerning traveler. Beaches, reggae, and guaranteed sunshine."

"Not to mention the great coffee," Jed interjects, turning the gauges on his espresso machine, causing a great hiss to emerge from the depths of the chrome engine.

Dan stands, rolls up his newspaper carefully and sighs. "There will be package holidays for American tourists with their white socks and trainers before we know it." Shaking his head, he leaves some cash on the counter and bids goodbye to Jed and Virginia.

"Shame he's such a grouch." Virginia sighs and turns to Jed. "Such great bone structure." She looks wistfully out of the window. "Are there any attractive, single, straight men left out there?"

I laugh, and Jed rolls his eyes. "Virginia, you got one of your own. Don't be greedy, now."

"Oh, I know." She performs a theatrical sigh. "But that's the trouble with being married to a surgeon. He's never around. He lives at the hospital, thinks the place would crumble should he leave for a coffee break. It's me and the cat, and she only wants me for food. You'd understand, Billie." She gestures toward me, seeking agreement. "What I need is a toy boy; a nice distraction." She smiles at the thought, finishes her cup and takes it to the counter. "Thanks, Jed, fabulous as usual."

"Thank you Virginia… all the ladies tell me that."

"Oh, you're a devil. Have a fabulous day, and you too, Billie, darling. Take care of those gorgeous babies."

"I will… good luck with the toy boy."

She waves and follows the same route as Dan, heading for work only a few blocks away.

"Okay, Billie girl, here we are. Sorry for the wait but as you know, rushed coffee is never as good." Jed smiles and plops two perfect flat whites on the counter.

"Thanks Jed." I slide a ten dollar bill across the counter and he rummages for change in the till. "Funny how everyone's so fired up about the new airport. Evan's so excited about the project, says there will be nothing like it. He calls it his 'dream job.'"

Jed passes me a few coins as I stir some sugar into my coffee. "Oh, take no notice of all the negativity. A lot of people have lived here their whole lives and aren't too keen to see things change." He shrugs, "It's nothing to do with Evan's work; they just wonder where the money's coming from and how we can afford such a big investment. People are saying the city needs another school, the hospital a new wing, the sea wall on the north side needs strengthening. They're just worried we can't afford it, and they're not sure the changes it'll bring will be good ones."

I press two lids onto our coffees, mulling over Evan and his airport. "Do you think it'll go through? God knows Evan's done nothing but work on it since we arrived." I worry about how much he has invested into this project. He is passionate about the structure and its completion. It seems the project has combined all of Evan's passions into one perfect design. Art, architecture, and flight.

"You know, I reckon it will. Johan Evander is an ambitious guy, and if enough private money is behind it, I'm sure Evan's airport will get the go ahead."

I'm about to reply, but I hear Sunny wail from the stroller and realize our time is up. Coffees in hand, I rescue Zoe, and we power walk to the park for the promised play and picnic.

* * *

Evan drives a few blocks and turns inland from the beach into the center of town where his firm is situated. Pearl Jam serenades his route, the stereo full blast. Eddie Vedder waking the city's remaining sleepers. The red Ford turns hard right, pulling into the underground parking lot of Evander Associates. He snaps the engine off and gathers his thoughts before entering the building.

The company is small compared to what he is used to, but somehow the pressure feels bigger. He feels it from all angles, and although overwhelming, it's strangely inspiring when he's in the right frame of mind. This project is his chance to make everything right. If he can do this one design perfectly it might wipe the slate clean. He has the chance to show what he is capable of and his reputation in the industry will speak for itself. Surely then he will be remembered for his skill in architecture as opposed to one stupid-ass fuck up. Three lives depend on him now. The thought takes his breath away.

His phone vibrates on cue. Text message - "Will you be home for dinner? Please say yes. Pick up some milk on the way. Bx." Squeezing his eyes tightly closed, he tries to readjust his focus, blowing a controlled breath of air into the stale confines of the car. He opens his eyes and hits the delete button. The only thing he seems able to control these days is work, his drawings, and buildings. The rest is fucking chaos, and most days it feels like demands come from all sides.

The phone slips to the floor, and he lets his head slump on to the steering wheel, forehead flat on crossed forearms. He stays like that until his head quiets, takes a deep breath and exits the car, phone and briefcase in hand, expression now steely and focused. The transition is so smooth it seems impossible that the confident, self-assured man striding toward the elevator could be the same one from moments before.

Evan has made the switch; he pushes aside the deeper underlying self-doubt. That tireless voice telling him he is not enough is silent for a time, and he decides today will be the day he proves them all wrong

8:45 a.m.: The numbers gleam from the belly of the red bird, and he's sure the dumb thing is smiling at him. The clock was a present from Billie. It's a brightly-colored plastic parrot whose tail hangs low like a pendulum, moving side to side as it marks each passing second. It's a cheesy thing she bought from a market in East London, and he hates it, but somehow it always seems to end up on his work desk.

"Christ almighty!" Evan picks the bird up and shoves it into a desk drawer before slamming it shut, takes a deep breath and tries once again to regain the focus he had yesterday.

There's a noise in his ears like angry bees—buzzing, stuck, bouncing off the insides, unable to find their way out. He stops, sucks in his breath and leans back on the swivel chair, letting his gaze wander out of the window to the street below. Just beyond he can see the ocean: a glistening patch of blue in the corner of his vision.

He should go outside, get some air, maybe take a walk, but he can't switch off from this project. When he gets his head straight, the ideas come in a constant flow. They link together and form bigger and more comprehensive pictures, lines, and angles. Contours form shapes and structures. While images come and the structure is evolving, the plans tell themselves to him, and he must draw and write, get it all down on paper and let it take its form. This is the magic, his magic, working its way through him into form and shape, building and structure. While the ideas flow, he has to be here, at his desk, ready to get it all down to be examined more carefully later and worked into the bigger plan. This project is his most inspirational yet, and he will make it perfect.

Every now and again a wave of distraction washes over him that has nothing to do with the project, the heat, or the need for air. He thinks of home, Billie, and the twins, and how unsure he has become about how to do that part of life. How to be a father and a husband.

Things at home haven't been easy. The twins are everywhere, and the noise and neediness is too much. He gets home, and Billie looks at him with a mixture of desperation and frustration like he's messed up before he's even in the door. He doesn't know what to do to make it any better and as awful as it makes him feel, he stays late at the office because it's easier than the madness his home life has become. Chaos and responsibility—he's never been good with either.

Reaching over for the cup of cold, black coffee on the desk, he sips and vows today he'll do better. Bringing his attention back to the page, he sketches. The pencil works quickly, moving this way and that, focusing on fine detail, and then flattening its edges to shade and create depth. The image takes shape: a bird, wings spread in flight. He sketches without thought. He's drawn this image many times before. It helps him think, opens the door for the right idea to come to the page.

"That's good man. You're in the wrong trade for birds, though," comments the tall figure standing close behind him.

Evan starts. "Hey Joe, how you doing? I thought I was the only one here."

"I got to get these drawings in before the end of the week so I'm here till they're done," Joe answers. It's hard to sound remotely stressed when you have a soft island accent like Joe's. He rubs a hand over his face and strolls to his desk. "I dunno how you do it, Evan, boy. You'll have sores on your ass if keep up these hours."

Evan looks up from his pile of papers with a smile. "Thanks for the concern, but so far my ass is holding out just fine. It's my brain that's the problem."

"The airport project stressing you out?"

Evan lets out a slow breath. "It's more than that. I just get to thinking there's so much that can be done. An airport like this could change the island, there's so much potential. Jesus, can you imagine?" He shakes his head, arms folded across his chest. "The effects on the island's economy…tourism and jobs… it would change everything here for the better. It's more than just a building. It could be a new fucking chapter for the island."

Joe stands over Evan's shoulder, looking down at the mess of notes, sketches, and plans; his expression a mixture of confusion and awe. "Simmer down there kid, I'm ready for siesta just listening to all that enthusiasm! I'll stick to the shopping mall. Less controversy."

Evan leans back in his chair, focusing on Joe, keen to make him understand. "You can't tell me you think it's a bad idea She's going to be beautiful." Evan's arms are in the air, his fingers tracing imaginary lines; an invisible picture forming before him.

Joe shrugs and smiles, impressed but not envious of Evan's energy. It looks too tiring. "And what if all that work's for nothing, eh? Have you thought of that?"

Evan's turn to shrug. "It won't be, it never is! Christ, it's a dream design. Home of flight, a start and end point to a journey, set in the tropics, a gateway to and for the whole fucking world. I don't understand all the bullshit around it." Evan leans forward in his chair, excitement flooding all earlier frustration. "Believe me, this airport's a sure bet, you have my word. Honestly, I can see it, and there will be nothing like it!" his tired eyes sparkle with possibility.

"Of course there'll be nothing like it. We're a thousand miles from nothing." Joe laughs. "Evan, I gotta hand it to you bro, you love your job." He sits down at his cluttered desk and sighs. "I just hope you get all those grand ideas and drawings accepted." Joe rolls up his sleeves, kicks off his shoes, and cracks his knuckles before buckling down to work on his shopping mall.

"Yeah, me too," Evan says, focusing back on the drawings—distraction through obsession.

The day ticks by, and busy morning turns to the slower pace of hot afternoon. Few are left by two when the sun is at its most intense, but Evan remains, his position unchanged. By four the office begins to fill again, his colleagues returning from their afternoon break, siesta, or surf. They smell of sunshine, a welcome contrast to the heavy, humid air of the office where overhead fans turn listlessly, distributing the oppressive heat evenly.

"Does anyone do air conditioning in this fucking country?" Evan pushes back on his chair and runs two hands through slightly damp hair. There are a few smiles in reply; the people of St. Cloud are used to the heat and the lack of air in summer. Evan stands and heads to the water cooler. Filling his glass and drinking its contents in a few blissful gulps, he closes his eyes and relishes the in brief cool that the water brings his hot, tired body.

"Evan Skylark, have you a moment?" Evan jumps, looking for the source of the voice.

Johan Evander has entered the open-plan office area and signals him over.

"Sure." He walks toward the tall man, the solo director of the firm, and smiles. Evander likes his work, and Evan appreciates the older man's experience and input. Although an unscheduled one-on--one meeting with Evander is usually rare, Evan finds himself in the boss's office frequently. Johan Evander runs a tight ship and is keen to be closely involved in the airport project. He likes to be kept in the loop, see each draft, and stay on top of the direction things are moving. Evan respects Johan and admires his skill and management; he makes decisions quickly, doesn't take bullshit and has an uncompromising work ethic. Johan Evander is the steady force behind the company's success, and Evan feels privileged to work for him.

The ride up in the elevator is comfortably silent, and as the doors open out on to a light-filled lobby, the two men walk side by side to the spacious office. The room is bright. Its shuttered windows open to a view of the city below and the beach beyond. Evan is taken with the scene, the city bustle, a glint of ocean and the small boats in the harbor.

"I need an update on the project Evan. I'm under some pressure for this thing to come off." Evander sits behind his desk and motions for Evan to take a seat on the other side. "There's a great deal of political agenda behind the debate now, and things are heating up. I want to be sure you're on top of things." His gaze is unflinching. "Much rests on our success." His tone is stern and Evan feels a small jerk of anxiety.

"There's not really too much more to report since last week Johan. The drawings are close to completion, and I'm working on the written proposal. I'm still confident we'll be ready for first submission in two weeks."

Johan nods and rubs his chin. "Good, I want to go through the proposal with you fully before submission. The pitch is as crucial as the perfection of the design, do you understand? This project can't go wrong. You're good and I believe that if anyone can get this through, it will be you. You have an edge to your work that the others have lost. Too many siestas." He smiles at his own joke as Evan stands, hands in his pockets, always uncomfortable with compliments.

"If accepted this will be the biggest project our company has managed, and it will be the biggest God damn construction on the island." For a minute, Johan Evander is far away, ambition clouding his view.

"I'll do my best," Evan manages as he glances to the door, eager to be out of this meeting, back at his desk using his time productively.

"One more thing Evan." His tone is laced with imminent warning. "I know that there was an 'issue,' let's say, involved with your departure from Sans Limites. I chose to ignore it. Personal dramas are of no interest to me." He sits forward on his chair, sets his elbows on the table and laces his fingers together, chin resting on extended index fingers. Evan freezes by the door, the room suddenly hotter than before despite breeze from outside where the birds fly free.

After a considerable dramatic pause, Evander launches in for the strike. "Your personal indiscretion in Europe has tarnished your reputation within the architectural world. The business is tight, and companies rely on recommendation in hiring. I should like to keep you and help you reach your potential despite this, but let us be clear; I expect great things from you." Another pause, time enough to let the words sink in. "Starting again in Europe will be a challenge for you, so remember what I offer you here. I expect the best."

At this, Johan swivels his chair to the window, signaling their meeting over. Evan all but runs from the room for fear his temper betrays him. Without a word, he closes the door quietly and walks determinedly to the elevator. As the doors close, he slumps against the wall chin to chest, open palms over his perspiring face, pushing back the anger threatening to overwhelm him. "Fuck!" The word holds all the fury and frustration of a past mistake. His fist curls and lunges at the steel elevator wall, and pain reverberates through his hand, but nothing changes. He's still here, still fucking up, never able to outrun the past. Blood oozes down his white shirt as he bangs the elevator's illuminated buttons. "Fuck, fuck, fuck…" The words are quiet now, low and threatening.

Sliding doors open on to the entrance lobby, Evan exits, striding across the polished floors to the revolving glass exit leading to the main street. "Mr Skylark… shall I sign you out?" calls a confused receptionist. Evan doesn't turn around and keeps walking, head down, till he reaches the nearest bar.

* * *

Chapter Seventeen

Turbulence

On an island like St. Cloud, people live in a reality subtly different to that of those people on the continent. There is something about life on an island, especially an island far from mostly everywhere else, something that is reflected in its people.

Maybe this is only obvious to me being raised in 'flat land in every direction,' Kansas, closely followed by a bustling overcrowded city like London. St. Cloud could not be more different for me. And its people? Well, I like their differences. I like the pace of living, the easy-going attitude of the community. I love the community! I love the sense of belonging that we all feel, even after a short time here; if you're not already related to half the island, the odds are you soon will be. We are an island where half the population is far from home, so in this paradise, we make our families: a collection of friends who become as important to our lives and well-being as the ocean, the rain, and the sunshine.

The morning has been muggy and hot, cloudy and humid; no place to escape the heavy heat. I bundle the twins up and walk to the beach. It takes half an hour longer than it should because I push one twin in a buggy and carry the other in a backpack. The narrow streets around Frontiere Point don't fit our double buggy. Laden down with sweaty babies, crackers, raisins, beach towels, and sand toys, I walk to Settlers' Cove where we strip off to swimming togs and play in the cool water till the twins are good and tired.

The cove is one of the few tidal beaches here in St. Cloud, and when the tide is out, the shores become a veritable science project. All manner of seashells, creatures, and weeds are revealed naked and shivering to be poked and prodded by children or collected in plastic buckets to take home and dry in bedrooms that will end up smelling of old fish.

The beach is a chance to sit for a minute if I'm lucky and watch my offspring race around, safe, within reach, always visible, mostly always happy. They are water babies; just the feel of the cool sea between their chubby toes is enough to send them into fits of hysterical laughter, soon followed by much splashing, chasing, and sand-sculpture building. Watching their little bodies toddle around in the sand, fat bottoms and big tummies, it's a wonder that the human race has made it this far. A species whose young are so utterly dependent on their parents. Dependent not just for a few hours until their legs are strong enough to run around a paddock, or a few weeks till tiny wings are ready for flight, but years. Years and years of feeding, caring, cleaning, and nurturing.

This thought is strangely comforting but terrifying. I cannot think of ever losing them to the big wide world, yet the thought of decades of responsibility is more than my brain can manage. Days pass, minute by minute right now, and in order to make it through the sticky quagmire of nappies, pureed food, and sleepless nights, I must operate in this slow and steady fashion. Like the hiker in for the long, arduous climb, I try not to think of the climb ahead but of each sacred footstep. Although sacred isn't a word I'd associate to my moments and days. If I were more Zen, I might bathe in the glow of my innocent children always, and I'd see the challenges as mere hurdles in my road to serenity. I'd never curse under my breath at the whining and crying. I'd welcome every sleepless night as a blessing—another chance to spend wakeful hours with them at this tender time in their little lives.

Newsflash: presently Zen is not in my vocabulary. We could try "exhausted, wrung out, grumpy with moments of mania fuelled by coffee, and a sense of humor (most of the time)."

Evie throws a handful of sand into Sunny's face. Direct hit, and much screaming ensues. There's a counter attack and tussle before I reach them, grabbing one under each arm and trekking back to our picnic blanket to distract them from battle with some well-timed snacks. Yes, moment by moment because honestly, years of this viewed as one long continuously playing track is too much for me. I adore my dimple-thighed cherubs more than I knew possible, but life as a mother to toddler twins is hard. I'd take CEO at IBM any day.

"There we are; some juice for you, and some juice for you, too." I plonk a juice cup into each unsuspecting sandy hand, and the battle is forgotten. All smiles, they slurp happily, free hands trailing the sand for shell treasure. I lean back on my elbows and feel just the tiniest bit Zen. I welcome it into my vocabulary like an ex-boyfriend. An awkward hello followed by a happy reminder of something once good. Yes, it will all be fine.

A car horn makes me jump, all Zen thoughts gone as I look around, irritated at who dares disturb our peace. Back on the road by the dairy, a green, dirty Jeep pulls up, two dogs leaning out of the back, barking excitedly. They race for the water, yapping and jumping. I sit up and see Jack wave as Louie and Bets barrel toward us, falling over each other in the double excitement of the cool water ahead and their best friends, Sunny and Evie, on the sand. Ensuing squeals of delight, barking, and giggling are interrupted by Jack's voice as he calls the dogs back. There's comfort in that voice.

I wave, and he nods in our direction, walking over the sand to where I sit, practically obscured now by the onslaught of fur, tails, and dimpled thighs. The twins jump on me in delight as Bets and Louie lick their hot little legs, then push us all in the direction of the water.

"Hey! Can you get these slobbering fur balls off me?"

Jack approaches, laughing at the mayhem. He whistles once and motions to the water. Louie and Bets respond immediately, racing for the waves, the twins barreling after them.

"Can you train my children to do that?"

"I only deal in four-legged creatures. You should know that." he plops down beside me on the sand; denim work shorts and bare feet, he passes me a cold beer.

"I don't know if I deserve this." I take the sweaty green bottle from his rough hands.

"Then give it back." He elbows me and makes to grab the bottle.

"Are you kidding? I didn't say I didn't want it, only that I didn't deserve it… entirely different things." I take a long, cool gulp, then clink my bottle with his.

"Sometimes the pleasure is sweeter knowing you shouldn't." Jack grins at me. "Have you been in?" He gestures to where the twins and furry friends play in the shallow water.

"No, I'm afraid if I do, both twins will follow me in too deep and then instead of having a leisurely swim, I'll be in the midst of a near drowning incident, left with the dilemma of which child to save first. Then, of course, I'd be so confused and torn they'd both drown while I was making up my mind, and I'd have to jump off a cliff myself, having been such a terrible mother…"

Jack looks at me quizzically.

"So… no… in answer to your simple question, no, I haven't." I grin at his raised eyebrows and have another swig of beer.

"Have you spoken to many other adults today?" asks Jack, looking like I've just run him over.

"Can you tell? You are the lucky one. Apart from Evan, and that was too early to count, you are the first human over the age of eighteen months today."

He turns his gaze back to the water and nods. I can't help but watch his legs lying in front of him. Their sheer size makes me want to reach out and touch them, but thankfully I keep this exploratory mission as thought not action.

Where Evan is long and lean, Jack is tall and heavily-muscled. Where Evan's body is smooth and angular, Jack is rough and well… hairy. Not in that most awful monkey man sort of a way where you can't look but imagine an awful hairy back, but soft-looking dark hair on his legs and chest, and the beginnings of that beautiful V-line leading down from the shorts.

Again carried away with my own train of thought, I glance at the top of Jack's shorts only to find he is watching me, amused. Blushing, I point to the beach and jump up, pretending I have just seen the most fabulously interesting thing I must show the children *right now*. They are delighted to see me and try to drag me into their mud pie project by the water's edge.

"I think Mom wants to swim. What do you say guys?"

I glance behind and Jack has hands on his hips.

"No, honestly, I'm fine. I'm doing mud pies for tea." I grin, trying to cover my embarrassment at being caught gazing at his crotch! What the hell is wrong with me? It must be hormones.

"No, I think you definitely need a swim." His tone is menacing, and his eyes flash.

The twins clap their hands in glee, and I take a few steps back. "No, I'm really quite all right. I'm not… you know. I think I've actually changed my mind."

He steps toward me, and I put both palms up to him. "I said no. Yes, I definitely said no!" I continue walking backward as he comes toward me with a determined expression.

"There was a yes in that sentence, Billie."

"Yes, I know, but I mean no. *No!*"

"There it is again, definitely a yes." He sprints toward me, grabs me at knee level, throws my squealing form over his right shoulder and sprints into the waves. I'm thrown high in the air and splash deep into the cool water, every nerve ending screaming in shock. The twins run in, squealing with laughter, finding the whole episode a fabulous big game. Soon, we're bouncing around in the water, Jack with Evie, me holding Sunny, and the dogs swimming and woofing their approval.

Joy is unpredictable.

Life twists and turns, and the things that bring us joy change and mutate with our life journey. That a parent is only ever as happy as their unhappiest child surely leaves childless individuals at an unfair advantage. Their happiness still within the realms of self-control. As one of life's minor control freaks, I prefer to keep the fluctuation of my own happiness up to me. However, as a hapless mother, I don't hesitate in saying that those of us with children are the lucky ones.

Parents surrender all control. Control in how life might turn out, which child will do what, get this, hurt that, and so on, and the frustration it brings is overshadowed by the joy that sweeps unexpectedly over a parent at the most unlikely times. A sandy picnic on a smelly tidal beach with two half-naked toddlers in the sun, innocent words chosen by little people trying to be understood, and those small steps to independence and right back to dependence. Warm little bodies finding their way to you at night, milky-sweet breath, and joyous children's laughter guaranteed to warm the coldest of hearts.

In the same way, such joyous experience is a welcome surprise, for every new joy gained, something that used to bring guaranteed joy before suddenly changes, flips, and becomes a source of angst. It reminds me I must live always on tiptoes, ready to jump, and swap direction. Be ready for the next surprise. Change is the only constant.

I remember the days not so long ago before babies when Evan and I lived differently. We found joy in each other and those predictable things we did together: late night meals, long talks into the night, a shared passion for film and art, poetry, and books. We pursued our creative dreams and drove each other to be better. A bottle of cheap wine was on the menu most evenings, and life was a little rosier with booze on board.

All of this changed dramatically after babies. The life we had before is a distant memory; the "us" that came before must be searched for, dragged out and dusted off like an old photograph. In the midst of crying, feeding, and teething, and the grey haze of sleep--deprivation, I remind myself of how we were before. That I will get beyond this tired, frazzled version of myself and give poor Evan a break for not being perfect. Exhaustion leaves me grumpy and oversensitive and I overreact, sick of feeling like I'm doing it all alone.

Tiredness is with me always, making conversation past 9:30 p.m. miraculous. Evan gets frustrated and tries to hide it, but I know. There's no joy in dealing with two demanding toddlers all day on three hours of sleep. My nights are still so broken, and right now, I forget what it felt like to not be exhausted, not to fantasize about a full night's slumber, to wake up refreshed and ready to face the day.

I'm not alone. I know this is a part of motherhood. I have enough friends in St. Cloud who, like me, walk through their days with the baggy-eyed awareness of one only just coping. So no joy comes to me from drinking. The odd beer is a pleasure, but beyond that, I'm happy to have ice cream. Sad, I know. Maybe I'm experiencing symptoms of middle-'agedness'; a preference for chocolate over sex and an addiction to daytime TV. Am I soon to develop bingo wings and a flat bottom?

The thought makes me laugh aloud and Jack turns to me questioningly, missing the joke. "What?"

"I just had a vision of my future self."

"You did? That's funny; I'd have sworn you were snoring just a minute ago."

"I was not asleep! I was relaxing and enjoying the scenic ride home." I lean back further in the passenger seat of Jack's Jeep and pull my cap further down over my eyes.

"With your eyes closed?"

"With my eyes closed."

"Snoring?"

"I was not!" I throw my cap at him and instead of hitting target, it sails out of the window.

"Your aim is terrible," Jack says, pulling over.

The twins and I have hitched a lift home with Jack, Louie, and Bets after our swim. Exhausted from their afternoon in the sun, Evie and Sunny fell straight to sleep as soon as the engine started, and Jack agreed to drive around for a half hour so they could have a decent nap. What a guy. I had fallen asleep too, and my bingo-winged vision was the edge of some random dream I drifted into, but I'm sure there was no snoring. I think.

Jack steps out and detangles the hat from a tree. We're halfway between Settlers' Cove and La Misere. The road is narrow, high up on the island, and framed on both sides by dense bush. The sound of tree frogs is loud and rhythmical as the heat of day recedes. Jack walks around to my side of the Jeep and pushes the cap down on my head.

There is an almost imperceptible pause as his hand touches the back of my neck, then the moment passes so quickly I wonder if I imagined it. The cloudy fantasies of Jack are becoming guiltily well--formed, and the more I push them away, the clearer they present themselves.

I am in love with Evan, I am happy with Evan, and my life is with Evan. What am I thinking?

We drive in silence along the winding road leading back to our street. I close my eyes, this time not asleep, but embarrassed by my own thoughts and confused at their persistence. I'm lonely. Things are different here, and Evan is hardly around. Thoughts of Evan while driving in the dusk with Jack make me feel ashamed and disloyal. I give myself an internal slap, vowing to give Evan my full awake, alert attention tonight.

The Jeep's tires crunch over the gravel driveway as we pull up to the house. Everything is dark, the sun having just set. Jack helps me with the sleeping twins, and I fumble my keys in the lock, opening the front door and tip toeing into the living room with a dozy Evie cradled in my arms. Jack follows closely behind, and we creep to the twins' room where we lay them into their adjacent cots.

Sunny murmurs and snuggles into his favorite blanket. I sigh. They will be awake in a few hours, hungry for missed dinner, and their routine will be up the spout.

The day has been worth it though, and I will enjoy the next few hours of quiet. We creep back to the living room, and I'm about to thank Jack for the afternoon and the ride home when a light springs to life, making us both jump.

"Where the fuck have you been?" Evan sits back in a chair by the window, glass in hand, whisky bottle on the table beside him.

"Jesus, Evan, you scared me. I didn't know you were home yet." I smile warily because there's something in his manner that frightens me.

"I'll bet you fucking didn't." He glares at us, but doesn't stand up. I don't think he can. His eyes glaze, and the room smells of booze.

"Easy, Evan. You're drunk. I'm gonna help you to bed." Jack takes a step toward Evan.

"Get the fuck away from me. That'd be just about right, eh? Take the drunk husband to bed then fuck his wife. That's what you came back here for, eh? To fuck her. I'm not fucking stupid."

I slap my hands to my mouth, speechless at the poisonous words; my knees are shaky as I sink to the floor in front of Evan's chair. "What are you talking about? Stop this." I reach an unsteady hand toward him. "Stop this now. We've been to the beach with the twins… they fell asleep. We drove the long way home."

He shakes his head at me, disgust on his face. "You think I'm a fucking idiot Billie? Are you making me pay? Showing me how it feels?" His words slur, and I begin to cry.

"Stop this, please."

He pushes my hand away and Jack steps in, grabbing him by the arm, forcing him to his feet. "No one thinks you're an idiot, but you're acting like one. You need to lie down."

"Get your fucking hands off me." Evan struggles, then flops into Jacks arms. His eyes flicker, and he vomits violently down Jack's front and down onto the floor. Momentarily paralyzed, I watch, unsure of how to use my limbs to stand up or just fall over.

Jack closes his eyes and sucks in his breath, jaw clenching as he picks up passed out, vomit-covered Evan and carries him in a fireman's lift down the three steps to the den. While I cry on my knees next to the pile of puke, Jack lays Evan on the sofa, removes his vomit-saturated clothes and finds a basin, which he leaves on the floor beside Evan's head.

I manage to stand as he walks back toward me.

"I'm so sorry Jack, he's just drunk. He didn't mean any of that. I don't know what's gotten into him. I… Oh God, look at you." He's covered in vomit. "You should get cleaned up."

He shakes his head and places an arm on my shoulder. "Don't leave him alone tonight. He'll be sick a lot more, and you'll have to be sure he doesn't choke."

"I'm so sorry." I'm repeating myself, but I don't know what else to say. "He won't even remember any of what he's said tomorrow. You shouldn't have had to see that." Shame colors my cheeks.

"How often do you see that?"

"He hasn't been like this for a long time. Something must have happened… I…"

"It's okay." he stares at me. He can see the lie.

"I'm going to go. Will you be okay?"

"Yes, of course, please. I'm fine, I'm sorry… you're covered in vomit."

"Will you stop apologizing? It's almost worse than the drunken Irish rant." He offers a small smile and leaves, Louie and Bets following, tails between their legs, wondering where the fun has gone. I head to the laundry for a mop and bucket, hearing Evan retch downstairs. Taking the whisky bottle, I swig a mouthful for courage, pour the remainder down the sink then check that Evan is still breathing.

I cry and mop sick, then curl in a chair opposite the comatose brewery that is my husband, trying to find a story to make sense of it all. Words to explain, understand, justify, and forgive. Nothing comes but words of anger and self-pity. I stifle a sob then rise slowly to the cries of two hungry, entirely innocent babies who need me.

* * *

Sleep comes slowly; at 4 a.m., I fall into a fitful restless sleep plagued with wild, panic-filled dreams. I hear the Tuis trill good morning as daylight seeps into the room. The air is thick with the toxic smells of alcohol and vomit and I don't want to open my tired eyes and admit that last night was real.

"Billie…" The voice is a hoarse whisper, but I keep my eyes pressed tight shut. "Billie…" A plea, a hand on my leg. "I'm so sorry."

I know that when I look at him, broken and remorseful, I'll want to forgive him. I'll want it all to be better, to move on and put it behind us like we have done so many times before. We will blame it on the booze—he wasn't himself, he didn't know what he was saying—and I'll make excuses for him and tell myself that love was never meant to be easy.

I open my eyes unwillingly. Evan kneels in front of the armchair I'm curled up in, his face crumpled, deflated. I take in the sorry sight, bleary eyes finding focus in the early light.

"Billie, I'm sorry."

I look at him steadily, but can't respond, not trusting myself.

"Christ, what happened? I was driving home… I came back early… I drove past the beach, and you were there with Jack and I was angry." He rubs his head, trying to massage the memory back in or push it away. "I came home and waited, and I don't remember the rest… I don't know, I was angry…"

"You are an asshole." I say the words slowly, deliberately, trying to keep my voice from wavering.

He tries to pull me to him, but I push him away.

"I'm so tired of the drinking. It's too much. I can't deal with this anymore, the drama, I can't do it. You scared the crap out of me and tried to beat up Jack."

He stiffens, the memory rushing back, and sinks onto his heels, both hands on his head. "Fuck." He breathes the word, bringing his hands down to cover his face. "Jesus Billie! What was he doing here anyway?"

"He gave us a lift home from the beach."

"Why were you at the beach with him?" His tone is accusatory.

"We just bumped in to him. He…"

Evan cuts me off. "I came home early because I needed you. I had a shit of a day, and I needed you. I'm your fucking husband, and where are you? You're off with Jack, you and my kids with Jack, frolicking around in the water wearing a fucking bikini! Christ, what am I supposed to think?"

"You are supposed to think, 'Oh, there's my wife at the beach with a friend and our kids, and I trust her!' Or how's this for an alternative thought. 'Maybe I'll go join them, spend some time with my wife and kids.' Maybe, 'I'm home from work early for a change, so let me surprise them and go meet them at the beach.' No, let's just head home in some weird, irrational jealous rage and get wasted!" My anger and upset flows freely.

Evan is stricken. "I thought for a minute… just the way you were with him, Billie. I was watching. I saw you together." He looks confused now, unsure of everything.

"Why is that a big deal?" I ask, knowing that the guilty feeling in my belly should answer my own question. "You don't decide to drink a bottle of damn whisky and start ranting at Zoe when I go out with her."

"Look at me and tell me you don't see the difference." All his anger dissolves and he looks lost. "Are you in love with him?"

He is serious and the words suck the breath from my lungs. I grab him by the shoulders. "What are you talking about? Listen to yourself. How could I be? I love you. Jack is our friend."

He stares at the floor, elbows on his knees, hands in his hair.

"I'm here on my own all day and half the night while you're at work. He's been nothing but kind and supportive since we got here. How can you even ask that?"

The anger resurfaces. "You make it sound like I'm abandoning you! I'm at fucking work. I'm trying to make a living for our family while you play at being Mommy. Don't put it on me!"

"Stop it!" I press my hands against my eyes, hot tears spilling over flushed cheeks. "Get away from me!" I push his hands away and try to stand up.

"Wait, Billie, I didn't mean for this. I'm sorry. You're right. I'm an asshole. I'm a jealous, drunken asshole and I'm sorry." This sudden change of tack throws me and I sob trying to push him away. I need to be out of his range.

"Stop, Billie, please stop. I'm so sorry. I'm a fucking drunk, and I love you, and sometimes I don't know how to do any of this… please… " He kneels in front of me, the weight of the world on his shoulders, and I just can't do it anymore.

I flop backward on to the chair, exhausted and empty. There is a moment, maybe more of desperate silence, quiet that comes from a room of used up emotion, stillness that follows great turmoil.

Raising my chin hesitantly, Evan whispers, "Tell me you still love me." His voice is thick as he moves himself over me, kissing my eyes, my neck, and my hair.

"I love you."

"Say it again."

"I love you."

"Say my name."

"Evan, I love you."

Four words spoken aloud, a reminder of what is real and what's worth fighting for. The touch and taste of him erase the jagged edges of the night before, and I pull him to me, returning each kiss with increasing need, knowing that perfection is a dream and this? This is real.

The night's emotion breaks into soft, regretful daylight. He touches me with shaking hands, his body suffering from the night before. Fumbling fingers waste no time seeking relief, hoping to somehow cleanse, take away the words and the hurt, remind himself he is mine and I am his. He moves inside me, whispering in my ear, words desperate and broken, giving himself to me the only way he knows how.

"Evan." I push him away, hands on his shoulders. I say his name slowly, deliberately, packing the sound with the weight of my love. I watch his face tenderly; his intensity melting to confusion, his sudden weakness fuels my need to take care of him. I'll make him better. I'll be strong for him. I'll be his rock, and we will make it like we always do. It's my turn now, my turn to call the shots, to show him I can be in control. That I can take care of him too.

Pushing him backward to the floor, I move on top of him, taking him away from himself and into me. His eyes are closed as he reaches for me. Hands on hips, then breasts as we move together trying to make things right, till finally he shudders and cries out, pulling me down beside him to the floor where we lie naked and tangled till our babies herald the next chapter of the day.

* * *

Chapter Eighteen

First Flights and Free Fall

"Come on, then, Mrs Skylark. If you're coming, we need to get going."

Opening my eyes groggily I find Evan, bright-eyed, sitting on the edge of the bed, hand on my shoulder. *Get going, get going, where are we going?* My tired brain attempts to puzzle together pieces of the day and decipher what the heck Evan is talking about. The room is dark and the digital clock flashes 4:30 a.m. "Oh my God, this is madness. Did I actually agree to this?"

"You did, and you won't think it's madness once we're there, just wait." He smiles, and his eyes glint with boyish excitement. "Come on, up you get!" He pulls on my arm and yanks the sheets from the bed, leaving me no choice but to comply.

Once up, dressed and bundled into the car, I enjoy the feeling of adventure, being up and off somewhere before the rest of St. Cloud is awake. Just being out of routine is exhilarating.

Sunny and Evie doze in the back, having been transferred in their pajamas from cots to car seats. They rustled and objected at first, but the purr of the car engine sent them back to sleep. So far, this whole adventure malarkey has a thumbs-up, and we haven't even left the carport. "Right, all set, there we are. We're good to go." Evan slides into the driver's seat, pushing a travel mug of hot coffee into my hands. I shake my head, impressed. Double thumbs-up.

Reversing out into the dark street, we travel the winding drive that takes us to the String Road and eventually the opposite side of the island to Tanners Point. The predawn mission was Evan's plan for some family time in his bid to gain some good Dad credits.

Some men might take their kids to the park and follow up some playtime with an ice cream chaser. Not Evan. We are off to see baby birds take flight from the cliff face nests of Tanners Point, a small, isolated rocky cove on the southern bay. It's St. Cloud's only bird sanctuary. Evan comes here alone from time to time to be a bird--watching geek, and before the arrival of the twins, we would come together. Many varieties of birds nest in the crevices of the high, rocky cliff face where the crashing ocean below provides food and the high cliffs ensure safety from predators. Evan tells me that only a few types of birds lay their eggs in the cliffs. He thinks if we're lucky enough, we might see some of the young ones take their first flight.

"Awake?" Evan squeezes my leg, driving on the dark roads with only one hand on the wheel.

I nod, staring up at the moon, its pale glow the only light in the sky. There are still no signs of sun at this early hour.

"Do you remember the first time we went to Tanners' Point together?"

I smile as he recounts memories of our first few weeks in St. Cloud. Everything felt like this—adventure.

"You cried when you saw all the broken eggs smashed down below, and you asked me if the mothers knew they'd lost their babies."

I nod, eyes still focused on the bright overhead moon, remembering clearly how sad I'd felt for the little lives never completed. Tiny beginnings of hearts, feathers, and wings that would never be. I turn to him. "You told me they knew alright, but that birds go with the flow of life and death, unlike people, who mourn and hold on and try to control all of it, when everything is as fragile and impermanent as the little blue egg, smashed on the rock." I recite his response verbatim, word for word, exactly as he told me then as we sat side by side looking out at those birds and their young and the remnants of those that didn't make it.

I remembered his words because they stayed with me, and sometimes in the chaos of life and my desperate attempts to control it, I think of that little blue egg and hold onto his words.

"You remember." I feel his eyes on me in the dark, and I smile, nodding, watching the road wind through the trees and thick bush that surrounds the road on all sides. The moonlight is obscured for a time, leaving only the light from our headlights, the darkness softened with shared memory and togetherness.

Color seeps into the day, fingers prying over the horizon, golden tipped and radiant. St. Cloud is transformed and we descend through the cooler morning air to the gravel road leading to Tanners' Point. Evan parks the car in the last roadside bay and we each carry a dozy baby down the steep, treeless pathway to a grassy bank. It looks across the cove and over the squawking, calling community of waking birds.

Rugged rock, pitted with holes and crevices, forms a large semicircle, its contours shaped by the constant waves from the ocean. Tanners' Point ends where the land reaches the furthest edge toward the sea. The point is the far corner of the cove curving behind us. There is no beach below, no rock or shingle to walk on. The drop is sheer and leads only to white-capped waves crashing against the rock. Long mermaid tails of seaweed sweep back and forth with the waves, constantly shaping and changing the edges of the island. Birds soar and cry out, swooping downward to dive into the waves, then returning back to nest, feed their young and rest a while. The spectacle is a wild show of flight and noise, and from our vantage point, I feel almost afraid—the outsider, the intruder in the tight community that lives, breeds and flies here undisturbed by humans.

Evan grabs my elbow. "Right there Billie, look!" He points to the rocks. Amongst the crowds, a black and white bird swoops and soars, resting for a time in the rock before taking flight again.

"What am I looking at, exactly?" I'm amazed Evan is able to differentiate the birds when there are so many.

"There." He points again to the black and white bird. "It's a Murre. I've never seen one here before. I didn't think they came this far south. Keep watching him. If there's a young one in the nest, we might get to see him fly."

Evan's eyes lock on the bird, and Evie, who is snuggled in his arms, rustles at the excitement.

"A Murre." I say the name aloud, watching the bird. Beautiful, I think, but not necessarily any more so than any of the others soaring overhead.

"They're not common here. In fact, I'd bet not many people would have seen one here before." Evan carries on excitedly as Evie wriggles, unhappy at being held tightly now she realizes she's outdoors and there's fun to be had.

"So tell me about them. What am I looking at?" I want to soak up his enthusiasm.

"Well, they always lay their eggs in the rock face, never the sand or trees, and they never build nests. And here's the thing. Their eggs are specifically designed to survive on a ledge. You see, more so than any other bird's egg, the egg of the Murre is really pointed at one end and rounded at the other, so that if it's disturbed, it won't roll off into the sea. It rolls around in a circle!" He has an incredulous grin. "Isn't that amazing?"

"It is." I'm intrigued, but also distracted by Evie, who has gotten out of Evan's arms and wobbles on sleepy little legs over to me to prod Sunny. I grab her hand, conscious of our child-unfriendly location.

"Look at the birds Evie." I point behind her matted curls, bedraggled from sleep, to the cove where the birds circle noisily overhead. She turns, momentarily distracted.

"Bidies." Her little hand extends, reaching out in their direction. Her face changes to mirror Evan's, and for a second, the likeness is astonishing. "Bidies." She repeats the word again and again, smiling at Evan, proud of herself, knowing she is clever.

"That's right kiddo, birdie." Evan points with her, scooping her onto his lap. "Let's look for the baby birdies. Can you see any?"

Evie frowns and looks intently, keen to please. Sunny, awake now, hears her voice and joins in the chorus of "Bidie, Mommy, bidie," clapping his hands together.

Evan's eyes are still on the flight of the Murre and the entrance to its rocky nest. "That's it, I fucking knew it! Look!"

"Evan!" I can't believe he has sworn in front of the twins and nudge him hard in the ribs.

"Christ, Billie, get off." He glares at me, oblivious to Sunny, who tries to get his tongue around the unfamiliar word. With his lisp, the word sounds more like "thucking."

I roll my eyes and shake my head as Evan points to the Murre's nest. "There it is. It's a young Murre." He glances at me to check if I'm displaying the same ecstatic expression as him; of course I'm not, and he looks exasperated. "A young Murre will dive from the nest at twenty days old knowing it can't fly."

"But, why?" I'm vexed for the poor Murre, who might soon be splattered on the rocks. "If it can't fly, why does it jump?"

Evan doesn't look at me when he answers. "Because it has to."

The adult Murre returns to the nest, and seconds later, in perfect synchrony, the adult and the young Murre dive from their home in the rock. As though privy to our discussion and keen to contribute, they glide together gracefully, harnessing the wind and warm air. They descend toward the ocean in a dance of sorts, gliding and soaring to the waves.

I hold a hand to my chest, afraid for the smaller bird, but it glides peacefully, the watchful parent at its side until the moment they reach the ocean and disappear beneath the waves.

"Where did it go?" Both birds are gone. Above, the circling mass of wings in flight cry out.

"Just below the surface." Evan smiles. "They'll find some breakfast, then head to shore."

"And the baby?"

"It'll survive on the lower rocks and in the water now until its wings can fly. That was its first taste of flight, although it was only really gliding. Now that wee bird knows flight and before long, it'll learn how to do it properly."

"So, it's on its own now?" Twenty days old, unable to fly and set out into the world seems a little early to me. Evan looks thoughtful, and Evie squirms, desperate to get closer to the "bidies."

"Mother nature's pretty tough."

Sunny suddenly wriggles free and starts running and Evie makes to follow before I have time to reply. Evan jumps up. "Hold on to him, for fucks sake, Billie, or he'll be off the side."

I have already scooped Sunny up, and I'm stomping back to where Evan holds too tightly on to a crying Evie.

"Yes, I know. Thanks for the helpful comment, and could you please stop swearing?"

He glares at me as I sit back down. Evie howls for me, and Evan can't make her stop. He stands, shoves her down on my lap beside Sunny and walks away, muttering under his breath.

"Where are you going?"

"Away." He strides down the steep path winding precariously around the cliff. Away. Away from the noise, away from the twins, away from me.

The morning turns on its head, the mood shifts in seconds with no warning, and I watch him retreat out of sight without a backward glance. Even the call of the birds seems angry and frustrated. They shout at me in my inadequacy, and I want to run after him and fight it out. I want to yell and tell him things don't always work out like he wants them to. Things aren't always perfect, and it won't ever be like it used to be before when it was just the two of us. I want to shake him and tell him to take example from his fucking birds and go with the flow, but I don't.

The twins scream. I focus on calming them down and distracting them till Evan returns, shamefaced and sorry.

An hour later, the rain begins, and Evie and Sunny are hungry and bored. We had walked in from the cove and settled on a small grassy flat near the car where I could let them run around safely. We had played tag, told stories, and sung nursery rhymes and still no Evan. Now the grey clouds splatter heavy raindrops all around and I begin to worry. Where is he, and why hasn't he come back?

At first, the rain is entertaining, and the twins run around, wet and giggling. Evan has the keys to the car, so there's no shelter. I am beyond mad, then amidst my anger is worry growing bigger by the minute. I make a small tent over the twins' heads with my jacket and we wait under the shelter of a gum tree. When I see his slumped form in the distance, head down, hands in pockets, I want to kill him. Now that I know he's safe and hasn't been washed out to sea, I want to thump his goddamned thick Irish head for leaving us. It's been two and a half hours, and the twins are howling. I'm ready to do the same myself. I can't run up to him and give him the slap he so deserves because I hold two screaming babies, and so I wait for him, watching him approach, trying to imagine how the hell he will explain himself.

"Pretty much as I left it then?" He shrugs and pulls the car keys from his pocket.

Incredulous at this total lack of apology or explanation, I wonder if I misheard him. "What did you just say?"

"I said, pretty much as I left it then. You pissed off, the kids screaming. I'm really glad we came."

I'm so mad I could spit. He makes to take howling Evie from my arms. "Get your hands off her. Don't touch them and don't touch me. I don't want to look at you right now." I struggle to my feet, legs cold and stiff from sitting on the ground, twins in my arms.

"Have it your way." He shrugs, gets in the car and starts the ignition.

Angry tears course down my cheeks as I fasten Sunny, then Evie into their seats and pry a sandwich into their little hands, their lunchboxes still full. We drive home in silence, Evan scowling, me too angry to trust myself to speak in front of the twins.

Fifteen minutes into the drive, they are fast asleep and I feel marginally calmer than before.

"Where the hell were you?"

Evan drives carefully, eyes on the road, determined not to look at me. "Walking."

"That's your answer? You were walking?" I raise my hands incredulously. "Well, I hope you had a nice fucking walk, Evan. I hope you had a real good time, some peace and tranquility, just you and the birds. By the way, great family outing, let's do it again sometime." I slam my arms across my chest and glare out the passenger side window. He doesn't answer or look at me, and we drive home in angry silence.

Much later that night, when the day has drawn its last few breaths, I head to the peace of bed, thankful the dreadful day is finally at a close. I spent the remainder of the afternoon in the garden with the twins, playing with Louie and Bets, finding solace in ripping weeds up by their sorry roots. I didn't see Evan and didn't care to. I was still too mad and could hear him banging away in his studio. I made supper, but he didn't show. I ate alone on the deck, and then went to bed where the cool sheets and soft pillows are reliably predictable. I leave the blinds open to watch the blackness of night and twinkling appearance of stars. This is my favorite way to fall asleep, watching the world sleep too.

As my heavy head leaves the day, dragging my mopey heart along, I think I hear the door creak and hope it might be a dream. The creak persists becoming gradually louder, then softer, the very real sound of our bedroom door opening and closing. Damn, I can't face any more drama today. I want sleep to wash over us both, then maybe tomorrow we'll talk rationally about the day that escalated from nothing to something for reasons I don't understand.

I feel Evan edge into bed, and for a moment, all is quiet. He keeps his distance, doesn't touch or move in toward me. Then a hand strokes my hair and a voice whispers so quietly I barely hear the words. "I'm sorry." I don't respond. I can't bear to talk, to drag it out, to have him explain why and how, to justify and apologize. I lie still, listening, feeling his hand stroke my hair tenderly, whispering his apology, believing I'm asleep. "I'm sorry, Billie… I'm so sorry."

I should open my eyes, tell him it's okay, that I forgive him, and it's not a big deal. I should kiss him on his sorry face and let him make love to me, and in the morning, we'd wake and it would all be gone. But tonight, I don't do any of that, because inside, I don't forgive him. I'm angry and hurt, confused and upset, and I want him to feel sorry a bit longer. I want him to feel sorry that he let us down, sorry that he left us there, and sorry for making me feel that we make his life harder rather than better. This thought sticks and remains planted hours after Evan is asleep and the moon is high in the sky once more.

Finally at three, I make a decision to let it all go, to surrender to the flow Evan so admires, but can't ever catch himself. Tomorrow,

I'll forgive him, and we will start again like we always do. Turning on my side, I watch him sleeping; life can be so very complicated. With this thought, I lean in, kiss his forehead then curl in to his open arms where I finally fall asleep.

* * *

"Don't forget, people, it's the midwinter carnival this Friday. Get down there and get ready to party. It's the best night of the year here in paradise. Tomorrow's best tide for surf will be 4 p.m. so shake off your work clothes and get to the beach. Jed's special at Beau Jangles will be dark Sumatra blend, bottomless cup if you're there before ten. Last notice for the day: Mrs Moody's cat is still on the run. She's a tabby and answers to the name Mildred. Mrs Moody is offering a reward of a crate of Mr Moody's homebrew for anyone who finds her."

Dan stops for breath. "Okay, folks, it's late and time for me to wind right down and sign off for the night. In tribute to a good Irish friend of mine, I'll leave you listening to the mournful sounds of Damien Rice." The track starts slowly, a quiet piano melody graduating into loud acoustic guitar and a sad, then angry Irish male voice. Perfect tribute to Evan I think. Dan is fond of playing music for people he knows on his weeknight show, and although he never names any names, we usually know exactly who a given track is dedicated to. He's gotten on the wrong side of quiet a few islanders with his choice of songs and dedications. But they are mostly fitting and taken in good humor.

St. Cloud is dark and all is quiet in our little house. From my seat at the computer, I can see Jack's kitchen light burning in the heavy darkness that surrounds our homes. Lights from windows dot the night's blackness here and there. Up on the hill, Zoe and Felix will be collapsed on the sofa eating takeaway curry, watching a DVD with subtitles, their energetic boys finally asleep.

Further away in town, Jed will be heading home after preparing Beau Jangles for a busy Saturday ahead. I know he stays late every night after the cleaning and cashing up is done. He will devise the specials menu and prime his darling espresso machine. I hope Sadie is waiting for him when he gets home. They have been together for almost a year, and the relationship has changed Jed in a good way.

Sadie is Canadian and was taking a year out to travel. She stopped in St. Cloud for a few weeks, weeks that turned into months when she unexpectedly fell in love with the guy that served her coffee every day. Jed is happier since meeting Sadie. Before, his identity was so tied to the business; it was a mission for anyone to drag him out socially. He seemed uncomfortable with a life that existed beyond the safe walls of Beau Jangles. In the café, he knows who he is. He runs the show, and the days have a predictable pattern. Life on the outside can seem a little more complicated. Since Sadie, he seems to have happily merged both lives. With Jed in love, Beau Jangles is an even happier place to be. As the face of the café, a gloomy Jed means gloomy locals and worse still, potentially gloomy coffee—we need to keep the guy happy!

Dan will be strolling through town, hands deep in pockets, heading to his own bachelor pad where he'll listen to jazz, pour a glass of red wine, and check his e-mail (he's in a long-distance relationship with a man called Ambrose, who lives in Tasmania). Dan's sexuality is common knowledge to all, even though he rarely discusses it, and I'm sure there are many women who still can't believe he's not heterosexual. It's small community living; people don't tend to believe what they haven't seen with their own eyes. No one in St. Cloud has ever known him to be in a relationship, but I think Dan is merely discreet. Rightly so, being a GP and a DJ means everyone knows him, and he has to work hard to keep some things private.

Virginia's house is three along from ours and is slightly elevated, her upstairs windows visible through the tea trees. Soft light from within catches the shadows. I wonder if she ever winds down; I wonder if they ever wind down. Her husband, Mike, is a workaholic, and Virginia is one of the busiest people I know. I can't imagine her ever lying back on the sofa with a book and a glass of wine or lounging in a bubble bath. I wonder if conversations in their house are ever around anything other than work. Time together must be so limited. Would there ever be room for talk that isn't critical to family business functioning? I am judging, and the critical thoughts are a bitter pill. It's easy to think the worst of another and their relationship woes when you're submerged in your own.

Evan is in the back bedroom working on his models, cool and untalkative. His moods still fluctuate unpredictably, and most nights, I'm anxious at which husband will arrive home from work. Will it be happy, excitable Evan or quiet, sullen Evan? A consistent somewhere--in-between would be so damn good.

Of course, the moods are not new. The darkness was always apparent, an undercurrent that from the very start came with the territory, understood and accepted. Evan has always been intense. Fiery and creative, funny and spontaneous. The flip side of these characteristics, evident now after almost three years of marriage and the loss of my rosy-tinted lust spectacles, is the ever-present tension arising from living with unpredictability. Darkness or anger can come so unexpectedly, filling the room, its dark cloud leaving a trace on everything.

I become a voyeur of my own drama, watching helplessly as I do what I've always done—blame myself. What did I do? What did I say? How can I make it better? When you do this for long enough, you become a sort of chameleon for the moods of your lover. He changes, I change. He's happy, I'm happy. He's sad, I'm sad too. I try to take a step back and listen to the advice of my rational head which tells me

300 | *Skylark*

that I'm good and reliable, that I can't always be to blame. I'm not responsible, but I find myself constantly at odds with the guilty voice that nags me to make it better.

I am on chapter nine of my second novel, and my progress is slow but steady. Evan is busy with work on the project for the airport so once the twins are asleep, I have most evenings to myself. Even an hour of uninterrupted writing makes me feel that I'm moving forward. Right now, the quality of my prose may be questionable. I have reread nothing. I just know I need to sit down each night when possible and write—get the words down and edit later. Jack tells me I'm probably more productive in my childfree hour than most writers would be in a work day. My words build up, desperate for their time to be delivered to a page. I like to think this is true; I can't waste a second when my time is my own, and so I have to trust that whatever comes out has a purpose in the final drafting of my book.

In the world of my novel and its characters and places, I am God. I plan and conspire our heroes' destinies. I get to say who lives and dies, who loves and loses love, where the story begins and ends, and this control, so lacking in my own life, gives me a heady rush of adrenaline.

A loud banging sounds from the back bedroom, followed by The White Stripes turned louder, then louder again. The spare bedroom at the back of our house has become a sort of workshop/studio for Evan, who retreats there regularly to paint or build. His fascination with flight is obsessive like Frank Senior, the Daddy he doesn't like to talk about. He builds models, tinkering like a little boy, suspending each finished work of art from the ceiling. All sizes of flying crafts, some resembling birds more than planes and others the reverse. The skeleton structures are finely planed pieces of native wood, tea tree and kauri. Dead branches saved and resurrected from our garden. Shimmering wings of paper so fine the light shines through making it almost impossible to see where the wing starts and ends. The structures are so delicate and beautiful, I feel sad that somehow this cannot be Evan's means of making a living. Like most artists, he merges uncomfortably into nine-to-five life in a career that's not art exactly, maybe close, but pays the bills.

Evan is lucky; he loves his job. He's passionate about architecture and design, and he looks at buildings in the same way others look at fine art. He takes in the angles and lines, the contours, and impact on surroundings. He views towns and cities differently than most, seeing a city as a whole rather than segments, districts, streets, and structures. When he designs, he works to include the new structure into the body of the city. A building compatible with the whole, either complimentary to existing beauty or a focal point, standing alone, enhancing its surroundings but bringing a new level of beauty and style to a community. He relishes his work and the ability to change an environment for the better with the creation of structure. It may not be flight, but it is art for Evan, and he works with passion on every project he leads.

Designing an international airport on an island that until now has been fairly isolated and remote is a mammoth task. Not only because of the structural challenges, but that the essence of the structure must work in harmony with the landscape. This, combined with the charged political atmosphere surrounding the project, sees Evan working all hours, trying to keep everyone happy. Not everyone *is* happy about the idea of St. Cloud being a tourist destination, and there have been many local debates, petitions, and protests around the topic. As yet, the plans are not confirmed; the government's aim is to pay half of the total cost of construction, they are applying for capital to fund the remaining half. Without funding, our island cannot afford the airport. Many say without an international airport, St. Cloud can't develop and grow.

Evan has much on his shoulders. His heart is in this small community, his friends are the communities' life blood, and many of them oppose change, tourists, and new commercial enterprise. But the design is the biggest project he has led, and he's passionate about seeing it to completion. There's pressure on him from his company, and although he hasn't talked about it, I know the stress is difficult. Hence, hiding in the back bedroom and the larger-than-usual consumption of local beer.

The banging continues, and now the music has changed to Johnny Cash. Never a good sign. I have just about had enough, and I'm about to tell him to keep it down when another sound takes my attention—a scream from the twins' room. One short, piercing scream followed by sobbing.

Funny how there exists a language in a baby's cry, one you recognize quickly without translation. Some cries are hungry, bored, or tired. Some are wet diaper or upset tummy… But the others, the other cries that come less frequently, the cries that make you drop what you are doing, that tell you in that language you have learned: "I need you. Please help me. Something terrible is wrong." These are the cries you dread.

I run to the twin's room and find Sunny on the floor howling. The side of his cot is down, and he has tumbled to the floor. A large gash is above his right eye and blood flows freely down his face, pooling on the floor. Despite my first reaction to scream in horror, I stifle the sound in a large intake of breath as I bend down to scoop up the hysterical little body. The fall had not been high, but his head must have hit the corner of the dresser and the gash is deep and gaping. I hold him to me, trying to calm him down, and press my palm against the cut to stem the blood flow.

How the hell did the cot rail come undone? They are fixed and locked into position every night. My mind races through the different ways this neglect of our babies' safekeeping has happened while I cradle Sunny and hurry to the bathroom for a damp flannel. Could Sunny have undone the catch? Then I remember. Evan.

Evan had insisted on tucking the twins in. He'd been home early tonight, a rare occasion. It was a treat for Sunny and Evie to have Daddy read them a story and tuck them in to their little cots. It's not fair to blame, I tell myself. There is no time for this, but as I hold the damp flannel to Sunny's head speaking soothingly to him, I remember that Evan had been drinking before he came home… I could smell it, and I chose to ignore it… and this is the result.

In moments, Evie is howling from her cot, but Evan hears nothing, absorbed in his models and music. "Evan!" I scream. Nothing but the dulcet tones of Johnny Cash in reply. "Evan!" Louder this time, still nothing. Carrying a squirming, screaming Sunny, I barge into the bedroom where Evan has his back to me. A spotlight shines down on his worktable, a pile of fragmented wings and wood pieces at his fingertips.

"Jesus Billie! What's going on?" He sounds annoyed until he sees the blood oozing through the flannel I hold to Sunny's head. Evan is on his feet and across the room, his expression foggy, eyes struggling to focus. "What happened?"

"You didn't lock the cot gate!" It's wrong of me to throw the blame at him, but I'm scared and angry. The strong smell of spirits hangs in the air and a half-empty bottle of Jack Daniel's sits on the shelf.

"What? No! I must have done!" He is emphatic.

"You didn't. He fell out and hit his head on the dresser."

Evan's face is white. "Oh Sunny, wee man, come here." He tries to lift him from me, but Sunny howls louder and Evan shrinks back.

"We need to get him to A&E. It needs stitching."

"Right, of course." Evan runs a hand through his hair, eyes still glazed and unfocused. Sunny is becoming limp in my arms and this is worse than the screaming and thrashing. His little eyes flicker as though struggling to stay open. I try to stay calm, pressing my lips to his cheek. "It's okay baby, we're going fix it. Mommy and Daddy will fix it. It will be okay. Evan, get Evie. We'll just have to bundle them both in the car. You drive, and I'll hold him and keep pressure on his head."

Evan takes a breath and rubs a hand over his face as though trying to wipe something away—disbelief maybe? The feeling that all this is perhaps a dream? I have the same feeling. That things can turn around so quickly with children is terrifying, the knowledge that in a moment life can change from quietly predictable to life-threateningly dramatic. This is our first real accident with either of the twins; so far, we have been lucky to have experienced only the usual coughs, colds, and occasional viruses. Itchy spots, teething, and high temperatures I can deal with. Head gashes and concussions are new and frightening territory.

Evan goes to step around me and stumbles. He swears and rights himself, struggling to find his balance.

"You're drunk!" I throw the words at him.

"I'm fine." He moves to get Evie, steadying himself on the doorframe.

"Jesus." I breathe the word, a cuss and prayer together if that's possible. I follow him, holding Sunny tightly to me, still pressing on the head wound to contain the bleeding. "Leave her!"

"What?" He looks around carefully, trying to appear sober.

"I said leave her. You can't drive. Evan, you're drunk!"

"I'm fine," he says, trying to sound forceful, but the words slur.

"You asshole, I need you, and you're fucking drunk!" I am beyond angry now, angry with him, angry with me, angry and afraid.

"Billie..."

"Shut up!" I yell and grab the telephone, calling Jack's number.

Ten minutes later we're speeding through the dark and twisty roads of St. Cloud to reach the city's only hospital. Evie sleeps peacefully in the back; I sit beside her, cradling Sunny, keeping pressure to his head. We are silent, and the journey feels like hours, although it's barely fifteen minutes.

I had brought Evie rather than leave her with Evan, who was as good as useless. He had protested, gotten angry, and as I left with Jack for the hospital, he watched us all go… leaning against the gate, swearing and shouting, unable to stand up without its support. What will he be doing now? Worry jumps into the mix, pushing anger momentarily to the wings. I imagine Evan's guilt. He has such limited coping mechanisms; none of this will be dealt with easily. Anger bubbles up and over my worries for Evan as Sunny whimpers in my lap. I close my eyes and kiss his moist head. Sunny is my priority; Evan can wait. By now, he will be passed out and won't wake up till I arrive home and even then, his memory will be selective.

Despite the season, the air is warm and heavy, the smell is of night—a rich, oppressive scent that hangs around us as I climb from Jack's truck cradling Sunny to my chest. The hospital is inland and without the cooling breeze from the ocean, the night feels as warm as day.

"Go, get him inside. I'll meet you." Jack has taken full control since I called him at midnight. He didn't ask questions or react in any way to Evan's aggression as we left for the hospital, and I'm beyond relieved that someone is here with me; that I can rely on someone.

Sunny is admitted quickly, and we're ushered through triage to an emergency room where they clean and stitch his wound, and then admit him for the night, fearing he is concussed. Weak with relief that he will be okay, I sink into the chair beside his little bed and cry openly, not caring who might see or hear. Sunny lies fast asleep, stitched and bandaged, we will wake him every hour due to the risk of concussion.

"How is he?" Jack's takes up the doorframe and I smile at him through my tears.

"He's going to be fine," I sniff. "Ten stitches and a suspected concussion."

"Well, that scar will be a lady-killer when he's older." Jack walks in and looks down at Sunny's peaceful form. "Lucky it wasn't his eye."

"I know. Where's Evie?" I'm experiencing that strange phenomenon where after something unexpectedly bad happens, you believe anything is possible and expect the worst in every situation.

"Come here." Jack motions for me to come to the door. I follow him warily, not wanting to be too far away from Sunny. A hospital baby cot is in the corridor, sides fully secured, and inside, fast asleep, thumb in mouth is curly-haired Evie, oblivious to the drama around her.

I smile and blow my nose. "Thank you, Jack. I'm so sorry."

"Why are you sorry?"

"It's two in the morning and rather than asleep in bed, you're here with me. I'm sorry I had to call you."

He shakes his head. "Don't be. You did the right thing."

"I didn't know what else to do. Evan… well, he couldn't drive, and I didn't want to leave Evie and…"

"It's okay."

I start to sob again, and Jack holds me against him, his arms tight and comforting, and I cry until I'm all cried out. And after the crying and holding, I feel tired beyond belief. We wheel Evie's cot into Sunny's room, and I lie down beside the sleeping, bandaged baby.

"I'll check on Evan and tell him everything's okay," says Jack. "Get some rest if you can." I nod and give him a watery smile before slipping into a broken sleep haunted by blood, dead babies, and Jack Daniel's.

* * *

There is a hard bang at the front door, and Evan jolts awake, disoriented, his head pounding, and his heart heavy. What happened? He's on the floor, stomach down, left cheek imprinted with the groove of the floorboards. The jump to his feet almost makes him lose the contents of his fragile stomach. He opens the door to Jack, hands deep in pockets, head down, face dark and angry. What happened? His head begins racing through broken events… dream or reality? Nothing is clear. Billie, where is she? What the hell happened? Shards of memory stab him and words ring in his ears: "You're drunk, Evan… you did this."

"Jack," says Evan.

"They're all spending the night in hospital. Sunny's okay, some stitches and a concussion. Billie and Evie are there with him."

The words bring a rush of broken memories and Evan lowers his head, a hand covering his eyes. "Oh, Jesus. I'm a fucking idiot. I'm sorry."

"Don't apologize to me, I didn't help you. I helped Billie and the kids."

"Right." Evan looks up at Jack, taking in his dark expression. His words are unflinching, but there's something else in his eyes—an understanding, an empathy. Evan's artist's eye sees things others sometimes miss. Jack somehow understands the dark pit he is sinking into. "I love her, you know, I just… I love the kids more than anything. I'm just…"

"You're just what?"

"I'm a fucking mess."

Jack nods. "Do you even know how lucky you are? She loves you. She'd do anything to make you happy. You need to sort your shit out, or you'll lose her."

Evan hangs his head and exhales a shaky breath.

"Get yourself dressed and go see them. It's 6 a.m. By the time you get there, it'll be 7, and they'll let you in." It's an order.

Not long ago, being told what to do by Jack, a man so obviously in love with his wife, would have sent Evan into a rage. He'd have told Jack what to do with his fucking advice; he might even have swung for him, but not today. Crushed and hung over, Evan feels like half a man; he left his wife and kids to be taken care of by another because he was too damn drunk to function. What does that make him? Just like his useless father. Just like his drunken brothers.

Jack leaves, hands deep in his pockets, shaking his head.

* * *

Chapter Nineteen

Chaos & Coffee

There are things you think you'll never accept, behaviors you're sure you'll never put up with, standing on the threshold of independent singledom, weighing up the attributes of the perfect partner. Then, one day you've found him, and it's all so great you let a few key "no-no's" slip through, believing the rest of the package to be so goddamned great you'll compromise. There's also that self-assured belief that somehow you'll manage to change all the bits that don't work for you; that somehow you can mold almost perfect to perfect.

The flip side is that the small things—minor annoyances at first—grow and mutate more regularly than shrink and die. In my experience, those things you thought you could change or accept become bigger and overwhelmingly pushy. Their presence in the more mature relationship becomes settled as the shiny veneers of best behavior become tarnished with time.

So I become more controlling, anxious, and busier while Evan gets distant and unpredictable. Seeds of dysfunction grow steadily, pushing against the confines of the small world we have created around ourselves. As Evan pulls away from me, I mirror the withdrawal, reacting in frustration and anxious worry, busying myself with the details of life with small children and praying that if I leave him be, he'll come back to me. We carry on, circling around each other, coming together and pulling apart. There's a voice whispering, "Stand still, be his rock. Let him come and go." I hear the words, but I'm incapable of complying, so tied am I to him. He moves, I move, this way or that, a magnetic force that joins and determines my position relative to him..

And so as life's minutiae distracts and obscures, our vision of what stands before us and the direction we're headed becomes hazy and unclear.

* * *

Grocery shopping with twins is as close to total insanity as it gets. To even attempt such a feat, one has to be either completely mad or absolutely desperate.

In my case, it's desperate. I can do without most things, but when there's no coffee for a morning fix, the situation is critical. Without coffee, I'm useless.

The morning started badly when Evie woke up at five-thirty with Evan as he left for work. She decided that if Daddy got to go play, she should be able to do the same; thus, we were all awake shortly after. Evan left with an apologetic grin. I know it makes him happy to have the twins awake with him for half an hour before he leaves for work. With the long hours and late evenings at work, he gets little solo time with them.

Days pass when he doesn't see them at all. He's only home when they are asleep, and I worry it's not enough for them. They need their Daddy and he needs them. Evan assures me that the long hours will ease off once the airport project is done. I must admit, at this point I couldn't care less about St. Cloud's damn airport. I just want Evan back.

It had been an early start, but not an unpleasant one. Everyone was happy, and that is a gold star beginning to my day. Things would have continued on in that happy vein if when I opened the cupboard to get the coffee beans, there had been some! The morning was a little harder for me than usual without the assistance of caffeine, so here I am at the store with two energetic twenty-one-month-old babies who are not keen to sit strapped in a trolley. But believe me, to let them walk would be beyond disastrous.

"Okay, I can do this. You hear me, you two? We're going to manage, and afterward, we'll go to Beau Jangles for a juice." Sunny claps his hands together, and Evie stares out the window, picking her nose. Rallying my nerves of steel, I fetch a two-baby trolley and secure Sunny in with a seatbelt and a kiss on his nose then scoop up Evie, who isn't as eager to comply. After a minor battle in which I only just emerge victorious, both twins are safely secured, and we enter the store. I allow myself to breathe. This might be okay.

Knowing that stopping for too long at any given display or shelf will probably spell trouble, I do my best to grab the required items while on the move. This is easier said than done, especially in the fruit and veggies aisle. All the colors and shapes seem to excite the twins. It's an edible jungle gym! They reach out to grab anything within grasp, and before I know it, we have several oranges, a kumquat, three oddly-shaped courgettes, and some random parsnips in the trolley that had been empty moments before.

Frowning, I retrace my steps to return the goods to their rightful homes, but realize I'm headed for trouble as the twins get squirmy, desperate to grab some bananas and a red onion or two. Screw it, we'll keep the veggies. I twirl the trolley around and push on, grabbing food on the go: porridge oats, yogurt, raisins, muesli bars, flour, sugar, honey, bread, on and on. I zip through the aisles, grabbing at a jog as the twins giggle with glee at the flying trolley ride.

Just as I am about to preen my Mommy feathers and congratulate myself on a successful mission, Evie yells, "Momma, pee. Evie pee!"

Right. Quick turnaround. Are there any bathrooms in the grocery store? Of course not! Dang. Evie and Sunny have been out of nappies during the day for a few weeks now and have been doing so well. I ought to be congratulating Evie for telling Mommy she needs to go pee, but bypass that moment of positive parenting in my frustration that she needs to go right here in the supermarket, where of course there are no toilets.

Only one thing for it. I take both twins from their seats and with one on each hip, leave my trolley mid-aisle and race for the doors before there's an unfortunate accident on the floor. "Almost there Evie. Hang on, sweetie, hold it in."

She does, but Sunny doesn't! Having forgotten to mention that he needed to go, he smiles with a relaxed look on his face, and I realize we are leaving a wet trail down the tinned goods aisle. My blood pressure rises as I make a snap decision on whether to tell an employee there is wee on the floor lest an old dear slide and break a hip or race outside to find a bush and let Evie relieve herself before the puddle is double the size.

"Crap!" I carry on running. I'll have to hope no one steps in the offending wee before I can get back in and offer to clean it up.

"Cwap," says Sunny as we pass a few confused customers, wondering what has happened inside that I am racing panic stricken out of the 'entry only' doors with a baby under each arm.

There are several accommodating bushes at the back of the parking lot, and I set Sunny down, gently telling him to stand still with one hand on Mommy. I pull Evie's pants down and hold her while she wees. It's all terribly undignified, but we're beyond caring. Mid-wee, Sunny decides he's had enough and, spotting a brightly-colored bird on another bush, runs from my side.

Ruthie Morgan

Thankfully, the run of a toddler isn't too hard to keep up with. However, I'm holding Evie and her little bare bottom mid-wee. As I turn to chase him, she continues to wee, and now it's down my leg and all over her pants. I lunge for Sunny and grab him, securing his wriggling form under my arm again. Poor Evie howls, her pants still round her ankles and her bottom in the air. Raising my eyes to the heavens, I count to ten, but only get to two. Abandoning the store for now, I get the twins into our car where I clean them up, change their clothes and wipe myself down.

"Okay, let's try that again." "Cwap!" shouts Sunny, clapping his hands as we re-enter the supermarket and meet the stern gaze of the duty supervisor. I suddenly remember the trail of pee we left on the floor. Mortified, I try to apologize, but I think it's too late; some poor staff member has mopped it up and a yellow 'Wet Floor' sign bears witness to my bad mothering.

As quickly as humanly possible, I find my abandoned trolley, replace the twins in their seats, grab three bags of coffee beans, and head for the checkout. Of course there's a line, and only one operator on duty.

I take a deep breath and do my best job at distracting Sunny and Evie from the display of confectionary conveniently lining the checkout queue. Progress could be slower, but only if the checkout operator keels over and karks it. And believe me, she looks as though it's entirely possible. Her name badge says Eileen, and as she scans each item, she examines it and discusses it with the purchaser, then follows all this with lengthy gossip about the customer's well-being, aches and pains, family dramas and the like.

My feet are twitchy. I just want to get out alive. The twins are about to spot the Chupa Chups, and then I'll really be in trouble.

Too late. A few minutes later, Evie's arms are outstretched toward the colorful display of lollies, and she yells like the world might end if she can't have one. Sunny looks bemused, but soon figures with all the attention she's getting she must be on to something and joins in. Withering stares are coming at me from all angles and there's still another person in front of me. I've come so close. What the hell!

I grab two fucking Chupa Chups from the display and unwrap them for my howling, spoiled brats. Of course, they're not spoiled, but that's how it looks and I know it. And have you ever tried unwrapping a Chupa Chup under duress? It's like the Krypton Factor for stressed parents. I wonder if there's a hidden camera and a stopwatch, the audience breathless as I fumble with the tricky wrapping and the children wail. Can she do it before it all turns to shit?

Finally, it's my turn, and Eileen looks at me and wrinkles her already wrinkly nose. Instead of talking to me, she does that thing where people will say what they want to say to the adult by talking in saccharine voices to the kids. "Oh my, aren't you two sweet little things? But you're too little for lollies. Doesn't your Mom know that? Your little teeth will fall out."

I stare her down with my fiercest "don't mess with me, Grandma" look, but she's oblivious, cooing at the twins. I swear if I weren't so desperate for coffee, I'd abandon ship, taking my lolly-sucking twins with me, but I swallow my pride, pay finally for my groceries and get out of there in as dignified manner as I possibly can. I hear Eileen click her tongue at my retreating back.

* * *

"Jed, coffee please, quickly… You have no idea what I've been through this morning."

Jed laughs and sets to work at the coffee machine as I relay my woes from the supermarket experience. Having lost the will to live post-supermarket trauma, I decided I couldn't wait for home to mainline some coffee. The twins are bundled in the double stroller which only just fits through the door of Beau Jangles, happily sucking their Chupa Chups, having had just the best morning.

Jed places a large bowl on the counter. It's one of his specials that I treat myself to on mornings of desperation: triple shot, flat white in a bowl. I'm reminded of Paris—strong coffee in a bowl with a pastry to dunk—a million years ago.

"Jed, have I told you I love you before today?"

"Only every time I make you coffee Billie." He rolls his eyes, wiping the counter before starting on the next order.

"No, but today, I really mean it. This looks like your best coffee creation ever. Total genius." I take the bowl and sit against the wall at a small, round table with the buggy pushed in beside me. Beau Jangles is quiet, and after my first sip, the morning's trauma has all but disappeared.

"How's Evan?" asks Jed from behind the counter, but my eyes are still closed, savoring the taste and the zing as it rushes into my poor, caffeine-deprived body.

"Can't talk, I'm having a coffee appreciation moment," I answer without opening my eyes.

Jed laughs again, heading into the kitchen to emerge with a tray of still-warm muffins.

"Evan's good." I open my eyes, caffeinated and ready for conversation. I wrinkle my nose thoughtfully at my answer, which is partly true. Since Sunny's night in ER, Evan has been trying hard. We've had a good week, but if I'm honest, the "good" feels a little forced. A happy plastic sort of a front, so in answering 'Evan's good,' I'm not lying, just omitting the remaining details.

Evan is good fifty percent of the time, and then he's not. It's hard to know how he's doing because when he's up and behaving like the

Evan I know and love, he doesn't want to talk about being down and partly I don't want to either.

When he's down, which seems to happen more frequently than ever before, he doesn't talk at all. He shuts down and is totally unreachable. Just when I'm in total despair, unsure of what to do anymore or how I can cope, he emerges good as new, better than new, like nothing happened and there's no cause for concern. If I do bring it up he shrugs it off. "I've always been like this, Billie. Sometimes I just need a little space."

Hello! Doesn't everyone? Do I have the option of shutting down for a day or two? So I swither between concern and frustration, and we carry on in the same pattern, not unhappy, just not quite right.

"He still underground with the airport design?" asks Jed as he transfers the warm blueberry muffins onto a tray.

"Yeah, it's really something. I just hope after all his work that they decide to go ahead." I'm a little sick of hearing about the airport but try to be polite.

"You know, not everyone feels that way." Jed looks serious as he sprinkles chocolate powder on to some waiting cappuccinos. Despite my frustration over Evan's obsession with the project, I can't help but support him whenever the debate comes up. I believe in him and his work and want others to as well.

"I know, I just think it's mad to try and delay progress. The island's going to change anyway. It doesn't have to be for the worse."

Jed nods, his eyes narrowing as he weighs up pros and cons in his head. "I'm not sure yet, but I am sure that whatever Evan has designed will be amazing. He's a talented guy."

"Yes, he is," I reply with a small sigh as my gaze wanders out the window to the busy street.

"You okay Billie?"

I jump, realizing my face must betray my worries. Smiling, I assure

Jed I'm just great and help myself to a muffin and leave some money on the counter. Returning to my little table, I notice to my surprise and joy that the terrible twosome have fallen asleep with their heads, one fair, one dark, leaned in toward each other, two little mouths hang open and a spill of drool drips down Sunny's chin. There is a God.

I sit back and sip my coffee, determined to enjoy the small window of peace the heavens have so generously gifted. Sleeping children are adorable. You can watch them carefully, admiring their cuteness, thinking about who has whose nose, dimples and so on, and for a short time, they don't need anything at all.

Sunny twitches, moving into some dream which no doubt features trucks and Buzz Lightyear. Evie gives nothing away, her face a picture of innocence hiding the mischievous urchin that lies beneath the dimpled chin. So like her father.

Smiling to myself, I take out my journal and begin to write.

Wherever I go I always make sure that I have copied by hand the last few lines recently written in my book so that if the occasion presents itself, I can continue on by hand and type up my progress later. My story plan is stuck in a folded up sheet of A4 to the inside front cover, so I grab a Biro and get cracking; even a few paragraphs these days is progress.

The loud sounds of the café don't bother Sunny and Evie at all; in fact, the busy atmosphere seems to assist their peaceful slumber. Jed makes coffee, clatters cups and plates, froths steamy milk, and talks loudly to all who enter. The door swings open and closed as music thumps all around, yet still they sleep. Absorbed in writing, I don't notice anything else until I hear the voice. Looking up from my corner I see Claudia at the counter, all high heels and bouffy hair.

"Hey Jed, I need a double shot, decaf, trim soy latte with a sprinkle of chocolate on the top… oh, and no sugar. I just can't process the stuff. My new yoga guy, he says sugar's the devils spawn, and it's killing us all slowly. You should bear that in mind!" She gestures around the café where little sugar bowls decorate each table, brown crystals threatening to corrupt the soul.

"Is that right? Well, I'd say I'm done for then. I like a little sugar in my coffee." Jed winks at her, smiling wickedly. It's funny to see how most men flirt with Claudia, despite her reputation. They are men, I suppose, ruled by their willies.

Claudia, sensing Jed's flirtation, smiles slyly and swats a hand at him. "You are too naughty. Now, what can I have to eat?" She peruses the counter, tracing a long, pink fingernail along its edge. "Oh, you really are a doll. I'll have one of those little pink macaroons; all to take away please."

Jed packages the macaroon with a smile. "You do realize the first ingredient in these is…"

"Don't tell me, and I'll pretend I don't know!" Claudia says. "Then I haven't really cheated. Just don't tell Nathan." She gives him a winning smile, grabs her coffee (which isn't really a coffee, is it? I mean, come on… soy decaf!), her packaged pink macaroon, and spins on a heel to head for the door. She catches me watching and feigns a smile, her heels click across the floor toward me.

"Billie! So lovely to see you!"

I'm wondering if I missed something and we became BFFs some time ago. "Um, nice to see you too," I reply, hoping her high-pitched nasal voice doesn't wake the twins.

She pulls out the chair across from me and makes to sit down. *No! This can't be happening. This is my sacred time. Go away, crazy vamp lady!* I don't of course say this, but manage what I hope might pass as a welcoming smile as she parks herself across from me and coos at the sleeping twins for a moment.

"I am so glad I bumped into you." She leans in. "I was thinking we should catch up sometime."

Ruthie Morgan | 319

"You were?"

"Of course. I was thinking about you over in that quiet, old street next to Jack with no girlfriends, and with the babies, oh and that gorgeous husband of yours just never around."

I'm not sure what to be offended at first: her insinuation that I have no friends, her comment on Evan's looks, or his absence. "Oh, I'm just fine, thank you," I answer as politely as I can. "I have plenty going on; I see Zoe lots and Evan's home as much as he can be. He's pretty busy right now."

"Zoe, do I know Zoe?" she asks, wrinkling her nose, signaling indifference. "Oh, yes. Solid girl, curly hair, married to the big German bloke, runs everywhere."

I smile at this disparaging description of my dear friend, imagining how Zoe would respond, and remembering her recent, equally disparaging description of Claudia. "Anyway," Claudia carries on, "I just wondered, being that you live next door to my husband."

"'Isn't he your ex-husband?"

"Well, yes, but is it relevant?" she snaps. I think it is, but decide that's not the answer she's looking for. "I was wondering… do you ever see anyone, well, you know… come and go?"

"Come and go? Could you be a little more specific?"

She shakes her head in mild frustration. "You know, women friends? Does he seem to have any women friends? Ladies visiting?"

I want to laugh, but manage to keep a straight face as I take a swift gulp of coffee. "Um, not that I've noticed. He keeps himself to himself pretty much; always in his workshop as far as I can see."

"Really?"

"Really."

"Do you see much of him? I mean, how do you know he spends most of his time in his workshop?" She looks a little accusingly at me now and I hope I don't flush as I answer.

"He's my neighbor. Of course I see him around. Our backyards are practically connected."

"Of course." She looks embarrassed. Taking a sip of her coffee, she sighs. "I loved him, you know."

Oh dear, I don't feel ready for this kind of confession.

"He really screwed me over. I know he's still in love with me, but I just won't take him back."

"Oh."

Her confidence isn't the intimate sharing of heartfelt feelings I was expecting after all. I should have known. Claudia the Viper is trying to spread another rumor about poor Jack. No wonder the guy is scarred. "You know, he didn't treat me well," she says, opening the bag holding the pink macaroon.

"This is really none of my business," I interject.

She continues as though I haven't spoken. "You know, he was a big drinker, and I mean a big drinker. Used to come home plastered and useless. I don't know how I lasted as long as I did." Her tone suggests she's rather proud of herself.

"Jack's not a big drinker!" I reply in his defense. "I've never seen him have more than a beer."

She scoffs at me, spluttering fragments of pink macaroon onto her lap. "That's now. You should have seen him before. Just like a typical man, he gets his act together after we break up." She scans the café and street outside for someone more interesting to talk to. "Anyway, been nice chatting. We must catch up again soon." She smiles that overly-sweet smile, tosses her hair over one shoulder and stands. I'm about to tell her she has one of the twins' rice crackers stuck to her bottom, but decide against it.

Whether or not her story of Jack has any truth to it doesn't matter. I wouldn't blame the guy for being drunk during a marriage to a woman like that. How else would he survive? It does surprise me though that Jack would ever have had a problem with booze. The subject of drinking once again pushes its way into the forefront of my mind. I'm sick of it and choose to give it no further thought.

My phone vibrates on the table and I check the message.

11:35 a.m. Hey baby, where are you? Tried calling home. Can you get a babysitter for tomorrow? Mid-winter carnival—we could go, have some fun—just like the old days. Ex.

I feel lighter reading his text. Fun is what we need. It may no longer be the old days, but we could have a night out and pretend.

11:39 a.m. Yes, yes, yes. Sounds great, let me work on it. Marlene owes me a favor. Bx.

The mid-winter carnival is St. Cloud's biggest festival; a night filled with street performers, live bands, street food, and fireworks. So far, Evan and I have never managed to go together because the twins were too little and I didn't feel ready to let anyone babysit yet. Evan went along last year with some workmates, but to go together would be amazing. A night out together might be just what we need.

I text Marlene, our neighbor on the other side. Her children left home a few years ago, and she is always offering to look after Sunny and Evie. Time for me to take a small step back and ask for a little help. The thought is comforting, and within minutes, Marlene has texted back saying she would be delighted.

I finish my last sip of coffee, thinking what an interesting morning it has turned out to be. Fully caffeinated and ready to face the rest of the day, I wave to Jed and gently maneuver the stroller and still sleeping babies out on to the street.

* * *

Pulling into the gravel driveway, I see Jack checking his mail and wave. He smiles and strolls over to see me.

"Hey, how's the day going?" I ask, turning off the ignition and removing my seatbelt. The twins yell excitedly from the back, seeing Jack's face at the window.

He opens the door and helps pry them out of their car seats. "Actually, pretty good, thank you for asking," he replies a little mysteriously.

"Really? Why?"

"Don't sound so surprised that I'm in such a good mood." He smiles. "Here, come look at this." He starts walking back toward his house, Evie on one hip and Sunny holding his hand tightly.

"Do I have a choice?" I ask, following anyway, although no one is listening.

Jack walks down the driveway and underneath his house to his workshop, Louie and Bets at his heels. I follow, intrigued.

"Now, wait here a minute." he puts Evie down and lets Sunny's hand go. "Wait here with Mommy just for a minute."

I stop and hold their hands while he disappears into the workshop. The lights from inside the windows become brighter and he pokes his head around the door. "Are you ready?"

"I think so."

He opens the door and ushers us inside. There, fully illuminated under spotlights is a work of art, a boat so beautifully restored that it takes my breath away. It's an old vessel, and Jack has painstakingly brought it back to its former glory. All dark wood and brass... The curve of its underside usually invisible underneath the water is perfectly smooth; its contours gently curving, lovingly planed and finished. I can't help thinking there is something quite female about those curves.

"Jack," I breathe. "She's beautiful." The twins skip around the workshop, not entirely sure what the fuss is about, but happy to be playing with the dogs.

"Thank you," he says. "I think so, too. She's been quite a project."

"How long have you been restoring her?"

"Almost a year now. It was a big job, but she's done. She just needs a name."

"I knew she was a she."

"Boats are always 'she,' Billie." He smiles.

"What will you call her?"

"Well, it's not up to me. The guy who bought her will decide. Tomorrow night at the carnival, we'll launch her, and then she's off on new adventures."

I nod, gaze never leaving the boat. She's so stunningly beautiful. "Oh, that's perfect. A launch at the carnival." I imagine the scene then realize he will probably never see his creation again. "Oh Jack, it just seems a little sad to me."

He folds his arms, head cocked to one side as we stand side by side, both mesmerized by the boat. "Why?"

Suddenly overwhelmed by the great loss Jack must soon experience, I touch his arm and continue. "That you found her and could see the potential in her, you saw what she once was and brought her back to life, and now someone else gets to sail her. You don't even get to give her a name. You must love her, but she won't ever be yours." I sense I'm being dramatic, but the whole thing seems so close and so terribly sad. The saving and the giving away, not knowing what will become of her after.

"Billie, this is what I do. I buy old boats, make them beautiful again, and sell them. That's how I get by. Of course, I'd love to keep her. I think that about every boat I ever finish, but I have to sell her and start again."

"It's just so sad." I run my hand along the smooth curves of her hull. "It's like never being able to commit. You fall in love, you invest everything you can, then give it all away, and someone else gets to love her." I feel broken-hearted for poor Jack.

He laughs, lifting me up to stand inside and admire the interior. "Not really. It's more like having kids, I imagine. You do the best job you can to make them the best they can be, then you send them off into the world knowing you'll always love them, but so will other people."

I turn to him, looking down at his upturned face, hands out to lift me safely down. "What?" he asks, looking a little embarrassed. I shake my head and smile taking in his strong reliable face and for some reason feel the onset of irrational tears. "Billie, are you…?"

"Nope," I say quickly, drying my eyes with the back of my hand. What a moron. I can't control these hormones. The wave of sadness that just washed over me makes me weak at the knees. I reach out for him and he lifts me down, knowing I'm crying, but not asking any more questions. "I'd best go unpack my groceries."

"Right. Leave the twins here for a bit. They can play with Bets and Louie. I'll bring them over later."

"Really?"

"Really."

I head back up the driveway and into the house, groceries forgotten. Curling into a ball on my bed, I cry for reasons I don't understand and lie there like that till the crying stops, wondering what in the hell is happening to me.

* * *

Chapter Twenty

Fiesta

Evan is home by seven, early by usual standards. He looks worn, but heads to the twins' bedroom to squeeze in a story before they fall asleep, and another day passes when he has barely seen them.

I'm happy that he's home before nine. I bustle around picking up toys, replacing them into their accompanying plastic boxes, scooping food remnants from the floor and sofa. Popcorn, crackers, raisins, and apple slices hidden away in secret stashes. The evening sun throws the room into shadow sliced with dashes of dark orange and crimson. The sounds of the evening begin quietly, tree frogs and crickets rousing, calling to each other, the cooler approach of evening a welcome respite in the surrounding bush.

Arms laden down with the rolled-up rag rug, I head to the back deck and shake its contents onto the grass. As it unravels and flaps, a shower of crumbs and Play-Doh pieces soar through the air. The flash of color attracts Jack's attention as he sits on his neighboring deck, immersed in some small project involving a knife and sandpaper.

He waves, and I wave back. I'd like to walk over and say hi, but hesitate, not wanting to be the reason Evan's mood spirals downward. Jack and Evan have spoken little since the night in ER, and mention of his name creates visible tension with Evan so I avoid talking about him for now.

I go indoors, frustrated and torn at compromising my friendship with Jack because I don't want to make Evan angry or jealous. Part of me yells, "You've done nothing wrong," and the voice is right. I haven't, but I can't pretend the thought isn't a fantasy that keeps me entertained in the long hours Evan is away.

I push the feisty, outraged voice further down, determined for peace; whatever the cost. I don't want to be the catalyst in another drinking binge that will inevitably end in tears.

Heading to the kitchen, I open the fridge, pushing my frustration aside, assuring myself that all of this will work its way out. Tomatoes, olives, anchovies, and crisp, green leaves. I distract myself by finding ingredients and put together our supper. Chop, toss, tear. I arrange the bowl, colors and textures perfect, flavors a simple but beautiful contrast, each complimentary to the other. I slice crusty bread, drizzle olive oil, grind the sea salt, and lay the plates; pour some wine? Maybe not tonight.

Half an hour later, Evan has still not emerged from the twins' room. I tiptoe to the door, knowing I will find him asleep on the floor, storybook still in hand. The door creaks as I peek inside to see, as expected, Evan asleep on the floor between the cots, open book face-down beside him. Evie is asleep on his tummy, and Sunny is curled in the crook of his arm. I watch them for a while, quiet peace in three who, when awake, are rarely still. Tiptoeing into the dimly-lit room, I gently lift each sleeping baby up and into their cots. Evan stirs as I prise Evie from her preferred sleeping position; tummy to tummy.

He smiles up at me with the soft expression of one still on the edge of a dream, stress-free and relaxed. I extend a hand and lead him next door to our bedroom, where he stretches out on the bed, and I crawl beside him, my back to his tummy, his arm relaxed and around me, pulling me closer. We should eat, it's late, but these undisturbed moments together are rare and Evan, still and peaceful, wanting nothing more than to lie together rarer still. I can't tell if he has fallen back asleep, his body is warm and relaxed, his breath on my hair and neck.

"Are you happy Billie?" The question is asked softly, honestly in a tone suggesting he is entirely unsure of what my answer might be.

"Mostly." I want to say "yes," or "always," but I can't lie to Evan. I never have.

"Do I make you unhappy?"

"Sometimes."

He breathes into my hair, and we lie quietly before I return the question. "Are you happy?"

"Sometimes."

His answer is honest, too, but I can't help feeling crushed that he didn't say yes or always. I can never shake the unrealistic expectation that his happiness is my job, that I should take care of and control it, that any unhappiness must be my failure. I turn onto my back and look up at the ceiling, his arms still around me and his face burrowed into my hair.

"I want to help. Tell me what to do."

He opens his eyes and moves back to look at me. "Sometimes I feel like you're watching me, waiting for me to fuck up." He pauses, closing his eyes, trying to mask the feelings that lie in their depths. "Everything I do affects you. I can't breathe without you sucking in my air, reading in to every single thing I do or don't do."

The words hurt, but they are true. I do watch him. I can't help it. It has become my pattern, trying to predict which Evan he will be next so I can prepare myself.

"Of course I'm watching. How can I not notice? One minute you're fine, then suddenly you're not, and I'm spinning trying to work out what happened, what I did, or how I can make it better." Frustration bubbles over into hot tears. "I just don't get it. How am I supposed to not notice when you shut yourself away and won't talk to me?"

"I do that to try and protect you."

"Protect me? From what? Do you think watching from a distance, trying to guess what's going on, wondering if you're ill, if you're about to leave me, if you just wished things were different… do you think that's protecting me? If you could just talk to me, we might be able to figure it all out."

"Christ, that's what I mean." He moves his arm and places a hand to his forehead, exasperated. "That's exactly what I mean. I need space and take myself away, and you freak out, thinking the worst possible thoughts. I can't be responsible for your happiness Billie. You've got to stand alone. I don't want to sway you. I don't want my head to screw you over, too. Do you understand that? Right now, I can't control my own fucking moods, and I can't be responsible for yours."

I press my palms to my eyes and suck in my breath, trying to gather myself. I don't want an argument. "Don't you see? It's too late for that. I'll always be affected by you, just as you're affected by me, by the twins, by the fact that we're a family. It's not that easy. I can't shut myself off from worrying about you in the same way I can't stop myself from loving you." I stop for breath. "And yes, there are days when I think that would be easier. Life would be so much less complicated. The fact that I care how you're feeling and worry when you're down should be a comfort to you. I love you Evan; that's just how it is."

For a moment he looks angry, but the spark in his eyes dissolves into something gentle and sad. "Can you just know, please, that it's not about you? I'll figure it out. Can you try, please, to ignore me, separate yourself, until I'm back to normal?"

"What the hell is normal these days?"

"I mean, the best thing you can do for me is to understand, just give me some space when I'm like that, because I promise you when I'm in that head I've nothing to give, and it's all I can do to scrape my ass to work and get through the day." He pauses and then the words spill over undeterred. "If I come home quiet, that's not the time to try and talk to me. I've nothing to say, and if you force it, I'll be an asshole." He tries to slow down and find the calm he had moments ago. "I'm sorry, but I'm trying to explain it, and I don't understand it myself."

"It wasn't always as bad as this."

"I've always been the same. You just didn't see it before. Now your whole fucking focus in life is happy families and the babies. I'll never be the perfect guy, Billie. This is it, and some days it's shitty. I get it. I have to live in this head."

Angry and hurt, I turn my back to him. "My whole focus is our family because that's all I do. That's all I am these days. Isn't it enough?" I stifle a sob, and he sighs. Here we go again, the inevitable conclusion to any discussion of late. Evan angry, me pathetic. He pulls me back toward him and leans in, stroking my hair and tucking it behind my ear.

"It is enough; it's me who's not." The words are quiet and resigned.

"Evan, I…" He cuts me off before I can talk around the subject some more and tie us in knots we can't undo.

"I'm tired Billie. Some days it's all so fucking hard." His tone changes, all the edges smooth, soft, quiet.

I turn to face him, placing my hand on his cheek. "Maybe you need to talk to Dan. Maybe he can help."

"I don't need to talk to Dan." He takes my hand in his and kisses the palm. "I'm sorry, baby. I hate making you feel bad. Everything's fine. Quit worrying about me; just take care of yourself and the twins. I'm fine."

"You're working too hard" I cup the strong line of his face, cheekbone to jaw, watching his expression.

"No, it's fine. Once things calm down and this project is finished, we'll take a holiday; maybe head over to Joe's beach house. What do you think?"

"I think that sounds perfect."

He kisses my forehead then closes his eyes. We lie there together till the room is dark and the tree frogs serenade the momentary calm lasting in the room till morning. Supper forgotten, we sleep, nothing resolved, but having found comfort in a few words plucked from the confines of silent worry and fear.

* * *

Leaving your beloved babies with a sitter is always epic.

Despite the fact that I'm in desperate need of a break from their impish faces, planning the leaving part is exhausting. But tonight, I am determined to go out, to do something different, have a few drinks and some fun with our friends, and enjoy a night with Evan. No kids, no work. So, despite the marathon involved in getting the kids ready, pre-empting a bemused Marlene for all manner of baby behaviors and potential disaster, I remind myself it's all worth it. We need this.

I hear the others outside laughing, the engine of Felix's car humming in the driveway. They holler my name, hurrying me to say my goodbyes.

"Okay Marlene, I think we're good to go here!" I fuss around a little longer than necessary, enjoying the imploring looks of adoration the twins send my way, knowing that they want me more than anyone else. For a time in their lives, I am the most important person in the world. The fact that I'm bustling around, ready to leave means the imploring looks are about to turn to tears: my cue to run.

"Goodnight beautiful!" I kiss Evie's head and she pulls on my blouse. "Goodnight handsome!" I kiss Sunny, then make for the door. His clear blue eyes fill with panic.

Marlene shoos me with a hand, smiling and shaking her head, no doubt remembering when her children were this age and leaving them was so hard. Now her grown-up children do the leaving, and return on holidays with laundry and empty wallets.

I feel the layers of tension slide from my shoulders as I am out the door and on my way to the car. Zoe leans from the window, grinning mischievously, and the boys look on impatiently as I stop, and bend down to rustle in my handbag, knowing I'm sure to have forgotten either my phone or keys.

Evan leans his head back on the headrest, eyes closed in exasperation. He's used to this. I'm not terribly experienced at leaving the twins, and it takes me a while to get out of the door.

"For fuck's sake Billie, are you sure you don't want to go back in and say goodbye again?" Evan asks, shaking his head in my direction and looking at Felix for support.

Felix flashes a grin at me, and then turns to ease the car out on to the road. Zoe claps hers hands together in delight and whoops, "Bring it on!" and we are off, into the dark night for our much needed escape from the confines of our everyday lives.

Evan squeezes my hand, the motion of the car evidence that we are in fact going out, and, regardless of my delays, we're on our way. He smiles, moving his hand to my thigh where it remains. I feel a memory of a time before… the feeling is old and dusty, unfamiliar nowadays in this life of sleepless nights and diapers. I feel happy in my own skin, blue jeans, and sandals, skin brown from the sun, and hair brushed and out of its usual ponytail. I feel beautiful, and although the thought makes me wince, embarrassed by my own vanity, the feeling is good. Evan's hand is on my leg, warm air rushes in the open window, we're with friends, and the lush green scenery of St. Cloud frames my vision from every angle.

Down the winding hill, thickly lined on either side by bush, Palms, Tea Trees, Pungas, and Ferns, the air is thick and heady; an ecosystem in full swing. Life growing, multiplying, spreading roots, bearing fruit, decaying, dying, and beginning again. The forests from my childhood memories were so different; less alive, drier, and lighter; the air thin on the lungs. In these native forests, life oozes stickily from tree sap and drips from constantly damp vegetation. I've always felt there's a Grimm's fairytale quality to the depth and dark green light of the bush here in St. Cloud. Things always moving, spreading, growing right before your eyes, creeping roots, and thickening undergrowth, vines that might entangle and hold you in. I'm plagued by a creeping claustrophobia when surrounded by the thick growth and damp air.

The dark green bush frames either side of the cove, but the long sandy beaches are clear and smooth, a contrast to the dense surroundings. Settlers long ago cleared the beaches for boat travel and fishing although there was a time when most of the island was bush covered. I often feel I'm only a visitor here, not just because of where I've come from, but because it seems that the land is old and people settling here are new and temporary. Years of settlers traveling, claiming land, and destroying part of the natural habitat to make way for buildings, sandy tourist beaches, roads, and houses. One day all this will be gone, and St. Cloud will return to its more natural state where the only balance is between flora and fauna.

"Earth to Billie… are you with us?" Zoe is swiveled in her seat, frowning at me, having obviously asked me a question I didn't hear, caught up in my musings over the dark bush and the islands history.

I smile and reply, "Zoe, I'm always with you."

The car winds its course past the beach and around the bush--lined roads heading into town for our much anticipated mid-winter carnival. "I just can't believe we did it; all of us, kid-less and off for a night out! I was sure all day that either Sunny or Evie would vomit, and we'd have to cancel." I squeeze Evan's hand on my thigh, and he smiles, shaking his head, eyes focused on the view.

"I know," Zoe commiserates. "I was convinced there would be some sabotage in our place. I lost count of the times Matty asked why he wasn't coming with us. Oh, and then Felix practically drowned Nate in the tub."

"You can't drown when all the bath water is on the floor," Felix answers.

Zoe barrels on. "You wouldn't believe it. Honestly, in the space of thirty seconds, Nate managed to tip an entire bath full of soapy water on to the floor using a plastic watering can. Those boys are wild!" She throws her hands up in the air. "Good thing they're cute." She throws a quick glance at Felix. "I don't know where they get it from!"

He rolls his eyes and sighs. "Okay ladies, I'm making a rule. As of right now, there is to be no discussion of children, babies, twins, diapers, pureed food, or anything remotely related to offspring! Are we agreed?"

Evan concurs, "We will drink beer, eat child-unfriendly spicy food, swear loudly, and forget we are supposedly responsible adults. Are you with me?"

"We're with you!" Felix is the first to answer, of course.

Zoe and I exchange amused smiles then concur, and the rest of the drive passes in relaxed conversation and laughter; the topic of little people avoided completely.

Bright-colored lights of town blink in the distance as we reach the crest of the road that links St. Cloud's east side to west, where the bustling town creates a division between bush and ocean. Although officially a city (boasting a cathedral built at the turn of the century, and a university specializing in marine biology and engineering), the residents of our island are more likely to refer to St. Cloud's main drag as "town"; its size gives a feeling of community that most cities don't.

Culturally, St. Cloud is diverse; its population heavily weighted by immigrants like us. People enticed here by the lure of a slower pace of life amidst the luxuries a small city provides.

I muse briefly over the stubborn attitude of some regarding the international airport Evan is designing. They rally against progress, hoping to keep St. Cloud in a timeless bubble when change is inevitable anyway. St. Cloud has much to offer, and there's only so long it can remain as it is. Shouldn't we be welcoming the progress? I wonder at that tendency toward the negative many people exhibit. The airport should be seen as a huge positive. The fact is we are still a zillion miles from most places—we're not about to get the regular tourists desperate for beach loungers and English fish and chips.

Right now, the journey to St. Cloud is long and complicated, full of transfers and delays, arrivals re-routed via Costa Rica or Peru. Flights into St. Cloud from the mainland are few and via smaller planes. Despite this, people do come, some to holiday, others, like us, to make a new start. The climate and familiar language ensure the transition to island isolation is an easy one. The airport will simply make the journey easier and less expensive.

Despite negative rustling in the underbelly of our community, there are many who will benefit directly from a busier, more prosperous island. The university is the best example. Historically, its intake of students was mostly island inhabitants, from St. Cloud or its neighboring isles. Now, many come from much further afield to benefit from our university's excellence in marine biology and engineering, but the indirect journey is a definite limiter. All this could change.

The flip side to our isolation is that businesses here in St. Cloud thrive. Competition is minimal and comes only from other island businesses or the odd chain enterprise that takes a chance out here. This makes our city center a wonderfully eclectic mix of mostly locally-run quirky stores and boutiques, cafés, bars, and restaurants.

I love it; it's a place that appears to have everything it needs and sits comfortably as the center point of the island. There's a noticeable absence of the frenetic pace and competition felt in most cities: the nervous energy of people and companies out to be the best, screw the others over, make the biggest margin and succeed with the smallest output in a cutthroat market. St. Cloud has thriving industry and competitive business, but the atmosphere is one of relaxed productivity, a symbiotic balance where each person, business, or company benefits the other directly or indirectly, allowing the city to operate harmoniously.

It's a mixing pot, and together, we form the secret ingredients. So many races, colors, and languages populate the streets and work in the fragrant, brightly-colored stores and market places. All of this diversity is gently coated in a layer of something specifically St. Cloud: a pace of life that moves just a little more slowly, a smell in the air of papaya, salt water, sun lotion, and music; always music—a slow beat with a reggae bass.

As the car winds down the road, I catch my first real glimpse of the carnival lights. St. Cloud sparkles and glitters like a party princess; the streets decorated with colored paper lanterns and banners. The air is warm and muggy; no breeze despite the late hour. The road becomes busier as the car reaches the edge of town, and I feel a quiet thrill of anticipation.

"Where are we meeting Dan?" I ask, extending a bare arm out of the window, trailing the warm air with my fingers.

"At Santos," Felix answers, distractedly negotiating the chaotic road.

We weave through the busy streets full of St. Cloud townsfolk, beer bottles in hand, warming up for the big night.

"Where should we park Evan?" Felix asks because Evan is the one most used to the city bar scene at night.

"We could head to the beach lot. It'll be quieter down there, and we can walk up to town. It'll only be a few minutes."

Felix maneuvers the car through the one-way streets and new diversions which open the town for the parade and evenings revelers until we reach the beach. The palm trees are strung with fairy lights and colored streamers, and the sand is littered with couples and families finishing up evening picnics or drying off from late night swims.

As the engine quiets and the car stills, sounds and smells of night move in through the open windows. I close my eyes and let it all wash over me… I am stepping into a different world, a world once known but carefully wrapped and tucked away so memory of its loss wouldn't be a burden in the years of baby rearing. How long since the last night in a city with Evan? A momentary flashback, a forgotten life, the memory triggered by simple smells and sounds.

I let one long, slow breath escape out into the fragrant evening and climb from the car. It will be a good night. Overwhelmed by an urge to feel the ocean, I give a loud whoop for joy, whip off my sandals and sprint for the water's edge.

"I'll catch up!"

"Wait up… Billie, you daft cow; get back here!" Zoe yells from the parking lot, but my toes are already in the water, and a surge of pure joy takes my breath away. Despite everything, the minor dramas, and worries of late, at this moment, I know it will all be okay. Closing my eyes, I clap my hands together and say a silent word of thanks for everything; all of this, Evan, our babies, St. Cloud, and the rest.

My moment of serenity is interrupted by another loud holler from Zoe. "Billie May, get your sorry ass over here. I will not drink my first cocktail alone tonight!"

Laughing in response, I turn and run through the soft sand, bare feet leaving a trail of hope for the future.

Felix and Evan walk ahead, deep in conversation. Evan is passionately describing some design specifics on the airport. He likes to talk to Felix about work because Felix gets it; he appreciates the engineering, the design, and the concepts. He shares Evan's passion for flight. They are good friends: Felix, the staunch German; and Evan, the mad Irishman. They talk animatedly; happy to have each other's company. I love that Evan has good friends here. Life is easier on all accounts with friends you can talk to.

Felix bends his head as he listens, concentrating on Evan's words. Evan's head moves in line with his hands, describing something in great detail, fingers excitedly sketching a shape in the air. Felix nods and asks questions here and there. Zoe links her arm through mine, and we follow our men along the bustling streets, laughing like excitable teenagers double-dating for the first time. A local band kicks off in the square, and the sounds of bongo drums, guitars, and voices in harmony float up and around the buildings and townspeople, and I feel the shift in energy; the move from pre-party to party.

Santos' is a small bar whose outside seating area is double the size of its dusty interior. Inside the music is loud and conversation louder. Through the throng of bodies we spot Dan perched on a barstool, beer bottle in hand, a deep smile on his tanned face, his perfect hair flicked carefully to one side. "I need some of his hair product!" Zoe yells in my ear as we weave through the crowd to reach him.

He has spotted us already, and our drinks are waiting by the time we arrive beside him. "You made it!" he extends his arms regally, then gives Evan and Felix manly slaps on the shoulders, then Zoe and I an affectionate kiss on both cheeks. "Drinks!" He passes the bottles around, having obviously sunk a few himself already.

We settle into the evening, drinking beer, followed by brightly-

-colored fruit cocktails garnished with paper umbrellas. The boys avoid the cocktails, afraid to be seen with a pink frothy drink and a straw.

Dan, however, *is* happy to sip from his straw; a pink frothy cocktail no threat to his sexuality. At 10 p.m., Dan gives us the signal to move on. "The parade starts soon. Let's get out on to the streets and get a good view." He hops from his bar stool and wobbles slightly as he hits the floor; the pink cocktails working their magic.

Outside, the streets are a mass of moving bodies, laughter, raised voices, dancing couples, and loud music. Someone is blowing a horn over and over again, and as if by magic, the crowds part, drawing up on to the sidewalks and clearing the roads. In moments, the loud Caribbean-style music becomes louder and decorated floats turn into the main street, each themed as a different mythical figure. Greek Gods, legendary heroes, and monsters seem to be the general theme: Zeus, Perseus, Medusa, the Kraken, a three-headed dog, Centaurs, and Minotaur's. Paper mâché masks and extravagant costumes hang from the slowly moving floats while loud music surrounds the moving chain of people and vehicles. The atmosphere is suddenly wild, people dancing everywhere, drinks in hand; the scene could be Rio de Janeiro in carnival time.

Evan seems to know everyone. He high-fives and hellos, claps backs and kisses cheeks. He has become party boy, and for a moment, this Evan seems unfamiliar. These days I'm used to the after-party Evan, the Evan who slips home too late smelling of booze and smoke, the Evan who is overtired and cranky in the morning. I haven't seen Evan at his peak for a long time, and the experience sends conflicting emotions through a head already fuzzy with a few cocktails. There's a nagging thought that pokes and prods through the haze of happiness, but I push it away. Tonight, Evan shines; funny and handsome, joking and making people laugh. He buys the drinks, and he is "where the fun's at". Everyone loves Evan.

Someone pushes him accidentally from behind, spilling beer down his shirt, and he turns around, sharply, swearing. The overreaction makes me flinch, but I look away, leave him to manage himself. I take a large gulp of my drink as Evan gives the man a hard push back to where he came from.

"Oh my God, is she topless?" Zoe yells, her breath sweet and alcohol-fumed. I have already had too much to drink and think that maybe the vision greeting me as I turn from Evan, tucking my anxiety safely away… must be a result of the cocktails. Alas no, traveling along the street atop a white float, clothed in a white toga, an olive wreath around her head, perched on glittering heels higher than should be humanly possible to walk in is Claudia.

She stands at the top of what is supposed to look like a mountain. Her face is composed, obviously going for the Goddess look. She doesn't turn her head or acknowledge the cheering crowd but stands stock still, looking into the distance like a blond, leggy statue. Her breasts poke over the top of the toga ensemble and her nipples are covered by glittering tassels. I scream at the hilarious scene, slapping a hand to my mouth in an attempt to push back the peals of laughter already rising as I stare, open-mouthed, at the Greek Goddess vision that is Claudia. Below her statue-like form is a banner which reads: "Aphrodite: Goddess of love, beauty, pleasure, and procreation."

"Holy fuck!" yelps Evan, recognizing the form traveling past, all tasseled nipples and aloof expression. "Is that…?"

"Claudia. Yes, I'm afraid it is," answers a deep voice from behind us.

"Jack!" I can't help but be relieved he's here, another emotion that confuses me. "Great to see you! I didn't know you were coming down."

"I wasn't, but they're launching the new boat at midnight down at the docks, so I thought I'd best be here to see her off." He nods, greeting everyone, looking a little embarrassed—his association with Aphrodite not quite forgotten.

"Hey Jack!" shouts Dan, passing Jack a beer he seems to have conjured from thin air. "Being married to Aphrodite must have been hell; I mean all that pleasure and procreation!"

Jack raises a hand, smiling. "Well boys, I leave that to your imagination, but unfortunately, as you all know, Aphrodite never fucking shuts up." Everyone laughs, and Jack, looking a little less awkward, settles into our company and watches the rest of the parade go by, all a bit of an anticlimax after the nipple tassels.

Jack is here and so is Evan, and everything is fine. I'm relieved they can be civil, in fact almost friendly to one another, although I'm not sure whether the civility is just a show for my benefit. It seems the drunken outburst and accusations of a few months ago have been forgotten; Evan apologized eventually, and Jack somehow seemed to understand. No one has spoken of the evening again, but I do feel that Evan can't let go of some underlying mistrust of me, of Jack, or maybe simply of himself.

The carnival continues on in its bright celebration of everything that is wild and fun and bright and loud: an escape from reality, a chance to be someone else for a few hours, to let our hair down, and to dance like no one's watching because really tonight, no one is. I crane my neck to see the wild collection of floats and characters passing by. They throw gifts to the crowds, balloons, candies, glow-sticks, and other paraphernalia gifted by sponsors of each passing spectacle. Some distinctly camp-looking Minotaur's throw condoms, and the crowd scream with laughter.

The final float approaches: a forest scene, four muscular men dressed in dire wolf costumes, fierce, paper mâché heads, open-mouthed, sharp-fanged, and wild-eyed. Their torsos are bare and shine with sweat, their lower halves fur-covered. Positioned on all fours, they rear up and bay to the moon, occasionally jumping on to two paws to bust out a few dance moves to the cheering crowd. As if by magic, the passing of the dire wolves signals an end, like a curtain closing on a final act, the wolves leave a trail of silence. Lights flicker out as they pass, and behind their wild forms, all is dark and the revelers fall quiet. Soon, the main street is black as night; all lights extinguished and music silenced, in the excited hush I turn for Evan but can't see him in the crowd.

"What happens now?" I ask Jack, who stands behind me quiet and smiling. There it is again, that gratifying feeling of safety in his presence. Jack leans down and speaks quietly in my ear, "Wait and see."

Zoe, lost behind a man of average height, squeezes her small frame toward us. "You guys, that was so great, aren't you glad we came?" She clasps my hand and stands on tiptoes, trying to see over the crowd for what is coming next. A familiar laugh sounds nearby, and I turn again to look for Evan, but can't see him… cocktails and beer playing havoc with my vision.

Jack, senses my concern. "Are you okay?"

"I was just wondering where Evan is. He's had a lot to drink."

"So has everyone. Don't worry. He's over there." He gestures behind us into the midst of the crowd, but before I have time to look, the sound of a loud ticking clock booms from the speakers. "Tick, Tock, Tick, Tock…" A countdown has begun. Someone somewhere yells "Ten," and the crowd responds counting backward in progressively louder, decreasing numbers: "Nine, Eight, Seven, Six." Jack squeezes my hand. "Five, Four, Three, Two, One!"

Fireworks crackle and boom from the top of a high-rise building on the main street, and sparkling confetti falls in heavy showers, coating everyone below. Fairy lights burst back into sparkling strings of color and spotlights shine onto a suddenly illuminated stage assembled in the very center of the street. A male lead guitarist strums four consecutive chords, and a drum kit bursts to life behind him. Two more guitarists and a female voice join the sound, and people everywhere begin to move. Bodies jumping and dancing to the band gravitate without thought to the front of the stage where already there has formed a sort of mosh pit: a mad crowd of happy, mostly drunken, dancing, shaking, jumping bodies—a small section of the islands finest. For now, the slower more relaxed beat of the island's usual reggae sounds are gone, replaced by thrashing guitars and a loud drum beat; St. Cloud is rocking.

Zoe is on Felix's shoulders heading for the stage, and I slot in behind as Felix's bulk cuts a path through the heaving bodies. We are soon on the dance floor, and all inhibitions have left the vicinity with the last of the dire wolves. Soon my overworked mind takes a happy backseat to my body, which does its best to remember how to dance. Gone are all worries, thoughts, plans, and concerns. In this moment, this is all we need, and it's perfect. We are intoxicated by the night, the music, the lights, the freedom, the cocktails, and the sheer energy of all those gyrating bodies who just want to cut loose and have fun.

Dan plays air guitar, and Felix jumps around thrashing his blond hair like he no doubt would have to Iron Maiden in the eighties. Virginia and her husband, Mike, twist and spin; Virginia, normally so composed, stumbles in her high-heeled sandals, grabbing on to a tall, dark man wearing a muscle vest. She steadies herself on his bulging bicep and holds on a little longer than is necessary… batting her heavily mascaraed lids, forgetting momentarily her husband is beside her. But Mike seems not to have noticed her absence and is busy getting down, twirling and jumping to a beat he hasn't felt in years.

I close my eyes again, feeling the night form in a stream of descriptive behind my eyelids; if I weren't so drunk, I'd stop and write a poem on a paper napkin.

Maybe later; for now, I decide to pull my head out of my creative ass and just dance. I laugh loudly, toss my hair back, and jump to the beat. Zoe has found Jed, and together they are working some classic eighties moves, all Bananarama and Ultravox. The band keep playing and playing, afraid if they stop between numbers the magic will be lost. The lead singer picks up the mike stand and swings it high above his head, channeling Iggy Pop. Zoe grabs me by the waist and twirls me around, singing along to the cover. "God, I am so glad our babysitters are staying over!" she screams practically in tune to the band.

I squeeze her hands as we twirl. "Me too. I'd forgotten how to do this."

"Do what?" shouts Zoe, only half listening as the band launches into another number with a fast, heavy drum beat.

"This, you lemon… dance, drink, forget I'm somebody's mom!"

She laughs in response, grabbing my hands again and dragging me close to the stage. The air is thick with sweaty bodies and the smell of beer, spirits, and the acrid tang of fireworks. I dance, letting my eyes gaze up at the dark night above; the quiet stars watching the happy mayhem below.

A hand cups my bottom, and I turn more slowly than if I were sober to confront the asshole who's copping a feel. Evan stands behind me grinning, his eyes glazed and forehead damp with sweat. "I've been looking for you," I say, hazily reaching an arm out to him.

He grabs both sides of my face, pulling me in roughly, kissing me hard. "Here I am," he replies with a grin. I kiss him back, and then pull him by the hand through the thronging mass of dancers. Evan rolls his eyes but lets me lead him, and in no time, is doing a fine impersonation of Shane McGowan from the Pogues crossed with a little Skylark Jackson. Laughing as he grabs me by the waist, lifting me high, I wrap my legs around him as he struts and shimmies around.

A series of piercing wolf whistles sound from all around, and as we turn our attention to the stage, we see Zoe with the microphone. She has somehow managed to climb up onto center stage, the band are laughing and start up with another number. Zoe's singing has not progressed beyond the shower or, at best, a drunken karaoke solo. Tonight she is Cindi Lauper and struts her stuff up and down the stage, pointing at the crowd, bending on one knee, beckoning to handsome men, and singing (really quite badly). Felix appears beside us, unsure of whether to leave her to it or race up and pull her down.

"Holy shit!" cries Evan "What is she on?" Dan appears beside us, and we all stand, stunned. Jack, Virginia, Mike, and Jed all aghast.

"She is going to die in the morning!" I squeal before slapping my hand over my mouth as Zoe swings the microphone like a Poi and tries to catch it before it lands on her head.

"Right, that's it, I've got to get her off." Felix looks set to get up there and physically remove her, but Dan pulls him back.

"No, leave her a minute, she's just cutting loose. I won't need to prescribe anti-depressants around here for a while. This is pure gold."

All around, people are cheering for Zoe as she grooves with the band and gets the words to the songs all wrong. She is having the time of her life.

"My God, I just can't take it." Felix strides forward and tries to make eye contact with her, but in her rock star moment of fame, she is oblivious to his blond head, although it towers above most others in the crowd.

Finally, she sees him and whoops with joy. Pointing to his approaching form, she hollers to the crowd "… and this here's my man! Let's give him a big up!" At this, she throws the microphone to the lead singer, sprints to the edge of the stage and takes a flying superman leap into Felix's shocked arms.

Doubled over, I laugh hysterically at the scene while the others high-five and back slap Zoe as she is returned to us in a fireman's lift; Felix not looking quite as amused as the rest of us. Jack appears with cool pint glass of ice water and hands it to Felix, who lowers his giggling wife to the ground and tries to make her hydrate a little.

Evan has disappeared again, but I'm having too much fun to care. "What time is it?" I ask Dan, who's chatting with an attractive man with dreadlocks.

"Who cares!" he answers with a smile. "The night is young, sister; relax."

Rolling my eyes in reply, I shimmy toward the grassy verge where I find Jed collapsed, exhausted from dancing. I sink down beside him and lower myself back on to the cool grass, slowly catching my breath. "How you doing there, Jed?"

"Never been better." He rests his elbows on bent knees, watching the crowd and the band still in full swing.

"Where's Sadie tonight?" I haven't seen Sadie around for a while.

"We broke up," he answers, his voice all matter-of-fact.

I try to conjure up my sober "agony aunt" self before replying. "Oh, when was that?"

"Couple of weeks ago."

"Oh… I'm sorry, Jed, what happened?"

"Well, she wanted to travel, move on from St. Cloud, and I just can't. I have the business and well… I'm happy here."

"Are you okay?"

"Sure, I knew it was coming. I felt pretty bad a few months ago when I realized that it couldn't work out, but I'm okay. She's got to do her thing, and I've got to do mine."

"Where is she now?" I sit up in case Jed might need a shoulder

346 | Skylark

to cry on, but he's being very manly about the whole thing, despite the fact he made it clear for a while he thought Sadie was "the one."

"On her way to Australia."

I frown. "Did you ask her to stay?"

"No." Jed turns to look at me now, his face confused. "Why would I?"

"Why would you? Because you love her, and because you wanted her to stay, dumb ass!" I raise my hands in exasperation. "What if she wanted you to ask her to stay? Did you think of that? Of course she wouldn't have made it obvious she wanted you to ask her to stay; she'd have been thinking she shouldn't have to. She'd have been hoping you'd ask her anyway. You know how it is, the stronger you feel the cooler you play it. She was mad about you, Jed. She's probably waiting for you to go bring her back, tell her she's the one and you want to make Sadie babies with her." Stopping for breath, I slap a hand over my eyes and fall back on the grass. "Why's love always so complicated?"

Jed shakes his head, staring at me incredulously. "Holy shit, I'd say you *women* are complicated." He pauses, taking in my rant. "Listen, if she'd been mad about me, she'd have stuck around. Anyway, it's different. I'm older than she is. She needs to do her thing now or she'll only end up hating me for stopping her. I'll be here if she comes back." The words are strong but his face looks a little shell-shocked, and I wonder if maybe I've hit a nerve.

"You're a good guy." I throw an arm around him. "And Goddammit, you make good coffee!" I check myself, realizing I just slurred, but carry on anyway. "Now does that have any correlation with how good a lover you are? I mean, man, you can work that espresso machine. It's like watching foreplay, the way you stroke her and turn those shiny knobs." I feel myself flush. "Did I say that or think it? Sorry, ignore me, too many cocktails. That was not a come on!" I feel a fit of giggles coming. "I'm just paying homage to your barista skills."

Jed is laughing at me, "You pay homage to me any time you feel the urge, Billie."

We sit comfortably side by side, people watching, lost in our own thoughts when I jump, remembering the evening's other big event. "Hey, where's Jack? We don't want to miss the launch of his boat down at the quay. Do you know what time it is? Seriously, it could be 4 a.m. and I wouldn't know."

Jed checks his watch. "Just gone eleven-thirty light-weight; plenty of time," he laughs. "Jack went in to get us a beer. He shouldn't be long now."

* * *

Inside the bar, Evan's in conversation with a few characters known to be trouble. The four men stand in a corner of the bar; heads bent, talking about something that seems too serious for a fiesta night. It's been a hell of a couple of weeks, but tonight, Evan finally feels good; in fact, better than good. He's high on everything; the night, the crowd, the music, and the feeling that for a short time, he hasn't a care in the world. Nothing can touch him tonight, and what the hell, what does it matter if he tries something new. He spends his life critically judging himself; tonight, he shuts those thoughts down, he's going to have a little fun. Reaching into his pocket, he takes out the rolled up notes and leans in to the man across who smiles slowly in silent agreement. An almost imperceptible exchange takes place, and Evan nods, replacing his hands in his pockets before heading to the bathroom without a backward glance.

With shaking hands, Evan locks himself in the bathroom stall; exhilaration mixed liberally with fear. It's only a small hit, and it's only this once. The gaudily painted bathrooms are dimly lit, and for a second, he looks down on the scene, grim and seedy. The image fades fast as the hit of cocaine speeds through his system, blanketing the reality in pleasure. He sucks in his breath and smiles; holy shit, it feels good.

He hears the door bang and a loud familiar voice. "Evan, are you in here?"

Jack's voice would normally get his back up, 'Mr Fucking perfect', but not tonight. Tonight, Evan is invincible, and even Jack isn't going to ruffle his feathers, not tonight.

" Evan get your ass out here!" Jack's voice is angry, but Evan pauses before opening the door, just to wind his righteous ass up a little.

"What's the drama, Jackie boy?" Evan is glassy eyed and rubs his nose absently. "Do you need to go? Get on in there."

"What the hell are you doing man?" Jack's voice is even, but his eyes are dark. He grabs Evan tightly by the arm waiting for an explanation.

"Let the fuck go, what's wrong with you?" Evan struggles to release his arm, but Jack's grip is firm.

"Let me go Jack, I've no beef with you. I've already apologized for before; I was drunk, it was a mistake."

"I'm not talking about that. What the hell are you doing? Do you really want to go down this road Evan?"

"What road are we on here Jack?"

"Isn't it enough?"

"You've lost me here; what?"

"Isn't it enough that your drinking is fucking up your family; don't start this stuff too." Evan suddenly registers that Jack knows, but the cocaine is hitting home and he feels invincible.

"You don't know what you're talking about Jackie boy; go home and build boats and get out of my way." He's beginning to feel pissed off now, and it's killing his high. He tries again to shrug free his arm, but it's caught under the steady glare of Jack's judgment.

"Do you know where this will end Evan? Do you think Billie can take it?" He releases Evan's arm, "What about the twins; is this what you want for them? Think about it, you have too much to lose." Evan shakes his head in disbelief; this conversation was not in his plan for tonight. Tonight, it was to be all happy, all good times, and no guilt trips or reminders to his guilty self that he is screwing up.

"Get the fuck away from me Jack; you don't know shit!" He makes to push Jack out of his way but then changes his mind. Laying his palms flat on Jack's shirt front, he hangs his head, shaking it gently before looking up with a slow smile. "You know Jack; I like you, and I think if you didn't want to screw my wife, we might even be friends."

"This isn't about your wife."

"Then what is it about? You're in here being the drug counselor, good Samaritan guy, because you think I need a fucking twelve-step program? Because you want to help me?"

"I'm in here because I saw you talking to those assholes outside; they're trouble, Evan. Don't get messed up with this stuff; you'll risk it all. I'm in here because I know. Look at me! I'm still trying to scrape my ass up from the sorry place this stuff left me years ago. It will screw you over."

A moment of clarity flashes briefly past Evan's glassy eyes, and he does stop, only for a moment. There's an internal risk assessment going on in that clever Irish head, and he pats Jack on the shoulder nodding. "You know, you're a good guy Jack, and I'm sorry I said those things about you before. I know you'd never mess with Billie; you're a good friend to her, and God knows she needs it." He looks to the door as though checking for anyone who might be listening to his upcoming confession. "Listen, I'm not taking any risks; you should know that. I love my family, and I'm just cutting loose tonight for the first time in a very fucking long time so please… I don't do this stuff; I'm having a little fun is all. I can handle it," he closes his eyes in a sort of plea, "so cut me some slack; I'm all good. Now piss off and go cut loose yourself." Evan strides out of the bathroom putting the incident behind him, his judgment blurred by alcohol and cocaine, feeling too good to let any part of his high brain admit he is slipping.

* * *

We sip the night's last drinks by a dwindling fire made of driftwood. The glow of orange flame and the quiet lapping of the ocean nearby have changed the mood from mad to mellow. The smell of burning wood and salty air rests on our clothes and hair as we sit cross-legged or lie stretched out on the still-warm sand.

"Man, that was one beautiful boat." Jed shakes his head remembering the scene at the dock; the small crowd cheering as Jack's boat slid into the water. There had been champagne and some more food and dancing, and we'd all watched in awe as the gorgeous craft sailed off with her new owner to begin her new chapter.

"She should be. Jack's done nothing but work on her for a year." answers Dan.

"Where is he now anyway?" Felix looks around distractedly.

"He'll still be at the dock, hanging around till everyone leaves." Dan roots around in his pocket, which is quite a struggle as his jeans are ridiculously tight. Not many men look good in skinny jeans, but Dan pulls it off. "Aha, I knew I had one in here! Who wants a hit?" He tries to straighten out the squished joint that has miraculously appeared from the pocket of the dreadfully tight jeans.

"You're kidding me... Doctor Dan? I would never have expected this of you." Zoe grabs the joint, examining it fully before sniffing its contents. "Ooo mama; smells like the good stuff."

"Give that here crazy!" Felix grabs the joint from Zoe, who clearly doesn't need it. He pops it into his mouth and leans forward, letting the embers of the fire touch the other end, sucking in with the expertise of one who has done this many times before. He holds his breath, eyes closed, then gradually exhales; the pungent smoke making me convulse in a fit of coughing.

"Pass that baby over here." Jed pushes me over as I laugh and cough simultaneously; he reaches a hand for the joint, gesturing with his head toward me. "Don't give this one any; God knows what she'll start talking about. Earlier she was getting horny over my espresso machine."

"Pass it on coffee boy." I laugh, extending a hand to Jed. "Anyway, it's a fantastic espresso machine." I take one long suck on the joint, trying not to show that I haven't actually ever smoked one, but give myself away choking and spluttering. Everyone laughs. "Okay, okay. I'm doing my best to look cool. Give me a break here."

"Where the hell's Evan now? He'll be pissed he missed out." Dan looks around lazily and takes another long draw.

"He must be back at the wharf with Jack," answers Jed. "I'll have his share."

"Yeah, that's right," I hear myself giggling, flopping onto my back to make sand angels with my arms and legs. "Cause those two are just best buddies." I'm startled by the sound of my own voice, and the whole scene seems wildly funny.

"It's working," says Zoe. "My turn, hey, I'm fine, Felix; pass it here or else!" She lunges for him, and they roll around in the sand together, Zoe unaware that Felix actually doesn't have the joint.

A loud voice whoops from behind us, and we turn to the source. Evan stands a few feet away, arms outstretched like the mountaintop Jesus in Rio de Janeiro.

"Rest your eyes on fucking genius!" He remains stock-still waiting for us to pay homage. Jed throws a paper cup at his head and

Evan raises his hands to fend off the following missiles. "Hey! Respect, I'm serious. You'll all think I'm crazy, but I suddenly got the answer in my head and had to go draw it out. It's fucking brilliant. I'm finished! The airport project! I couldn't get my head around that last image; it's the design piece that brings all the elements together." Evan talks quickly, animated, like we should all get it, understand and be as enthusiastic about it as him. "I knew what I wanted to do but I just couldn't get it right. Well, there I was, drinking and dancing with all you good people, and it all came to me. I had to race like a mad bastard to the office to draw it out. I couldn't get in at first and spent half an hour persuading security I wasn't there to clear the place out, and once I was in, I finished the fucker. It's all done. Divine fucking inspiration, let me tell you." He stops, looking around at our stunned faces.

"You mean to say you've just been working, right now… tonight, in the middle of the party?" Dan talks to Evan in the careful tones of one who thinks the other might need psychiatric intervention.

"Yeah, that's right!" Evan claps his hands together, looking around at us with a wild expression. His eyes glint but his face is pale and clammy.

I sit up slowly, sand-covered and confused as my addled brain tries to find some steady ground. His excitement in inspiration, such a clear reminder of a time not so long ago in Paris. A scene in my head: Evan home late, wild with happiness that he'd found the missing piece of another puzzle, me at my desk, Evan kneeling before me. It's his intensity I've always loved, but there's something right now that doesn't feel right, something spoiling the scene. I squint, trying to change my viewpoint. I can't figure it out, but then I'm high—what do I know?

"Evan, you're mad!" is all I manage to say, looking at him, eyes still trying to find focus.

"I know baby, it's amazing."

Ruthie Morgan | 353

"I know baby, it's amazing," I repeat in a deep-voiced Irish accent, suddenly finding the whole scene entirely hilarious. Evan doesn't seem to notice anything. His eyes are now fixed on the ocean. I watch him, and there's a small voice shouting, "Danger, Evan alert, weirdness warning," but I'm too stoned to care. We are all a little steam-rolled by this wild-eyed frantic version of Evan; he is a condensed, multiplied version of himself. Evan to the power of one hundred.

"The office is miles away. How did you get there?" asks Zoe.

"Oh, I grabbed someone's bike and cycled like Lance Armstrong. And don't worry, I put the bike back where I found it and jogged down to find you all. Anyway, get up off your asses. It's time for a swim!"

He strips off in a flash and races into the water without a backward glance. The men, taking little encouragement follow suit, losing at least twenty years in maturity as they race butt naked into the water and proceed to dunk one another and handstand, bare bums in the air. The scene is hilarious, and I want to join in, to soak up every ounce of fun to be had and keep laughing because it feels so good.

"Zoe!" I yell her name even though she is lying on the sand beside me. "Come on!" I tug her arm, pulling her to a sitting position. "We have to swim. We women can't be left on the sidelines!" Stripping to bra and knickers, I race after them, screaming as the cold water hits my warm skin.

Zoe, never one to be left out, is right behind, and in a mad rush of childish joy, we too splash and tag in the black water, the waves barely visible at this late hour.

The sensation of water is exquisite, and as Zoe swims off to dunk Felix, I float on my back, head half-submerged, eyes to the heavens, ears below the surface. What strange and terrifying peace can be found under water. When the body is submerged and the mind numbed with cold. When your heart beat rises in your ears like a drum, and the sounds of the world above are blanketed by water. When the weight of the ocean is crushing yet comforting and the pull of the undercurrent seems to point the way.

I bob on the surface, content in a small world of my own. After the chaos of the evening, the small hours of morning are beautifully still and quiet, even the ocean seems to be recovering. Even the low-hanging moon seems weary, too tired to pull itself high to its usual spot in the night sky. The water is blissful and after the night of dancing and drinking, its cold, cleansing waves are medicine to the tired soul.

* * *

Jack is waiting on the sand when we emerge much later dripping and shivering. Zoe gives a Jack a hug, but I reach quickly for my abandoned clothes, aware I'm next to naked.

Dan and Jed follow laughing about something. Unabashed, they challenge each other to a sprint down the beach and back to warm up: naked men sprinting—a comical sight. "You know, some things should definitely be done wearing undies," says Zoe looking disgusted. "There's just too much flapping around if you ask me. Felix, are you ever getting out?" she yells at the blond head still treading water. "I swear that man feels no cold."

"I'm just waiting for Evan."

His voice is distant, soaked up somehow by the water that lies between us.

Strange that this simple statement causes no alarm. Waiting? What do you wait for in a dark ocean? Where could someone possibly go that you'd have to wait? We girls are fully dressed as Jed and Dan return, out-of-breath, and are thrown their jockeys by a disdainful Zoe.

Felix shouts from the water, "Did Evan get out already?"

Now passes one of those long, drawn-out moments when the world stops and a single second morphs into a silent minute. A thousand scenarios flash through my mind and panic nestles into my chest cavity, my heart rate rising steadily.

"No," calls Zoe, the first to find her voice. Here follows a multitude of questions without answers. The panic settles, growing quickly out of proportion, filling lungs, pushing out breath and allowing none in.

In seconds, everyone is back in the water calling his name, swimming in different directions, trying not to think about what might have happened. I strain to control the hysteria creeping higher and higher, threatening to overwhelm. I'm in the water wading back and forth, diving under, holding the panic at bay, calling his name over and over.

Jack, the only properly sober one amongst us, takes control sending the boys in different directions, instructing Zoe and me to walk along the edge of the water. Everyone is calling his name, a chorus of "Evans" all trying desperately to sound less fearful than we are.

It takes seven minutes from Felix's question to the discovery of a limp body, face down, close to the wharf. Knowing the ocean better than most, Jack had followed the current and found him floating like a piece of driftwood. It takes three minutes to get him to shore, his long naked body glistening in the moonlight, white and still. It takes two endless minutes of mouth to mouth, air pushed from Jack to Evan, each breath into damp lungs serenaded by my hopeless cries.

In the second that life splutters wet and salty from his mouth, time resumes its course; second by second, beat by beat. His chest heaves to rid itself of the ocean and his heart finds its rhythm, pulse gaining strength, life not yet ready to stop. Steadily, my world rights itself; time returns to its reliable form second to second, minute to minute. I clutch his head, saying his name over and over, telling him it's me, it's okay, he'll be okay, wondering hopelessly if he will.

They roll him over, water clearing from his stomach, air flooding his hungry lungs noisily. Jack collapses on the sand, the others crumple in relief, and I sob into his listless hair.

Is fate our master or self-will a saboteur? Are the cards drawn for the choices we make or can a single second, a decision, a turn of tide alter destiny? Can life possibly be so fragile, so easily shaken, like the sycamore seed flying in circles blessed by nature with all the potential it needs to survive, wings given to fly its small form to a place which will predict its future to grow or wither? All this perfection and potential left to the whims of the breeze.

We wait in silence for the ambulance, each facing our own demons. The night's events have altered us irreparably, shaking us to the core. This brush with near-death brings our own mortality into clear view; we are guilty and afraid, relieved and full of shame, painfully aware for now of life's fragility.

Evan will recover, and tomorrow, we will start again, but I feel the tide pulling him from me; the seed of something beautiful shuddering in the wind, wings broken and future unsure.

* * *

Chapter Twenty-One

Silent Regret

I watch him sleep, and in the early light, his face is peaceful and his breathing steady.

He breathes, a steady flow of air in and out, breath flooding his lungs, rushing through his body.

He breathes.

Since the night on the beach, I have dreamt many times of the alternate outcome. In the dream, he does not breathe, and there is only water. He floats facedown, and I'm alone, trying to pull him to shore, turn him over, let his face feel the air. The struggle feels endless and still he floats face down, water lapping over his body steady as a heartbeat—but there is no heartbeat.

Daylight creeps into the room, a soft grey hue dousing the room in monochromes like an old black and white movie. There's just enough light to see his face, pale but relaxed, shedding years in sleep. Dark hair falls over one eye, curling in glossy fronds, a contrast to the pale sheen of his skin.

Few words have been said since he returned from his night in hospital. That evening's latter events leave us speechless, filled with feelings that don't transmute to spoken words. Emotions still raw and painful are best kept blanketed in silence for now. As I watch him, finally peaceful in sleep, I understand we feel something equally painful but significantly different.

I experienced the loss of Evan, a lifetime without him in seven minutes: pain, grief, anger, sorrow, and guilt. Guilt that I lost sight of him, did not take care of him, or save him, and the nagging question. Was this an event of chance, or was there a series of steps leading to its inevitable conclusion? Steps I saw but chose to ignore. Evan's quiet manner suggests a complex soup of emotions stewing behind those sleeping eyes. We need to talk, but until he is ready, we will dance around each other pretending nothing is a big deal.

As with every other day, the morning chorus begins slowly; a solo bird in song rousing his feathered friends to join him. As though orchestrated by a fine conductor, the bird is joined by another, then another until the song rings in natural harmony signaling sunrise.

Evan stirs, his arm reaching to find me and pull me in. An eye cracks open, still half in the peaceful world of dreams, the other half finding its way into the real world. These moments are precious to me, the short time where I have him back where he has not yet fully found his wakeful self, the burdens and worries that lie heavily on his shoulders still asleep.

"Why are you awake so early?" His voice is husky from sleep. I try for a funny one-liner, something to make him laugh, a smart comeback, anything but the silence; the words I can't say and he won't hear. But no words come. Instead, the sounds pool and constrict my throat. I smile and close my eyes tight, pressing a finger to my lips as though heading back to sleep. I will those tears to hold fast, but they don't listen. They come when they please and always when he watches.

"Don't."

He throws the word toward me, and it smarts on my barely composed face. I shake my head, and he pulls an arm over his eyes, turning his back to me.

* * *

"Look, all I'm saying is you need to take care of yourself." Dan leans back in his swivelly doctor chair, a ball point pen resting against his lips.

"I do and I am… it's just." I feel my bottom lip quiver and know what I must look like.

"Well, you can't shift this chest infection, and you're not sleeping. That doesn't sound like great care to me." He frowns, pointing the ballpoint pen in my direction.

"Okay, so give me some rocket fuel antibiotics." I fold my arms across my chest, feeling defiant and not sure why. Fixing my gaze on the Punga trees outside the window, I sigh, wondering why everything feels like a battle.

Dan leans forward in his chair and scribbles in scrawly doctor's writing on his script pad.

"Any chance you can throw in something recreational?" I work on finding my smile, hoping a little joke might help.

"You need more than drugs girlfriend," says Dan, shaking his head as he finishes the script with a flourish of his pen. He passes it to me. "You look like you need some home help and about three solid days of uninterrupted sleep!"

"Ah, genius. Can you write that in a script, please, and I'll pop it into the pharmacy right now?"

At that moment, Sunny wails mid-snore from the double buggy parked in a corner. Both twins had miraculously fallen asleep in the pram as I power-walked to my doctor's appointment this morning. His cry rouses Evie, who springs to attention, alert and wide-eyed, checking exactly what sort of fun she's been missing.

"Well, look who's awake," says Dan, smiling a white-toothed Dr.

Kildare grin at the twins. "My favorite little monsters. Let's have a look at you two." He walks over and unfastens the straps of the buggy. The twins climb out; Sunny heading straight for me, arms outstretched to be picked up, and Evie heading straight to the red plastic toy box in the corner. Sunny is soon on my lap, thumb in, staring at Dan with a little frown, trying to figure out where we are, and then wondering if this means Dan might stick him with a needle soon.

Evie, however, remembers only the fun stuff: the memory of doctors' offices post-immunization treats registers in her head, and she toddles over to Dan, climbs on to his lap and says, "Jelly bean, pwease?" Chubby hand extended and waiting.

Dan obliges, passing brightly-colored jelly beans out of a clear jar with a teaspoon. With the twins distracted, mouths full of e-numbers, he turns to me again. "So, do you want something to help you sleep?"

"Oh my God, no, I'd probably never wake up again. It'll be fine. I just need to re-find my rhythm. I just can't seem to wind down like I used to. No biggie, it can't go on for too much longer."

"I hope not, those black shadows are getting beyond the powers of concealer. Promise me, if things haven't improved in a week, you'll come back in."

"I promise. Thanks, Dan; you're the best." I stand up and lean over to kiss him on the cheek, and then scoop up the twins.

"How's Evan?"

"He's good."

"Good," he repeats, and we look at each other for just a moment before I turn away. This is my standard reply to enquires about Evan. It has been a month since the night on the beach, and it seems we are all still shell-shocked from the experience: the panic and desperation, fear and guilt. The intensity of those few minutes has left its mark on us all, and after the initial joy of finding Evan alive, we all went quiet, receding to the safe confines of home and routine, taking renewed pleasure at life's simple beauty—a joy never more keenly experienced than when laid next to a brush with death.

Evan has been quiet and withdrawn. A somber, less exuberant version of himself. He works, comes home, helps put the twins to bed, then shuts himself away in the spare bedroom/workshop where he spends his nights listening to Bon Iver and Sigur Ros, building things, fiddling with models and painting, maybe. He has asked for space, and I have given it to him, despite my desperate need to go to him, hold him, even just sit quietly in the same room together. I respect his request, knowing the solitude must be what he needs. It will pass, this cold, quiet phase; there is some internal conversation happening that is only his to hear.

It was an accident. He drank too much, shouldn't have gone swimming, and had we been paying attention, if we hadn't been so drunk ourselves, we would have stopped him.

Evan has been down before, but not like this. Lying with him at night, a dull ache emanates from his sleeping form. A heaviness that seeps out in slumber: anger, frustration, grief, despair. It leaves as he sleeps, tired mind exiting the conscious realm, and as it departs, it seems to find its way to me.

And as I choose to love him every day, forever, I choose to share the pain, to bare some of it for him, to take some weight, and to let him rest. I lie awake as traces of his despair and fear alight on my heart, nerves springing to action, adrenaline coursing through veins, my frightened body sensing danger. Fight or flight, get ready to run. I lie beside him, his cares gone for a few precious hours, and I feel them all but understand nothing. For a time, his emotions become mine, and I carry them like a faithful caddie till morning when the gentle light brings him back and I pass the baton.

Daylight pulls me free, permitting the return of those burdens not mine to carry, and I pass them back hollowed out and worn.

He wakes, eyes clear and bright for a few short moments before a heavy heart reminds him of the load to bear. The spark dies, dullness returns, and the cold fortress he has erected stands securely till nightfall. Daylight brings rational thought back to my tired brain and I remember that this too will pass. There are far worse situations. No one is dying, we live in paradise, we have children and a house and a job and food on the table. All of this, yet the space where his despair sits in my chest remains, until the evening, when finally he sleeps.

I have spent so much time replaying the scenes from that night, wondering why it happened and why we didn't notice. Angry with Evan for being so stupid, blaming him, blaming me, blaming the alcohol—but what's the point in any of that? Nothing changes, and after many sleepless nights of over-analyzing, I realize none of the hows and whys really matter, and accidents happen every day.

But as every day passes, Evan still drifts, his mood far away, floating out somewhere he might have ended up if Jack hadn't found him. Instead of drifting, I remain stuck in the same place, waiting for him to forgive himself, to step outside of the drama, to look at himself with kinder eyes. Waiting for him to come to me and tell me it will all be okay; that together, we will be okay. I wait for him.

And so when our friends check on how Evan's doing, I say he's fine. I smile and say it, knowing he will be soon and I must wait it out; let the dark cloud pass as it has done many times before. Even though the cloud is darker this time, I try not to worry. He has me. We have each other. We have a family, and we will get through.

* * *

"Once you have tasted flight, you will forever walk the earth with your eyes turned skyward, for there you have been, and there you will always long to return."

Leonardo da Vinci

Sweat prickles his scalp, and he takes a long inward breath, slowly, deliberately pulling what cool air is left into his overheated body. The office is hot, air conditioning on the blink again. An engineer tinkers with a unit in the corner, in no hurry to take the heat from the room and replace it with something cooler.

Dampness around his temples deepens black curls to ebony. Using the base of his palm, he pushes back the heavy dark strands from his eyes. "Christ, it's hot! Is anyone else dying in here?" he asks irritably to the four other men who huddle over desks and drawing boards.

"You Paddies aren't used to this, are you?" Dean Hobson looks up, smiling; he's Australian, used to the oppressive heat.

Evan scowls, Dean's nasal accent irritating him almost as much as the term paddy. "If they'd hurry up and fix the fucking air conditioning, I wouldn't have to get used to anything." He raises his voice and inclines his head toward the maintenance men as he speaks; they ignore him, continuing to work at St. Cloud pace.

Dean notices he got a rise from Evan and presses on. "So, are we due to see any Jumbo Jets taking off from St. Cloud soon, mate? You're looking pretty busy over there. Must be close to finished, right?"

"Close enough." Evan's voice clips, suggesting an end to the conversation, but Dean is undeterred. He had wanted the airport design contract himself and being ousted by the new boy back when Evan joined the firm never sat well.

"When's the bid?"

The final plans and proposal are to be presented to a board of government officials, business investors, and venture capitalists. Three other companies are making bids to design and construct the international airport, and none of the others are from St. Cloud. Evander Associates are the only national firm given the opportunity to gain the contract. Other international firms could produce the structure for less, but Evan is sure that what is saved in finance will be lost in integrity. His plans are for a structure that works with the landscape and local resources. His plans use only local construction, labor, and materials; his structure is sustainable, has a lower carbon footprint, and is, he believes, architecturally beautiful.

Evan has spent countless hours on the designs. Drawing after drawing, measurements, more measurements, research, models… his work has been obsessive, but the end result is close. He has gone through the plans time after time with Johan Evander and is now on the final version. Almost ready for delivery, he prays it will be well-received; the pressure for the company to win the contract is everywhere.

The subject of the airport is hotly debated. Will they build? Won't they? Will the island have control and will the economy benefit? Or will they be forced to accept a cookie-cutter plan, imported from abroad, built by imported workers, an eyesore rather than an art work and built in a less environmental manner using resources not from St. Cloud. He can work himself into a frenzy in moments thinking of all the work that will be wasted if the bid goes to another firm.

The contract is then only viable if the private investors agree to invest. The strength of the design and the thoroughness of the bid will determine the outcome. Even at this late stage, after so many months of work, the investors could decide not to opt-in or worse still, in Evan's opinion, they could simply choose another design, another architect, and another company.

"Two weeks," he replies, standing to signal a definite close to the conversation.

"You feeling confident?" Dean leans back on his swivel chair, his gaze following Evan skeptically, words following Evan's striding form heading for the door. "Jeez, did I say something?" Dean smirks, palms turned to the ceiling, mock-innocence.

Out on the street, the air is still warm, but at least the stifling feeling of claustrophobia is gone. Evan strides toward the beach, head down, hands in his pockets, thoughts tumbling one over the other. One problem never resolved before the next feverish worry pushes through leaving the question before unanswered, then back in line to continue the endless cycle of worry.

He has missed lunch and breakfast, and he registers this only as the smell of grilled meat wafts from a street side stall. Grabbing a steak sandwich, he heads for the pier, the air and smell of the ocean a welcome change from the stuffy interior of the open-plan office. Since the night of the mid-winter carnival and its aftermath, Evan has avoided being too close to the water. Even the smell of the ocean is overwhelming; the jumbled events of that night rushing back in a blur of fear and panic.

Frighteningly, it's the longing he can't put away, the ache to return to the brief exquisite peace of the middle ground between life and death. Those seconds that passed as a lifetime in the quiet bliss of peace and acceptance. In those moments, the noise of the world was gone. The demands and desires, the needs, the voices in his head—all gone. Those words: what will you do, who will you be, when does it really begin, and when does it stop? Have you found it yet, are you good enough, do you deserve this? Do more, be more. Where do you fit, and why are you here? All of it, all the words, the fears, all of it gone, leaving a quiet blanket of peaceful acceptance gently warming and reassuring a frightened heart that all was as it should be… let go, let go, let go.

Spray from a rogue wave splashes his legs and bare arms; his shirt rolled to the elbows, legs crossed at the end of the dock as he looks out beyond, reflecting on before. A bird soars overhead, swooping and diving, calling out in joy to anyone and no one. The sun breaks from behind a hazy cloud and the sounds of children laughing float from further down the beach. He watches them running in and out of the cool water, sheer delight in motion, in sand and waves, shells, and the promise of ice cream.

Guilt now; how can he fantasize over the notion of escape when he has everything he could want and more? Remembering Billie that night, sobbing over his barely conscious body, the sound of her scream as he surfaced noisily back into life. Seeing her grief as she thought she'd lost him leaves him numb with self-loathing that he could be so stupid. One dumb decision could have screwed over her life, their life.

He'd known the cocaine would be too much. What possessed him to think that one time would be any different? He's always known he can't mess with any of that stuff, but in the moment when it was there being offered, such an easy escape, he didn't think; he just did.

She doesn't deserve any of this. Since that night, she edges around him, almost afraid, and it's too hard right now to be there and see her like that—afraid of him and what he might do. He doesn't understand her. Unshakeable, she continues to love him, and he keeps messing up, but she stays, and her commitment to him scares him almost as much as his lack of self-control. How many times can he break her heart?

Another whoop of joy as the children splash their mother who runs shrieking from the water's edge. A man approaches, racing into the water with the children as the mother looks on, a hand shielding her eyes from the glare. Happy fucking families. The thought accompanies the knowledge that he should be with his own family, making his own kids laugh, spending time with his wife. He takes a slow breath of air before biting down on his sandwich. He chews deliberately, resolving to be better. He can be who they need him to be; he can shake the darkness. He's done it before.

"Half day?" a familiar voice calls to him from below, the deep timbre causing his stomach to clench uncomfortably.

Jack waves a hand from down by the water. He is pulling in on a small sailboat on the other side of the dock, and Evan has been too absorbed in thought to notice.

"Jack," he answers, nodding in his direction, hoping Jack won't join him. There have been few words between them since "the night." What do you say to someone who breathes life into your failing lungs, who pulls the water from your drowning body, and brings you back? Where do you begin, and when do you stop? *Thank you. Thank you for saving my life. Thank you for rescuing my sorry ass. Thank you for being the hero and revealing me as the pathetic loser I truly am. Thank you for making me owe you my entire life when I don't even like you, and before I forget, thank you for making my wife believe you are her guardian angel; the contrast between you and me glaringly obvious to all: saint and sinner, good guy and fuck up, provider and piss head.*

"How you doing man?" Jack sits down beside Evan, looking out to sea, eyes on the waves ahead.

"I'm good." A moment's awkward silence passes between the men, side by side looking out to sea.

"Work okay?" The conversation is forced, both feigning some kind of normality between them, trying to erase the memory of this beach, this dock, not so long ago.

"Ah, the airport project's coming to a head; everyone wants to see it accepted, and it looks like I'm the whipping boy. Damned if it goes forward, damned if it doesn't."

"Do you think it will?"

"I do." Another silence, broken as both men try to speak at the same time, a muddled jumble of "Evan/Jack" in Irish lilt and deep, island tones.

"Sorry, go ahead," says Jack, motioning for Evan to continue.

"It's okay. I mean… oh, fuck it Jack. I don't know what to say. You saved my life, and what do I say to you? I'm talking about my stupid fucking project."

Jack shakes his head, motioning for Evan to be quiet. "Leave it man, you'd have done the same for me. Let's move on. Drama over. Don't carry it around."

"Right."

"Right." Evan can't argue. Jack is the good guy, he's being gracious, so why doesn't Evan feel any better?

"How are Billie and the twins? I haven't seen them around much the past few days."

Evan stiffens as Jack mentions her name, but checks himself before answering. "Away, I thought a few days somewhere different might be good for them. I've got the bid coming up, and I haven't been home much, so I thought they should get away for a bit. A friend from work has a holiday place over in Seacrest."

"They've gone on their own?"

The question irks him. "Uh-huh. Billie is pretty competent. Anyway, what's the time? Best get back to the office. Air con is fucked, and it's like an oven in there." Evan claps a hand on to Jack's shoulder as he stands to leave. "Take it easy. You building anything just now?"

"Yeah, I've just been out sourcing some wood."

"Another boat, that's good. Keep you out of trouble, right?" Evan attempts a smile and Jack tries to return it. "Be seeing you then." Evan turns to leave, but Jack isn't done.

"Evan, hold up!" Evan turns around slowly, mentally preparing himself for the brotherly lecture, words of wisdom or warning he is about to receive. "The other night, in the bathroom… tell me you're not using that stuff."

Evan sucks in his breath, a deliberate slow inhalation to allow himself time to reign in a rogue reaction, speak levelly, and not punch

Jack's lights out for being a condescending prick. Does he have any idea how many times Evan has gone through this already in his head, how many times he wished he'd made a different decision? The self-judgment is enough to live with without Mr Perfect giving him a lecture right now. *Breathe, don't react. He isn't trying to goad you, breathe.* He faces Jack, but his hands, stuffed deeply into the pockets of his Levi's, ball into fists, his head down, eyes focused on the wooden planks below. "I don't 'use' that stuff, no." The emphasis lies heavily on the word 'use' as though grammar somehow divides addiction, to 'use' would make it a problem, and he doesn't have one. "It was a one off; I don't mess around with any of that. It was a dumb decision." Evan is still, careful with his words, a full-blown rant close to the surface. He feels anger ripple beneath his skin. Why should he have to justify himself to Jack? Why is he explaining? How could he possibly get any of it, understand what it feels like to need that sort of escape?

"Don't go there. You have too much to lose." Jacks words are sincere, but anger tinges the edges of his well-intentioned advice.

Evan runs his hands through his hair, his face alight with barely--contained fury. "You think I don't know that? You think I don't know what I've got? You think I don't deserve any of it. You're fucking transparent. Don't give me the 'I'm helping you because I care.' I get it Jack. I see it, you're not fooling me, so save the lecture. I know what I'm doing, and I know I fucked up." He stops for breath, hands on hips, head down again. "Jack, you have my eternal gratitude for saving my sorry ass, but now will you just leave me the fuck alone?" He turns on his heel, back down the dock, heading for the city; his long stride moving purposefully through the hot streets to the hotter office where he will stay at his desk till midnight, then return home to an empty house.

✳ ✳ ✳

Chapter Twenty-Two

Seacrest

"Complacency is sudden death in the mothering business." I write the words in spidery black ink in my notepad, circle the words then begin adding notes around the little encapsulated bubble - words, ideas, and trains of thought till the page resembles a detailed map; my sentence a small island in the center.

The sentence seems like a good headline for my column this week. I would like to be able to write about something different. Strangely, there's been a surplus of columns on mothering and babies since I began writing for the St. Cloud Chronicle's weekend supplement. Thankfully I've had no complaints from the editor, Lenny Horrows, and I have nothing else to write about. My life consists of variations on a theme entitled "Mommy!" The name, more familiar than my own; in fact, since the twins could say the word, it's probably the most used word in our household. It is who I have become. Say goodbye to Billie; Billie the writer, daughter, colleague, friend, partner, wife, lover… in no particular order. I am Mommy! Always with a capital, sometimes all capitals, and always with an exclamation mark.

The twins are asleep. For how long, I can't say, so I take the moment, grasp it with both hands, and type feverishly on to my laptop. If I can get the bare bones of the column down now, I can edit later when things are busier, and my brain doesn't mind a little distraction. For now, during the creative part, the act of writing straight from the thought bank, I must have quiet. I have no idea how long the quiet will last so I write feverishly.

By complacency in mothering, I mean the feeling that you've got it, you know what you're doing; you have this particular part of the mothering thing figured out. My experience is limited. In fact, 23 months of experience exactly, but I wonder if you can double that to 46 being that I have twins. Does it work that way?

My limited experience so far has taught me that the minute you think you've got it figured out, those babies pitch left field, taking you by surprise, and generally do the unpredictable just to let you know you're not actually in control and you'd better get used to it. I wonder if this is one of the biggest lessons parenthood can offer, that the modicum of control you thought you had and the small boundary you might draw around yourself is gone. Erased, annihilated, AWOL, undercover until further notice. Control is a thing of the past, and you must look back at it like an old, dear friend, fondly remembered.

Control is out of the window, and acceptance of that one fact can make the first few years of motherhood just a teensy bit easier. The minute I think I've got the twins in some kind of a routine, they show me otherwise. If I think I've figured out the sleep thing, the eating thing, the foods they like and when they like them, the way they'll fall asleep and the time I can expect to have them in bed, they change without warning—up till midnight for no reason and no longer a fan of mashed bananas. When I think I have their capabilities and lack of understood, like she can't possibly get through the gate or he won't manage to climb that, he'd never stick his fingers in there and so on, they are bound by the law of Murphy to surprise me.

If I find myself preening my mother feathers for even a second, it's a sure sign things are about to get ugly. Complacency at any age or stage spells trouble, and after every near-disaster, sleepless night, food fight, etc., I'm left wondering what the hell I was thinking imagining I might get it. In these moments, it pays to remember the wondrous values of birth control.

Head in hands, eyes bleary from lack of sleep, I trudge heavy-footed back to the beginning, ripping up the notes thus far on what I think I know about my babies. Out comes the new lined page of A4, and the exercise begins again. What's funny is that each time I manage to forget that the notes in the margin say, "Don't forget to write in pencil. Many corrections and rewrites are inevitable." I plan and create routines and try to predict while they cry "Mommy!" clapping their hands together in glee at the fabulous display of incompetent parenting I put on time and time again.

"No darling… Mommy wants you to eat your veggies… no, it's nap time now, not play time… I said don't eat sand, don't hit the cat, don't climb on the kitchen counter, put the hot coffee mug down… gently… I said it's nap time, be nice to your brother… did you say "please Mommy?"… that's the third wee on the floor today… inside voices, please," and so on and on and on it goes.

You see, I can write about being a new mother, but the parallel roads my life once displayed seem to have dwindled, and only one highway exists. Road sign above flashes neon: "Mad, sleep-deprived mother of wild toddlers this way—destination 18 years of age, x kilometers, and a face full of wrinkles. Do not speed or diverge from the concourse. Take a break when tired. Warning: teenagedom is dangerous territory—do not stop the car for any reason."

I write feverishly, trying to put all these mad, jumbled thoughts on parenting, good and bad or lack thereof, into a semblance of something that resembles a witty, insightful column. To lay weight to my topic, I hear a wail 200 words in.

After lying with Evie in the strange little single bed, she finally falls back to sleep. It's only 9 p.m., but there is still light in the room the twins share. Seacrest lies on the far west side of St. Cloud. It is a small fishing town known for cooler nights and shadier days. Its beaches are long, uninterrupted stretches of pale sand graduating to shingle, visible only when the tide draws the ocean away from the land. Small homes and fishing huts rise from the edges of the beach, their views breath taking; from these precious spots you can see the weather move and change, and clouds threaten before the rain comes sweeping across the wide expanse of ocean. Here the sea is a less vibrant blue; its tones deeper, cooler, a greyish tinge reflecting the changeable sky.

The cottage has three small bedrooms, an open-plan living/kitchen, and a deck looking over the ever-changing ocean scene. Two weather-beaten Cape Cod chairs sit at angles on either side of the deck and fragrant blossoms grow from an overhanging bush, heavy flowers spilling onto the wooden planks and balcony. Evan's friend Jo from work owns the cottage, and we have enjoyed a few short holidays here, the four of us: Evie, Sunny, Evan, and me, all together.

This cottage is the only place we have ventured to for more than a night since the twins arrival. Their first six months are a complete blur as I fully expected them to be. There's no getting away from it; twins are tough when they're tiny. It's double of everything. Double the breast feeding, double the tiredness, double the crying, double the colic, the projectile vomiting, the poopy nappies, and so on.

For the first six months, I operated like the walking dead, managing to function, feed, wash and change the twins, cook badly, just about launder the nappies, and that might have been it. I was steam-rolled; not only did we have no family close by to step in and help, I had very little idea of what to do. There's only so much you can learn from reading books, and the rest you have to figure out as you go.

Evan was overwhelmed. We both were. He tried to help with the feeding and changing, but with breast feeding, there wasn't much he could do, and often the twins would only settle with me. After a while, exhausted and trying to maintain long hours at work, he left me to it, helping if I asked but never volunteering. In moments of despair, it seemed to me that Evan was happy to leave for work in the morning, returning at night to a disheveled, exhausted me; he had the look of one lost in his own home. Everything had changed, and who was this wretched imposter posing as his wife? And the crying? Did it ever stop?

Things got easier, and we slowly found our feet, but things change with babies. They come first always, and although I thought this would be an easy thing to accept, we both struggled with the transition. Ours had been such an insular relationship. We were divinely happy in our own bubble; then along came our babies, and nothing was quiet or simple or controlled anymore. Gone were conversations late at night, uninterrupted sex (if I was ever awake long enough to have any), gone was any sort of tranquility or peace our life had before, and the worst was that neither of us knew if it would ever return.

We would come to Seacrest for a holiday, and without the distractions of work and the city, Evan unwound, like a coil losing tension day by day. We would talk again, laugh more, and he became the easy presence I'd known before. We'd spend our days on the beach, in the rock pools and tidal coves, playing with the twins, catching crabs, paddling, and swimming.

At night, with the twins finally asleep, Evan would pull the chairs together and bring out a blanket. We'd sit, looking at the changing view, watching the sun set and making grand plans for the future until one of the twins would wake, and I'd scurry off to feed or change. Of course, this would happen as Evan was getting amorous, spreading the blanket on to the deck, pulling me down, fiddling with my ridiculously unsexy feeding bra. By the time I returned to him, he was always asleep, so I'd bring out some pillows and curl in behind him and sleep too with the sound of the waves close by, the sweet smell of sea air a heavenly sedative.

Tonight, I am alone outside. I sit looking out to the sea as the light fades. The beach, the smells, and sounds are the same, but everything feels different. I'm sad thinking about him, and the last time we were here together. He was happy, less edgy. The twins were smaller, not crawling yet, and somehow everything seemed to fit. It feels as though a piece has been mislaid from the jigsaw that made our family portrait. One piece that makes the picture incomplete, and I don't know when it disappeared or where to find it.

My laptop has run out of battery and sits on the ground beside me. I lean back in my chair, darkness surrounding, moving in so gradually that I hear the ocean but can no longer see it. Like the change in Evan, gradual and slow, until finally I look up from my baby distracted haze to notice things are different. I raise my bare feet and rest them on the balcony, folding my arms across my belly, closing my eyes and trying not to dwell on the things I can't control. The space is good; it will give us both perspective. It's just a phase, part of being a couple, and it will pass as all things inevitably do.

The telephone rings, startling me from introspection. I race inside, trying to stop the screen door from banging on my way in, desperate not to wake the twins.

"Hello?"

"Hey baby."

"Hey." I smile hearing his voice because ultimately, despite everything, I know Evan loves me, and that one fact shines a light through any dark imaginings.

"Everyone asleep?"

"Yep, offspring drooling on their little pillows as we speak."

"What are you doing?" His tone is soft, the question hesitant.

"I was on the deck, writing a little, then daydreaming. Then I can't be sure, but I might have done a little sleeping myself."

"That's good, you need the rest."

"I wish you were here. I came close to a conversation with a potted plant tonight. I miss you." I sink back into the weather-beaten Cape Cod chair, twirling the telephone cord around my finger.

"I miss you too, but I'm useless right now. I need to get this bid done, and then I'll be better." His tone is soft, worn-out, and tired.

"Better at what?" I ask, opening the subject to any number of things. There is a pause and I picture him covering an exasperated face with a tired hand.

"Better for you… I don't know, just better. I'm not much good right now, and it's better for you to hang out there with the twins."

"You don't have to do it all on your own. You don't have to send me away to spare me. You can lean on me. I want to help." I catch myself sounding desperate.

"You can't help, do you see that? Watching and worrying over me isn't helping. I'm trying to do the right thing, get you all the hell away from me for a few days till I finish this thing and sort my shit out." His tone isn't soft anymore, it's edgy and he's angry.

"Evan, things are worse. I know work is stressful right now; I get that, but you need to deal with the other stuff. You just don't seem to be…"

"Be what?"

"Be yourself." I pause, gathering the words I feel I have one chance to say. "Cope with things like you used to. It's like a switch has gone off, and I don't know how to turn it back on. I don't hear you laugh anymore… life shouldn't be this tough."

"Where have you been living Billie? Life is fucking hard whichever way you look; however many fucking switches you have on!" He pauses and I hear him draw breath before continuing. "Things are different, and I don't like it either. I want it to be the same."

"The same as what?"

"The same as before."

Ruthie Morgan | 377

The words sting as I personalize their meaning: a reflection on me and my failure to be the gatekeeper in our relationship, that somehow amidst change and chaos and new life I have neglected him. And although I could have predicted his words, prepared for the burn, their sound smarts, and my cheeks redden in anger and hurt. "Before what? Say it… before I got myself pregnant. Isn't that what you mean?"

"That's not what I mean."

"Isn't it?"

"If I could explain, don't you think I would?" The discussion has gotten out of control, and I don't like it, but I can't stop myself from pushing further.

"Am I part of the problem Evan?"

"Shut up." His voice snaps with anger, sharp and steely, glinting down the line, piercing through the thin layer of togetherness that cloaks my shaking shoulders. "You have no fucking idea." His slow, controlled release of the words warn he is ready to blow, but the command to "shut up" is too much for me, and my own fuse blows without warning.

"Then give me one! Give me an idea what's going on. Is this what I have to expect every time you have stress at work? You quit talking, you drink till you fall over, and shut yourself away building your fucking planes! Or maybe it's not work at all, maybe it's me; maybe it's the whole picture, and you're too much of a coward to say so. You don't touch me anymore unless you want sex, and even then, you can barely look at me. Jesus Evan, you're absolutely right. I have no idea!"

There is a long silence as I sink to the floor, sobbing silently, the trickle of hot tears releasing all the anger that's left drop by drop.

"Calm down." The anger has gone from his voice. It's like I sucked it right through the phone line, and there's none left. "I don't want to argue anymore." He speaks with resignation, and I feel like

I've slapped him verbally around the head. We are both quiet for a time, reeling in how quickly unsaid words become big and ugly when delivered in anger.

"I'm sorry Evan."

"I'm sorry too."

I hang up the phone a minute later, a sorry sight, slumped on the floor, eyes red, face blotchy. An image of despair. My heavy head leans on bent knees, and I cry for it all: the past we have lost and an unknown future, for him and for me, our children sleeping next door, and family far away. Evan's despair curls its way into my heart, and I cry, feeling I might never stop.

* * *

The music is too loud for this time of night, but there's no one around to care or complain. Evan huddles over a work table, a spotlight shining down on his work-in-progress. He works on a delicate structure, painstakingly woven together with native grasses and flax, the skeleton a complex scaffold of fine wood, whittled down and shaped from Kauri and Gum branches. Bright light illuminates the model, and the focused arc of light casts the remainder of the room into shadow. The only movement comes from his hands, translucent under the spotlight. They work carefully, long fingers steady, each movement carefully controlled.

The sounds of Sigur Ross float around the room, adding a dream-like quality to the scene. The music takes him away from himself, helping the smooth transference of frustration from head to hand, from destructive thought to constructive craft. He builds, weaves, and shapes; the structure taking form: a strange and beautiful hybrid, part bird and part plane.

Evan leans back, looking at his work; his body thrown completely into shadow, hands stretching above his head. So uncomplicated. How easy it is when there are no instructions, no intention or deadline, when the only reason is the simple joy of the act. The end result is often a surprise. Lack of criteria and functionality open the doors for beauty in simplicity. He tilts his head to one side, then rubs a tired eye with his palm before reaching for his glass. Empty, he extends a long arm for the bottle, pouring the amber liquid. Just one more.

The conversation with Billie is still too recent to imagine sleep might come. Her words sit in his chest, stinging with each breath of warm, humid air. What the hell is wrong with him? Why can't he shift the weight, and why can't he talk to her? The feelings frighten him. Before, when he felt this way, the bleakness might last a few days then shift unpredictably. Suddenly, it would be gone, and the world was so fucking bright he'd feel like the luckiest guy alive. Those moments in the darkness were almost worth it just to feel the shift back to reality. Normality became an instant high, and his appreciation for the world and his place there was keen, sharp and bright. This time the shift just won't come. He feels stuck and afraid, mired in an ocean of grey.

Being around Billie is too hard. He can't pretend. He's never been able to keep anything from her. Beside her, he becomes more of everything he doesn't want to be and can't seem to change. The contrast is blinding, and the voice in his head taunts him. *She deserves better than you, she deserves better. Be more, sort yourself out, and quit trying to fool everyone; be a man, be a man, be a man.*

She's right; it's more than the bid, the job, the pressure. More than her, their relationship, the twins or the island. It's everything and nothing; all of it, and none of it. Dull despair covers the color and erases its memory day by day. A crippling guilt goes hand-in-hand with gloom, a parasitic guilt that attaches to everything. For each blessing, the guilt grows, proportional shame to the power of joy. The overpowering flavor of guilt is everywhere, knowing he has everything, but none of it matters. The despair has no basis, a phantom without foundation, weak and insubstantial, yet still it remains.

The phone rings in the living room, but he ignores it. Downing the drink in one gulp, he exhales, lowering his elbows onto his knees, gaze fixed on the incomplete shape. What does it need? Evan does what he knows best: turning the negative to positive through form, he builds and constructs; the small structure becoming more detailed as each fragment of frustration passes from head to fingertips. The answer phone picks up in the background and through his haze, he hears Billie's voice, pleading and tearful. He leans over, turns up the music, and refills the glass.

* * *

Chapter Twenty-Three

Displaced

It's been two days since we last spoke; two days since the ugly words said in anger and the despair that followed. I can't seem to settle, can't find a place to set my worries down.

I explore with the twins, make mud pies, gather sea treasures in buckets and bake cookies, feeling only half a part of these activities. My other half is in Frontiere Point, waiting for Evan to come home, waiting for things to be okay.

The sun is low in the sky at 7 p.m., and I take the twins inside. We eat noodles, read stories, and begin the routine that signals bedtime is approaching. My goal is bed by eight-thirty, late by usual standards, but here in Seacrest, I have no one else to hang out with, and the promise of another long evening alone is disheartening.

The telephone rings as I'm dealing with a toileting accident, a small offering that almost made the toilet but missed. I hear the ring but can't get there. I was hoping it might be Evan, and I really would like to hear his voice. I have Sunny under one arm trying to clean his nether regions with some wet wipes when Evie toddles through holding the phone to her ear talking jibberish to whoever is on the other end.

"Evie, give that here." I urge her to pass me the handset, despite knowing I'm currently unable to manage a conversation, holding a half-naked, poop-encrusted baby under one arm. Evie grins and toddles right out of the bathroom, chatting into the receiver in the adorable but nonsensical language of the cheeky almost two-year-old. I finish with Sunny hoping that whoever called has had the sense to hang up. But as I emerge with a fresh bottomed Sunny five minutes later I find Evie still blabbering away into the handset.

"Evie Skylark… you are not to play with the phone, now give that here!" I make to grab the phone and place it on the receiver, but Evie scowls and runs, phone in hand, diving for cover under the bed. "Okay, get out right now, you little monkey, and give me that phone!"

She grins and shuffles further back. Sunny joins in the party, crawling under the bed frame and giggling like this is the best game ever. If I could put my hands on my hips and stamp my foot I would, but I'm under the dusty bed, chest to the floor. I have a scary flash--forward to teenage Evie and feel thankful that right now the battle is only over the telephone… and I'm so going to win. As I edge toward her, determined to pry the phone from her sticky little mitts, I hear a familiar voice calling my name.

"Billie? Billie… can you hear me? BILLIE!… that's it, I'm hanging up now… "

Iris! I lunge forward in a slick belly slide and grab the phone from Evie, who lets out a high-pitched wail. "Iris?… Is that you?"

"Billie! Where the hell have you been? I've been chatting with your mini-receptionist for ten minutes now!"

"Oh my God, I can't believe it's you!" Iris and I have lost touch over the past year, me absorbed in my mad life with babies and Iris with her career. "It's so great to hear your voice… and so crazy! How did you get this number?" I shuffle backward from under the bed, trailing dust balls as I go.

"I managed to get Evan to answer the phone. I had to let it ring about twenty-four times right enough. What's up with him, anyway?"

She doesn't wait for an answer but barrels on; this is the Iris I know and love. "I was just desperate to talk to you and told Evan I'd just keep calling all night till he gave me your number."

I'm smiling listening to her, and the simple act of smiling and meaning it feels so good.

"Billie, you've no idea; I've so much to tell you. Why the hell do you have to live so bloody far away? I know Ireland's not as warm but could you and Evan not have stayed here in Belfast? Anyway, don't answer that; we haven't time. I need to tell you the latest." Iris races on, and it's so good to hear her voice I flop back on top of the bed and let her chat away, giving me all the news at top speed. There's a lot to tell.

The twins are still under the bed, Evie having forgotten entirely about the phone. Sunny has taken a few toy cars and broom-brooms them over the dusty wood floor beneath me. Hearing my watch beep the hour, I check the time and do a quick calculation in my head.

"Iris, it's 3 a.m.! What are you doing awake anyway?"

"Bloody hell, is it that late? Shit, I've to be up for work at six. Well, here's the thing; I went out for drinks tonight with Marcus and…"

"Marcus… not Marcus from…"

"Yes, the same one, 'luscious Marcus' from university. I met him again in Dublin a few months ago; turns out he's an accountant here. Well, we've been seeing each other since then and…"

I cut her off again. "That's too funny; you're actually going out with luscious Marcus? I can't believe it. Is he still luscious, or does he look like an accountant?" I remember Iris back at university and her obsession over Marcus, a handsome third-year Economics student. In fact, I'm sure it was Marcus she dumped me for the night I met Evan.

"These days I'd say he's luscious Marcus crossed with a wee bit of middle-aged accountant." She stops, then continues in a breathy voice, "Well, at least I think he's luscious, and here's the thing; get this." She pauses, building up to something, and I wait for the inevitable conclusion to the gush about Marcus and his lusciousness. The conversation has transported me right back to university, an excited Iris raving about her latest love flame.

"Are you still listening Billie May?"

"Yes, of course; well, get what? What am I getting?"

"Well, we went out for drinks tonight and then… well… Billie, he bloody well asked me to marry him!"

"What?" I yell into the phone, giving the twins a fright—both come scurrying out from under the bed, toy cars in hand, wide eyed. "Are you kidding me? Oh my gosh, you're not kidding… and you said yes?"

"Yes!"

We both whoop and screech into the phone like teenagers, Iris giddy with excitement and me incredulous at the thought of Iris married to luscious Marcus. The laughing and congratulating and hilarity are so gorgeous I feel light as a feather. It's another half hour before we finally wrap up the conversation and say our goodbyes.

"Ok cowgirl, I need some beauty sleep. I couldn't go to bed till I'd told you. Who'd have thought; me in a wedding dress? It's mad."

"Go get that beauty sleep, and thanks for calling to tell me. You've made my day. No, that's such an understatement, you've made my year!"

"Take care of that mad Irishman of yours and those two gorgeous babes."

It's gone quiet again and I jump, having lost track of time on the phone. Peering over the side of the bed, I find them asleep, curled up together on the rug. Just listening to my conversation with Iris has tired them out. I smile then yawn myself.

"I will. Miss you."

We sign off, and I untangle the twins from each other, and tuck them carefully into their little beds before making my way to mine.

I smile at the unexpected call and the happiness in Iris's voice. Another Irish wedding. The thought sends me back for a few moments to ours and how life has moved on since then. But instead of feeling sad or worried as I did earlier, my heart is light and full of hope. And as I lie in bed with the window open, smelling the sea air, I have faith in the power of love and its ability to overcome all things.

* * *

The darkened room is eerie in the half-light, pale and ethereal. Sepia-tinted shadows flicker in the yellow glow a single candle throws upward to the ceiling. Suspended by nylon threads, hanging at varying heights, hovering angles of wings outstretched, representations in form of moments in the motion of flight; Evan's creations.

The structures hang in scattered order, visible evolution from a form which closely resembles a double-winged plane to something far more abstract and complicated, neither machine nor creature. The last creation looks almost human, an abstract but hauntingly beautiful face and wings that are largely out of proportion from the rest of its frame.

In between plane and flying woman, each creation shows development, metamorphosis from beginning to end, the subtle change that moves the structure from something mechanical and stiff to something fluid; hauntingly human. The only constants through each suspended form are wings. Each has a carefully constructed, molded, shaped, planed, sometimes woven set of wings. The gradual change from mechanical to animal, the final creation akin to angel wings.

Icarus in the quest of the sun. Carved and woven from wood and flax; although paper thin, the impression is of lightness, feather, and flight.

Evan sits cross-legged on the floor of the darkened room; elbows on knees, fingers laced together, eyes closed in thought. He has been to work every day this week, and he's worked fourteen- or fifteen-hour days. The details are complete. The drawings, designs, the pitch; the whole package is finished, and he has nothing left. The bid is next week, but Evander wanted it first, wanted a week to make sure Evan was as good as he'd hoped. Now is the time everyone will start with the judgment, the work will be tainted with the shitty details, opinions, and nit-picking from other people's agendas. The beauty could be sucked right out of the design. It's happened before. He sees it all the time.

He's torn. Part of him wants to hand it all over and be done, saying, "Here she is. This is my best shot, and she's beautiful; she's all yours. Good bye and good luck, time to move on." Another part wants to fight for her, to defend her through others' criticism, see her through to completion, and ensure she's built exactly the way he designed her. All his creations are female, they have to be; they are his other lovers. Now, nearing the final stages of a long relationship, will they make or break, and will he stand by her or wave goodbye.

She is his best work; the pinnacle in a short career. Blood, sweat, tears, and the rest have gone into the planning and creation and she's finally ready. This one structure a symbol of everything that brought him here, to this moment. A slice of his life and the exposure of this project feels like the prospect of an incoming tidal wave. Anxiety bordering on cold fear with the knowledge that he can't escape overcomes him. It's inevitable, and he must stand firm and wait to see what remains. It's become too important, like painting your life on a canvas then hoping the world likes it. Being forced to care what others think is something he's never been good at.

Raising his eyes to the view from the window, there is nothing but darkness. Out here, the dark is weightier, pressed down by deep growth and damp air. There is nothing to distract him from this mood; this feeling that nothing fits anymore, that the color has been sucked from the world, and it's his job to find it: a toxic mix of depression and pressure, expectation and despair. If Billie was here… but she's not. He sent her away. He didn't want to be around her or the twins. All that hope and expectation, the pressure to be perfect for them, to be better… he just needs time, just time. Despite this, the space where she fits inside him is cold and empty. He misses her.

Images run in slow reels through his mind, and in each scene is Billie. He feels all of it slipping away—her, the twins, this life, all of it colored grey. He can't stop any of it, and he doesn't know when it changed. The waves of all-encompassing moods are hard to deal with, more frequent these days, leaving him exhausted and unsure of himself. It's such an effort to stay in one place, to retain one feeling, keep steady. The world moves and lurches like never before.

The pressure of the week, lack of sleep and too much whisky sees it intensify. His head flits from high to low, from well in the world to the "fuck it" attitude of the gambler with nothing to lose. Letting himself roll backward, hands over his eyes, legs bent, back to the floor, he realizes he needs her—not in time when he's sorted all this out, but now, selfishly; he needs her now. He stays there for a time, wallowing in the darkness of the moment, eyes closed, trying to quiet the noise in his head.

"What the fuck am I doing?" The loud words in the silence of the room bounce from the dim walls and no one answers. He sits up, back aching from the hard floor. Bending his head forward, he runs both hands through his unruly dark hair, takes a deep breath then suddenly, forcefully smacks himself hard on the face. The sound and accompanying pain knock him back against the wall and once again, he asks himself the same question. The reply comes in silence. His jaw smarts from the blow, but the pain is real, the sensation somehow welcome; something real in a head where the lines have become blurry.

"Get a grip Skylark; you're a fucking waste of space." He's heard the words before; the memory is deep, engraved and associated with pain, pain given by someone else, a father, angry and drunk, a son who never seemed to get it right, a mother too afraid to stop it.

He stands up shakily, head dizzy from the blow. Who'd have thought you could practically knock your own self out with a good right hook? If he wasn't so pissed off, he'd laugh. Heading for the bottle on the shelf, he pours a shot and swirls the glass as though a momentous decision is at hand. He'd promised himself that he wouldn't drink today. He'd have a day where he didn't touch the stuff; prove to himself he could do it. Its 9 p.m., and he watches the dark amber glow of the thick liquor as it whirls around the glass, leaving a trace behind as it moves. He knows he can't.

In one hard gulp, the contents of the glass are down. He breathes, drawing air into his mouth a little at a time, feeling the whisky evaporate on his tongue. *Isn't that what he taught me?* "Breathe when you drink it, son. Taste it with your tongue and your nose; smell it and feel it. It's magic, stuff of champions." Some fathers taught their kids how to play football. Evan's Dad took him to the pub.

Part of the anger is in recognition: like father, like son. For all these years, he tried to be everything his father would have hated. "A fucking artist? Who's going to buy that bollocks? Get yourself a real job, gob shite!" He can still hear him, clear words sound over years passed. The voice is a blow as real as the ones leveled by his father's hand. Now, here he is pissing it all away with the drink. He's got everything he wanted, and it isn't enough. He doesn't know when the change happened, when he stopped paying attention and the drinking began to compete with all the good things in his life, pushing them out slowly, one by one. He doesn't know, and he's afraid it's too late.

But then there's that other voice. It's like his Mammy in the other ear. "You're not like him son. You've got a job, and you're a clever boy. Look at you. University, an architect, a wife, kids, and a fancy job abroad on one of them islands where they grow coconuts? You've done well, son. You're not like him."

He knows he's not; his Mammy's right. He can make it work. He's not his father. It's just been the changes, the babies, the move, and the job. It's been a lot, and he'll ease up on the booze after the airport bid is over; once it's done and dusted. Right now, he just needs something to take the edge off.

One shot down, and he's beginning to feel better, the jagged edges of life a little smoother. He pours another and leans against the wall, stretching his long legs out, feet crossed at the ankle. *That's better.* Looking up, he admires his work, suspended mid-flight. It's beautiful, and he knows it. When he builds, paints, and creates the models he's designed in his head, nothing else matters; nothing can touch him. He breathes out and takes a slow sip, presses the remote on the stereo and Radiohead interrupts the silence.

He's feeling good now, his cheek and jaw numb, the pace slowing to one he can manage. He'll call Billie. He needs her. Or maybe he'll just drive down there, spend the night and go in late tomorrow. That's what he'll do; it's all going to be fine.

The models move in the light as if dancing to Radiohead's "Fake Plastic Trees," Someone is banging at the front door. Evan's not answering.

✱ ✱ ✱

It's past midnight when I hear the car on the gravel road. Fumbling around for my robe and phone, I peer from the corner of the window, trying not to move the curtain. Headlights illuminate the front of the beach house, and with a jolt of joy, I realize it's Evan.

The car seems to stutter, and it stops abruptly just beyond the driveway. Why is he here so late, and why didn't he tell me he was coming? I unbolt the door and push open the screen, thankful that the twins are exhausted and deeply asleep; I want to see him more than anything. Moving to the edge of the porch in the darkness, I lean against the handrail, watching, waiting; waiting for Evan.

The lights flicker off, and the car door opens. He steps down from the driver's seat and sees me on the porch. I don't wave or speak, and neither does he. Without stopping to close the car door, he walks toward me, hands in his pockets, eyes on my face, only just visible in the dim light. Our last words were angry, and neither of us wants to talk. He looks so worn, hollowed out somehow, a shadow of himself.

He comes to me, and my arms reach out, ready to hold him.

For now, there are no words that fit the silence falling around us. My fears are extinguished with the car lights; he has come to me, and as he walks to the deck he looks at me like this was always the plan. That he'd break my heart then come back and refit it, good as new.

Reaching the bottom of the steps leading to the small front porch he stands, hands in his pockets, looking up at me with still, careful eyes. I can smell the whisky on his breath and see the glaze in his eyes, but those eyes are on me, and for now, it's all I need. This is the Evan I know, he is my past, and as far ahead as I can see, here now; looking at me like he's lost, and I can tell him where he came from. All the things I'm not sure of are pushed aside till morning; for now there's this and it's enough.

He climbs the steps slowly, eyes still locked on mine, and wraps me closely to him, squeezing the breath from me. "I missed you," he whispers into my neck, kissing my hair, rubbing his unshaven chin over the side of my cheek.

"What took you so long?" I answer quietly as he raises my chin, exposing my neck to his mouth.

"It's only been a few days." I feel the slow smile spread while his lips touch my neck. "I'm here now."

"I know."

"Is everyone asleep?" His hands press into the small of my back and I move closer, eyes closed, silently willing the twins to have a full twelve hours of uninterrupted sleep.

"They are."

"Just us?" There's disbelief in his voice.

"Uh-huh." Tonight I want to remember how it was before.

He holds me at arm's length and runs his finger down the side of my face. Damn, I haven't noticed I am crying until he wipes a stray tear away with the back of his hand. "Will you forgive me for everything?" the words are soft and quiet, and I nod as he watches me carefully, his expression unchanging. "I don't deserve you."

"You are so right, goddamn it" I reply with half-laugh half-sob. "But somehow you're stuck with me anyway."

Evan nods slowly. His breathing is steady and controlled as he grasps my shoulders. "I want to see you."

"Here I am." I smile, knowing this is not what he means. With one hand, he pushes the cotton robe from my shoulders, and it slides to the floor, leaving me waiting, watching him, wishing I'd worn something less Brigitte-Jones-in-mourning to bed. "Are you wearing my boxers?" he rubs his chin thoughtfully, eyes focused on me in my singlet and men's undies in the moonlight.

"I wasn't expecting you." I think he's smiling but clouds have obscured the moon and his face is in shadow.

"Take them off."

"You." I stand motionless, wondering why this feels like the first time, wishing heartache didn't seem to be the pre-requisite to great make-up sex.

Evan slowly pulls the singlet above my head before stepping back again, watching—an endless minute, his expression never changing. Shaking slightly from anticipation, not cold, I wait for him to call the shots, letting him have this one slice of control. He traces a finger around a breast, one then the other, slowly at first then with more force. Bending to me, his mouth finds mine, hands gripping my arms, raising them high above my head, my body responsive and vulnerable. He knows me so well and I'm lost. We kiss and caress softly then more insistently, as urgency takes over and the pace moves from slow and controlled to desperate.

Dropping to his knees, he pulls my shorts down roughly, and I gasp as he reaches forward, his long fingers between my legs before I can catch my breath. My hands are in his hair, and I pull him closer, forgetting to suppress the moans which escape with his every touch. Delayed gratification gone with the shorts, Evan is suddenly unable to wait and hoists me over his shoulder before striding through the house to the little bedroom where he closes the door gently, then takes me roughly.

It takes some time before everything, all of it, is out of his system—all those pressing emotions fighting for their place in line, all the frustration and self-loathing, all the misdirected anger and lingering guilt. He rhythmically thrusts his way out of the mire, letting it all fall away as he brings me to climax twice, before finally coming noisily, collapsing spent and somehow cleansed on top of me where I hold him and sob quietly into his dark, wayward hair.

In the morning, he is gone. Even the space where he lay beside me is cold when I wake wondering if maybe I dreamt him. I sit up drowsily, my aching body testament to the night's activity. Walking to the kitchen, I expect to see him there, drinking coffee, waiting for me to wake, but there's no trace, no note, no sign that he was here at all; that for a while we were fine.

It shouldn't have to feel so final, so definite, so cold, but it does, and I can't shake the grief that sits in my chest. I go out onto the deck and sink into a chair propped against the wall of the house, facing the ocean. The air is cool, and the briny smell of salt water strong. The sun begins to rise, creeping fingers of pink and gold fully prying open the box I hid my troubles in only last night. A cry sounds from indoors, followed quickly by another loud wail, and the day begins; another day like the one before.

* * *

Chapter Twenty-Four

Past Shadows

The house is already dark when he gets home, but he doesn't feel guilty. No one is waiting for him, and tonight that feels good. He's exhausted. After a long day at the office going through the bid for the last time with Evander, Evan's brain is fried. All that after barely four hours sleep.

He couldn't stay and face her or the twins this morning; he didn't have it in him. He took what he needed last night and went straight to the office this morning to start all over again. What a dickhead; she'll be upset and confused, but for now, he just has to get through. He'll call her soon. Billie will understand; she always does.

God, he needs a drink. Barely in the door, and the whisky is poured. Two sips down the hatch—better, much better. The red light of the answer phone flashes from the corner, and he strolls over, pressing the button to relay the messages.

Beep:

"Hey Evan, it's me. You must have gone straight to work. Call me when you get home. I love you. "

Beep:

"Hallo? Hallo? Oh, right, of course, answering machine. It's me, Cam, just calling to see how things are going. Give me a call when you can."

Beep:

"Evan? Pick up, Dan here. Evan, are you home? What's going on, man? You were supposed to come by and see me yesterday. You're mucking up my schedule. Come meet us for a beer tonight at Santos or come by the surgery tomorrow. Take it easy. "

Beep:

"Evan, hi, it's Zoe. Just following up on my message from yesterday, can't seem to get you home. Hope you're definitely coming over to Seacrest; Billie's going to love the surprise. She doesn't even know we know it's her birthday. There's a few of us going over now, just the usual crew, let me know if you want a ride or you'll just meet us all there. Chow. "

Evan sighs and sinks into a chair, takes another swig of his drink and picks up the phone. It rings twice, and then she answers, expectancy in her voice. "Hello?"

"Hey."

"How was your day?"

"Good. Look, I'm sorry I ran off this morning. I didn't want the twins to see me then get all upset when I had to leave."

"It's okay." He can tell by her tone it's not, but carries on. "Did you have a good day?"

"It was nice. A little the same as yesterday; paddling, shell collecting, a picnic, that sort of thing. Sunny and Evie are loving it."

He can't help but feel pissed off that she sounds so fed up. What he'd give to be doing nothing but paddling in the rock pools and having picnics. "Stay till next week, and have a good break. I think Zoe's planning to come over for a night this weekend."

"She is?" *I haven't spoken to her.*

"She left a message, mentioned something about visiting. Listen, I won't stay long. I just wanted to check in."

"Okay. How was work? Are you ready for the big presentation?"

"I think so. It'll be fine."

"Of course it will. You'll be awesome."

"Hug the kids for me, will you?"

"Of course… Evan?"

"Uh-huh?"

"I love you."

"I love you too."

He clicks the phone down and closes his eyes. Someone knocks at the door, and he's tempted not to answer, but he just pulled in and the blinds are open, lights on. He sighs, puts down his drink and walks to the door.

He's tempted to smile as he opens the latch to find Jack standing in the doorway, his bulk blocking out the light. Of course, it would be Jack, fucking Jack. He's everywhere. "Dan asked me to call round; he thought maybe your phone wasn't working. He wants you to call him." Jack nods and makes to leave, having relayed the message and seeing no reason to stay.

"Is that it?" Evan asks, an edge to his voice. "Did you want to come in and strip-search me for drugs or check how many empties are in the trash?"

"I'll leave you to it," Jack says without emotion, turning from the door.

"You do that, Jack, you leave me to it."

He slams the door, kicks off his shoes and heads back to the studio where he turns up his music and works quietly on some wings for another craft until he's tired and drunk enough to sleep.

* * *

Seacrest is beautiful at night. The ocean quiets to low ebb, and birds serenade nightfall with all manner of flight display and song. I had fallen asleep watching the sunset and awoke cold and stiff, disoriented and unsure how long I'd been out. My head struggles to orient itself. The dream I was immersed in was so vivid.

We were back in Paris, and my first book was finished and published. Life had taken a different turn. We were living on the money from my book deal, and Evan was selling art. The twins looked like they might be four or five, and they spoke in French, but in the dream, I understood them perfectly.

Rubbing my eyes and yawning, I head inside, pulling the blinds and wrapping a soft wool blanket around my shoulders. Some force that comes before thought makes me pull out my laptop and find the file *St. Germaine*, a novel by Billie Skylark: 19 chapters and 274 pages. A complicated love story set in Paris in the 1920's; passionate characters you loved and hated, unrequited love and a cheeky twist in the tale. I'd been proud of it then. Why didn't I ever try harder to have it published?

Everything seemed to fall to the wayside after pregnancy, then after that, there was no time for anything. After the twins were born, I knew I had to write for my sanity; thus, a second novel that is ongoing, but the first completed and perfected was never given the chance to be read. I'd called around a bit, asked if various agents might be interested in reading it, but my confidence was so low that after the first few rejections, I launched the manuscript into the filing cabinet where it was lodged and left.

Curiosity makes me open the file and read the prologue and first chapter aloud, and there is such joy in remembering where I was and what I was thinking when the characters and plot sprung to life.

What the hell. I don't know whether it's the full moon or the reckless lack of control I feel regarding my future—but I find myself googling literary agents and publishers. I plow through a list of companies, wondering why I'm bothering, but urged by my dream and that feeling of having nothing to lose. I write a cover letter and short synopsis then send the letter and file with the novel off to four of the listed agents. Why not?

Around ten the phone rings again and I'm happy to answer, the voices on the other end my only contact with the outside world this past week.

"Hello?"

"Okay, don't freak out, I've decided we're going to have another baby! I haven't told Felix yet, but I just have that feeling, Billie. I just realized it this morning; it's meant to be."

"Hey Zoe." Only Zoe, no, I take it back, only Zoe or Iris would start a phone conversation this way; no introductions and straight to the point.

"So, I'm just wondering how to pitch it. For now, I'm going to be on my total best behavior, cook his favorite meals, bake some cookies, listen to his boring work stories… that sort of thing then…"

"Wait a minute…" I'm racing after the conversation thread, trying to run at Zoe pace "I'm all confused, are you pregnant?"

Zoe whoops with laughter "Oh my gosh, no, whatever gave you that idea?" I roll my eyes and smile. I really do seem to be a magnet for girlfriends who wear their 'weird' on the outside. "Not yet, but that's stage two of the plan."

"Zoe, you're mad."

"I know. Anyway, enough about me, why didn't you tell me you were going away? And, more to the point, how long are you away for?"

"Oh, it was a little last minute; we thought a break would do us good. I came over to Joe's place with the twins on Tuesday."

"We thought?" Zoe emphasizes the word 'We' and I feel an unwelcome interrogation coming. "Well why didn't Evan go along?"

I sigh in exasperation and hope she hasn't heard. "He's got a lot of work with the airport bid coming up so he stayed behind."

Zoe, both nosy and perceptive smells a rat. "But you guys never do stuff like that; you're like, the couple that can't 'bear' to be apart!" She emphasizes the word 'bear.' "I remember you telling me Evan was proud he'd never slept without you since he met you! What's up with that? Have you got a man on the side?" Zoe laughs at her little joke, the idea of faithful old me ever having an affair too ridiculous for words. I don't laugh back, and Zoe falls quiet. "Is everything okay, Billie? Sorry I'm being an ass; note to self, engage brain before dialogue."

"Everything's fine, sorry. I'm just tired; the twins were up a lot last night. You know what it's like in a new bed."

"Of course; hey it's good, you're having a break. In fact, it's great. When Evan told me you were away, I had just the best idea." Here we go, I smile to myself, knowing she is about to invite herself over. "Well, I just thought that maybe I could head over there on Friday, and we could have a bit of a girls' night. You know, PJ's, cheesy movies, wine and pizza… that sort of thing. What do you say?" She waits expectantly but my hesitation speaks for itself.

"That would be nice Zoe" I try to sound enthusiastic but I'm not sure I'm fooling her. I love Zoe but don't know if I have the energy for her. I'm worried about Evan and don't want to talk about it.

"Nice? I mean really, Billie, since when did we use such crap descriptive… 'nice' is for cups of tea, Gran's fruit cake, sweatpants, and big knickers. I'm needing an 'Awesome', 'fabulous', 'wonderful'… that sort of thing."

I can't help but laugh, Zoe is an infectious force of energy. I decide right then that her visit is exactly what I need. "Okay, okay…

awesome, fabulous, and most wonderful; please come, my dear friend! Visit me, but don't bring granny's fruit cake or your big knickers!"

"That's more like it!" Zoe giggles, and we chat some more before hanging up, grateful for our easy friendship. After hanging up the phone I decide that maybe I'll leave it off the hook for tonight. After a good dose of Zoe by phone, I don't think I could handle a call from Iris.

Much later I head to bed, exhausted from the few hours' sleep last night and the tension I've held all day, but I'm unable to sleep in the big empty bed. I climb in beside Sunny and Evie in the adjoining bedroom. It's a cozy fit, but their small, warm bodies are comforting, and after a time, I fall asleep too.

* * *

He wakes early the next morning convinced that after today, he'll make a new start. He'll stop drinking for a while, drive over and get Billie and the kids, make it up to them, start exercising again, who knows? The sunrise is beautiful, and he showers and shaves early, pouring a coffee and standing on the back deck watching the full lightshow as the sun rises over the ocean, casting fingers of colored light over his world.

Evan stretches, sips the last dregs of coffee, and glances over to Jack's house before heading inside for his keys. He feels so good he decides he's not even mad at Jack today.

Today is a new beginning.

The truck sails effortlessly around the bends and past the sweep of ocean. He makes the drive into the office feeling an overwhelming high of adrenaline and anticipation. At 7 a.m., he will make the bid to the board of directors and foreign investors, and by the end of the day, he'll know if all his work has been worthwhile.

He feels goods for the first time in a long while. He knows the plans are perfect, and he is sure it will all go well. Evander will get off his case, and he can begin the process that will take the plans to the next level. He will see his baby born, become part of the landscape, see the people benefit, and the community develop. He'll prove to Evander he was worth the risk. He'll have done something people will remember, and they might forget he's the guy that got fired for messing around with the company director's wife.

Taking the stairs two at a time, he bounds through the open-plan office to his desk where he reviews his notes and presentation files a few more times, counting down the minutes till seven.

Inside Johan Evander's office, the technician fumbles around with the large screen and high-speed connection that will link them to the board, where they'll put forward their proposal and field the questions they'll no doubt be fed. Evander feels confident this will be a coup for the company. He's been through the plans thoroughly, every detail, and he is impressed with Evan's work—not just the attention to detail, but the beauty of the designs. They are stunning, quite unique, his talent obviously untapped till now.

He takes the lift at six-thirty and joins Evander in his office, ensuring all is ready before they go live at seven. The board is on London time, hence the early hour of the presentation.

"You ready Evan?" Evander is tense and unsettled.

"Yes." Evan is confident.

Evander glances up from the pile of papers on his desk, eyes narrowing. "What the hell have you done to your face?"

Evan pales, remembering the self-inflicted welt on his cheekbone. He'd forgotten they would they would see his face; it had been the last thing on his mind.

"I walked into the cupboard door," he answers, feeling the angry bruise with his fingers, but Evander is already on the intercom hurrying his assistant through to disguise the welt with some subtly applied powder from her handbag.

At six-fifty-five, the screen flickers to life, and Johan Evander chats with unfamiliar faces Evan can barely make out as he mentally rehearses his opening. Moments later, Evander introduces Evan and gestures for him to begin.

This is what he's good at, and he knows it. In these moments, he escapes all insecurity and self-doubt. His words are clear, his manner engaging, and he delivers the information, taking them through the plans slide by slide. He discusses the bigger impact of the structure, its economic viability, its environmental impact, its future effect on the economy, and finally, its sheer beauty in design. There is much nodding and many complex questions, but Evan has succinct well-versed answers to them all. Evander stands quietly at the side, arms folded, one hand rubbing his chin thoughtfully, a smile playing on his usually stern face. It's in the bag; it's got to be in the bag.

Evan is charming and smart. He woos them with words and plans, and finally after two hours of presentation and discussions, he asks for any final questions, breathing an inner sigh of relief. He didn't fuck up; he did it, and now they must decide. He has given it his best shot. Now the rest is out of his hands. He can make that new start, take the pressure off, and give himself a break; give Billie a break, too. God knows she deserves it.

There are a few board members slightly out of camera shot, and as he waits and watches the screen, counting the seconds till all this is over, a sharp, heavily-accented voice breaks the silence. For a moment, Evan believes he has misheard. Something clenches involuntarily in his stomach, and an icy tap of dread trickles down his neck as he waits to hear the voice repeat itself and confirm what he hopes he imagined.

"I would like to know if Monsieur Skylark plans to oversee the project to completion if we choose 'Evander Associates' plans."

Johan Evander nods vigorously while the blood drains slowly from Evan's body. She turns to face the screen, and he catches her profile briefly before she looks him in the face, blond and petite, her eyes narrow and smile stiff.

"Of course. Evan would see the project through to completion. He has worked solely on this since his employment with us here at Evander Associates." Evander continues, oblivious to the cold stares emanating from Juliana Dupont to Evan Skylark. "Evan is very passionate about the project, and we are very proud of what he has achieved."

"Indeed," she replies tonelessly, eyes fixed on Evan, who has barely breathed since recognizing her spiteful form on the screen.

The past follows wherever you go.

Formal thank yous and goodbyes are made, and the board assures Evander they will be in touch by the end of the working day. The screen goes blank, and Evan blanches, sinking into the nearest chair.

"Well done, Evan. That was a marvelous job. You have done the company proud. Now we wait."

"Now we wait," Evan repeats the words aloud, lowering his head into his hands, wondering why he can't ever make good. Evander tells him to go home, take the rest of the day off, relax and get some air. He promises to call as soon as word of a decision comes through.

The truck winds and weaves its way to the topmost point of the island. He needs to clear his head, he needs the cool air; he needs to breathe… he wishes he could fly.

"Fuck!" He bangs his fist on the steering wheel and the truck swerves. "Fuck!" again and again, but there is no release from the frustration. How could it have worked out this way? Could it be a coincidence that she ended up on the board which will decide the next chapter of his future in architecture? Did she know they had moved to St. Cloud? Would she even have cared? For a woman like her, surely the incident with him was a drop in the ocean to the many dramas she must attract. Could she have tracked his career? Planned this? Surely not, that would take too much energy and spite. He remembers her words: "You will finish this."

This is madness. Surely she wouldn't take it to these lengths. He's overreacting. She's well-respected professionally in the European circuit. She will have been voted onto a board, and it's pure coincidence that it happened to be the board to decide the fate of his treasured project.

He wants to call Billie, he needs to talk to her, but what would he say? How can he tell her he's fucked up again? If he loses his job, they have to up sticks and move again. Where to this time? Billie is finally settled. She has friends, and he has friends; people who care about them and their kids. They have a new life, and only this morning, he was ready to make it all better, to stop the drinking and turn it round because looking back, it was the drinking that started all of it.

He gets out of the truck at the viewing bay where the road ends on the way up to St. Anne, the place they stopped and watched the birds together after finding out they were to have twins. Evie and Sunny, still so little and innocent to everything, looking at him every day like he's Santa Claus, like he's the best guy in the world, knowing nothing and caring only that he loves them… yet he pushes them away.

The wind whistles over the eastern side of the island and as he sits by the cliff edge, watching the waves crash below; he focuses on each bird soaring in the breeze. The arc of their wings, the effortless motion that harnesses the energy of the wind; hovering gracefully, plummeting, soaring, freefalling, then whipping up to head once again for the sky before the next exhilarating dive.

The sun is low in the sky when he stretches out and stands, heading for the warmth of the truck and the road down the hill to a future predicted by the past following like a dog with its tail between its legs.

* * *

By nine-thirty, Evan can't figure out what has happened. Why hasn't Evander called? Have the board delayed their decision? What does this mean? He checks his phone over and over, and then finally decides to call Evander himself.

"Evan." The tone of Johan Evander's voice suggests that he was expecting the call.

"Johan, I… well, I couldn't relax until I knew what the decision was. Have you heard anything?"

"Where are you?"

"At home."

"Can you come back in?"

"Of course, I'll be there in twenty." Evan puts down the phone, his heart racing, unsure of what any of it means. He grabs his keys and heads to the truck.

Another elevator, another eternal journey upward; this time there is no one else in the building, but still the rise from level one to nine feels endless. Exiting on the ninth floor, Evan strides across the lobby, past the unmanned reception desk and knocks carefully on Johan Evander's door, waiting ajar.

"Come in."

Evan does as he is bid, finding Johan and two suited men in the room. All waiting, it seems, for him.

"Have you heard from the board?" Evan asks before sitting down. He needs to know.

"We have."

"And?" Fucking hell. Does he have to pull it out?

"And, we are thrilled that they have decided to go with your proposal. Evan, your designs and concepts were second to none, and they were most impressed by the detail and fine edge to your work. Most impressed."

Evan lets out a huge sigh of relief and sinks backward into a waiting armchair. "That's amazing, great news. That's just great." He can't quite believe it. They love it, they will build his airport; but why the seriousness and apologetic tone from Evander? Suddenly, he is nervous all over again. "Is there a problem?" The room is still, a second passes, more time, seconds, minutes, everything is quiet and the weight rests back on Evan's shoulders. "What is it?"

"The board appears to have a problem. Not with the plans or the designs or any of the details. Let me say again what a wonderful job you did."

"What do they have a problem with?" he asks, knowing the answer.

"The condition with which they accept our proposal and plans is on the basis that you are removed from the project. They have requested we reassign the management of the project to completion to another Evander Associates employee, and if we have no one of suitable experience, they will assign someone themselves."

The air in the room is thick and uncomfortable. Evan can't seem to find his feet to support and transport him from the room, to make a stand and leave. He sits silent and stunned.

"I am very sorry. This is unprecedented. We are very happy with your work, but it seems… well, it seems a personal issue has arisen, and I assume it may be connected with a conversation we had some time ago."

Evan's face gives nothing away. He stares straight ahead. A personal issue—and now the worst of humiliations. All his beautiful work to be handed over to some monkey to see through and no doubt fuck up. To oversee without a fucking clue as to the way each angle came to be, each contour took its form, all of it. He has to give it away.

"We understand your passion regarding the project, and we value your skill immensely; however, it is entirely out of our hands."

Evan nods and stands, willing himself to leave without a scene, to slip away, to deal with it later. Just get up and walk out. With immense effort, he walks from the room.

Evander speaks to his back. "You will, of course, remain with us Evan. This is no reflection on your ability. Please understand. We will see you on Monday."

He leaves without fuss and walks slowly to the truck. He gets in, doesn't slam the door, turns the ignition and pulls out of the parking lot. He doesn't stop; he goes home and bolts the door. There is darkness moving in on all sides, and it's all he can see.

You never leave the past behind. He is his father's son. He always knew he didn't deserve any of this, and he found a way to fuck it up, over and over again. It's always been the same.

Sinking to his knees on the hardwood floor, he wills himself to calm down, but the room is swimming. His heart beats wildly in his chest; a trapped bird straining to fly. Darkness closes in on all sides. There's no air; he can't fly and he can't breathe.

* * *

Chapter Twenty-Five

A Birthday

It's Friday, and I must admit it's been a very, very quiet week. Aside from Evan's visit, I have been on my own with the twins for what feels like forever. That's not to say that the quiet thinking time hasn't been good. The fresh air and ocean, the simple cottage and lack of things to fuss over, plan and do has been wonderful, but I'm beginning to crave the company of adults. Friends to bring back perspective and give my melancholic self a kick in the ass. I'm excited Zoe will arrive today. She will roll in, mad and frenetic, and she'll make me laugh, and somehow everything will feel normal again.

We are constructing sand sculptures; it's an activity that can take an entire morning with the twins. It goes a bit like this: Sunny and I build, Evie knocks over gleefully, Sunny cries, Evie sulks, and we start again. Just when I think I might bury myself in the sand and start digging for Australia, I hear the distant sound of a car on the quiet road.

"Zo-Zo-Zo !!" shouts Sunny waving his spade. He stops and claps his hands together while a more wary Evie pokes her head around from the back of the house, her fist grasping a pile of green and brown seaweed. Recognizing Zoe's face, Evie squeals, and soon Zoe is walking up the driveway laden down with French bread, wine, and a baby under each arm.

"I'm here to save you! Quick, get a corkscrew and two glasses!"

she yells, approaching the deck, the twins squealing with laughter. We hug happily, and I unburden her of the wine and bread but leave her with the squirmy babies. It's not long till she's unpacked and standing in the kitchen opening the chilled wine with a cheeky smile. "Look at you! It's a good thing I'm here. You look positively bereft from lack of adult company. Here, let me take care of you." She plants a glass of cool white wine in my hands and pushes me down at the kitchen table. The twins toddle around, chasing each other, giddy with happiness to have another adult to entertain them.

"I've been fine. It's been a nice break; you know, sort of quiet and…"

"Boring?" interjects Zoe, laughing. "Honestly, you can't fool me, girlfriend. I've done the solo trips with toddlers before, and I'm telling you that after two days in confinement with nothing but preschoolers for company, no TV, and not a coffee shop for miles, it's a recipe for insanity. You're lucky I'm here, or you'd have been running screaming for the waves given another week on your own."

I feel my face fall. Zoe stops and pales. "I'm sorry, bad analogy. Will you ignore me, please? You know I speak regularly without my poor, tired brain being fully in gear."

"It's okay." I wave her concern away with a hand. "Anyway, I haven't been entirely on my own. Evan came down for the night on Wednesday."

"Did he? He didn't mention that, the sneaky devil. I spoke to him on Wednesday, and he didn't tell me he planned to come see you."

"I don't think he planned it."

"Aha… that kind of an unplanned visit? Oh, if only I could get Felix to feel as desperate as that to have sex with me. I mean, he wouldn't drive across town, never mind across the island in the dead of night just because he had to be with me." Zoe flops down across from me; her wild curly hair a little tired and flat.

"Well, I'm not sure that was exactly the case."

"Oh come on you… I know how you two are; it's so obvious. I just wish I could inject a little of that back into Felix. You know, it's always a little… well… the same." She swirls the wine around the glass thoughtfully.

"What's wrong with the same?" I ask, feeling a little jealous at the steadfast security Zoe has with Felix.

"Well, same is fine with cookies, you know. You find a recipe you like, you stick to it, but with sex after ten years with the same person, well… it's just not like cookies."

I want to laugh but Zoe is completely serious, lost in thought over the cookies-sex debate. "Nope, it's not like cookies. Here try one of these babies." I throw a box of triple chocolate chip at the wistful Zoe, who whoops and rips open the cardboard.

"You know, forget what I said; cookies rock!"

We laugh and tuck into the box before finishing another wine and sorting out a few big debates on husbands, children, sex, and lack thereof.

By nine-thirty, the twins are fast asleep, their path to slumber a little delayed due to the excitement of Zoe's arrival. Tired and a little drunk, we slip outside to the Cape Cod chairs facing the horizon and the moon.

"Now, this is what I'm talking about," Zoe drawls in her best American accent.

"Oh yeah baby. All this paradise and it's just you and me."

"Thank God for that. Men are a pain in the ass!" We giggle like schoolgirls before I shush her with a finger pressed to my lips, not keen to put the twins to bed all over again.

"You know, I agree. Sometimes I just wish I could marry you Zoe. We'd share out the jobs, you know; the groceries, cleaning the loos, cooking, that sort of thing. At night, we'd drink wine and watch cheesy movies and just buy out for sex when we got horny. Wouldn't that be so uncomplicated?"

"That would be so uncomplicated." Zoe is enthusiastic.

I cross my legs and blow my breath out in a long exhale, hair lifting and flopping over my eyes. "And so boring."

"Yep." Zoe nods disconsolately. "And so boring. We are such losers. I do love my Felix, but I think I'm going through midlife crisis."

"I love my Evan, but he's such a dick sometimes, and I do think your baby idea is midlife crisis."

"Really? You know, I wish I could agree, but I can't. It won't go away, and I can't stop thinking about it." Zoe twists a lock of hair around her finger.

"What does Felix say?"

"Well… I guess I haven't really given him the chance to say much of anything." She smiles mysteriously.

"So you don't know how he feels about it?"

"Well, actually, I sort of do."

"And?"

"I suspect it's not an affirmative."

Zoe untwists her hair and turns to me, eyes sparkling.

"Right, and what are you going to do about that?" I ask, knowing a plan must already be underway.

Zoe smiles and winks, rubbing her hands together like an excited child. "I have my ways."

"I bet you do! Poor Felix!" I throw a cushion across the deck at her as we both dissolve in drunken giggles.

"Anyway, Mrs 'I've got all the answers' Skylark, what about you and Evan?"

"What about us?"

Zoe isn't buying and presses on. "What's the deal? Why are you here on your own? Are you guys fighting?"

"No."

"Then what?"

I feel my face pale but know it's too dark for Zoe to notice. I fold my arms and sigh, trying to choose my words carefully. "He can just be real intense. He's always been that way, but recently it's been harder… I don't know; he's just been darker. Not all the time, but unpredictable, like best husband in the world to worst in ten minutes when nothing around has changed. I spend days trying to figure what went wrong. Then, all of a sudden he's fine again. Oh, I dunno, Zoe, I'm not making sense. Too much wine."

"Do you think he's like, depressed?"

"No," My response is quick, "Nothing as serious as that; it's just work. He gets so absorbed in work or his art, gets all strung out. Anyway, let's not spend the night talking about our other halves who aren't actually even here!"

"Oh my God, you are so right! Listen to us. Let's have another wine and watch a movie."

We head inside arm-in-arm to watch something featuring Brad Pitt, Zoe exclaiming loudly that she once was sure Felix looked just like him. I try to agree but we are soon laughing hysterically at the thought before settling down, finally calm, with some kettle chips and popcorn for a brain candy movie and the fantasy of forever love and happy endings.

* * *

Evan cradles the phone like a lifeline, he needs to talk to Billie. He needs to hear her voice but can't seem to dial the numbers. Her voice would help bring him back. Back from where? Where is he? What's happened?

He lies on the sofa, still in the same clothes he walked in the door wearing last night. He didn't drink; he didn't do anything. He lay there all night somewhere between sleep and wakefulness; his head a mess of jumbled thoughts. All the things that would normally rescue him from a period of bleakness—Billie, the kids, whisky, the sun in the trees, the birds—none of it feels good. The thought of all the things he has worked for, everything he has, feels undeserved and tarnished.

He presses the sides of his head, trying to squeeze out the noise, the constant fucking noise, all the words. He needs quiet, he needs sleep, but it won't come.

Billie… her birthday; he needs to pull himself together, he needs to try. He'll lie here for a bit longer, wait it out, it'll pass if he just holds on.

* * *

Down at the beach, I sit in the damp sand with Sunny and Evie, digging for crabs, and each time we find one, they squeal; Sunny desperately frightened of the many-legged creature, and Evie desperate to squish it with her handy spade. Each time we catch one, I quickly scoop it up in the bucket and deposit it back to sea and we begin the whole thing again.

The day is beautiful; sunny but not overbearingly warm. The breeze is gentle and soothing, and I try to think back to my last birthday. What would we have been doing? The twins would have been barely eleven months old. How quickly time slips away. I remember the cake. I made a cake and we ate some in the afternoon with Jack, saving a piece for Evan later when he got home. I cooked salmon, and Evan came home late with flowers, but I barely made it past the overcooked salmon, practically asleep at the table. The twins were both teething and hadn't been sleeping. I remember Evan was frustrated that I was so tired, and he'd just gotten home. Angry words, and I threw his flowers at him. What a birthday!

I roll my eyes at the memory, then moments later find myself smiling, remembering the make-up that followed.

"Mommy is twenty-five today," I tell an uninterested Sunny, who looks up at me, spade in hand, and replies by throwing his shovel full of sand into my hair. "Happy birthday to me!" I squeal grabbing his chubby thighs and tickling him mercilessly until Evie approaches to defend her brother and soon becomes embroiled in the tickle fest.

Sometimes this visible slipping away of time takes my breath away: hours, days, and years I have with them slipping past; snapshots of their little lives growing and changing before my eyes. Evie and Sunny are soon fighting over who gets to sit on top of me and run their sandy hands in my hair. I take a deep breath, hoping for patience, and try to iron out the small dispute fairly. Attention must be so carefully delivered, love poured out in equal measures always. Despite knowing this, I also know that no matter how hard I try to treat them equally, try to divide my attention and time perfectly between the two, one will always feel loved less.

*　*　*

By mid-afternoon things are quieter, much quieter.

"I can't believe you arranged for Marlene to come get the twins, Zoe. I mean, do you think they'll be okay?" I sit bolt upright on my striped sun lounger. "Do you think she'll be okay? Oh my God, what if they cry all night they've never been away from me overnight before… " I lay a panic-stricken hand on Zoe's sun-kissed forearm. I'm not sure if she's even listening; her body supine, eyes closed, enjoying the sunny afternoon.

"Will you stop it," she answers lazily. "This will be the best thing in the world for the kids and for you… absence makes the heart grow fonder, blah, blah, blah, and all that. You'll be all rested and ready to embrace motherhood with new vigor tomorrow." Her tone is lethargic.

"Did you rehearse that little embracing motherhood bit? I liked it," I say, lying back down with a sigh.

She smiles, finally rousing herself to sip the cocktail which waits on the side table. "Oh, and don't forget you can thank me any time!"

I blush, realizing I have been so perturbed about the twins being snatched by maternal Marlene for a sleepover at her place I haven't thought to thank Zoe for arranging the whole thing. "I'm sorry; I'm a terrible friend. Maybe after the cocktail I'll lighten up."

"Right," she replies, clinking my glass derisively.

The rest of the afternoon slips by on the striped sun loungers, a little chatting, some dozing in the sun, and some cool cocktails. At around 4 p.m., I hear the sound of a car crunching over the seashells and stones that line the long driveway. Someone bangs on a car horn, and I scream and jump in my lounger, very awake.

"Oh my God, who is here?" I yelp, hands to my breasts, feeling a little exposed, asleep in my bikini! Zoe claps her hands and whoops as the doors to Dan's Chevy open, and our friends peel out singing happy birthday in (quite bad) harmony. I squeal, and then slap my hands to my mouth in surprise only to quickly return them to my bust as loose bikini straps threaten to expose me amidst the happy birthday serenade.

"You planned this!" I punch Zoe affectionately on the arm, and she screams and punches me right back. We fall into giggles that are quickly overpowered by yells of, "Surprise!" from Dan and the crew.

Dan resembles James Dean with his sixties attire and coiffed hair, a look he is partial too when driving his vintage Chevy. I am swept from bear hug to bear hug and kissed happy birthday by my nearest and dearest till I'm giddy with joy.

"You guys are amazing; I can't believe you planned this, Zoe. All that girls' weekend nonsense! What will we do with the excess Brad Pitt movies?"

"Did someone say Brad Pitt?" queries Dan, his sixties quiff wilting slightly.

* * *

Soon, we are on the beach, swimming and drinking more cocktails concocted by Dan, complete with umbrellas and maraschino cherries. I'm so touched that they care enough to put life aside for a time and come spend my birthday with me. Once Evan arrives, the day will be complete. It feels somehow wrong to be so happy when I can't share it with him.

The day is hot and the lure of the cool ocean soon wins over, and we race in to swim before dark. "He's coming, don't worry," Zoe says in a frustrated voice. We're treading water, cool waves lapping around our shoulders. Dan floats on a pink Lilo trying to maintain his hairdo, and the others dive around the pale sand throwing a Frisbee.

"Did he say he definitely would?"

"Of course… and will you stop with the 'can't survive without my man' puppy dog look?"

I feign horror and dunk her under the water. Feeling decidedly happier, I wait until she emerges and splash her laughing face again for good measure. "You are such a cow… since when did I ever do the puppy dog look?"

Zoe spits a mouthful of salty water and splashes me. "Oh my God, you have no idea, Billie; like, every day. It's nauseating!"

"Oh, you so deserve to be dunked!" I dive for her again until a voice from the shore calls us in.

"Are you guys getting out of the water today? There's a ridiculous amount of wine here to be drunk and the grill is just hot enough for the steaks. Come on and dry off!" Jed's voice, always the caterer, calls from the water's edge, Frisbee forgotten. He has taken control of the barbeque.

An hour later as the sun sinks low in the sky, we sit around the small fire Felix has built, drinks in hand, steaks long gone. Dan has lost the cardigan and looks unfamiliarly disheveled: swimming shorts, bare sandy arms, and hair in spiky vestiges of a once coiffured quiff. Zoe lies on Felix's lap, Jed and Sadie are entwined (Sadie having just arrived back from the short sojourn away from Jed, it seems it took only three weeks away to realize she couldn't be without him). Then there's me and Jack—the last remaining singletons sitting in between the couples, our eyes meeting over the fire from time to time.

No one has mentioned that Evan hasn't arrived, and I try to forget about it. There will be no more puppy dog eyes from this girl tonight. I feel a sassy sort of an alter-ego emerging and decide to embrace her just for a while. The entire world has a rosy happy glow around it, and tonight it's all happy endings and good friends and birthdays and bubbles. The sun is on its best behavior, and as its sinks to its lowest point in the evening sky, I urge everyone to walk to the water's edge and bid goodbye to the daylight.

We walk to the point where the ocean laps gently onto the sand. The last crescent of sun hovers over the horizon, dark pink and red, reflecting its final burst of color on the calm ocean.

"Who needs fireworks" I whisper. Jack stands behind me, which is lucky as I feel a little wobbly, and everyone seems to be leaning on someone—except Dan, of course, who is back at his car, straining with something in the trunk.

I lean into Jack, and he lets me. "Thank you."

"For what?" he asks quietly.

"You know." I turn to him and pushing on my tiptoes kiss his cheek before taking off to help Dan with the large amp he's trying to maneuver drunkenly down the path to the gathering by the fire.

"Now, hang on," says Zoe, always the organizer. "Before we all get totally sozzled, can I just check where in God's name we're all going to sleep? Just so you know, I'm not up for an orgy!"

Jack jogs over from behind the little cottage moments later to inform us he has set up camp: four two-man tents, all with sleeping bags. "No, no." He raises his hands in mock deflection of imminent praise. "You can thank me later, just be grateful I was in boy scouts."

We all laugh and toast Jack and his tents, glasses raised in the air but stop, all eyes on the driveway as another car pulls in. My heart lifts… Evan?

A loud English female voice hollers from the open passenger seat window. "Could you have made this place any more difficult to find? Honestly, I told Mike we should have followed Dan here, but he insisted he had to check in at the hospital one more time and 'apparently' he knew the way." Virginia is talking to us but her tone suggests the words are for Mike, who exits the driver's seat stiff-legged and sheepish.

"Hey guys!" He salutes with the expression of the war weary; Virginia rolls her eyes and throws her hands in the air. "Oh, it's so good to be here! How wonderful; we just made sunset. Divine, it's just divine… Billie!" She extends her arms out to me, and I push my disappointment away in time to smile and give her a hug.

"I'm so glad you could make it!"

"Happy Birthday!" She puts a bottle of expensive champagne

into my hands and starts making the rounds, greeting everyone, embracing them in hugs, and I feel touched once again that I have friends that care this much about me. I push the bottle into the sand and lunge at an awkward Mike, enveloping him in a hug. Glasses are pressed into Virginia and Mike's hands, and Jack heads off to the smooth grass behind the house to set up an extra tent.

It isn't long before Mike has relaxed fully and sits barefoot on the sand, trousers rolled up around his knees, regaling funny work stories. Virginia sits beside me, Zoe, and Sadie, and having downed four glasses of bubbly in quick succession, she's feeling chatty about work and the challenges of the female anatomy. Sadie looks shocked, but Zoe and I listen, amazed, at the stories she regales; the difference in threshold for the weird and wonderful dramatically altered post labor. The birthing of babies eliminating any taboo regarding the vagina.

Near eleven, Dan wanders over to the amp he has connected to his iPod and powered magically from the car battery.

"Ladies and gentlemen," he announces, sounding like Jim Carrey. "It's time for Karaoke with Doctor Dan. Select your song and get in line!" He whoops and grabs an empty beer bottle, being that he hadn't been quite organized enough to find a microphone. He has selected a Kings of Leon number. Looking like he has rehearsed this many times in his bedroom mirror, he holds the beer bottle and sings, the clever app leaving the original soundtrack blaring without the artist's voice. Lyrics display on his iPad, and now and again, he glances toward it for guidance in between pointing to his crowd and singing with his imaginary band about 'Sex on Fire'. When the guitars hit the final chords, he drops to his knees and holds a pose while we cheer.

A list of songs on his playlist have been conscientiously printed and distributed, and we check for our favorites, ready to take our turn on the sandy stage. Self-consciousness has gone out with the tide, and we vie for next spot to have our turn.

"Me next, me next!" Virginia pleads, jumping to her feet, her tie-dye skirt trailing behind as she grabs the beer bottle from Dan and selects Katy Perry, "I Kissed a Girl." We hoot and holler as she grooves and gyrates, singing and shimmying up to Mike, who laughs, no longer awkward, fully into the rare evening out with friends.

Mike follows Virginia's lead singing a cheesy Guns N' Roses number. We cheer, boo, and throw paper cups as he sings on, oblivious, playing air guitar. Jack leans back on his elbows, laughing hard, and I catch his eye across the fire.

He's watching me, and it feels good. Scruffy in denim cut-offs and a bikini top, my hair is sandy and tousled, but tonight, I feel gorgeous, comfortable with myself and the people around me; everything is perfect—almost. I'm trying, but I can't ignore the tiny seed of anger over Evan not bothering to come, and it makes me feel feisty and a little reckless.

Next up is Jed, who does a convincing rendition of Eddie Vedder with Pearl Jam singing "Don't Call Me Daughter," the lyrics not entirely fitting, but the effort commendable. Sadie follows bashfully, choosing Madonna's "Don't Tell Me to Stop." She dances, channeling Madonna's vibe and attitude, the onset of the music pulling her out of herself and into "sexy lady just got me my man back" self.

I grab a giggling Zoe and drag her up to sing a duet of Martha and the Muffins "Echo Beach." She protests for just a moment, then on hearing the intro gets excited, grabbing the beer bottle from me before I can begin. "Tick-tock, tick-tock." The track begins slowly with the guitar solo and rhythmic beat, and Zoe goes wild, jumping like she's back on stage, forgetting entirely to sing.

Throwing my arms around her I commandeer the bottle and sing in my best rock star voice, moving, jumping, and bum bumping into Zoe. Fans going wild, (not really) I practice my moves. "Echo beach far away inside, echo beach faraway inside." I don't need the words;

this one has been practiced in my bedroom mirror with a hairbrush many times.

Zoe suddenly remembers she's supposed to be singing too and grabs the bottle, joining in for the chorus. We finish to a raucous of cat calls and wolf whistles before collapsing hysterically into the sand.

It takes some time before everyone calms down. I'm laughing so hard I think I might wet my pants, and Zoe won't give the bottle back to Dan, desperate to choose her second number.

Felix takes control and commandeers the beer bottle selecting Iron Maiden, which everyone is incidentally surprised to find on Dan's iPod. Felix is in his element, all Germanic stiffness thrown off with his sweaty t-shirt. He "air guitars" and sings for the glory of the motherland. We whoop and holler in applause, and Zoe throws herself onto him, legs wrapped around his waist, kissing him like it's high school prom.

"Get a room!" yells Dan from over by the amp. The others continue the applause while Felix takes a bow with Zoe attached, and then hoists her higher and strides to their tent, his testosterone fully boosted by his Iron Maiden performance. Raising one hand in salute, he slaps Zoe's bum with the other and continues on unembarrassed by the wolf whistles accompanying their departure.

I have a feeling Zoe won't mind the cookies tonight.

Everyone is shouting Jack's name, but he shakes his head, refusing to take the stage. Poor Jack. I play the birthday girl routine. "Do it for me, Jack, you have to… it's my birthday." I bat my eyelashes, channeling a little Marilyn Munroe. "Go on, get your hairy ass up there!"

Jack shakes his head in quiet despair and grabs the bottle, fiddles with the iPod, clears his throat, and waits head-down for the intro before starting to sing in a low, gravelly voice which screams of too much partying in a previous life. Bon Iver's 'Skinny Love' breaks the quiet of night, Jack's low voice is a contrast to the high-pitched sound of the original, but somehow it works, and we sit drunkenly in awe.

I listen and watch and wonder guiltily. Why not him? Why wasn't he the one? How might life have been if I'd met him before Evan? My thoughts betray Evan, but I'm too drunk to push them away. What if I lived with him, had his babies, and let those hands be the ones that touched me at night? What would life be like? Would I be waiting for Jack, too?

He sings and I listen. "Come on, skinny love, just last the year…" Stunned with the tuneful voice he's kept hidden deep in his secretive personality, I wonder what else he might hide.

Soon everyone begins to fade, one by one, couple by couple, and I know Evan isn't coming; he was never coming, but my anger is all gone, and the moment seems simply inevitable. Here I am again, waiting for Evan. The waiting so much a part of our relationship that it's almost comfortable—an inevitable component that comes with the territory. The saddest thing is, I know I would wait as long as it took if I knew that in the end he would come, but tonight there will be no Evan, and in this moment, the feeling is crystal-clear and cold: I am done waiting.

Soon it's only me, Jack, and Dan left sitting around the last embers of the dying fire.

"Don't go guys. I don't want the night to end," I say mournfully, but Dan stands, takes a bow and almost keels over in the process.

"Good night darlings. I bid you adieu, keep it tight!" And with that, he wobbles off to the twins' room inside the house. Dan doesn't do tents.

I smile up at Jack. It's a smile that might tell a story, one that only he would understand; complicated and a little sad. He smiles back a similar tale, eyes sparkling and dancing in the fire light. I break the moment, cheeks flushing, returning my gaze to the red and white charred logs of the fire. Jack jumps to his feet.

"Wait here, I just remembered." He jogs off to his truck and is back before I have time to wonder what it might be he almost forgot. Sitting back down beside me, he pushes a small package into my hands. He shrugs, and the gesture makes me smile. He looks like an embarrassed teenager.

"What's this?" I hold the brown paper-wrapped package in my open palms and smile up at him.

"I made it, for your birthday, it's just…"

"Jack, thank you."

"You haven't seen it yet."

"I don't have to. You made it for me, and I'll love it."

He rubs his face with a hand while I carefully unwrap the small parcel whose contents leave me speechless for a time. Jack watches as I stare wide-eyed at the perfectly carved wooden bird. It sits in my hand; its small face expressive, head tilted slightly to the side as though watching us, perfect wings tucked alongside its body, shape, and texture of feather carefully carved in to wood.

"She's a Skylark," Jack says, trying to explain but he doesn't need to. I know, and the gesture makes my eyes fill as I hold her at arms' length and examine her beauty.

"She's perfect," is all I can manage when I'd like to say so much more.

We sit side by side, shoulder to shoulder as the moon casts a pale yellow glow through the darkness. And the understanding hits me so strongly that I have no choice but to say the words aloud. "I love you Jack." I breathe out, eyes ahead, taken by the drama of the waning moon.

"You love everyone tonight," he answers with a smile.

"No. I really love you."

"I know, I know, like the hairy big brother you never had, right?" He nudges me affectionately, knowing I'm drunk, not wanting to take advantage.

But I turn to face him. "No, not like that at all." I lift a hand to his stubbly cheek and hold it there till he brings his hand up to cover mine.

"Billie…" He gently pulls my hand down to rest in his, safe in his lap. Sucking in my breath, I pull my hand free, cupping my palms against my mouth, shocked by what I'm about to do. "Jack, I'm just telling you in case you need a little warning."

"Telling me what?" he's concerned and turns fully to face me.

"I'm going to kiss you, and you're not allowed to say no, so don't even try to stop me. It's my birthday, and it doesn't have to mean anything." I hear the words and wonder for a startled second who said them.

He's taken aback. "Billie…" he tries to protest, but I've got him, hit him in the Achilles. He's never been able to say no to me.

He tries to move away a little, but I move closer, more than a little drunk but fully aware of what I'm about to do. At this moment, nothing else matters. Evan didn't come, and he doesn't care; he's drunk somewhere else that's not here with me.

Jack is here, he has always been here, and the truth is I love him, too. "Let me kiss you."

He is still, dark eyes bearing down on mine, unsure of what's happening but not about to stop me.

"Let me kiss you." I say it again, and he does.

I lean in to him, lips grazing his gently at first, softly till he lets me in. I take his rough cheeks in my hands and pull him to me.

He responds slowly, letting me have this, until there's a shift, and I feel him give in completely, moving his tongue into my mouth, taking control, and the taste of him is every fantasy I've guiltily pushed away. He is strength and trust, security and honesty, rough and unpretentious, and he smells like the ocean. He pushes me softly back on to the blanket by the dying fire, and this time, he kisses me. Softly at first, then roughly, and I feel him, every part of him in that kiss, longing rising inside, pushing through layers of self-control. His tongue tasting, finding mine, telling me that this was always how it would end. I am pinned beneath him, unable to move, but I want him closer. I need him and am at the point of no return. In a single moment of sobering clarity he stops, pulling his mouth from me, pressing his forehead to mine.

"We have to stop."

I quiver beneath him, and he kisses my forehead, curling his body around me, stroking my hair as I sob quietly, apologizing over and over again.

* * *

Chapter Twenty-Six

Fallen

I wake early with a pounding head, and for a few cloudy moments, the bright glare of reality doesn't filter through the warmth two large enveloping arms provide. A few disoriented seconds pass when my head hurts, and I don't know why. I don't want to move from the comfortable embrace holding me fast, but know that for some reason, I must. Something is wrong. Each following second shines a brighter, harsher light behind my eyelids, which remain closed tightly, willing the real world away. Hesitant memories of the night before play out like trailers from a movie I've seen before, and with each flash of recollection, the pounding in my head increases its heavy beat. Without warning, the haze clears; the dark sheet of confusion whipped away in one sharp tug, and the night comes rushing in noisily, clear and in full focus. The arms holding me are not Evan's; the body I'm curled against is so very different—solid and unflinching, so dissimilar, yet so very comforting.

Oh God, Jack.

What was I thinking? Memory suddenly sharp and the night's events crystal-clear: my tactless come on, his unwillingness, the kiss. My body freezes in horror at the memory; my pushiness and instigation of the kiss, and worse still, the wanting and needing and knowing that I didn't want him to stop.

Oh fuck, what have I done?

Slowly, carefully, I open my eyes. We are on the sand, curled together on a blanket, an arm wrapped around my waist, curled snugly and protectively behind me, his soft breath on the back of my neck.

A sob catches in my throat, and I will myself to be quiet, to gather myself. I must get up, tell him I made a terrible mistake, run back to Evan and leave this confusing relationship I have undeniably built with Jack, irrevocably broken. I want to lie here in his arms and weep at the unfairness of life, but to stay will only hurt him more, and Evan… what the hell have I done? How could I have done this to Jack, knowing, as I have always known, how he feels? How could I have done this to Evan, knowing, as I have always known, how he is?

Jack senses my movement and jumps, releasing me from his protective hold. His eyes say it all, and I know already what must happen, as does he. I want to have something better, something more meaningful to say; something that will mend the damage. Instead, I shake my head tearfully. "I'm so sorry, Jack."

"Don't be, I'm sorry too. Can we…?"

"Yes, let's forget, please. Blame it on me, on the cocktails. You don't have to feel guilty; it was me. Please…" I push away his hand as he reaches to comfort me. He can't protect me from the way I feel about him, and the realization that I feel this way is more than I can bear.

"Billie, I should have…"

"Jack, stop; please, just stop. I can't think. God, I'm a terrible person." The world spins, and I can't find my center point: Evan. What have I done? Raising my hands to my eyes I press my palms into my sockets, pushing everything out, all the flashes of light and memory until all I see is black.

What happens now? What do I do?

"I need to see Evan. I need to talk to him."

A seed of panic settles deep in my heart, and my guilt and uncertainty is overshadowed by an unprecedented foreboding.

"Why didn't he come?" I ask the question aloud, although only to myself. The feeling that settles deep in my heart grows into something frightening as dread rushes over, leaving me gasping for breath and afraid. "Something must have happened." I am on my feet running from Jack, who doesn't try to stop me. He watches me go, watches me run from his arms to find Evan.

I race inside to find the keys to the car. Head pounding double-time to each footstep, but worse than that, worse than the guilt, worse than the confusion and longing that accompanied the kiss is the feeling that something is very wrong; that Evan needed me, and once again, I was with Jack.

* * *

Inside the small house, a gradual transition from the depths of night to dawn sees darkness lift to pale grey. The shapeless black room takes on shadows and form, and the scene becomes disturbingly familiar. He's awake, and all of this is real, not some dark imagining or anxious dream. But despite the light of another very real day, the disorientation remains. There's no sense of time or day, just the grey light as he lies there, motionless but alert, waiting for the birds to sing. The harsh sounds of life are everywhere, loud and clear; voices shouting his name—music, children, the noises surround him in the quiet dawn. Everything but birds. The noise in his head won't let up, and he can't hear the birds. Where did the birds go?

Shakily, he rises from his curled position on the sofa, eyes glazed and unfocused. He walks to his studio knowing only one thing: he must stop the noise and set the birds free. He needs to hear them, only the birds, then he can move on and begin again.

The studio is dark, the light dim, a bottle standing alone on the shelf with its golden contents—a warm contrast to the grey everywhere. Before everything, this comes first. Opening the bottle with unsteady hands, he raises the slim neck to his dry lips and drinks till it's done.

Nothing.

Everything is as it was before, and still the birds are quiet.

Raising his head, he sees them all, frozen in motion, stuck in a moment of flight, ugly and stiff, unnatural and tainted. In a sudden burst of energy, he strikes out; the whisky bottle smashing to floor as he reaches for the first flying creature he can touch. Hands pulling, grabbing, tearing, feet smashing and stamping. In five minutes of pure destruction, nothing is left. Every flying form painstakingly created by hand gone. The detritus of years of beauty in wings crushed and flattened on the floor.

Amidst the chaos and noise in his head, a persistent call trills softly, its pitch perfect; the beauty of nature's song breaking through the thick layer of madness quilting his every sense. Birdsong.

Evan stills, afraid for a moment, wary and unsure. He shakes his head, bringing splintered hands to hair. Black curls momentarily cover bloodied fingers. Eyes pressed shut, hands to his head, listening; he hears it clearly this time, and his spirits soar. All other noise fades to this, the joyful call of a single bird.

No thoughts accompany the action. He follows the sound, shaking legs heading slowly to the source of the call. Sliding the back doors open, he sees her, just a glimpse, a flutter of wings and a dive in amongst the thick bush. Evan walks carefully, eyes on the bird, eyes on the bird. He mustn't lose her. He just needs to hear the song and watch her fly.

The grass is wet and dewy. He kicks off his shoes, never missing a footstep, tracing her path. The cool air a blessing on his skin, and he lets his suit jacket fall to the ground as he walks on, following and watching. He's half-dressed, the creased best suit a reminder, countless hours curled indoors waiting. He loses each item, letting it all drop away, piece by piece as he follows her into the bush, winding his way through trees. Thorns tear at bare legs. He walks; the air; such cool comfort, the sound of birdsong a prayer.

Shards of early morning light break through vine and palm, splitting the dark with the beginnings of day. Shaking his head in wonder, he sees the shades of green as though for the first time, but keeps his gaze fixed on the bird calling him forward.

"She's a Skylark, Billie, you won't believe it! She's a Skylark!" The words aloud, spoken to her, although she will never hear them.

The trees clear, and the Skylark soars ahead, gaining height, higher and higher she flies, and the ocean opens wide in front of him, beckoning, willing and quiet. With a final song and dizzying poise, the Skylark floats for an imperceptible second before plummeting, head-first, wings like a dart, for the ocean. Evan reaches out, hands ready to catch her, hear her, fly with her. He steps out beyond the cliff edge.

There is no imperceptible moment of flight before the fall, just the plummet. The singular twisting, turning, freefall of man without wings, falling with gravity to the ocean below; tragic yet strangely beautiful. White skin against the grey light, and later the luminescence of his body, quiet and free, floating peacefully in the waves while the Skylarks soar above.

Evan's world is silent and finally peaceful.

* * *

Tires screech into the driveway, and I tear from the car, banging on the locked door, fumbling for keys before pushing wildly into the dim, quiet house. A breeze blows through the open back sliders, and curtains shift and billow in the rare breath of wind. I drop my bag, calling his name, running to the open doors, standing, two feet planted firmly on the ground, calling his name over and over.

All around, the morning chorus sings, but no voice answers my call.

I run. Long grass clinging to my legs and clothes, pace steadily quickening in time with my heart. I find his shoes, his jacket, his tie.

Down the overgrown path, my legs scream as thorns rip skin and heavy undergrowth pulls and tangles. I find more of him: a shirt, trousers, socks, all of it, piece by piece—a pathway to the cliff. Like a child leaving stones to find their way home, he has left me a trail, and I scream for him as I pass each marker, his path from this life to that.

"Evan!" Voice strangled and desperate I reach the abrupt end to the pathway, beyond the point where the fence should have been. The ocean stretches out before me in welcome and the birds sing overhead to his body floating somewhere below. Sinking to bloodied knees, I cry his name in reply, seeing it all clearly. Too late, too late, too late.

I stay there until they find me hours later, shaking and rocking, holding his clothes, refusing to move. His body is found the next day, floating out into the calm open water beyond St. Cloud. Floating or flying free, on his way home: wings rendered useless by water.

Evan Skylark.

* * *

Chapter Twenty-Seven

Final Flight

"Death makes angels of us all and gives us wings where we had shoulders smooth as ravens' claws."

Jim Morrison

Death by drowning is quiet; peaceful they say. The victim of death by drowning feels nothing. So busy trying to swim and stay afloat, they don't feel the water seeping slowly into their lungs breath by fractured breath.

Death in a close community is not quiet; it is a loud affair, the grieving united. It is a rush of voices and words, grief that spills over airwaves and coffee cups… shock, guilt, denial, and blame. Tears flowing into quiet conversation, floral tributes and food offerings. Tangible symbols of sorrow and respect when words have no currency. Talk, so much talk. All the whys and what ifs, misinformed reasons and explanations; people looking for a way to make sense of tragedy. Sadness settles like a mist over St. Cloud and remains, a solemn reminder, a shroud cocooning the island in sorrow.

Evan's funeral is a small affair; simple, attended by few despite a community in mourning. Friends organize the intimate service and gather together afterward at the parking bay en route to the summit of St. Anne, where the birds still fly and the Skylarks sing and dive toward the water below.

* * *

Each step is a meditation toward calm, a movement closer to him, to where he is now. Each careful step toward the cliff, where down below the ocean reflects only brightness and joy.

But I feel nothing.

I look through eyes that are no longer mine. The hands that hold the ashes I must scatter to the wind shake uncontrollably, but I don't feel them. A shutter has closed on a world I once lived in, the lights gone out, and I can't see my way, nor care to. A cool breeze shifts us, the small collection of shattered friends who have become our family. They gather with me, support me from small distances; I cannot be touched. I don't want to see their eyes or hear their words.

I want his.

To walk on would be easier, to join him, to leave it all behind— the pain, the loss, the guilt, and the blame, all of which will drown me when this numbness fades. Our babies keep me here. For them and for him, I stay on this side of life, praying that somehow I'll make it without him.

Stopping unsteadily at the furthest point before the land drops away to the waiting ocean, I lean against the guardrail trying to breathe. I want to remember him alive and vibrant, beautiful and crazy, funny and wild. Eyes pressed tightly shut, I try to see him on the first night we met, on our wedding day, Paris in summer, Scotland in the rain. I try to see him discovering he would be a father, holding the twins for the first time, telling me it would all be okay; we'd always be okay.

But in amongst the fleeting images are darker scenes hovering in corners of my vision: anger, drama, drinking, sadness, despair. I can't push them away, and part of me doesn't want to. All of the memories are Evan, everything he was, everything I loved and have lost. I hold each memory too tightly, they slide from view and before me is the glistening ocean—his last memory in this life.

Our entry and exit from life so often violent and unceremonious, our path along its course so unpredictable. Even in tragedy, we must hold onto beauty, onto life in its entirety, beginning to end. So I cling to each memory of him, because life is no less miraculous minus the happy ending. We are no less beautiful in human frailty. To live fully, we must feel it all, storing each moment like a new and wonderful word, studying its meaning, enjoying its sound. We learn as we go, and we make mistakes, but we live. Our lives a series of moments scattered to the wind to sink or soar, and in the face of my despair, I must hold fast to the wings of joy when they catch the current.

With shaking hands, I unscrew the lid of the canister and scatter the ashes. A flash of grey then gone, taken by the wind to fly.

I am no longer waiting for Evan, and the thought is a blow, another wave of reality to pummel my unsteady self, floating numbly in rough waters. I say goodbye quietly. Someone plays a guitar as the birds swoop and fly overhead, and my broken life pries itself up from its curled and frightened position to carry on slowly, so slowly.

* * *

St. Cloud. (Eighteen months later)

I had lost him, lost sight of him, stopped paying attention, and he drifted, drifted away from day to day as softly and soundlessly as though floating out to sea. That his last moments were in flight are no comfort to me. There is no comfort except knowing that now he is peaceful and flying somewhere with his beloved Skylarks.

I returned to a life smashed and broken as visibly as the detritus of shattered wings and carefully carved bodies in Evan's decimated studio. Knowing that in his last desperate moments I lay in Jack's arms, peaceful, happy, having betrayed him, crushes the breath I have left, and I wonder if the broken pieces of this heart can ever be mended.

"Not your fault. Nothing you could have done... mental illness, manic depression, psychotic episode." The labels banded around following the investigation into Evan's death, and the possible causes give me no peace. My heart breaks for him again with every new justification or reason for his suffering. That I didn't know, that I didn't help, that I couldn't see.

"Accidental death," the coroner's report stated. Accidental death. I like to think Evan was at peace in those final moments, that somehow he found escape in flight, the freedom in wings he had always dreamt of, the comfort I could never give him.

I talk to Evie and Sunny of Evan and reassure them that in each moment we miss him, a little bird looks down and flies for us, sings for us, and that it's Daddy—always there, just not here. A small wooden Skylark sits on the bedside table, and its perfect form spreads happiness and pain in a glance. A reminder of what I had, of how it slipped away, and that love in all its complicated forms and guises is precious. I dream of our past and a future I pray might one day hurt a little less. Running my hands over the small carved Skylark, I feel

Evan and know that he's smiling. He saw me that night and understood, loved me through all my failings as I loved him.

I slowly picked myself up and carried on with half a life, pushed forward by our children and our loving friends. I returned for a time to Scotland where I was able to grieve and know the twins would be okay, smothered with love from Cam and Nell. Our friends urged me to sell the house on Frontiere Point, start again, move somewhere new nearby, somewhere I wouldn't see Evan in every room, but I couldn't. As time passes, his face becomes less clear, and I need to be here to keep the clarity in memories of him as long as they will stay. I painted the house from ceiling to floor, outside and in, planted fruit trees in the yard, and Jack erected a fence strong and tall enough to withstand the biggest of winds and the most agile of small children.

"St. Germaine," my novel, was published six months after Evan's death, fulfillment of a long-held dream providing little joy. But words saved me as they so often have, and I continue to write every day; the act a quiet meditation, a conversation with myself, with him. My despair and self-pity channeled into fictional characters who wear it better than I do.

Zoe and Felix welcomed a baby girl, Freya, to their family—a small miracle of life sparked on the same night Evan left.

Jed and Sadie married a year later out at Seacrest and now both run Beau Jangles, still making coffee and playing reggae.

Virginia and Mike are exactly as before. Virginia, a wonderful support to me since Evan's death. She is a surrogate super-auntie to Evie and Sunny, and without her, I would be lost.

Dan still doctors and DJs, and through everything has been a rock, always there with the best advice, a shoulder to cry on, a pill to help me sleep, and a sense of humor that manages to rescue my lost laughter. His relationship with Ambrose fizzled out, and he has yet to find Mr Right.

Evan's international airport was built, and every day, people from all over the world fly to and from St. Cloud. Outside on a grassy lawn where a small water fountain trickles away time stands a plaque with Evan's name. People and planes pass this small tribute every day, unaware of the significance of the name and his work. It truly is a beautiful structure, and despite everything I know, he would be proud.

Jack is still next door, building boats, watching over us, always there but never intrusive. He waits for me, and I know one day I will be ready. One day, I might start again, but for now, I'm still working on today—day by day, word by word—and for Evan, always bird by bird.

Billie Skylark, 2009

Acknowledgments

Thank you to all the gorgeous friends who put up with me as I talked and obsessed my way through this story. To Rachael and Eleanor, my first readers who gave me confidence that Skylark was a story worth reading.

To dear Evelyn whose patient proof reading and geek's eye for detail were invaluable, and Kate, friend, lawyer and beta reader extraordinaire.

To all my beautiful book club AKA wine club girls who read and gave feedback always honest, insightful and careful with my wobbly ego. To Maari who reminds me regularly that even in these Maria Von Trapp years of my life I am a writer. To Robbie and Elaine a zillion miles away, and dearest Violet and Ian who raised me to believe that I could do anything.

Lastly, to my own little brood of wildlings; who love me loudly and fully, and to Richard, my daily reminder that the real stories are always the best.

Made in United States
Orlando, FL
08 December 2021